Praise for Pierre Pevel's *The Cardinal's Blades*:

'... a rollicking novel packed with rooftop chases, back-alley swordfights, epic tavern brawls, clandestine roadside meetings in coaches and cool diplomatic exchanges between men of power where what is left unsaid can be as important as what is voiced ... Overall, *The Cardinal's Blades* is a rollicking good book, full of action, adventure, mystery and some quite delicious intrigue'   *Wertzone*

'If you are looking for a swashbuckler, you won't be disappointed with *The Cardinal's Blades*, especially if you like your swashbuckling with a smattering of history'
Interzone

'If I had to sum up *The Cardinal's Blades* in two words, they would be: great fun. This is the France of Alexandre Dumas and Fanfan la Tulipe: a land of flashing blades and break-neck chases, beautiful women and gallant warriors, of masquerades and midnight plots and sword play'
Strange Horizons

'A fantasy novel of depth and style ... Thanks to Pevel's eye for detail, swashbuckling action and characterisation this is something quite original'   *SciFi Now*

'An enormously thigh-slapping, cheering, toasting, roaring, puking, bawling, galloping, adventuring hearty piece of fiction'   Adam Roberts

'A fast-moving fantasy of swordplay, disguise and deception in the Paris of *The Three Musketeers*, with the blood of dragons splashed across the unforeseen consequences of follies and tragedies past. Dumas would surely approve and I loved it'   Juliet E. McKenna

THE KNIGHT

A Tale from the High Kingdom

PIERRE PEVEL

Translated from the French by Tom Clegg

GOLLANCZ

LONDON

First published in Great Britain in 2014 by Gollancz
An imprint of the Orion Publishing Group
Orion House, 5 Upper St Martin's Lane, London WC2H 9EA
An Hachette UK Company

A CIP catalogue record for this book is available
from the British Library

ISBN 978 0 575 10797 7

1 3 5 7 9 10 8 6 4 2

Typeset at The Spartan Press Ltd,
Lymington, Hants

Printed and bound in Great Britain by
Clays Ltd, St Ives plc

The Orion Publishing Group's policy is to use papers that
are natural, renewable and recyclable products and made
from wood grown in sustainable forests. The logging and
manufacturing processes are expected to conform to the
environmental regulations of the country of origin.

www.orionbooks.co.uk
www.gollancz.co.uk

For Dylan.

For Irma and for Pierre.

Prologue

Summer 1544

1

'His name was Lorn Askarian. Some say he brought misfortune, while others claim that all was saved because of him. Through his veins ran the black blood of doomed heroes.'
Chronicles (The Book of the Knight with the Sword)

An ashen moon had risen above the capital of the duchies of Sarme and Vallence. Its light reflected off the surface of a lagoon whose black, shallow waters were criss-crossed by luminescent salamanders. It was summer and the Great Nebula filled the sky. The night was warm, stifling, invaded by the smell of sludge that emanated from the canals and crept even into the darkest and most secluded alleyways of Alencia's old quarters. A lantern was burning at the end of one of those alleys. Surrounded by a ballet of insects, it illuminated a door upon which Lorn Askarian knocked with a leather-gloved fist. Ignorant of the fact that he would soon be paying a price for his loyalty, he had come to rescue a man whose life seemed to be worth more than his own. The panel set in the door slid open.

Knowing that the hood hid the upper portion of his face, Lorn lifted his head so his eyes could be seen. He waited, his hand placed on the pommel of his sword, a dark, still silhouette in the flickering light.

The panel snapped shut and the door opened.

Lorn entered, closely followed by a man who until then had remained in the recess of a doorway. About sixty years of age, Odric crossed the street as quickly as he could, clutching the fabric of his black cloak about his frail shoulders. As soon as he was inside he heaved a sigh of relief. Then he took in the greasy walls, the floor covered in thick filth, the smoke from

3

the wretched yellow tallow candles and the ragged cloth split down the middle which passed for a curtain at the end of the hallway. Squalid, it was not the sort of place that the retainer of a prince of the blood usually frequented.

'This… This can't be the place,' murmured the old servant in a worried voice.

Lorn did not reply.

One shoulder thrust out, the man who had opened the door twisted his neck to gaze up at the sky. He was tall and heavy, massively built, perfect for the post he held. He closed the door with a preoccupied air and automatically turned the key in the lock.

'Still no storm,' he grumbled.

'I'm looking for a girl,' Lorn announced.

'That's not the speciality of the house.'

'Her name is Lidah. Do you know her?'

A hefty studded club tucked in his belt, the doorkeeper examined Lorn with a falsely indifferent eye. Lorn had just taken off his gloves but kept his hood up. His sword was a broad Skandish blade with a basket guard that enveloped the hand: a formidable weapon, but one that required skill to wield.

'Well?' Lorn insisted quietly. 'Do you know her?'

'Possibly.'

Lorn had expected to play this little game. He had a silver coin ready, which he flipped into the air and the other man caught on the fly.

'Lidah is here. What do you want with her?'

'Nothing.'

'And him?' the doorkeeper asked in an ironic tone, indicating Odric. 'Does he want nothing from Lidah either?'

'He doesn't,' confirmed Lorn without blinking.

The man shrugged before tugging on a cord that hung near the door.

A withered hand drew apart the curtain at the rear of the entrance hall, it belonged to a small dried-up woman wearing too much make-up, who bowed and waited, an obsequious smile upon her lips.

'I am Madame Veld,' she said. 'This way, if you please.'

4

Behind the curtain, a stairway descended into the silent, malodorous shadows.

The pipe smoke was the colour of gold in some cases, of copper in others. It rose up and formed a ragged haze of shimmering red and yellow arabesques beneath the low vaults, lending the cellar a dim tawny light. It was hot in here. The air was heavy and the heady scent of kesh made the atmosphere quite oppressive.

Lorn had to stoop in order to enter. Straightening, he squinted and swept the room with his gaze, paying no heed to Madame Veld's words. The different varieties of kesh resin that might be smoked here did not interest him. Nor did the nature and price of the other items on offer.

'Pay her, Odric,' he said.

The old servant took out a purse from beneath the folds of his cloak and plucked three gold coins from it, which he slipped into the woman's hand.

'Thank you, madam. We... We will not be needing your services.'

Taken aback, Madame Veld fell silent and stared at Odric. Then her eyes widened as she saw the small fortune gathered in the palm of her hand.

'Wait here,' commanded Lorn.

Was he addressing Odric or Madame Veld? Left in doubt, the old servant stayed where he was and watched Lorn walk away with an uneasy eye. Their hostess was no longer smiling.

A series of narrow mats were aligned along the dirt floor. Some were assembled into groups of three or four, but most were isolated by veils behind which shadowy figures could be glimpsed, seated or lying down, prostrate or moaning, sometimes locked in an agitated sleep. Men armed with long clubs stood watch, for although kesh seldom provoked outbursts of violence, they were sometimes called upon to break up a quarrel, expel an undesirable individual, or discreetly carry away a corpse. These men also kept an eye on the adolescent girls who silently made their way from one mat to the next. They poured drink, rolled balls of resin, prepared and lit the pipes, replaced those grown cold. Although a hand might stray and brush against them, these girls did not offer other services. Kesh did not usually excite the senses, but for those who desired company there were some prostitutes waiting to be called.

Three of them were chatting in low voices beneath a dark lantern. Weary and sad, they perked up and smiled upon seeing Lorn approach and remove his cloak. They knew how to judge a man at a glance and they liked the look of this one. He was young, tall, broad-shouldered and attractive, with brown hair, hale skin and bright eyes. He exuded a self-confidence which inspired respect and his clothes were finely made. The quality of his shirt fabric was excellent and the same was true of the leather of his boots. As for the silver signet ring on his third finger, it seemed to possess a goodly weight.

The three whores were in for a disappointment, however.

'I'm looking for Lidah,' said Lorn.

The trio immediately lost all interest in him, although one of them deigned to enlighten him with a movement of her chin. Lorn glanced in the direction indicated and saw a young blonde woman coming towards them slowly, her hair slightly dishevelled, tightening the lacing of her bodice.

She noticed him in turn and frowned, looking apprehensive.

'Lidah?' The woman did not answer. 'I'm called Lorn.'

She relaxed slightly only to bridle again when he took her by the arm to draw her away from the others.

'What do you want with me?' she asked, freeing herself with a movement of her shoulder after they'd gone a few steps.

'To speak with you.'

'Speak or fuck, it's the same price.'

'All right. How much?'

The prostitute thought it over, then lifted three fingers. So, three silver coins. A fortune, but Lorn paid it all the same. After which, he discreetly showed her a signet ring of gold and arcanium.

'How did you obtain this ring?'

The woman hesitated.

'How did you?'

'Your pimp resold it. Now, answer my question.'

6

She sighed.

'It was a gift. Saarda had no right to take it from me. But I know it was one of those bitches who told him about it and she'll get what's coming to her.'

She gave the three other whores a venomous look. They had been watching Lorn and Lidah from the corner of their eyes and immediately pretended to take no notice.

'A gift from whom, Lidah?'

'A customer. I don't know his name.'

'But perhaps you know where I could find him...'

'He's in the alcove, over there. The one with the red curtain.'

Lorn felt himself seized by a mixture of hope and anxiety. He turned round. Closed off by thick draperies, he could make out five archways in the rear wall.

One of the curtains was scarlet.

'I won't have any trouble with Saarda, will I?' asked Lidah.

'No,' replied Lorn in a distracted tone. 'No, none.' Then, perhaps realising he was making a false promise, he took off his own signet ring and gave it to the young woman. 'Keep that, or bring it back tomorrow to the palace of the de Laurens if you want to change your life.'

Looking down at the ring cupped in her hands, Lidah was rigid in disbelief at the chance that had just been given to her. Was he really offering her a place in service to one of the richest and most powerful households in all of Sarme and Vallence?

She wanted to thank Lorn, but he had already turned away and was signalling Odric to go over to the red curtain. The servant immediately obeyed and crossed the room to join Lorn before the alcove Lidah had indicated.

Lorn paused for a moment before opening the curtain with a sharp jerk.

2

In the alcove, a young man with long greasy hair was lying on the sheets and cushions of an unmade bed. Half-naked, soiled with sweat and urine, he was frighteningly thin and had a waxy complexion, dark lips and glassy eyes. A yellow beard ate at his hollowed cheeks. A mixture of bile and vomit was drying at the corner of his mouth. One might have thought he was dead, but this corpse was still sucking at his pipe.

His name was Alan and he was the son of a king.

Bringing a hand to his mouth, Odric stifled an exclamation before rushing forward.

'Master!' Trembling, he lifted the young man's head and gently brushed back the filthy locks that hung down over his face. 'Master...' he called in a choked voice. 'Master, I beg you. Answer me, master...'

Lorn was still for a moment.

Incredulous and deeply shocked.

Then he gathered his wits and gently pushed Odric aside to examine the prince. Crouching, he pressed his ear to Alan's breast. His heart was barely beating but it was perhaps not too late.

'We... We can't move him in this state,' he said.

It seemed vital to restore some semblance of dignity to his friend, to this dying man whose flabby lips were still trying to suck something from an extinguished pipe. He needed to be washed. To be dressed. And, hopefully, instilled with enough strength and lucidity to be able to place one foot in front of the other.

Odric nodded and, as Lorn backed away, started to clean the prince's face with the corner of a sheet dipped in some dregs of wine. Seeing that Alan hardly reacted at all to the touch of the damp cloth upon his skin, the servant tried harder. His movements were delicate yet clumsy, so great was his emotion.

'What have you done to yourself?' he murmured. 'And why, master? Why inflict this upon yourself? Of all the deaths available, why choose this one?'

'Do you need help?

One of the girls serving the smoking den's customers had approached Lorn. A brunette and rather pretty despite her thinness, she smiled sympathetically.

'Do you know what to do?' Lorn asked her.

'Yes. But it will be quicker if there are several of us.'

Nodding, Lorn paid her. Two other girls joined her and they got to work.

'Let them take care of it, Odric,' Lorn said.

The old servant reluctantly obeyed.

Lorn was soon admiring the three girls' skill. Washing and dressing an unconscious man was no easy task. They managed it ably and wordlessly, as if they were performing the ablutions of a dead body in the dim bronze light from the ochre smoke.

'May I ask who you are?'

The voice that had risen at his back had nothing friendly about it.

Lorn did not blink.

He looked over his shoulder and, in a glance, saw the bearded colossus who had come to speak to him, four guards standing behind him and Madame Veld observing from a distance.

Lorn turned back to the girls: they would soon be finished.

'No,' he said. 'You may not.'

He detected a rustling behind him. His reply had caught the bearded man short and his men did not know what attitude to take.

'Besides, we'll be leaving soon,' added Lorn, before turning to face the guards' leader, who took three steps forward and said threateningly:

'It looks to me like your friend doesn't wish to leave.'

'He's still coming with me.'

'Listen. I don't know who you are. But here, I'm the one who—'

He did not finish his sentence.

With his left hand, Lorn seized him by the back of the neck and drew the man towards him as he leaned forward. Their brows collided together roughly but Lorn tightened his grip, preventing the other man from breaking free. At the same time, he unsheathed a dagger and pressed it against the bearded man's belly.

At a loss, the other guards dared not budge as Lorn and their leader stood locked skull to skull, looking into one another's eyes, their breaths blending.

Then, barely opening his mouth, Lorn said:

'It's your turn to listen. The man lying there is my friend. We're going to leave with him and you'll do nothing to hinder us. Since I'm not an idiot, I know I won't come out unscathed from a fight against all five of you. But I also know that I will gut *you* at the first twitch your men make. Do you understand?' His head trapped as if by a vice, the man nodded almost imperceptibly. 'Perfect. Now, I'm going to do you a favour. No one can hear what I'm saying to you, so I suggest you laugh. Laugh as if this is a great practical joke, so you can save face and we can go our separate ways as friends. What do you say? Don't take too long to decide. One of your boys there, behind you, looks about to try something. Probably because he can't see my dagger. So think, think fast, and answer this question…' Lorn paused and then asked, 'Would you like to find out what a packet of guts splattering on the floor sounds like?'

They left the smoking den without mishap.

3

An hour later, Lorn was talking to Enzio – Elenzio de Laurens – at the foot of the gangway to a galleon about to set sail. It was still night and yet sailors were releasing the moorings while others were busy on deck and in the rigging. Lanterns lit the entire ship. But the vessel bore no flag and was making ready to leave Alencia as discreetly as it had arrived.

Wearing a large black cloak whose raised collar hid his face from view, the elder son of the duke of Sarme and Vallence seemed concerned. Nevertheless he remained focused and tried to be reassuring.

'The crew is reliable. As is the captain.'

'Thank you, Enzio.'

'I should not have let you go there alone. It was far too dangerous.'

'I had Odric. And you couldn't have accompanied me. If you'd been recognised…'

Enzio nodded gloomily.

One day, Alencia would be his capital and he would be at the head of a thriving merchant republic, particularly influential in the domains of the arts and diplomacy. He couldn't risk being compromised by scandal, even – and especially – for a child-hood friend like Alan. His father would never have allowed it.

Lorn knew all this only too well.

'I'll go and see how he's settling in,' he said.

He patted Enzio's shoulder before making his way up the gangway.

As he entered the cabin where the prince had been installed in secret Lorn met Odric, who was leaving. His arms loaded with his master's rags, the old servant looked concerned. He exchanged a grim look with Lorn and moved aside to let him pass before shutting the door.

Tightly tucked in, Alan was lying upon a narrow bunk. Kneeling in prayer, a priest of Eyral held his hand. The prince appeared to be sleeping, his face more gaunt and pale than ever in the light of the small oil lamp hanging from the ceiling. The cabin's walls creaked quietly in the silence and Lorn stood for a moment, not daring to move or speak.

Finally, his prayers completed, the priest gently released Alan's hand and rose to his feet.

'Good evening, my son,' he said in a low voice. 'I am Father Domnis.'

His gaze was calm. He wore a white robe cinched by a leather belt and embroidered in silk thread over the heart, the profile of Eyral, the White Dragon of Knowledge and Light.

'Good evening, father.'

Tall and solidly built, the priest's hair was cut short and his beard was neatly trimmed. He was greying as he approached the age of fifty and gave the impression of possessing a serene inner strength. Lorn thought he had the look of an old soldier about him.

'How is he?' he asked, with a glance towards Alan.

Father Domnis turned to look at the sleeping prince.

'I made him drink a potion to soothe him.'

'But beyond that?'

The priest sighed.

'The ravages of kesh have spared him nothing,' he said softly.

'Can he still be cured?'

'It's not impossible.'

Lorn plunged his steel-blue gaze into that of the white priest.

'Tell me, father.'

Father Domnis did not blink.

'If the prince truly desires it, then yes, he can be cured and freed from the grip of kesh. But it will be long and difficult. Painful.'

Lorn sighed, shaking his head gently.

He allowed a moment of silence set in, and then, collecting himself, declared:

'We'll be leaving soon. In a few days, we will reach the High Kingdom.'

'The sooner the better.'

Lorn looked down again at Alan and felt a lump growing in his throat.

'He'll need the best possible care, father. He is a prince of the High Kingdom.'

'And he's your friend,' added Father Domnis with compassion.

Lorn turned towards the priest and studied him for a moment, as if trying to take full measure of the words just uttered.

Then he said:

'Yes, father. That he is.'

Lorn met with Elenzio de Laurens again on the quayside just as dawn was breaking: it was time to take to the sea. The two friends embraced, and then Lorn said:

'Thank you, Enzio. And please thank your father. Without him, without you, without your spies who discovered that the signet ring was for sale, we might never have found Alan again. Or found him too late.'

Enzio smiled.

'Make sure he arrives home safely, will you?'

'I promise,' said Lorn.

Whereupon he drew forth a blood-stained letter from his doublet and asked:

'Can you deliver this letter to Alissia? I was hoping to see her, but—'

'I have a better idea. Deliver it yourself.'

As Lorn stood there in puzzlement, Enzio pointedly turned towards the entrance of the quay. Lorn followed his gaze and he saw her.

She was dressed in a riding outfit, looking tired and dishevelled, her boots covered in dust, but she was smiling and her eyes sparkled.

And she was so beautiful.

Alissia.

They rushed towards one another and embraced, exchanging a passionate kiss that lasted long enough to force Enzio, a tolerant friend but also a protective brother, to discreetly clear his throat. Lorn took Alissia's face between his hands and delicately separated it from his own.

Astonished and delighted, he smiled.

'I... I thought you were in Vallence,' he said in an emotion-filled voice.

'I jumped into the saddle as soon as I heard.'

'Heard what, Liss?'

'That you were here.'

'Don't tell me you rode all the way from—'

'Be quiet. And hold me tight.'

He obeyed, hugging Alissia with all his might, eyelids closed, inhaling deeply to fill himself with her presence.

It lasted a too-short moment, and then he said:

'I must leave.'

'I know. But let me believe you'll stay awhile.'

'I'd like that.'

'Then stay.'

Regretfully, Lorn drew apart from Alissia and looked deep into her eyes. He delicately brushed back a reddish-blonde lock that had fallen upon the cheek of the woman he loved.

'I can't. I must return to the High Kingdom as quickly as possible. My duty calls me to the king. They say he's ill.'

'Don't set sail on this ship, Lorn. I have a feeling the journey won't end well.'

'Come now, be reasonable. I shall return as soon as I can.'

'I share Alissia's foreboding, Lorn,' said Enzio, who had approached them. 'Stay awhile.'

'What's come over the two of you?' asked Lorn in surprise, with a hint of amusement which faded as he saw the worried expressions on the faces of both brother and sister.

'Something evil is brewing in the court of the High Kingdom,' announced Enzio. 'There are rumours of intrigue and plotting. It does not sound at all good to me...'

'Just a few days, Lorn,' insisted Alissia.

Lorn gave her a tender smile as he caressed her cheek. He was confident and the young woman's fears touched him all the more because he was convinced he was in no danger.

'What could possibly happen? Don't worry, Liss. Everything will be all right.'

He embraced Alissia again tenderly, and then exchanged a last manly hug with Enzio.

'Thanks again, my friend,' he said. 'I'll see you soon.'

He hastened back on board, just before the gangway was removed.

Spring 1547

'Black were the jewels of his royal crown. Black the veil that fell before his gaunt face, the extinguished fire of his eyes, the fold of his absent lips. Black the signet ring on his bony hand. Black the accursed days of his prolonged dying.'

Chronicles (The Book of Kings)

The High King had asked for his throne to be moved close to the window. He wanted to watch the rain falling on the Citadel that night. It was a white shower, loaded with ashes that left a pale shroud upon the tiles and the stones. A sinister omen. The announcement of a forthcoming war, famine, or epidemic.

Or a period of mourning.

Old King Erklant hoped any mourning would be for him. He was ready to die, readier than when he threw himself into a melee at the height of battle. Was it because he had challenged Death so often in the past that it was taunting him today? He suffered from an illness that the priests, the mages and the doctors did not understand. A mysterious illness that had made him a skeletal old man, who always felt exhausted and whose reason, at times, became confused.

A gust of rain blew through the open window and pattered at his feet.

He did not react, remaining immobile on his throne of ebony and onyx. He was lucid, however, not asleep behind the veil concealing his face. Immersed in his thoughts, he was reflecting on his reign, on his sons and his queen, on his kingdom threatened by rebellion and war. Thanks to the warnings the White Dragon had sent in his dreams, he knew the future would be dark and tragic.

But what could he do about it?

He had been a great king. For as long as he could remember, he had ruled, loved and fought like one. So what had become of this glorious and formidable king? Had he disappeared for ever? How had he become this old man who, hidden away in an empty fortress, was simply waiting to die? Now he only inspired pity.

Bitter and careworn, Erklant II allowed himself to be distracted by the drops splashing on the window ledge. Then his gaze followed the chalky drips that were forming a puddle inside and his thoughts started to drift away from him...

But he gathered them back in.

His bony hands gripped the throne's armrests and, pulling with his arms and pressing with his legs, the High King slowly rose to his feet. It was a small victory. He was weak, but out of pride had continued to dress the part of a warrior king. The leather and steel chain mail weighed heavily upon him.

Having drawn a deep breath, he took a step.

And another.

A third took him to the window.

He observed the Citadel beneath the white cloudburst: the rain-splashed rooftops, the tall curtain walls and their walks, the fires of the watchtowers and the dark outlines of the mountains.

Beyond them spread his kingdom.

The High Kingdom.

Erklant II sighed.

Long ago, during the Last War of the Shadows, other men had shut themselves up in this solitary fortress. Led by the man who became the first High King, several thousand warriors had waged what they believed would be their final combat, right here. For them, it was not a matter of vanquishing the hosts of the Dragons of Obscurity and Oblivion, but only of resisting them to the bitter end and falling with their weapons in their hand. Like them, the old king had come here with the intention of dying. The Citadel would be his tomb, far from prying eyes and murmurs.

But his plans had come undone.

The members of the Assembly of Ir'kans had spoken to

him. Or, at least, they had sent him one of their emissaries, as was their wont. The High King had received him. He had listened to him and found new hope. Perhaps he could still save his kingdom and end his reign with a semblance of glory. If the Assembly were not lying, that was the will of the Dragon of Destiny and only one man was missing before it could be fulfilled.

A man defamed and banished.

A man condemned to hell.

A man who must now be recalled to service.

Rain clinging to the veil covering his bony face, the High King raised his eyes and his gaze lost itself in a distance greater than he could see, looking towards a ship that seemed tiny on a storm-tossed sea.

2

'Dalroth was ringed by high walls and a distant sea. Some said it lay beyond our world. It had been built during the Shadows, against the armies of the Dragons of Obscurity and Oblivion. It had survived the patient wear and tear of time, but the Dark remained a powerful force there, able to corrupt the bodies and souls and dreams of cursed men.'

Chronicles (The Book of Shadow)

A violent storm broke out that night.

An angry sea raged around an island towards which a solitary galleon was making its way. The beleaguered vessel struggled to maintain its course – pitching, plunging and then rising again – its prow sometimes standing straight up before crashing down upon the foaming crests. The rain-filled squalls caused the sails to flap noisily. Black waves exploded against the sides of its hull. The gale swept across it from end to end. Its masts and wooden frame creaked ominously but the ship sailed on, illuminated at intervals by great purple lightning bolts in the sky.

Surrounded by tall cliffs, the island seemed inaccessible. Nonetheless the galleon, bearing the banner of the High King-dom, made landfall, finding refuge in a cove protected by a ruined tower standing at the end of a reef of jagged rocks. The ship docked at an old stone pier before lowering the gangway. The place was desolate, blasted by howling gusts of wind. Four soldiers disembarked and stood at attention despite the rain that spattered their helmets and inlaid breastplates. A young man joined them. He wore a sword at his side and fine clothing beneath a large cloak whose hood hid his face. Followed by his escort, he approached the cliff with a brisk step and, by means of a stairway carved into the rock face, began to climb towards the fortress at the island's summit.

Its sinister ramparts prolonging the cliffs beset by thundering waves on all sides, Dalroth stood massive and menacing in the shrieking winds and drenching downpour, seeming to appear out of nowhere each time the lightning ripped a scarlet wound in the night sky.

The governor of Dalroth was sleeping fitfully when soldiers burst into his chamber, pushing past the servant at the door. They were soaked and their helmets and armour gleamed in the light from the lantern held by one of their number. The governor sat up in his bed with a dazed expression.

'Wh— What's going on?' he stammered.

He saw the soldiers step aside to allow entry to a young man whose face was concealed by a hood dripping with rain. Without saying a word, the man handed the governor a scroll sealed in black wax. Through the half-opened curtains, bright flashes of lightning filled the room with a dazzle that froze the scene for a heartbeat.

The governor dithered for a moment.

Then he took the scroll with a trembling hand and unrolled it. The soldier with the lantern brought it close so that he could read what was written.

The order for the prisoner's release was delivered to the captain of the garrison, who picked six able men and placed himself at their head. The storm continued to vent its fury upon Dalroth and he knew what that meant: if the Dark inflicted nothing more than nightmares and morbid ravings before morning, they would be fortunate. They'd best perform their duty quickly.

In these times, the fortress of Dalroth was a prison so terrible that, out of clemency, judges sometimes allowed condemned men to choose death rather than be sent there. No one had ever returned from it entirely sound of mind. Too much blood had been shed there, too much suffering and despair had been witnessed, too many lives sacrificed. And although the era of the Shadows was long over, the Dark remained a powerful force in the bowels of the fortress where the prisoners were held. Each of them, in their cells, experienced their own special hell. Hounded even in their dreams by macabre visions and abject terrors, afflicted by twisted obsessions, all of them succumbed to madness. At the mercy of the slow corruption of the Dark, even the strongest minds could only resist for a few years.

The captain and his men advanced with a determined step, accompanied by the rattle of weapons and chain mail. To reach the gaol, they had to walk along empty corridors, descend increasingly dark and sinister stairways and pass through a series of gates that were locked behind them. The air was dank, charged with humidity and anguish – it was an effort to breathe.

Leading the way, the captain wore a sombre expression. As for the soldiers, they were already being nagged by a vague sense of dread, which was only one of the first symptoms of the Dark. They were aware of the effect and struggled to retain their self-control, resisting the urge to invent figments in the shadows, to feel a breath down their necks, to imagine a creeping presence at their backs.

Normally, the Dark only represented a danger at the very lowest levels of Dalroth. Elsewhere, it induced a sentiment of oppression and loss which one gradually became accustomed to, just another aspect of the prison's grim atmosphere. But on these nights when the purple storms raged, the Dark rose like a miasma from the island's entrails, aggravating fears and angers, reviving old resentments and suspicions, transforming sorrows into hopelessness. It could, in some individuals, provoke brief episodes of dementia. That night, moreover, the captain had not slept. He had been anxiously watching the storm from his window when the sergeant on watch had knocked at his door. He had expected the man to announce a suicide, a bloody brawl between soldiers, or some ominous unrest among the inmates. The arrival of a royal envoy had come as a surprise, but was hardly more reassuring.

The squad finally arrived at the last door separating it from the prisoners' quarters. At the bottom of a spiral staircase, in a room with bare walls, the noise of the storm was reduced to a distant rumble. The double doors were made of black wood, the panels reinforced with fat square-headed nails. A heavy bar held them firmly shut.

Upon the captain's order, a gaoler slid the bar aside before pushing open one of the panels. He strained, bracing himself, as if the fortress itself was resisting him. With a whisper of complaint, a breath of air slipped out through the narrow gap. The captain thought he saw a dark shape accompany this movement and immediately dissipate. From the corner of his eye, he watched for a reaction from his men, but they remained in orderly ranks and seemed to have noticed nothing amiss.

Had he imagined it?

The gaoler pushed again and the door opened onto a deep, dark, vaulted hallway.

A shiver ran down the spines of the captain and his men.

3

The light drove away the shadows as the door opened with a groan. The dungeon cell was divided in two by a cage. Damp straw was strewn on the grey flagstones. There was a pallet and a blanket lying behind the bars. Otherwise, the room was bare.

The prisoner was sitting on his bedding with his back to the rear wall, wrists on his raised knees, hands dangling and head bowed. He did not move when he heard the key turn in the lock, nor when the light reached him. He was wearing a shirt and a pair of breeches. There were scabs covering his forearms, his ankles and his dirty feet. His hair hung in long filthy locks before his face.

The captain stepped up to the bars.

'Knight,' he called.

As the prisoner did not react, the captain called again:

'Knight. Knight, do you hear me?'

Having failed to elicit any response, the captain turned to the gaoler:

'Is he still sane?' he asked. 'Does he even understand me?'

The gaoler merely grimaced in reply and shrugged his shoulders.

'Open up,' the captain ordered, trying to ignore the voices whispering in his ears.

Voices he normally heard only in his sleep…

The gaoler obeyed, unlocked the cage and drew back to allow two soldiers to pass. They seized hold of the prisoner beneath his armpits and lifted him up. The man made no effort to resist. He was tall and broad-shouldered, but his body had withered due to the rigors of prison life. He stank and seemed to lack any strength.

'Knight?' the captain tried again.

He still hoped to capture the prisoner's attention.

Worried, he took hold of the man's chin between his thumb and index finger, and gently forced him to lift his head. The hair parted to reveal a gaunt face with a blank gaze and drawn features. It was the face of a man who was still young, but who had undergone greater ordeals than any individual should bear. A dark stubble covered his hollowed cheeks and a scar marred his right eyebrow. His lips were dry.

The captain sought in vain for a gleam of recognition in the prisoner's eyes.

'Take him,' he said.

He felt oppressed. Spied upon. Threatened by Dalroth's shadows. Like his men, he had only one idea in mind: to flee this accursed place.

The prisoner was not so much marched as dragged along. He had difficulty remaining on his feet, stumbled often and struggled to keep up with the pace forced upon him by the soldiers. Several times, the captain asked those holding him upright not to mistreat the man, but like them, the officer was goaded along by a tremendous urge to leave the underground gaol cells.

A mournful groan rose from the depths of the fortress when the gaoler finally shut the black door behind them, as if Dalroth regretted allowing even a single soul to escape. For their part, the captain and his men felt a great relief. Liberated, they breathed easier and found themselves smiling for no good reason, except that they were safe and sound. The captain thanked the gaoler, signalled his men to follow him and climbed the spiral staircase to return to Dalroth's upper levels.

To the storm.

The storm had not abated. In fact, its fury seemed to have increased. Thunder shook the island like mighty blows of a battering ram. The lightning bolts ripped open dazzling slashes in the black, tormented sky. The rain fell in heavy sheets and the wind howled all around, whistling in the embrasures, rattling the windows, threatening to blow out the torches and

27

rustling the drapes. Loaded with moisture, the air seemed so thick that one needed to keep one's mouth half open in order not to suffocate.

They had almost reached their destination, but they still had to traverse a vast courtyard. The captain hesitated, but this was the shortest route. He beckoned his men to follow him before venturing outside.

It was the moment the prisoner had been waiting for.

Bent beneath the storm, the two soldiers supporting him thought only of crossing the courtyard as quickly as possible. Not anticipating trouble, they reacted slowly when the prisoner freed himself with a brusque movement of his shoulders. He did not lose a second, delivering an elbow blow to one soldier, then spinning round and striking the other with a knee to the groin. The man doubled over and collapsed to the ground with a moan. His companion was still reeling. With an incredible display of strength and agility, the prisoner lifted him over his shoulder and dumped him on his back. In the same movement, he stole the man's sword from its scabbard and was about to pin him to the ground when the captain shouted:

'No!'

The prisoner froze just when there was a flash of lightning. He turned wild eyes towards the officer.

'No, knight. Don't… I beg of you.'

Heedless of the rain slapping at his face, the prisoner stared at the captain, looking puzzled and uncertain, as if his words were somehow both foreign and strangely familiar. Then another flash of lightning tore open the night, splashing purple over the courtyard and the soldiers who stood silently with swords in their fists.

The prisoner bounded away from them.

'Knight!' the captain called out.

In vain.

The man was already escaping by a stairway.

The world was a nightmare. A haunted realm, filled with screams.

The prisoner was fleeing.

Blinded by the gale, disoriented by the thunder, he had no idea where he was going. Everything was strange and hostile. Scarlet chasms opened in the sky and threatened to swallow him. The wind carried the moans and laughter of damned souls to his ears. Lightning lashed at his heels.

Barefoot and soaked to the skin in his tattered clothing, he was oblivious to the chill. He could only think of escape, of fleeing at any cost from this maze of grey stone and from the men pursuing him. He did not know why they had come looking for him. He did not know what they wanted from him. But he knew that no one had ever left Dalroth and he preferred to die than return to the hell that lay within his prison cell.

The alarm had been raised. Shouts, orders and calls rang throughout the fortress, mixed with the din of the storm. At the top of an outer staircase, the prisoner halted when he saw three soldiers running towards him. They spotted him in turn and slowed, approaching cautiously.

He observed them.

Hanging back from his two comrades, the third man called out over his shoulder:

'Over here!'

Voices answered him. Some of them came from close by.

The prisoner examined the three armed men. He was still hesitating when, suddenly, the lightning illuminated their faces glistening with rain.

He plunged forward.

He surprised the first soldier with a sword slash to the shoulder, then spun round and gutted the second with an upward thrust of his bloodied blade. The third attacked with a yell. But Lorn easily parried two cuts before planting his sword to the hilt in the belly of his adversary.

Other guards were now arriving.

The prisoner pulled his blade from the body and fled towards the heights of Dalroth. He thought he'd succeeded in eluding his pursuers when, emerging from an alley, he saw a patrol coming towards him. He immediately reversed course, although he risked running into those he had just left behind.

Breathless, with soldiers at his heels, the fugitive turned off just as the others came into view.

The net was tightening around him.

Moving along galleries and climbing stairs, the prisoner continued to ascend towards Dalroth's summit. Out of the corner of his eye, he watched for the distorted shadows of the soldiers projected on the damp walls by each flash of lightning. It was a hunt in which he was the prey and the pack of hounds was growing steadily nearer.

At the end of his strength, he climbed a last flight of steps and reached the ramparts. A gust of wind took him by surprise, almost bowling him over. Here, the wind was deafening and the rain came hurtling down with force. The boiling sky seemed close enough to touch with an upraised arm.

The prisoner instinctively hunched his head between his shoulders and sought a way out. Soldiers were approaching from both directions along the rampart walk. Others were coming up the stairs he had just climbed. Behind him lay empty air, and at the end of a dizzying fall, the rocks dashed by the furious waves of the Sea of Shadows.

The soldiers deployed themselves carefully.

He was trapped. His eyes rolled like those of a hunted beast and anxious panting made his chest heave beneath the soaked shirt. His fists tightened around the sword's grip.

The circle closed in on him.

When a soldier advanced, the prisoner prepared to charge him. The man immediately retreated and he did likewise, keeping his back against the parapet to avoid being completely surrounded.

He waited.

When the captain finally joined his men, he tried to say something, but the prisoner could not understand his words. He knew that flight was impossible and that he could not overcome these opponents. But he would not let himself be recaptured. He had difficulty ordering his thoughts, as though he was drunk, but a sense of desperation even stronger than fear burned within him. One way or another, tonight he would escape from Dalroth.

At the slightest gesture by the soldiers, he retreated further. Towards the parapet, thin air, and death below.

'Lorn!' a voice shouted. 'Lorn, I beg you! Don't do this!'

The royal envoy passed through the row of soldiers. Alone and bareheaded, he advanced with slow deliberate steps. Keeping his gaze fixed upon the prisoner, he stretched out his hand.

'Lorn, it's me. It's me, Alan.'

He was slender, attractive young man with blond hair, who spoke in a calm and even voice.

'You there, don't move a muscle,' he said to the soldiers. 'If you make him jump, I'll have all of you executed. Understood?'

The soldiers nodded. Some had noted the royal signet ring he wore on his finger, or even knew his identity. The captain signalled to his men they should obey and the order from Prince Alderan, the High King's younger son, was relayed through the ranks.

The prince addressed the prisoner again. His eyes did not leave Lorn's for even an instant. The poor wretch stared at him, his gaze betraying doubt and suspicion.

'It's me, Alan. You recognise me, don't you?'

The prisoner nodded very slowly, without conviction. He still had his back to empty space, his hair whipping in the wind. With each flash of lightning, his outline stood out against a backdrop of tormented sky.

'I've come for you,' explained Alan, taking another step forward. 'I've come to fetch you. You've been declared innocent, Lorn. My father ordered a second trial that absolved you.'

Lorn frowned and seemed to lower his guard slightly.

Memories started to come back to him.

Lorn. Lorn Askarian.

That was his name.

He was slowly emerging from the twisted fog of an endless nightmare. But thinking remained a struggle. The wind and the rain harassed him. The lightning stung his eyes. His head ached and the thunder hammered at his temples.

With the hand that he had not held out, Alan undid the

31

buckle of his belt and let his sword fall to the ground. The soldiers exchanged anxious glances with their captain.

'You see? I have no weapon. I'm your friend, Lorn. You have nothing to fear. Not any more. I'm your friend and I've come to take you away from here. Far away, Lorn, never to return.'

'A— Alan?' the prisoner stammered.

'Yes, Lorn,' replied Alan with a smile. 'It's me. It's Alan.'

He drew closer and saw a change come over the other man. The fear and doubt disappeared from the prisoner's eyes, replaced by an immense weariness.

The sword slipped from his hands.

His knees gave way.

Exhausted, Lorn burst into sobs before collapsing into the prince's arms.

4

'The Assembly of Ir'kans traditionally met in an ancient hall, where the Guardians attended either in person or in spirit.'

Chronicles (The Book of Secrets)

The table was a stone ring at the centre of which floated an ethereal sphere. A column of pale light fell upon this sphere and enshrouded it with a pearly halo, which only provided faint illumination. Spaced at regular intervals about the table, the armchairs in which the Guardians were seated remained in shadow. Of the Guardians themselves, only their heads and shoulders could be discerned. They were all wearing concealing grey hoods.

'What is his name?' asked the Third Guardian.

'Lorn Askarian,' the Seventh Guardian replied.

'Is that his real name? The one he bears before the Dragon of Destiny?'

'No,' said the Second Guardian. 'He is the Knight with the Sword.'

'Do we know for certain? Who among us can vouch for this?'

'I do,' said the Seventh Guardian.

There was a moment of silence.

'The star of the Knight with the Sword has reappeared in the firmament,' said the Fourth Guardian. 'And it stands in conjunction with that of the Prince.'

'That proves nothing,' protested the Third Guardian in a hostile tone.

'Are you blind or have you gone mad?' exclaimed the Seventh

Guardian. 'It is written that the Knight with the Sword would return from the Fortress of the Shadows.'

'And that the Shadows would follow him.'

'That's true,' confirmed the Ninth Guardian.

'Then who is the blind one here?' asked the Third Guardian. 'Who has gone mad?'

The Seventh Guardian was about to reply, but the Third did not allow it, commenting to the others:

'We have gambled with the path chosen by the Dragon of Destiny. And if it is true that the Knight with the Sword's star now shines once again, it is also true that it does so with a dull glow. Perhaps we have made a mistake.'

The First Guardian now decided to intervene. He spoke in a firm, even tone. Beneath his hood there sparkled the stars of an immense nocturnal sky.

'The Assembly has deliberated and made its choice. There can be no question of reversing that decision.'

'Against my advice,' the Third Guardian ventured to protest.

'The judgement of the Assembly prevails!'

It sounded like a call to order.

The Third Guardian made no reply, but his silence was an ominous sign. He was powerful and proud. He had his followers. The First Guardian found it prudent to adopt a more conciliatory tone.

'We must sometimes act to ensure that Destiny's will is respected. It is both our right and our duty to do so, but only on very rare occasions, for we are all aware of the danger it entails. The extraordinary fate in store for the Knight with the Sword is certain, so we were obliged to permit his star to shine once again. But as the Third Guardian has said, it shines with a dull glow. That should worry us.'

'This dull glow is perhaps due to the Fortress of the Shadows,' stressed the Seventh Guardian. 'If we allow him more time, his star may recover its full brilliance.'

'No one can swear to that,' objected the Third Guardian.

'Nor to the contrary!' the Seventh Guardian retorted. And turning to the First Guardian he added, 'Are we going to give up? Turn our backs on the Knight with the Sword, now that we have recalled him? Think of all he is supposed to accomplish.'

Silence fell again.

Then the First Guardian said:

'Let's summon an emissary.'

'Which one?' asked the Fourth Guardian.

'The one who served us so well with the High King. Let him meet this Lorn Askarian and determine how strong a hold the Dark has on him. If he is the Knight with the Sword, and if his star is forever tarnished, then we shall know what to do.'

5

'It was an ever-raging sea, and even more so at night. It was
born of the cataclysm that shook the world at the end of the
Shadows. That explained its name. And its storms. And the evil dreams
and tortured nights of Dalroth.'

Chronicles (The Book of Shadow)

The royal galleon sailed away from Dalroth and the storm. The
waters of the Sea of Shadows remained agitated and treacherous, but less so than around the cursed fortress, where the forces
of nature confronted the Dark without ever winning the battle.
The winds abated. The swells diminished. The waves assaulted
the vessel with a reduced fury.

A cabin had been reserved for Lorn.

There was a bunk that looked comfortable, but he asked
for the wherewithal to wash first as he wanted to feel clean
and decent. Despite his fatigue, he made a thorough job of it,
requiring several ewers of water. He put on a fresh shirt and
breeches. Gave away his prison clothing to be burned. Resolved
to trim his beard rather than shave it off, out of fear of cutting
himself due to the ship's swaying and plunging into the dips
between swells, but also because his hands were shaking. Alan
assured him there was a ship's boy among the crew who would
be able to shave him, but Lorn would not hear of it.

And, at last, he lay down.

He was exhausted, stricken by a weariness that was as much
mental as physical. Yet sleep eluded him. It was as if he had
just awoken from a nightmare. Or an illness, a fever, a tortuous
dream from which he was still struggling to extract himself.

It was like a weight upon his soul that had lifted and left him naked.

Just before embarking, he had turned around and raised his eyes towards Dalroth to – so he hoped – look upon it one last time. Alan had waited until Lorn, his face splashed with rain, asked him in a hoarse voice:

'What year is it?'

Alan hesitated.

'Please,' insisted Lorn. 'I'll find out eventually, won't I?'

'You really don't know?'

'No.'

'The year is 1547,' the prince revealed, in as gentle a voice as possible.

He could not help feeling ashamed.

Telling Lorn the year was the same as telling him how long he'd been imprisoned. But saying it obliged him to face the awful truth. Sometimes the harshness of a fact becomes unbearable when it was spoken aloud.

As his friend remained silent, the prince drew in a breath and added:

'We are in the spring of 1547.'

There, all had been said.

Lorn took some time absorbing this information.

'So it's been... three years...' he murmured.

'Yes.'

Lorn had nodded slowly.

He had remained silent, but at that moment he had felt, for the first time in a very long while, an emotion that was neither fear nor dismay.

One of the most human emotions.

Anger.

Rocked by the strong swell, Lorn was drowsing when he heard a quiet knock upon his door. Amidst the creaking of the galleon, he doubted whether he had heard right and pricked up his ears.

The knocking came again.

'Come in,' he said in a voice that was still hoarse.

A white priest peeped in with a hesitant air. He was about fifty years old, with grey hair and a short, perfectly trimmed beard.

'Forgive me, my son. Were you sleeping? I can come back...'

As Lorn made no reply, the priest entered. He was tall and solidly built. Upon seeing Lorn struggling to sit up, he hurriedly said:

'No, no, my son. Don't trouble yourself.'

Lorn contented himself with rolling onto his side and propping his head on one elbow. 'May I?' asked the priest, pointing to a stool.

Lorn having nodded his assent, the priest sat down.

'I am Father Domnis, my son. Perhaps you remember me. We met three years ago when—'

'I remember.'

'As you might guess, Prince Alderan's asked me to visit you.'

Wary, Lorn asked:

'Are you worried about my soul?'

'It is no secret that Dalroth tests the spirit as much as the body,' said the priest in a conciliatory tone.

He was wearing the white robe of his order with a dragon's head over the heart, barely distinguishable as it was also embroidered in white, although with shiny silk thread. He worshipped Eyral, the Dragon of Knowledge, who was also the protector of the High Kingdom. Of all the Divine Dragons who had once ruled over the world and men, Eyral remained one of the most respected.

Lorn lay on his back again. He laced his fingers behind his neck and stared up at the cabin ceiling.

'I'm fine, father. I need peace and quiet. That's all.'

The priest knew Lorn was lying to him.

But he also knew Lorn was lying as much to himself, as was often the case with those who had been through a hellish ordeal. His lie was helping him combat the horror of what he had endured, what he had done, and, perhaps, what he had become. But he would need to confront reality eventually.

'I'm glad to hear that,' said Father Domnis. 'However, if

you feel the need to confide…' He left his sentence dangling. 'Or if you have nightmares, visions that haunt you,' he added.

Lorn did not reply, his eyes fixed on the beam that ran above his bunk. He was exhausted, but a dull anger continued to grip his belly. He had no trouble containing it, however. It was like a wild but sleeping animal curled up inside him.

After a moment of silence, Father Domnis proposed:

'Shall we pray?'

'I no longer have faith, father.'

The priest nodded gravely, like a man who believed he understood.

'No doubt Dalroth has '

'No, father. I did not lose my faith at Dalroth. I should even have liked its comfort there, but…'

He did not finish.

'In that case,' said Father Domnis, 'would you permit me to pray for you, my son?'

It had been a long time since anyone had worried about him. Nevertheless, Lorn did not feel the slightest twinge of gratitude, or reassurance. He wondered where this priest, and all the others, had been while he was screaming his lungs out, tormented by the spectres of the Dark.

'Go ahead and pray for me, father. It's what one does when there's no hope left.'

A short while later, Father Domnis joined Alan on the poop deck. Gripping the rail, the prince watched Dalroth recede into the night. The sea was still heaving, but they had escaped from the storm, its deluge of rain and purple lightning. The noise of the thunder had diminished.

His face lashed by the spray, the prince kept his eyes fixed on the cursed fortress.

'Well?' he asked.

'Your friend is strong. I have good hope he will one day recover. But he is not the man he was, and he never will be again.'

'The Dark?'

'Yes, although I don't know to what extent it has infected him. But even without that…'

The priest of Eyral hesitated.

'I'm listening, father.'

Alan's tone had remained courteous. But he was a prince, a son of the High King. He was accustomed to being obeyed and he knew, with a slight inflection of his voice, how to indicate when he was starting to grow impatient.

'You know that war changes men,' said Father Domnis.

He was concerned to find the right words, fearing that he would exasperate Alan by clumsily declaring a truth the prince didn't want to hear.

'It usually changes them for the worse,' said the prince. 'Some come back broken. Or mad. Incapable of settling down.'

'Some come back dangerous.'

Alan turned to the white priest, who saw in the prince's eye what he had feared most: a seething, indignant denial.

'Are you telling me that Lorn has returned from a war?'

'In a manner of speaking. A war against solitude. A war against madness. Against oblivion.'

'Against the Dark?'

'Yes, unhappily.'

'And did he lose this war?'

'I don't know. But I sense in him a terrible anger that only—'

Alan lost his temper.

'Lorn has been dishonoured, betrayed, abandoned by everyone! He lost the woman he loved! His life was stolen from him and he spent three infernal years at Dalroth despite his innocence. Who on earth, in his situation, would not be angry? Tell me! Who?'

Father Domnis had no reply.

Alan felt suddenly weary. He regained his calm, sighed, and leaned on the rail.

'Forgive me, father.'

'It's nothing, my son. I understand.'

The priest knew that Alan was not angry with him. And he also knew, the prince having confided in him several times on the subject, that his anger was not only inspired by the terrible injustice done to Lorn; it was also the expression of a profound sense of guilt.

Alan felt Father Domnis place a hand upon his shoulder.

'There's no cause to reproach yourself, my son.'

'Really? Then why do I have trouble looking my best friend in the eye?' asked the prince.

He had a lump in his throat.

'You wanted to rescue your friend. You blame yourself for not being there for him... But it's not your fault.'

Staring out again at the turbulent horizon, Alan kept control of himself and nodded.

'What can I do to help him, father?'

'First of all, you must summon your patience. Pray. Wait and be there when he has need of you. Don't pressure him. Don't oblige him to do anything. Listen to him when he wants to speak, but don't try to prise confidences out of him...'

'On the ramparts, he was ready to throw himself over the edge. Is he still a danger to himself?'

'No doubt.'

'And to others?'

'Yes.'

The frankness of the priest's reply surprised Alan. He absorbed the news and, looking worried, straightened up.

His gaze lost itself in the distance.

'Lorn is lucky to have a friend like you,' said Father Domnis after a moment. 'However...'

'Yes?'

'Be patient,' advised the white priest. 'But also be prudent.'

The prince mulled this over.

Patient, he believed he could be.

But prudent?

Born only a few months apart, Lorn and he had suckled at the breasts of the same nurses before being raised like brothers. When they were children, they had played the same games. Later, they had received their first swords together and, at the age of thirteen, lost their virginity in the same bed with two sisters renowned for their skills. The day when the king dubbed his son before the assembled knighthood of the High

41

Kingdom, Lorn was the second in line. And after that, their friendship never weakened. On the contrary, it grew stronger over the years through thick and thin, joys and sorrows, hopes and regrets.

'For me, Lorn is more than a brother,' said Alan. 'I have already let him down by leaving him to rot within Dalroth. I will not turn my back on him a second time. And you know what I owe him.'

'The Dark is both powerful and insidious, my son.'

'No, father!' said the prince, clutching the rail as if he wanted to plant his fingers there. 'I will not suspect Lorn of being someone else. What sort of friend would I be, distrusting him when he is in such need of help?'

'I understand,' replied the white priest as he turned towards Dalroth. 'But don't forget that the man you knew might have died in there.'

Lorn did not sleep.

Eyes wide open in the dim light, he stared at the ceiling above his bunk. He did not blink, he did not move and he barely breathed, trapped in a disturbing mineral stillness while the ship pitched, creaked and groaned around him.

There was a pale gleam in his fixed gaze.

6

Lorn awoke in the morning, when a servant brought him his meal.

It was old Odric, Alan's trusted valet. Thin, dry and wrinkled, he had been in the service of the prince since his birth. So Lorn, too, had always known him.

'Good morning, Odric,' said Lorn, noticing that the servant was avoiding his gaze.

'Good morning, my lord.'

In fact, Odric was uneasy and couldn't hide it. Lorn watched him set out the contents of his tray on the table.

'I'm happy to see you again, Odric.'

'Thank you, my lord.'

Then, his eyes still averted, the old servant enquired:

'Is there anything else you desire, my lord? The supplies on board are limited, but...'

'This will be fine.'

'At your service, my lord.

The valet withdrew, but before closing the door, he turned round.

'My lord?'

'Yes?'

He looked ashamed.

'I... I beg your forgiveness, my lord...'

His face expressionless, Lorn felt the anger that had faded during the night returning.

'Leave me, Odric.'

Once he was alone, Lorn rose and went to the window.

The galleon had not yet left the Sea of Shadows, but it was sailing on calmer waters, propelled by steady winds. Lorn watched the waves for a long moment, and then turned towards the meal awaiting him.

He ate without appetite.

Lorn was finishing his breakfast when Alan came to join him and, without ceremony, sat down to pick at his friend's plate. They exchanged a glance but said nothing.

Because they were true friends, silence had never embarrassed them. Yet the silence that installed itself between them now had a different quality about it. It was not the expression of a complicity that needed no words, but the manifestation of awkwardness, each of them hesitating to speak first. Lorn did not feel able to express anything at all, not even gratitude. While the prince did not know what approach to adopt, torn between the urge to take care of his friend, the fear of being tactless and an idiotic sense of decorum that inhibited him.

Moreover, he could not help but feel guilty.

'Your eyes have changed,' he finally said in a casual manner.

With the tip of his knife he was spreading a pat of butter on a piece of bread.

Lorn frowned.

'What?'

'Your eyes. They've changed colour. The right one, especially. At least, I think so.'

Lorn took down the little tin mirror hanging above the washbasin. Then he approached the window in order to see more clearly in the light passing through the small diamond-shaped panes.

Alan was right.

Lorn had been born with blue eyes. Now, the right one was a very faded grey. The previous evening, in the cabin's dim light, he had not noticed this. Besides, he'd avoided examining himself too closely. It had been years since he had seen his own face, and the one he'd glimpsed in the reflection frightened him.

'How did that happen?' asked the prince.

'I have no idea.'

But Lorn knew the cause of this change as well as Alan. He

44

tossed the mirror on the crumpled sheets of the bunk and sat back down.

'That's not so serious,' Alan commented. 'I'd even wager that it will please the ladies. It gives you a… umm… mysterious air.'

Lorn shrugged.

The truth was, he didn't care if one of his eyes had changed colour. He knew that Dalroth had done far worse to him, by stealing part of his soul for ever.

'Father Domnis spoke to you, didn't he?' he asked.

Alan's face grew grim.

'Yes.'

'And?'

The prince weighed his words carefully.

'He's afraid you've been corrupted by the Dark.'

'Do I seem to have lost my reason?'

'No,' admitted Alan.

That did not prove anything, however.

Both men knew that the Dark's contagion might not be apparent. It was furtive and patient. It could wreak havoc before it fully revealed itself. It might even go completely undetected.

Lorn sighed.

'And what do you believe?'

'I believe you are my friend and I will do everything in my power to help you.'

They exchanged a long glance that spoke volumes, before Lorn finally said:

'Thank you. Thank you for taking me out of that hellhole.'

He almost had to force himself to say it.

He knew that Alan had braved the storms of the Sea of Shadows in order to fetch him home from Dalroth. He was equally convinced that the prince had done everything he could to hasten Lorn's release. And yet he couldn't feel any gratitude towards Alan. The torments he had endured under the influence of the Dark were like raw wounds; still too painful for him to feel anything but his suffering.

'Don't thank me, Lorn. I owe you my life, don't forget that.'

Lorn said nothing.

'Furthermore,' continued Alan, 'there's no reason to thank me. Or anyone else. You should not have been sent to Dalroth in the first place. You were innocent and—'

Lorn stopped him.

He had no desire to hear his friend speak of his innocence and he knew perfectly well where he stood in this matter. His pain and his anger were on the verge of becoming outrage.

'Don't hold what I'm about to say against me, Alan. You... You are my friend. I know you couldn't help me these past three years. But others could, and they did nothing. Nothing at all. So forgive me if I hold a grudge against all of you. Even against you personally. I still have too much... too much anger in me.'

The prince nodded, with a profound sadness in his eyes.

'I understand.'

Lorn then regretted having caused his friend sorrow and tried to explain himself more clearly.

'No one deserves to endure what I did at Dalroth. The suffering, the nightmares, the madness, the Dark... No one deserves that and I can't...'

His voice choked. He could not finish his sentence.

The prince hesitated, and all he found to say was:

'Free, Lorn. Free and declared innocent. I wish I could have done more but I didn't know about the accusations made against you. I would have defended you, otherwise. And three years would not have passed before—'

Lorn's gaze hardened.

'I'm sure of that. But as I said: don't ask me to forgive you now.'

'Without you,' Alan continued nonetheless, 'I would no longer be of this world. And where was I when you needed me?'

'Stop it, Alan. Just stop.'

Lorn's tone had become icy and menacing.

The prince pulled himself together at last and, ashamed of his self-pity, fell silent with his head hung. He knew that he was sometimes selfish and he was angry at himself for giving in to his tendency to ease his own conscience.

There was another silence which, as it stretched, became embarrassing.

Alan noticed Lorn's left hand was bandaged and thought he had hit upon a safe topic of conversation.

'Are you wounded?'

Lorn gave him a cynical smile.

'In a manner of speaking.'

After a moment's hesitation, he removed the bandage and, fist raised, placed his elbow upon the table so Alan could see the seal on the back of his friend's hand. It was an ancient rune, that of the Dark, engraved upon a red stone medallion embedded in the flesh.

The galleon soon left the black and dangerous waters of the Sea of Shadows behind. The continent was still far away, but an island loomed on the horizon. The captain set a course for this island first, and then made for two rocky needles that stood behind it. A gigantic stone arch linked these twin peaks.

Alan and Lorn came out on deck to witness the spectacle. Standing on the poop deck, a mage from the Navigators' Guild had already started his incantations. The ship was loaded with arcanium. Even its sails were woven with threads of this metal. Reacting to the magic, the arcanium started to glow and to hum, while an uncanny breeze lifted.

Still weak, Lorn was overcome by dizziness. He had insisted on leaving his cabin in order to watch the ship depart from the Sea of Shadows. But he had overtaxed his strength and had not foreseen the effect the immensity of the horizon would have on him after three years in a gaol cell. He felt crushed and lost, tiny and vulnerable. The blue sky seemed infinite and the sun hurt his pale eyes. The air of the open sea was intoxicating. He had to take in several deep breaths, gripping Alan's shoulder as his friend discreetly held him upright.

'Are you all right?'

'I'm… I'm fine…'

'Sure?'

Lorn did not have to reply.

At the galleon's approach, the runes engraved in the stone

arch lit up. Shimmering coils spun in the air. They wrapped themselves around the ship, curled around the masts, slipped over the sails and crackled when they came into contact with the arcanium supports. A passage opened beneath the immense arch.

The ship entered it and disappeared in a blinding flash.

7

'The High King Erklant II was wed to Queen Celyane in a second marriage, after the death of his first wife. No doubt he never loved her, although she bore him two sons.'

Chronicles (The Book of the Three Princes' War)

The ladies-in-waiting busied themselves, finishing sewing on a button, measuring a sleeve, taking in a hem, adjusting a pleat. In their midst, Queen Celyane let them get on with it, holding herself straight and lifting an arm when necessary. Tall and slender, still beautiful, with dark eyes and a severe mouth, she was impassive but watchful, regularly ordering her entourage to step aside so she could see herself in the large mirror placed in front of her. This outfit was the one she would wear at an event that would mark the triumph of her policy and would establish her in the eyes of all the world as the reigning queen of the High Kingdom.

An event fit to be related in the *Chronicles*.

'Ma'am?'

The queen turned her head towards a young lady-in-waiting who presented her with different sets of jewellery on a satin cushion. She was pointing to one when it was announced that Lord Esteveris wished to be received. The queen sighed and permitted her minister to enter. Behind her, one of her dressers climbed onto a small stool to place the gold-and-ruby necklace she had chosen about her neck.

A man in his fifties appeared, plump and bald, luxuriously dressed, his fingers adorned with several rings. A former prelate, Esteveris was a cautious man and an able politician who always maintained a calm, unctuous manner. He was reputed to be aware of all the intrigues and plots brewing in the High Kingdom. Despite the countless spies in his employ and the accommodating souls who spontaneously came to him with information in the hope of winning favour, this was no doubt not the case. But Esteveris did nothing to contradict the rumour and even endeavoured to lend it credence.

He bowed.

'Your Majesty.'

'To what do I owe this visit, my lord minister?'

'News has just arrived, ma'am. News from the Citadel.'

'I'm listening.'

Esteveris said nothing.

When he persisted in remaining silent, Queen Celyane understood and dismissed her entourage. The room emptied in a few seconds and as soon as the door to her antechamber was closed, the queen demanded:

'Well?'

Looking concerned, the minister announced:

'The High King has received another emissary from the Assembly of Ir'kans.'

As the queen did not react, he added:

'It's the second time in only a few months, ma'am.'

But the queen remained expressionless. So he continued:

'After the first interview, the High King ordered the trial that absolved Lorn Askarian. And now I've learned that a troop has left the Citadel bound for Samarande. To Samarande, where Prince Alderan will soon be landing, ma'am. That cannot be a coincidence...'

Esteveris fell silent, convinced that the queen would finally react.

He was not mistaken.

With an impatient snap of her fingers, she pointed to a gold-and-vermilion service on a table. Bowing, the minister went to pour a cup of wine while the queen sat in a low-backed armchair. She took the cup that Esteveris brought her, but barely wet her lips.

'I suppose that you have no better idea of what was said during this second audience than at the first...?'

'No, ma'am,' admitted the minister in a prim tone.

'Don't you have spies within the Citadel?'

'Only a few, ma'am.'

'But very able ones, fortunately...'

Esteveris was sufficiently acquainted with Queen Celyane to know it was never a good sign when she resorted to irony.

'The High King receives the Assembly's emissary alone,' he explained. 'Even Norfold, the captain of the guard, remains outside the door. My spies cannot risk—'

Queen Celyane bade him to be silent with a gesture, and then, containing her frustration, tapped nervously on her armrest.

'What mission was this troop assigned?' she finally asked.

'I do not know.'

'How many men?'

'Twenty horsemen from the Grey Guard.'

'But there's no doubt that they are heading for Samarande.'

'None, ma'am.'

'At the order of my husband.'

'Yes, ma'am.'

The queen of the High Kingdom pinched her lips.

Samarande was the most influential of the seven Free Cities – their capital, in a sense. Long ago, the province of the Free Cities had belonged to the High Kingdom, before being invaded by the kingdom of Yrgaard. As soon as he was crowned, the current High King had reconquered it at the end of a military campaign that had driven the armies of the Black Dragon back across the Sea of Mists. Erklant had since granted a degree of independence to each of the Free Cities in order to win their gratitude and loyalty. They governed themselves as they saw fit, as long as they paid their taxes and never acted against the interests of the High Kingdom. After suffering under the Yrgaardian yoke, this newfound liberty allowed the Free Cities to prosper. Yet one of them was about to throw off the tutelage of the High Kingdom and return to the bosom of Yrgaard...

'Do you think the High King may try to oppose Angborn's cession?' asked Esteveris.

Rather than a question it was a warning, all the more prudent on the part of the minister as he had already posed it several times before. He was the principal architect of this political and diplomatic masterstroke that would make Angborn a full-fledged Yrgaardian city. Nevertheless, he was aware what this cession represented in the eyes of the High King and his last remaining supporters.

The queen shrugged her shoulders.

'That senile old man?'

'The province of the Free Cities was the most handsome conquest of your husband's reign,' Esteveris said. 'And throwing the armies of Yrgaard back into the sea was one of his most glorious feats. It's easy for our adversaries to claim that ceding Angborn to the Black Dragon means amputating part of our territories and bringing Yrgaard to our doorstep. No doubt the High King, however isolated, is not—'

'Leave my husband where he is, will you? Leave him in that fortress he has chosen to make his tomb. After all, isn't that what he wants? To die in peace?'

The minister bowed respectfully.

'As for our adversaries…' the queen continued. 'The cession of Angborn to Yrgaard shall take place, whether they like it or not. It will benefit the High Kingdom. It will re-establish diplomatic relations with Yrgaard and lay the foundations for an unprecedented alliance. The High Kingdom and Yrgaard! The two most powerful realms of Imelor allied at last!'

As her words grew heated, the queen had risen and took a few steps. She calmed down and added more thoughtfully:

'It will be a done deed in a few weeks, Esteveris. We will be in Angborn and before delegations from the world over we will sign a treaty with Yrgaard that will force all our enemies, within and without our borders, to carefully reconsider their… positions.'

Celyane was smiling and her gaze shone, fixed on something far away. She stood proudly, satisfied with herself, in the dress she would wear for the occasion, which, like her triumph, only required a few finishing touches.

Seeing that she was savouring her forthcoming victory over all those who contested her authority or doubted her ability to rule on her own, the minister refrained from mentioning the tribute Yrgaard would be paying to acquire Angborn. Of course, the political and diplomatic advantages that the High Kingdom would reap from this operation were assured. But it still came down to selling Angborn – and the formidable fortress that defended it – in order to fill the royal coffers. The High Kingdom was on the verge of ruin and needed Yrgaard-ian gold.

'The fact remains that the High King has just sent twenty horsemen from his guard on a mission to Samarande,' said Esteveris after a moment. 'If their mission does not concern the treaty, it probably has something to do with Prince Alderan's arrival.'

The minister paused before getting to the crux of the matter:

'Or with the return of Lorn Askarian…'

The queen gave him a steely glance.

'Lorn! So Dalroth did not get the better of him?'

'It's possible he's no longer alive, ma'am.'

'How long was he at Dalroth, exactly?'

'Almost three years.'

'And can anyone survive that?'

'Not with one's reason intact, so it's said.'

'In that case, what could the High King want with this man?'

'I don't know ma'am.'

Celyane of the High Kingdom pondered for a moment, then gave a haughty smile and clapped her hands loudly, which prompted the return of her ladies-in-waiting.

'It's another of that old fool's whims,' she said dismissively. Once again she became the centre of feverish activity and, standing straight, she stretched out her arms horizontally. 'Let him amuse himself as he pleases,' she added. 'We have other fish to fry.'

Esteveris returned to the luxurious apartment he occupied in the palace. He ordered a scented bath to be prepared and, dressed solely in a long ample shirt, he sank into the steaming water. The thin cloth clung, diaphanous, to the folds of his obese and completely hairless body. Fat beads of sweat ran down his ruddy face, wiped away at regular intervals by a servant.

The minister was worried.

Of course, the kingdom's situation was cause for concern. The empty treasury. The legitimacy of the queen's rule increasingly questioned. The peasantry threatening to revolt and the nobles plotting with the Duke of Feln. And the other Imelorian kingdoms massing their forces at the borders because they were hostile towards the rapprochement between Yrgaard and the High Kingdom.

But Esteveris was almost as tormented by the return of Lorn Askarian and the audience to which – he was convinced – the High King would summon him. Before ordering Lorn's second trial the old king had received an envoy from the Assembly of Ir'kans. That couldn't be a coincidence. The Assembly must have had a reason for wanting the man's liberation despite everything he had endured at Dalroth. What message had it sent to the High King? What had it revealed to persuade him to take this step?

Esteveris had to assume that the High King, at present, knew. A perspective that was more than worrying, especially when one thought of what Lorn risked learning if he harboured even the slightest desire for revenge. And how could he not, after what he had endured? Anyone in his shoes would want to discover who had plotted his downfall, and why.

Curiously, it did not seem to trouble the queen.

Why not?

How could she not see the threat that Lorn's return represented? How could she not be interested in whatever Erklant was up to in the Citadel? When the High King had shut himself away there, everyone had believed he was planning to end his days in peace, far from the scrutiny of others. But it had occurred to Esteveris that the king was actually seeking a refuge where he could act in secret. In hindsight, this hunch seemed to be correct...

You old fox, the minister thought to himself, smiling faintly as he reclined in the perfumed vapours of his bath.

The fact remained that the queen's lack of concern could be

dangerous and, if she persisted in doing nothing about Lorn, Esteveris would have to take care of the matter.

For the good of the High Kingdom, for the good of his queen.

And also, perhaps, for his own good.

Closing his eyelids, he called for more hot water.

8

*'The Navigators' gate having transported them to the waters of the
Sea of Mists, they arrived three days later within sight of the Free
Cities. The voyage had proceeded without incident since the royal
galleon left the terrors and storms of the Sea of Shadows. It was,
at last, the end of the crossing.'*

Chronicles (The Book of the Knight with the Sword)

'It's me,' announced Alan, as he knocked on the cabin door.

'Come in.'

The prince found Lorn stretched out on his bunk, reading.

'We're about to arrive.'

Lorn closed his book and glanced out the window. They had
passed the city of Angborn on its island and were now sailing
the calm waters of the Sea of the Free Cities.

Their heading was due south, as far as Lorn could tell.

'Thank you. We'll be landing at Samarande, won't we?'

'That's right.'

Looking preoccupied, Alan drew up a stool and sat down,
leaning forward, hands joined, elbows resting on his thighs.

'What is it?' asked Lorn.

'You've hardly left your cabin these past few days.'

'I found some books in an old chest. And since I needed to
catch up on my reading…'

The jest did not make Alan smile.

Lorn gave a sigh, sat up on the edge of his bunk and looked
his friend straight in the eye.

'I'm fine,' he said. 'Give me time. This will pass.'

His gaze, however, said something quite different.

But if Lorn had lied, it was not so much to reassure his friend as to be left in peace. As sincere and well meaning as it might be, Alan's often clumsy solicitude weighed on him.

'Really?' asked the prince.

'Really.'

The truth was that Lorn preferred to avoid the ship's crew.

Out of superstition, the sailors were wary of him. He was marked by the Dark and therefore cursed; he could only attract bad luck. Reason enough for him to be feared and despised on board. It had not taken long for Lorn to notice the hostile, worried glances directed his way whenever he left his cabin. And to make matters worse, the sunlight still dazzled him painfully; his eyes seemingly unable to readapt to the light of day. So he had fallen into the habit of going out on the deck only after nightfall, beneath the glow of the Nebula. He devoted the daytime to reflection, reading and resting.

'You seem to be doing better,' said Alan, rising to his feet.

In fact, Lorn did look better. To be sure, his face remained pale and drawn. But he had regained some strength. His mismatched eyes shone with a new gleam. He had trimmed his beard short and his black hair, neatly cut, now fell to his shoulders.

Alan went to serve himself a glass of wine from the jug placed on the table.

'Do you want some?'

'No, thank you.'

The prince drained his glass in a single gulp, and asked:

'Have you thought about what you'll do?'

'What do you mean?'

'Now that you're free. What are you going to do?'

Lorn looked down bleakly at his left hand and the leather band concealing the seal of red stone embedded in his flesh.

Free, he thought.

Was he really? Would he ever be, with this infamous mark? For it to appear, one had to have come under the influence of the Dark. But on its own, that was not enough: not all those who came into contact with the Dark were marked in this manner. Without anyone knowing why, it did not place its rune on just anyone. Did it prefer the strongest, or the cruellest, or those most inclined to serve it? It was in any case a terrifying privilege. To be sure, those whom it adopted survived. The mark spared them the worst of its corrupting effects and they seemed to escape the physical and mental degeneration that struck others. They always ended up paying the price, however. For although the Dark did not kill those it marked, it did bring them misfortune. And Destiny, sooner or later, came to settle accounts with them.

So, in a way, Lorn owed the fact that he was still alive to his mark. It represented the Dark's choice. Without it, he would be dead. Or mad, with his body eaten away and deformed. But should he rejoice in that fact? One did not escape the Dark. One did not ever become free of it.

'I would understand if you wanted nothing further to do with the High Kingdom,' the prince continued. 'But you should know that when you're ready, I will be glad to have you at my side.'

Whether he accepted it or not, Lorn knew what this offer represented: an extraordinary rehabilitation.

'Thank you,' he said.

'Don't thank me. I'm not doing you a favour. I really do need you.'

Lorn frowned and stood.

'What's going on?'

The prince hesitated, and then revealed:

'The affairs of the High Kingdom are going badly, Lorn. My mother's authority is increasingly called into question, and my father—'

His voice choked off.

Lorn waited.

In the past, he would no doubt have offered the prince the comfort of a friendly word, a considerate hand placed upon his shoulder. But he now felt incapable of that. Perhaps it would come back to him.

Alan served himself another glass of wine, promptly drinking half.

'My father no longer rules, Lorn. And he's doing very poorly indeed.'

'Is it that serious?'

'Yes. You… you would not recognise him if you saw him. He's more dead than alive. Gaunt and pale. He looks like a withered corpse. Dry. Wrinkled. It's frightening to see. And his voice… his eyes. They're—'

Alan was unable to continue. He finished his glass and stood gazing into the distance.

'I… I know that you have every reason to hate him, Lorn. But if you saw what he has become, you would pity him.'

Lorn doubted that but preferred to say nothing. Instead, he asked:

'What's wrong? What ails him?'

'No one knows. The doctors, the mages, the priests, all are powerless. People are starting to say it's the Great Affliction.' The prince grew animated. 'The Great Affliction! But why? For what crime would my father suffer the Great Affliction?'

Lorn did not answer.

According to legend, the Great Affliction struck culpable kings. It persisted for as long as the fault was neither redressed nor pardoned, and it could harm an entire kingdom. It brought famines, wars and epidemics. In the end, no one was spared.

Alan regained control of himself.

'If it does not happen before, then the High Kingdom will slide into war upon the death of my father. I will be forced to take up arms to defend the throne and I would like to be able to count on you. But as I said, I would understand if you refuse. I'm not asking you to give me an answer right away. Only to think about it.'

'I promise I will. But for now…'

'I know, I know. You need some time.'

They exchanged a smile.

'Do you know why your father ordered a second trial for me?' asked Lorn. 'He must have thought I was guilty when I was convicted, since he did not exercise his right to pardon me. So what changed after three years?'

'I don't know,' the prince replied. 'But shortly before he ordered that second trial, he received a visit from of an emissary of the Assembly of Ir'kans.'

'An emissary?'

'That's what they told me.'

'Nothing less than that...'

Lorn remained lost in thought for a moment.

'It seems I have a destiny,' said Alan casually. 'Perhaps you do too...'

But Lorn had no chance to formulate a reply.

'Did you hear that?' the prince asked suddenly, listening carefully.

'Yes.'

'It sounds like cannon fire...'

Intrigued, Lorn hurried to climb up on deck. Alan, who knew what it was about, followed him more slowly.

Shading his eyes with his hand, Lorn counted nine cannonades.

'The count is correct,' he said as Alan joined him. 'Nine for a prince of the blood. Something tells me you're expected.'

'Once again, Esteveris has done his job well.'

'Esteveris?'

'My mother's minister. Don't you remember him? Bah! You'll become acquainted with that snake soon enough...' Alan heaved a resigned sigh. 'Meanwhile, I need to play my part as a prince.'

Lorn suddenly realised how terribly weary his friend looked.

Samarande was bedecked in the colours of the High Kingdom when the royal galleon landed. Stages and barriers had been erected and people stood ready to toss armfuls of flowers from their windows as the procession passed. Kept back by halberdiers, an impatient and joyful crowd had gathered on the quays and in the neighbouring streets. The weather was splendid. The entire city was celebrating.

The galleon having anchored in the port's waters, a delegation of notables came out to meet it aboard a big, luxurious barque. From a distance, people recognised Alderan of Langre, prince of the High Kingdom, when he took a place in this barque to reach the shore. Cheers rose, but the crowds contained their joy until the prince appeared wearing a magnificent outfit with silver trimmings upon a tribune decorated with gold leaf and covered by a canopy of blue silk.

Trumpets sounded and it was a triumph.

On the quays, a movement of the crowd obliged the halberdiers to brace themselves and call out warnings. Their orders were drowned out by the cheering, the bravos and the redoubled applause. The spectators craned their necks and jostled one another, jammed together shoulder to shoulder. Smiling and waving, Alan received the acclaim.

Lorn had remained on the galleon. Wearing a hood which protected his eyes from the sun, he watched the scene and said in an admiring tone:

'I don't recall him being so popular...'

'He wasn't, before his return from Alencia,' Father Domnis informed him. 'It's almost as though he embodies all the hopes of the High Kingdom in these troubled times.'

Young and handsome, charismatic, Alderan of Langre enjoyed the favour of the people who willingly forgave him his old escapades. Youth must have its way. And besides, wasn't he already settling down? Hadn't he visited all of the Imelorian kingdoms as an ordinary gentleman, in order to deepen his knowledge of the world? And undergone a retreat in a monastery for more than two years? It was said that he was generous, attentive and brave.

'Some parties are starting to dream that he will inherit the throne upon the death of the High King,' the white priest said.

'That sounds a bit hasty,' said Lorn. 'Has Yrdel renounced the throne too?'

Alderan was not the only prince of the High Kingdom. He had two older brothers: Jall and Yrdel. And while Jall had abandoned his claim on the crown by joining the Church, Yrdel remained the firstborn and, by right, the heir to the Onyx Throne.

'As far as I know, Yrdel is very much alive, isn't he?' insisted Lorn.

Father Domnis shrugged.

'I don't get mixed up in politics, my son. But the High

Kingdom is divided and under threat. The people are worried. They dream of a great king and fear that Yrdel will not fill the role.'

Lorn remained silent.

He recalled what Alan had confided to him earlier in the day. His worry that a war would break out in the High Kingdom upon the king's death and that he would have to fight to 'defend the throne'. But take up arms against whom? And to defend whose throne?

His own, or Yrdel's?

Lorn reproached himself for imagining his friend to be a usurper. Such a suspicion would never had occurred to him previously. But did that mean he was wrong?

Calm and self-assured, the prince acknowledged the homage he had just received. He addressed a few words to the crowd from the tribune, following which he waved while the people cheered, and then he climbed into the saddle in order to take the head of the long and superb procession awaiting him.

Lorn raised his eyes towards a dazzling sun.

He was now free and the world seemed infinite to him; full of danger and uncertainty.

9

'The festivities in honour of the prince lasted an entire day. When evening came, a ball was held in the governor's palace, while banquets were thrown for the population in the neighbourhoods, streets, courtyards and gardens of the brightly lit city of Samarande.'
Chronicles (The Book of the Three Princes' War)

An hour before the ball, Alan returned to the apartment assigned to him within the governor's palace. There he found Lorn and only took the time to hang up his sword before falling into an armchair, his feet crossed upon a low table.

Lorn had spent the afternoon indoors, in the shade of the louvered shutters, away from a radiant sun he was no longer used to. At Dalroth, he had sometimes been permitted to leave his hellhole down in the cells to spend a few hours alone in one or another of the fortress's small, damp, enclosed courtyards. But the sky was rarely clear and it was usually raining or drizzling – the light of a tomb.

Alan heaved a long sigh as he stretched out.

'Look like hard work being a blood prince,' remarked Lorn.

Although the gibe was mild, his tone was not mild at all. Alan pulled a face and wondered how much bitterness and reproach really lay in Lorn's words. After all, if one of them had good reason to complain about his fate…

The prince chose not to comment.

'I can't bear it any more,' he said. 'And I have less than an hour to prepare for the ball.'

Standing, he went to serve himself a glass of wine and drained it in a single gulp. Lorn noticed the shimmering golden streaks that betrayed the presence of kesh in the dark wine.

The prince poured himself a second glass.

'I'm exhausted,' he declared in a weary, distracted tone.

'This ball is held in your honour,' Lorn said. 'I doubt they'll start without you. Or that anyone will remonstrate with you if you arrive late—'

'No, you misunderstand me.'

Lorn frowned and waited.

'I'm tired, Lorn. Really tired…' The prince began to slowly pace up and down the room. 'Tired of the honours and salvos and trumpets. Tired of putting myself on show. If you only knew how I missed the days of our youth. When I was simply the king's third son, the unruly young one who no one knew what to do with.' He halted and turned towards Lorn. 'We were happy back then, weren't we?'

Lorn gave a faint wistful smile, thinking of the carefree days evoked by the prince. The memories of wild horseback rides, laughter, games, wine and tumbling wenches rose to mind.

'Yes,' he said. 'We were.'

Alan's gaze was already fixed on a less distant and much less pleasant horizon.

'Now, he continued with a serious air, 'the whole kingdom thinks my father has abandoned them. Or that he is mad, or dead, or might as well be. And my mother is more hated than ever. As for Yrdel…' He shrugged. 'Well, you know him: Yrdel is what he is. He will make a good king but he will never be loved by his subjects. But the people love me. They cheer me. They organise feasts for me. They believe in me. Why? It's a mystery. Perhaps because I am the last one they should believe in, but there it is.' He snickered bitterly. 'So this is how my mother and her minister employ me. For no purpose but to be cheered and feted…'

Lorn had just realised how Alan's popularity could be a political weapon. It was hardly surprising that others had already sought to make use of it, for better or worse as far as the High Kingdom was concerned. That afternoon, talking with Father Domnis, he had learned that the High Kingdom was preparing to sell Angborn to Yrgaard. The news had shocked

64

and appalled him. But it was clear how Prince Alderan's visit to Samarande would reassure the other Free Cities.

'They did not want me to go and fetch you at Dalroth,' Alan was saying.

'They?'

'My mother and Esteveris. On the grounds that I was needlessly exposing myself to the dangers of the Sea of Shadows, when I should be attending to the affairs of the High Kingdom. They were furious that I cancelled a state visit at the last minute...'

Lorn had never met Esteveris but he knew where he stood with Queen Celyane. She did not and never had liked him, no doubt due to his influence over her son. That influence could only be harmful since he had often, deliberately or not, encouraged Alan to free himself from his mother's tutelage.

'But Esteveris is an old fox,' the prince continued. 'It didn't take him long to arrange matters more to his liking. The news of my courage has already spread far and wide throughout the High Kingdom: I did not hesitate for an instant to confront the dangers of Dalroth, flying to the aid of a friend, unjustly condemned. Apparently it's even thanks to me that your name was cleared.' Disgusted, he shook his head gently. 'And that's how history is rewritten...'

Alan fell silent.

He was sincerely sorry about the turn taken by events.

'I have not done this to further my glory or to serve Esteveris's plans,' he said. 'And certainly not to be greeted as a hero, when the High Kingdom should be bestowing honours on you.'

Lorn was surprised by the prince's candour and did not know what to say. But when he saw Alan drinking a second glass of wine laced with kesh, he blurted out:

'You should perhaps go easier with that, no?'

It was not truly a question, or even advice, but a plain observation.

The prince did not immediately understand.

Then, looking at his empty glass, he said:

'Oh, that?' He set the glass down. 'Don't worry, the kesh is merely there to give it colour...'

Kesh could be a formidable drug. It was an effective remedy for pain, but in strong doses caused a slow physical and psychological deterioration that often proved fatal. Alan had almost become one of its victims. Following relapse after relapse, he had fled, leaving all behind, and would have been dead in some sordid smoking den if not for Lorn. His recovery had been long and difficult. Rather than journeying to the other Imelorian kingdom or going on a religious retreat, he had undergone a painful cure in an isolated monastery, in the care of Father Domnis. And in deepest secrecy.

Lorn merely looked at him without saying anything and the prince displayed a wide but somewhat nervous grin.

'It's true! Don't you worry about me. I'm cured.' And he felt obliged to insist further. 'I swear to you! I am cured. But try some of this wine, if you don't believe me. You'll see it's harmless. Wine fit for a maiden...'

Lorn didn't know whether to believe his friend or not.

'All right,' he said. 'I'm glad to hear that the whole sorry episode is behind you.'

Alan clapped a friendly hand on his shoulder.

'I'm fine, Lorn. Of the two of us, I'm not the one you should worry about. Look after yourself instead, will you?'

Lorn nodded.

'Perfect!' exclaimed the prince with renewed enthusiasm. 'Now I need to get ready... Are you coming?'

'I don't think so, no.'

'Are you sure? Think it over.' Alan was already halfway to the door. 'We'll discuss it again in a little while, all right?'

Lorn didn't reply.

Leaning out at the balcony, Lorn listened to the noise and the laughter coming from the ball arranged by the governor in the prince's honour. All of the members of the city's high society had been invited. Once he was ready, Alan had again tried to persuade him to come along.

'It will do you good, Lorn. Who needs to have some fun more than you? To drink and to dance? And perhaps court a beautiful lady or two?'

But Lorn had refused. He was in no mood to meet strangers and endure their gazes. Already, aboard the ship, he had
noticed how the crew avoided him and talked behind his back.
He was returning from Dalroth, and the reasons why he had
been sent there mattered little. Innocent or not, he had spent
nearly three years locked up in the fortress. Innocent or not, he
bore the mark of the Dark.

Remembering Father Domnis's advice, Alan had not insisted
further.

'I would stay here with you, but—'

'I don't need you to hold my hand. Go and be a good prince.'

'If you change your mind—'

'I'll see you tomorrow, Alan.'

'And if you need anything at all, Odric is at your service.'

'Until tomorrow.'

Alan got the message and gave him an embarrassed smile.

'Right. Good… Until tomorrow.'

The apartment assigned to the prince looked out over the
gardens of the governor's palace and provided a magnificent
view of the city and its port below. Night had just fallen.
Illuminated by the vast grey and white Nebula, the splendid
starry sky was reflected in the black waters of the Eirdre. The
scent of flowers and trees lining the paths filled the air.

As did the noise from the party rising up to the balcony
from the open windows of the large salons downstairs. People
were chatting and laughing. Glasses clinked. The orchestra was
playing a lively reel, marked by the pounding of the dancers'
heels on the parquet floor.

Lorn regretted not having gone with Alan.

It had been a long time since there had been any gaiety in his
life. A long time since he had been joyful and carefree. Why
should he deprive himself now, after three years? He only had
to descend a few steps. Did he want to live like a hermit for
the rest of his life? Sooner or later, he would have to face the
world around him. He'd known tougher challenges and yet he
hesitated, as one hesitates to love again after a heartbreak…

The night being exceptionally fine, the party left the salons
and the orchestra moved out onto the terrace. More tables were

set up outside. Torches were lit. And an entire dancing parade of dresses soon brightened the gardens.

'Odric!' Lorn called out over his shoulder.

The old servant appeared promptly.

'My lord?'

'Is there an outfit in the prince's wardrobe that might fit me?'

Lorn appeared on the terrace wearing black leather and grey linen. Elegant but lacking confidence, he attracted little attention. Those present chattered and laughed without taking any interest in him. Their glances slid over him with indifference. Two lightly tipsy girls, laughing together, bumped into him. They barely noticed him and did not apologise.

Lorn was rooted in place for a moment, unsure what to do. He had the strange sensation of being lost on the stage of a theatre. He was thinking of returning the way he came when Alan spotted him and, stopping mid-sentence, immediately came over with a wide grin.

They exchanged a manly embrace.

'I know that doublet,' jested the prince.

'Yes, Odric—'

'Keep it. It suits you better than me.'

Lorn nodded.

'I'm so glad you changed your mind,' he said as he took his friend by the elbow.

He turned towards the people he had abandoned. They were waiting, looking intrigued. Lorn met their gazes, noticing an attractive young woman in the group as well as a man with a severe-looking face and hair plastered back, who was staring at him.

'Who's that grim fellow?'

'The ambassador of Angborn. A Yrgaardian by origin. He's delighted with the idea that his city will soon be under the Black Dragon's authority once more. She's such a pleasant being, after all...'

Since the Shadows, a Divine Dragon ruled over Yrgaard. A formidable and feared creature, intelligent but cruel, the Black Dragon nurtured an implacable hatred for the High Kingdom.

'Come,' added Alan, 'I'll introduce you.'

But Lorn refused.

'Actually,' he said in the prince's ear, 'if you don't mind, I would rather...'

People were starting to dart glances in their direction, wondering who this man was the prince treated with such familiarity. He must be the friend Alderan had brought back from an expedition to the Sea of Shadows. They spoke in low murmurs, heads tilted together, pretending to look elsewhere.

'He's said to have spent five years at Dalroth for a crime he did not commit.'

'Five years? I thought it was three.'

'But what was he accused of?'

'Who knows? Both trials were held behind closed doors.'

'To deserve Dalroth, it must have been something terrible...'

Ill at ease, Lorn rubbed the back of his left hand through the thin leather band that wrapped it. Alan guessed how he was feeling and immediately blamed himself for his lack of foresight.

'You're right,' he said. 'Besides, I'm getting bored... Let's go and have a glass of wine somewhere else. The governor has imported an Algueran wine at great cost. It's no match for our Langrian vintages, but it's not too bad...'

Lorn followed Alan towards the buffet tables set up on the terrace. The prince purloined a bottle and two glasses, and they took a few steps out into the gardens. All those whose paths they crossed watched as they walked as far as a balustrade where they could look out over a harmonious perspective of flowerbeds and paths. There Alan filled the two glasses with a slightly unsteady hand. Lorn deduced that his friend had been drinking, but kept silent.

'I... I'm sorry,' said the prince, staring at a spot on the ground.

'Sorry?'

The prince tried to choose his words carefully.

'Yes, I... I realise that I've been tactless...'

Alan was standing with one shoulder hunched, as he always did when he was sincerely, deeply embarrassed. It did not

69

happen often and one needed to know Alan as well as Lorn did to interpret this gesture. Prince Alderan had a calm, sunny personality, full of self-confidence, for whom dealings with others always seemed easy.

'I don't know how to go about this the right way,' the prince was saying. 'Yet I would like to help you, Lorn. I would truly like to help you.'

Lorn kept silent.

Alan had realised that he wanted the old Lorn back, as he was before. The prince had expected to find Lorn exhausted, to be sure. And bruised. Perhaps even diminished. He knew his friend had emerged from a terrible ordeal at Dalroth; but he wanted him to still be Lorn. Even though the road might be long and recovery difficult, he wished for Lorn to remain the person that he, Alan, had always known and cherished. The person he missed. And the one he wanted with all his might to find again. He'd been motivated by a sincere solicitude and affection, but also – he understood now – by a streak of selfishness and perhaps even capriciousness.

'I still want to be your friend, Lorn. And to succeed at that, I know I must comprehend and help the man you have become. But… But it is as though you are out of my reach,' Alan concluded, turning towards Lorn.

Their gazes met.

For the first time since they had been reunited, Lorn felt something of their old friendship stirring within him.

Restrained by an idiotic reserve, the two men merely touched glasses. Alan drank a mouthful of wine, contemplating the gardens for a moment, and then leaned back against the balustrade. Lorn did likewise. They raised their eyes towards the terrace and, beyond it, the governor's palace illuminated by the Great Nebula.

And because they had no need to speak, they fell silent – together – for a long moment.

Alan kept Lorn company for as long as he could.

Then, called away by his political and social duties, he excused himself, promising to return. It was a little before midnight.

70

Lorn waited for him a moment and then thought about leaving the party. But he knew he would have trouble sleeping. And even if he managed to, he also knew what awaited him: every night, nightmares took him back to Dalroth.

Lorn resolved to enjoy the gardens on his own.

They were quiet and fragrant, lit by paper lanterns, and he only needed to take one path or another and wait in a shadowy nook to avoid other strollers. As for lovebirds and couples of a single night, they had no desire to meet anyone else either.

Lorn found an isolated bench near an ornamental pond. Lost in his thoughts, he was rubbing his leather-wrapped hand as he looked up at the milky coils of the Great Nebula when...

'Good evening.'

He recognised the young woman. She had been part of the group Alan had abandoned in mid-conversation to come and greet him. About twenty years in age, she was beautiful and particularly elegant in a pearl-grey dress.

Now she was alone, sipping from a glass of wine.

Lorn rose to his feet.

'Good evening'

'Elana,' she said, extending her hand.

Lorn placed a kiss upon it.

'May I keep you company?' she asked.

Lorn nodded as she already began to sit down. After a moment's hesitation, he took a seat at her side upon the bench.

There was a silence.

Bringing her glass to her lips, Elana observed Lorn's profile closely over its edge. Then she offered him her drink.

'Do you want some?'

'No, thank you.'

'You don't drink?'

She insisted with her gaze.

'All right,' conceded Lorn with a small shrug.

He took a swallow and returned the glass to the young woman. The wine was nicely cooled, slightly flavoured with kesh liqueur. It added a sweetish note, but that was not the kesh's sole virtue. Perhaps it accounted for Elana's indolent air.

Sipping her wine, she resumed her examination of Lorn. It

71

was as if she were trying to detect in his face something that eluded her. Her black eyes flashed with mischief.

Lorn continued to look straight in front of him.

His embarrassment grew and he was about to speak when Elana beat him to it:

'A few days ago,' she said in a conversational tone, 'a royal messenger arrived from the capital. He announced that Prince Alderan would soon be landing at Samarande following a dangerous expedition to the Sea of Shadows.'

Lorn waited, and she asked:

'That dangerous expedition was you, wasn't it?'

He smiled faintly. He'd never been called a dangerous expedition before.

'My name is Lorn.'

'Lorn?'

'Lorn Askarian.'

'That sounds like a Skandish name.'

He made no reply.

'And you were imprisoned at Dalroth,' the young woman added.

Lorn discreetly slipped his left hand beneath his right: the leather band still hid the Dark's seal embedded in his flesh, but he felt as though anyone could see it or guess at its existence. His marked hand hurt for no particular reason. It was the first time he had felt that, and thought it must be a cramp.

As he said nothing, Elana continued:

'According to the messenger, you're a friend of the prince. An old friend?' she asked ingenuously.

'Since we were born.'

'So why did he do nothing, when you were convicted?'

'He was far away. He didn't know.'

'For three years?'

'For three years.'

Intrigued by her, Lorn turned to look at Elana. She held his gaze without blinking and, suddenly joyous, rose to her feet, leaving her empty glass on the bench.

'Let's go somewhere else,' she proposed.

'Pardon me?'

72

'Let's go somewhere else. Let's go for a walk!'

She took Lorn's right hand between hers and tugged him to his feet. He allowed himself to be led.

'Who are you, exactly?' he asked.

'I'm the best thing that could happen to you this evening. Come on!'

Lorn paused to take a closer look at her.

She had long black hair, a pale complexion, sparkling eyes and a pretty face: she was very much to his taste. Or at least, to the taste of the man he had been.

A suspicion, then, arose inside him.

It was as though the pain caused by the Dark's mark on his hand was heightening his wariness and sharpening his senses, as though it were warning him of a danger that was still vague and distant, but real all the same.

Was he mistaken?

He had to find out.

He followed Elana.

10

They left the governor's palace but did not go far, remaining on Samarande's heights.

With Elana on Lorn's arm, they followed paved, brightly lit streets, bedecked with flowers and flags, where the celebrations continued into the night. People strolled, laughed and drank. They danced in the torchlight and played skittles in front of the packed taverns. Accompanied by flutes and tambourines, joyful dancers pranced by, entering and leaving the houses. Orchestras played at the crossroads and everywhere jugglers, fire-eaters, acrobats and bear-baiters performed for the crowds.

Radiant and carefree, Elana talked freely.

Lorn, naturally taciturn, barely listened to her. The pain spreading through his left hand had reached his wrist. The crowds and the noise, moreover, were making him uneasy. It seemed to him that everybody saw, everybody knew. And that those who didn't, guessed. He was marked by the Dark. It was like a visible stigma, a shameful disease, a stain impossible to conceal. He caught people giving him furtive glances. And he felt others at his back.

In every glance, he read the same wariness, disgust and fear that he felt towards himself. And all of them were hostile.

'What if we went to my home?' Elana proposed.

Spoken with the most charming of smiles, this invitation confirmed Lorn's suspicions. He knew he should have felt an attraction and even desire for Elana. And yet there was only mistrust. Who could possibly want to be with him? How could such a young, beautiful woman be seeking the company of a man afflicted by the Dark, in flesh and soul?

She must either be mad or have a special motive.

And Elana seemed to have all her reason intact.

So she wanted something from him. He was convinced of it, as the Dark's mark grew more and more painful, to the point of hindering his train of thought.

'Are you all right?' asked Elana.

'Yes,' Lorn lied, flexing the knuckle of his hand wrapped in leather.

A cold sweat beaded his brow.

'Are you sure?'

He nodded.

'I think… I think I need some peace and quiet. Let's go to your home, yes. Good idea.'

She took hold of his arm.

'Come. It's close by.'

It was a discreet, tidy house at the end of a quiet little street. Elana opened it with her own key and apologised: to allow them to enjoy the festivities, she'd given her valet and her chambermaid the night off. Lorn realised that she was trying to put him at ease, thinking they were alone, which was no doubt untrue.

He entered, more on his guard than ever.

The interior was so clean and well kept it was difficult to say whether anyone actually lived here or not. Elana, however, seemed to know the place well. They climbed a staircase of varnished wood and passed into a pleasantly decorated salon. While the young woman lit some candles, Lorn went to the window and saw that, on this side of the house, they were not on the first floor but much higher. Like all of its neighbours, the house clung to the flank of a hillside and overlooked a river some fifty feet below, running between high banks and spanned by a series of bridges.

Lorn held back a grimace: his hand and his forearm were causing him increasing pain. It was starting to worry him. Not merely because the Dark's mark had never been painful before, but because he supposed the other symptoms he was experiencing – faintness and sweating – were associated with it.

What was happening to him?

'Would you like something to drink?'

Lorn got a grip on himself.

'Yes,' he replied, turning round.

She was standing close to him, a glass in each hand. She was smiling, with a mischievous expression, confident of her charm.

Lorn took the glass she held out, but did not drink from it.

'What is it?' he asked in an amiable voice.

'Wine. From Sarme, I believe. You don't like it?'

'And that's all?'

'What do you mean?' the young woman asked in surprise.

'Just wine. Nothing else?'

'Of course.'

Lorn's tone grew hard.

'Really?'

The young woman seemed perplexed.

'What? But...'

'Really? Answer me!'

She took a step back. She remained calm but her features grew tense. She sensed that something wasn't right, that the situation was getting out of hand...

'There's no drug in this?' demanded Lorn, advancing with a menacing air.

'What's come over you?' ventured Elana. 'I don't...'

'Answer!'

'I don't understand!' she said, keeping her eyes fixed on his.

She retreated slowly and cautiously, as if she were facing a wild, dangerous beast ready to pounce.

'Nothing that will put me to sleep?' asked Lorn. 'Nothing to knock me out or kill me?'

The young woman tried to flee but he was quicker.

He seized her and shoved her against the wall. With a swift gesture, he drew the dagger tucked in his belt and slipped it beneath Elana's chin. She immediately froze.

'Call,' he said.

'Wh... What?'

'Call. Call out for help.'

When she didn't seem to understand, he shook her roughly.

'Call out!'

76

She finally obeyed.

She called out, but not loudly enough to suit Lorn, who, eyes blazing, shook her again.

'Louder!'

This time she cried:

'Help!'

Satisfied, Lorn signalled her to be silent by placing an index finger against her lips, and waited.

He listened, alert to the slightest sound.

Nothing.

'No one?' he asked in an almost jesting tone.

'I… I told you…'

'Yes! I know what you told me!'

'Then why did you ask me to—'

'Because… Because…'

His face twisted by an inner torment, he struggled to think. He felt nauseous. He could not use his left hand without gritting his teeth from the pain and his vision grew blurry at times.

He needed to concentrate.

'Because I don't trust you!' he finally managed to say. 'You… You had me come here for a reason… and I want to know what it is! And don't tell me it's because of my pretty face!'

Enraged, he planted his dagger in the wall, right beside Elana's cheek. She flinched, quivering. He seized her by the throat with both hands and squeezed.

'You're going to tell me what you wanted,' he shouted, spattering her face with saliva. 'You're going to tell me why you lured me here. And… And I want to know who you work for. For the queen? For… For…' He searched his mind. 'For Irelice? For Yrgaard? For…'

Even if she were willing to answer, Elana would have been incapable.

Lorn was strangling her so hard that she could not breathe, much less speak. She needed air. Her eyes full of tears were bulging as she fought to loosen the vice around her throat. But she lacked the strength, and Lorn, prisoner of some inner demon, had lost track of the world around him. The pain in his left arm was blinding him. A red veil had fallen before his eyes. His voice sounded deep and slow in his ears when he repeated:

'Who is it? Who? Speak!'

Elana struggled, in vain, and more and more weakly. Finally, in a gasp, she managed to emit a pitiful:

'Mer... cy...'

And that word, that simple word uttered in a dying voice, had its effect.

Barely audible, it reached Lorn. He suddenly realised what he was doing. It was if he had snapped out of a waking nightmare. He released Elana, who fell to her knees, while he stumbled backwards and stood there gaping at his hands, his surroundings and, lastly, at the young woman before him.

'I'm... I'm sorry,' he said. 'I...'

He did not understand what had come over him. He did not understand why he'd suspected this young woman of...

Of what, exactly?

His arm was still hurting him. And he still felt ill, but he had recovered enough lucidity to appraise the situation, as if in a thick fog, and realise the gravity of his deed.

A deed he could not explain except as one of madness, of the Dark awakening in his soul as it had awoken in his flesh.

Elana had regained her feet.

Still gasping and shuddering, she leaned upon a small table on which rested a stoneware pitcher. Her long unbound hair hung before her face. Her shoulders lifted in time with her laboured breathing.

Lost, fragile, Lorn was wondering what he had become.

He wanted to aid and comfort Elana, not knowing she had recovered far more quickly than her appearance suggested.

The pitcher struck him in the temple.

A first blow made him stagger.

A second made him fall over.

And a third, breaking the vessel, left him unconscious on the floor, bleeding from the head.

Very coolly, Elana looked at Lorn lying stretched out and shook her head, in both disbelief and exasperation. She had not expected him to give her so much trouble, and certainly not to have been so quick to unmask her…

When he woke, Lorn did not move.

His cheek resting on the floor, he opened one eye and saw Elana making several passes with a lit candle in front of the window. He had both eyes closed when she turned round and pretended to still be unconscious when she inspected him, lifting one of his eyelids with her thumb.

She seemed satisfied with what she saw.

Nevertheless, she returned with a cord to tie him up. He let her, being in no state to resist. He lacked the strength. His head was spinning and his vision remained blurred. He was not certain his legs would bear his weight and his arm was still torturing him.

Driven by curiosity, Elana took the time to examine the stone seal on Lorn's hand. Then she bound his wrists, but was disturbed before she finished.

Someone was coming.

Lorn could distinguish the footsteps of several men. One of them exchanged a few words with the young woman. His ears buzzing, Lorn couldn't make out any words. Their voices sounded distorted and they seemed to be speaking a foreign language.

He nevertheless recognised one word:

'Irelice.'

If he had heard correctly, Lorn needed to escape at any price. There was no question of his remaining in the hands of Elana and these men. He did not know what they wanted exactly, but he had no intention of finding out at his own expense.

How many men were there?

Two or three? Four, perhaps?

It didn't matter.

Lorn knew he wasn't strong enough to put up a fight against even one of them. He was not even sure he could remain on his feet for very long.

And as for delivering a single well-placed blow…

He waited until they seized him and drew him to his feet.

79

Taking advantage of the fact that the men supporting him were not expecting a struggle, he freed himself with a shrug of his shoulders and charged forward.

He took a few long clumsy strides towards the grey, wavering rectangle that marked the window.

And threw himself at it.

'No!' Elana cried.

Lorn tumbled out into thin air.

11

'Woe to he whose body is embraced by the Dark. Woe to he whose soul it embraces. Woe to he who hears its Call and woe to he who answers. Woe to he who, in his entirety, is delivered unto it.'

Chronicles (The Book of Prayers)

Lorn plunged straight into the river and disappeared beneath its dark, swift waters.

The current carried him away.

Dazed by the shock of a fifty-foot fall, he resurfaced downstream. He took a great gulp of air and did his best to keep his head above water. But he was weak and disoriented. His movements were clumsy and uncoordinated. Moreover, he had to struggle in the darkness, with only one able arm, against treacherous eddies and whirlpools. His boots had filled with water and were pulling him towards the bottom. Luckily, the bonds that Elana had hastily knotted had come undone around his wrists.

Battered and tossed about, Lorn thought he was going to drown and almost knocked himself out against the pile of a bridge before grabbing hold of it.

It was a brief respite.

He did not have the energy to call out and knew that he would not be able to hang on for long. He looked for some means of rescue, a hope, anything. His troubled vision allowed him a glimpse of a stairway that descended from a quay to the river.

Perhaps he could reach it…

Lorn drew a deep breath, calculated his trajectory by instinct, and let go. The battle he waged against the current used up his remaining strength. He swallowed water several times, thought he'd missed his target, but finally succeeded in dragging himself out of the water onto the stone steps.

He remained still for a long moment, listening to the sounds of the celebrations and the conversations of people who walked by without seeing him. Then, shaking and feverish, he stood and climbed the stairs on trembling legs. His left arm was one great throb of pain. His clenched hand barely responded to his commands and when he tried to move his frozen fingers, a burning sensation radiated through them to the tips of his nails.

He was close to the port. The inhabitants were a more mixed and dangerous lot than on the city heights, but the neighbourhood was perfect for disappearing. Soaked and limping, keeping his head bowed, he slipped into the flow of passers-by without anyone taking notice of him or showing alarm at his state.

Yet he had never felt so physically ill. He was both hot and shivering from cold. There was a whistling in his ears. He was crippled by cramps. Steel claws raked his guts. He did not know the cause of his state and found it difficult to think. Impossible to concentrate or follow an idea to its conclusion. It occurred to him that he should return to the palace, but he quickly dismissed this notion out of fear that Elana's men would be waiting there for him.

Besides, he was thirsty.

Very thirsty.

Yes, a few glasses of wine would do him good…

Still dripping, Lorn entered the first tavern he came across.

He sat in a corner, having to start over twice as he counted out the money he had on him, and ordered a jug of wine. The tavern was seedy but he didn't care. He just wanted to drink and drink, hoping the wine would kill the fever and his pains.

So he drank.

A young girl brought him a second jug of wine. She was winsome, rather plump, with a pretty mouth and beautiful chestnut curls, not yet twenty years in age. She smiled at him and thereafter often caught his eye by smiling again. He responded mechanically. He even found some comfort in it, but soon perceived that he was attracting hostile gazes from a group of sailors seated at a neighbouring table. At first, he thought he might be mistaken, but no, it was him they were eyeing as they spoke in low voices.

Lowering his eyes he saw that the leather band around the Dark's seal on his left hand had come undone. In the dim light, the dark red stone medallion resembled a clot of blood and the rune looked almost black. As if caught doing something shameful, Lorn hid both hands beneath the table.

The sailors rose, looking grim.

Surmising they were about to have a go at him, Lorn decided to leave. He was in no shape to fight and had only one desire: to be left in peace until he felt better. He bolted, making a detour in the crowded room, trying not to cross anyone's gaze. He did not linger, wending his way among the tables and customers, leaving by a small door that led him into a sordid-looking alley. The sailors had already lost sight of him, but as soon as he set foot outside, someone shoved him from behind.

Lorn fell headlong upon the filthy paving stones. His breath cut short, it took him a moment to understand what had happened. The person who'd bumped into him so violently had meant him no harm: the man was being attacked by four others, who were amusing themselves by hitting him and pushing him back and forth within their circle. Lorn, too busy looking out for himself, had walked right into the middle of the brawl.

He picked himself up, wiping his mouth.

In the alley, there was no one else except Lorn, the four louts and the wretch, who, struck in the head, had collapsed and was now receiving a flurry of kicks. The thought of intervening occurred to Lorn. It mattered little to him what this man had done. He was on the ground and, four against one, might die if no one stepped in. His aggressors were running amok, drunk and relentless. Soon they would be kicking an inert, bloody heap.

But Lorn stayed rooted in place, hugging his left arm tightly against his body...

The biggest of the four men caught his eye. Leaving the others to finish their work, he straightened up and, displaying a nasty little smile on his lips, took a step towards Lorn. He was heavy and fat. Sweat beaded his brow and the knuckles of his fists were scraped raw. Intrigued at first, he calmly looked Lorn up and down, silently challenging him to make a move.

Lorn swallowed. He was trembling.

Without taking his eyes off Lorn's, the lout opened his trousers and turned to one side in order to urinate on the victim's sprawled body. As he pissed, he continued to stare at Lorn. After which he gave a loud snort and refastened his trousers while Lorn bowed his head and turned on his heels.

Sick, broken and defeated, Lorn slowly walked away.

Behind him, he heard the big lout snicker and spit scornfully.

Lorn vomited against a wall two streets further on.

The wine had added drunkenness to his fever without easing his pain. He felt lost and abandoned. Attacked by the Dark, his body was betraying him. And his will, his strength of character, was weakening as well.

He was delirious.

Dalroth had got the better of him. There had been the nightmares and the haunted nights. There had been the solitude and the despair in the shadows of his cell. And at the end of this long, slow ordeal, only two outcomes were open to him: madness or oblivion.

Lorn had believed that he'd defeated the cursed fortress by avoiding madness, cheating the Dark's spectres. But he was wrong. For although he had not become demented, he was now no more than the shadow of a vanished man.

He felt gazes upon him, gazes that perhaps he only imagined but were unbearable all the same. Leaving the animation of the festive streets, he entered a back alley.

Fleeing.

He disgusted himself.

Humiliated and distraught, Lorn was overcome by dizziness and vomited again. He hadn't eaten anything and had been drinking throughout the evening. He had no idea where he was and could not care less. He just wanted to disappear.

At the entrance to the porch of a building, he raised a

sweating face to the night sky. His gaze sank into those eternal depths and his thoughts took him back to Dalroth and the night he was freed, when he found himself backed up against the ramparts.

He suddenly burst into sobs.

'I should have jumped,' he murmured, letting himself slide down the wall.

He fell sitting on the ground and took his head in his hands.

'I should have jumped,' he repeated in a broken voice. 'Jumped...'

12

'Well! You look more in need of this than me...'

Lorn lifted his head from between his hands.

A man he had not noticed before was sitting in the shadow of the porch. A beggar. And he was offering Lorn a bottle.

Lorn hesitated, wiped his nose and mouth on the back of his sleeve.

'Go on, have a drink!' the man insisted.

Lorn took the bottle in a shaking hand. After all, anything would do to take away the foul taste in his mouth.

Though...

Lorn grimaced after the first gulp and swallowed it down with difficulty.

'Not exactly first-rate, is it?' the beggar commented wryly.

'Not really, no.'

'It's the wine the burghers gave to the city to celebrate the prince's visit. Believe me, they're drinking better stuff up there, at the governor's palace. But the rest of us are supposed to drink this and give thanks for it.'

The beggar fell silent for a moment.

'I'm called Delio.'

'Lorn.'

'Have another drink, Lorn. You'll get used to it, I assure you.'

Lorn obeyed and immediately regretted it. To be sure, the wine seemed less foul, but not to the point of giving it a third chance. He returned the bottle to the beggar, who drained it in a few gulps.

'And I wouldn't worry so much if I were you. I know what ails you. It will pass,' said Delio in a reassuring voice.

Lorn looked at him steadily and the beggar understood.

'Oh,' he said knowingly. 'I see.'

'What do you see?'

'It's the first time it's happened to you, isn't it?'

'You know what's wrong with me?'

'Well, that depends. Do you use kesh?'

'No.'

'Then yes, I know.'

Delio stood up and left the darkness of the porch. Intrigued, Lorn stood up in turn, leaning on the wall. His legs trembled a little, but they supported him.

'What...? What is it?' he asked. 'What's wrong with me?'

His impatience had made his voice hoarse and menacing.

Normally, he would have paid no attention to the beggar. But he was so far at a loss concerning the illness afflicting him that he was ready to hear anything, to listen to anyone.

And perhaps even believe what he was told.

'Where did you catch that?' Delio enquired.

With a glance and a movement of his chin, he designated Lorn's marked hand. Lorn realised that the Dark's mark was again visible. And once again he covered it up with his right hand.

'Don't trouble yourself,' said the beggar, removing the filthy hood that covered his head.

He had a craggy, badly shaven face, whose left cheek was eaten by a purple, venous crust. It was the purple plague, the plague of the Dark. It wasn't contagious, but there was no cure for it.

Lorn understood why the man stank of rotten meat as well as filth.

'Well?' insisted Delio. 'Where did you catch it? In the Deadlands?'

Without really knowing why, Lorn decided to tell the truth.

'Dalroth.'

The beggar's eyes grew wide.

'Dalroth?' he exclaimed. 'Well, damn me... My compliments.'

He was speechless for a moment, and then asked suddenly:

'Can you stand us a round?'

'You said you knew what's wrong with me,' said Lorn.

He was growing tired.

'You won't like it.'

'Tell me!'

Delio retreated a step, but obeyed.

'You must know what happens when a kesh smoker is suddenly deprived of his favourite drug…'

Lorn knew only too well. But he was too weary and too ill to be truly moved by the memory of Alan lying in his filth, a cold pipe in his lips. He was not even sure he was still capable of compassion.

'Withdrawal,' he said.

'That's right. Well, you're going through the same thing, but with the Dark.'

Ignoring the pain in his left hand, Lorn seized the beggar by the collar. His eyes flashed with anger.

'I… I said you wouldn't like it!' Delio yelped.

'What are you talking about?'

The beggar was gasping for air.

'It's… the Dark… Your body… It's… It's grown used to… It… needs…'

Lorn shoved him away violently before he could finish his sentence.

'You lie!'

Toppling backwards, Delio had struck a wall. He rubbed his neck and said:

'All right, all right… Perhaps I'm mistaken then…'

'And why should I listen to you?' rumbled Lorn. 'Why should I believe you? Why should I believe the ranting of a stinking, filthy wretch! A beggar! One who's being eaten alive by the Dark!' he spat. 'So? Why should I?'

His gaze was still filled with rage. But it was also the gaze of a man who was lost, adrift, for whom rebellion and denial were the last recourse.

'Because you're really not any better off than I am?' suggested Delio.

Lorn froze, struck in the heart.

Fearing he was about to receive another blow, the beggar cringed. But Lorn only stared at him and reflected, despite the torments of his fever, standing there shivering, his eye haunted by a painful uncertainty.

He suffered a dizzy spell.

His knees gave out and he would have fallen if Delio had not rushed forward to grab him.

'Steady now! Stay with me, friend…'

Smaller than Lorn, the beggar had difficulty holding him up. But Lorn leaned on his shoulder and eventually recovered.

'All right?' asked Delio anxiously.

'I should have jumped.'

'Jumped from where?'

'From on top of a rampart.'

'That's rarely a good idea. Can you walk?'

'I… I think so, yes.'

'And do you have any money?'

'A little.'

'That will do. Come on, we'll soon set you right…'

They took a bridge over the Eirdre and walked into Bejofa.

They dined on soup in a cheap eating place and then visited a series of squalid taverns. They went from alley to alley, crossed back courtyards darker than wells, descended into cellars where people drank to pass out and forget. It was a sordid and dangerous world. One's throat could be slit for a copper belt buckle, girls exchanged their favours for the promise of sleeping in a bed, and famished children begged at the doors of kesh-smoking dens. But no one asked questions in this world. And no one judged anyone else here.

Lorn ended up feeling at ease with Delio.

He had followed the beggar without thinking at first, and then out of weakness. He let himself be towed along. The soup had revived him some, while the darkness of the places they visited reassured him. The worst of his fit of illness seemed to have passed. He still suffered from cramps but he felt better and, despite his fatigue, was starting to enjoy the beggar's company.

The man was likeable. He only stopped talking to whistle for jugs and bottles which Lorn willingly paid for. Born in Sarme, Delio was a former sailor who had spent the first part of his life at sea and not re-embarked after a stopover in port. Delio himself could not say why. At the appointed hour, he'd ordered another glass of wine instead of returning on board. That had happened in Samarande, fifteen years earlier.

'I tell myself that one day, perhaps, I will leave on another ship. But I know that it won't happen. I'll die here. And as far as dying goes, this city is as good as any, am I right?'

Lorn had nodded.

The beggar was talkative but he wasn't inquisitive. Besides, he knew all he needed to about Lorn: the man had money and was willing to spend it buying Delio drinks. On that point, Lorn had no illusions. He did not doubt that Delio would abandon him as soon as he ceased paying and would forget all about Lorn by the following day. But it didn't matter. Delio distracted him. He was joyful and, when inebriated, proved to be a bountiful source of funny and increasingly bawdy tales. One of them made Lorn burst into laughter and cough up the mouthful of wine he had just drunk. It splashed on a man and they would have come to blows if Delio had not defused the situation with a jest.

As the night advanced, the celebrations came to a close in Samarande. The musicians put away their instruments, people went home and the streets emptied little by little. Soon there remained only a few drunks who were chased away by the city watch and some lovebirds who did not want the evening to end.

But Bejofa was a neighbourhood that never slept entirely.

They were going from one tavern to another when, passing a dark alley, Lorn detected presences in the shadows. At first, he acted as if he hadn't noticed and counted six men. Then he pressed a protective hand upon Delio's chest to keep him back.

'Careful,' he said.

The beggar retreated as the men revealed themselves. Petty criminals. Thugs used to performing dirty deeds. Dressed in thick leather and rough cloth, they had daggers at their belts and all of them held weighted clubs, except for one. He stood with his arms crossed. Tall and bald, his bare shoulders covered with black hairs, he seemed to be the gang's leader.

Sure of himself, he struck a pose.

'You gave us quite a chase,' he said.

'You were looking for me?' Lorn asked.

'You could have killed yourself throwing yourself out that window…'

Sincerely indifferent to his own fate, Lorn shrugged. He heard Delio, behind him, running away before it was too late.

The thugs advanced, ready to fight.

'It would be simpler if you followed us,' the bald man said.

'Where?'

'You'll see.'

Lorn let out a sigh.

The thugs slowly encircled him, moving cautiously, some of them slapping their clubs on the palm of their hands. Without doing anything to prevent them, Lorn considered his situation. He did not feel up to contending with these men. Indeed, he did not feel up to contending with anyone or anything. But the idea of surrendering to these brutes was unbearable.

'I won't follow you anywhere.'

'There are six of us.'

'Doesn't matter.'

Unarmed since he had planted a dagger in the wall at Elana's place, Lorn balled his fist and adopted a fighting stance.

'I don't want to hurt you,' the bald man told him.

'That makes me feel much better. I think that, above all, you want me alive.'

The man smiled. Most of his teeth were missing.

'You're cleverer than I thought,' he said.

'Because you actually think?'

The bald man's smile faded.

'As you like, then… Don't kill him,' he said to his men. 'And don't mess him up too badly.'

The thugs knew how to win a street fight: they attacked all at once. Before he had time to react, a blow from a club landed on Lorn's ribs, then a second upon his back, while a third almost broke his wrist. He let out a cry and did not see the blow that hit him beneath the chin and caused him to stagger backwards. He fell down at the foot of a crumbling wall.

The gang members tightened their ring around him. Their leader parted them to pass through.

He hadn't struck a single blow.

'It's over,' he said.

But Lorn got up with the help of the wall.

Tottering, he displayed a deranged smile and spat out a bloody gob. He raised his fists and once again took up a fighter's stance. He was unsteady on his feet and his gaze was blank.

'Go on,' ordered the bald man.

One of the thugs attacked. Lorn surprised him with a right hook to the temple, but he was powerless to counter the others. Blows started to rain down. On his sides. On his back. On his belly. Unable to defend himself, Lorn protected his head with his elbows. He gritted his teeth, reeled but did not fall. His opponents were forced to persist and the ordeal went on.

Finally, a blow to the back of his thighs forced him to his knees. The next blow, on the back, forced him to arch his body and lower his arms. The last blow, right in his face, toppled him.

Lorn lay exhausted and broken, his hair sticky, his face covered in blood and mud. His arms stretched out, he coughed up a thick bile that stained his lips. He was almost blind. A buzzing filled his ears. He was in incredible pain and wanted to die.

The gang leader towered over him.

'Why do you bring this on yourself?'

Lorn did not reply. He groaned and raised himself with difficulty on all fours. He was still trying to stand up.

'By the Divine Ones!' the bald man muttered.

Then there came one blow too many.

It was a violent kick to the ribs which blasted Lorn with pain. The thugs' leader thought it was the finishing blow. Looking satisfied and almost relieved, he gazed down at Lorn who had fallen back on the dirty paving stone and lay motionless. Was he still breathing? Yes, fortunately. But he would no doubt keep some traces of his injuries. No one could fully recover from the beating he had just endured.

A few seconds went by in the silent alley.

Then, just when the bald man was about to give the order for him to be carried off, Lorn rolled onto his belly. And slowly, ponderously, like a stone giant who had slumbered too long, he rose up.

On one knee first.

Then up on legs that did not tremble.

His chest lifted by deep breathing, Lorn straightened up his shoulders and head. He balled his fists. On the back of his left hand, the leather band slipped off and revealed the stone seal. A strange gleam shone in his eye. Running through his left arm, the pain had completely overwhelmed him and become welcoming, soothing.

It cradled him.

'What...?' managed the gang leader.

Abnormally lucid and calm, Lorn dealt first of all with the two quickest thugs. He dodged an attack by the first and delivered a palm blow to the base of the nose that drove his opponent's nasal bones into his brain. As the man collapsed, Lorn seized the second's wrist. He turned him round by raising his arm at his back, forcing him to put one knee on the ground, held his jaw in the crook of an elbow and, with a sharp twist, broke his neck from behind.

The cracking sound caused his remaining aggressors to freeze. They instinctively backed away and exchanged anxious glances.

Lorn released the corpse which slumped to the ground. He retrieved the man's dagger while the thugs and their leader kept their distance. He resumed a fighting stance, planted on bent legs, and challenged his adversaries with a look.

He felt good and smiled. It had been a long while since he had felt this...

Alive.

One of the thugs decided that the game was no longer worth

the effort and fled before his leader could retain him. The two others hesitated. In their eyes, the odds had changed.

It was Lorn who launched the next assault.

He leapt forward, avoided a clumsy blow from a club, spun round as he slipped beneath the guard of one thug and, rising up, planted his dagger several times in the man's body: three quick stabs, each of which pierced a vital organ. Returning to the one whose club he had dodged, Lorn sank his dagger into an eye. The blade broke off and remained in the socket, from which blood spurted.

The leader finally attacked.

He'd unsheathed a very long dagger. It was a blade of fine quality, which he'd looked after with care and knew how to use. It hissed twice in front of Lorn's nose. On the third pass, the knight grabbed hold of his opponent's wrist with both hand, drove his knee into the man's belly and followed up with an arm lock. The bald man grimaced and fell to his knees, incapable of making the slightest gesture due to his pain. He dropped his dagger and moaned:

'Mercy...'

But Lorn pressed down with his full weight and dislocated the man's shoulder. With tears in his eyes, the man choked with pain and vomited. Lorn bent down, seized him by one ear and obliged him to look him in the eye.

What the gang leader saw there terrified him.

'M... Mercy,' he repeated.

Lorn slowly leaned forward, until their cheeks brushed one another and the scent of the man's sweat and filth filled his nostrils.

'Thanks,' he murmured in the man's ear as he picked up the fallen weapon.

The bald man gave him a look of disbelief.

'Th... Thanks?'

He did not see the dagger thrust that passed through his throat. Lorn stood up and took a few steps back to watch the man choke in his own blood, his heels scraping the ground while a necklace of pink bubbles soaked his chest.

When the body no longer moved, Lorn took a deep breath

before walking over to a barrel of rainwater placed beneath a drainpipe at the entrance to the alley. He plunged his head in, washed off the mud and the blood covering his face, and brusquely straightened up, refreshed, his hair dripping.

But something wasn't right.

He sensed it just before the pain struck him in the abdomen like a hammer blow. He fell to his knees, moaning and grimacing as he held his belly. It felt like a small animal was devouring his intestines. He took hold of the barrel, trying to stand up, but his suffering was too great. And suddenly, he thought a red-hot nail had been driven through his left hand. He let out a cry. Incredulous, he lifted up his marked hand before his eyes burning with sweat and observed it as if it did not belong to him, as if he were seeing these curled fingers and muscles tensed to the breaking point for the very first time.

The pain in his belly intensified and blinded him.

He collapsed.

Rolled onto his back.

He retched and, before passing out, vomited a thick black bile which spilled across his cheeks.

13

'Exasperated by the queen, some great lords had reached the point where they nurtured projects of rebellion. They united behind the Duke of Feln, who was an inveterate plotter.'
Chronicles (The Book of the Three Princes' War)

A secret messenger had announced their coming.

The riders arrived in the night and, from his window, Count Teogen of Argor watched them enter the courtyard of his castle. It was a keep built on the side of a mountain and partly hollowed from the granite, an austere and solitary dwelling to which the count had retired after being removed from the High King's Council. He loved this place, no doubt because he flattered himself in thinking it resembled him: hard and cold, but solid and without pretence.

And belonging to another era.

The riders wore great dark capes which covered the rumps of their mounts. Swordsmen for the most part, they numbered a dozen, but only two dismounted, following the servants who had hastened to meet them with torches.

Teogen remained at his window, his gaze lost in the direction of the dark ragged silhouettes of his mountains. He knew what had brought the horsemen. He already knew what Duncan of Feln was going to propose and he was not yet certain what answer he would give. But the High Kingdom was in a bad way. According to some, the realm was poised on the edge of a deep abyss. It was all the fault of a king who no longer ruled, and an ambitious and hated queen.

There was a knock at the door.

*

As soon as he entered, the Duke of Feln threw his cloak on one of the armchairs placed in front of the fireplace and exchanged a formal embrace with Teogen.

'Good evening, count.'

'Good evening.'

They had not seen one another since the Count of Argor had returned to his mountains. The count remained a force of nature despite his fifty-seven years. Tall and massively built, he had grown stout but still seemed capable of crushing a helmet and the skull inside with a single blow from his mace, his favourite weapon on the field of battle. Although he wielded a sword instead, Duncan had also distinguished himself by his courage in combat, which had earned him the scar that marred his cheekbone. He was reputed, however, to be more a wily politician than a man of war. With a well-trimmed beard and a confident gaze, he was ten years younger than Teogen.

'My daughter accompanies me,' he announced. 'If you would permit it, I would like her to be present during our meeting.'

The count turned towards Eylinn of Feln, viscountess of Beorden, who entered the room in her turn.

'Just one word from you and I will retire, count,' she said, performing a curtsey that etiquette did not require.

'No,' replied Teogen. 'Since it pleases your father that you should remain...'

A humble smile upon her lips, the young woman straightened up and undid the lace of her cape, allowing a servant to take it away. She possessed a delicate beauty: a lily-white complexion, a sweet face and ruby lips. But the most striking thing about her was her eyes, eyes full of life, intelligence and cunning.

'Thank you, count.'

She was dressed as a rider, wearing black and red only as she was still in mourning for her husband, a very old and very rich lord whose fortune had refilled the chests of the Feln family.

Teogen invited the duke and his daughter to sit near the hearth, in order to enjoy the heat and the light of the fire crackling therein. Then he waited for the servant to pour the traditional ice wine of the Argor Mountains and leave, before saying:

'I'm listening, duke.'

'You already know why I've come here, don't you?'

'You want me to join your cabal.'

Without showing any sign of it, Eylinn was amused. It was Teogen's way to get straight to the point: he belonged to a different era and a different world from her father. But Eylinn knew this was also a role he played in order to hide his own game and destabilise whoever he dealt with. The duke was aware of this as well, for he did not miss a beat and calmly declared:

'I would like you to join the forces that will restore the High Kingdom to its former grandeur.'

The count smiled. He drank a mouthful of wine, keeping his eyes on Duncan's. The duke continued:

'If the High Kingdom was in a poor state when you were dismissed from the Council, matters are worse today. There are rumblings of revolt in the countryside. The harvests were poor and the people are overburdened by taxes. Nevertheless, the treasury's chests are empty and the funds are lacking to attend to the kingdom's essential needs. And what will happen when the High Kingdom is no longer able to defend its borders?'

Teogen frowned.

'How's that?'

'For the last two months, the soldiers in the garrisons of the North and the East have been on half-wages,' the Duke of Feln explained.

'I doubt that Vestfald will attack us.'

'I grant you that. But what about Yrgaard?'

'Yrgaard?'

'The High Kingdom is about to cede Angborn to it.'

At these words, Teogen's fists balled. Duncan noticed this but gave no sign.

He added:

'Selling it would be a more accurate description.'

His fists still closed, Teogen clenched his jaw while Eylinn, whose eyes flashed, contained a smile. She knew the count numbered among King Erklant's earliest companions, with whom he had reconquered the province of the Free Cities, defended his throne, and driven off the Black Dragon's armies. Abandoning, losing, or – worse still – selling Angborn was a breach of the kingdom's integrity, but also, for a warrior and a man of honour like Teogen, an insult to the memory of those who had shed their blood or given their lives to liberate the Free Cities from the Yrgaardian yoke.

'For the High Kingdom,' the Duke of Feln was saying, 'it's an opportunity to replenish its coffers. But for Yrgaard?'

For a moment, Argor thought the question was merely rhetorical, but Duncan evidently expected an answer. Annoyed that the duke was playing at being a teacher with him, he shrugged his shoulders, but nevertheless deigned to respond:

'Yrgaard acquires Angborn, of course!'

Duncan of Feln could not prevent himself from showing a small, superior smile. Eylinn saw this and raised an eyebrow: because he thought he was more intelligent than almost anyone else, her father was sometimes his own worst enemy.

'Yes, but more than that,' he said. 'Yrgaard acquires Angborn and its fortress. Which stand at the entrance to the bay of the Free Cities. Do you remember that island, Teogen? Do you remember that fortress?'

The duke nodded grimly.

Angborn had been the key stake in the final act of the Free Cities' reconquest. For several months, a terrible battle had been waged in its ditches and upon its ramparts, the Yrgaardians fighting to the last to defend it. How many men had perished there? Teogen could only name some of them, but all had fallen close by him...

Still watchful, Eylinn reminded herself that her father knew what tune he needed to sing to Teogen. Yet, wasn't he singing a little too loudly, forcing the note? Despite appearances, the count was not some easily fooled yokel.

'He who controls Angborn,' continued the duke, 'controls the bay. And he who controls the bay dictates his law to the Free Cities. Believe me, Angborn is only the first step in a campaign of conquest.'

He added:

'Armed conquest. The Black Dragon...'

Teogen ceased listening and raised his eyes towards a torn banner that hung on the wall. It was black and embroidered with a wolf's head – seen face-on – in silver thread. The emblem of the High King. Not that of the High Kingdom, but the personal symbol of Erklant II. The king had given him that banner on the evening after a hard-fought battle and, since then, the count had kept it as a talisman.

He was a warrior, an old warrior who knew the price of loyalty and the value of shed blood.

'The Black Dragon,' he murmured.

He had never met her, or even seen her. On the other hand, he had fought one of her offspring. 'Dragon-princes', as they were called. They were human in appearance, but bore within them a part of their progenitor's power. It made them formidable enemies, capable of releasing enough Dark force to mow down the front rows of an entire army.

Realising he had lost his audience's attention, Duncan of Feln had stopped speaking. He hesitated for an instant. More skilled at detecting emotions, his daughter took the initiative and stood, rousing Teogen from his reverie.

'I see that my presence here is superfluous,' said Eylinn with a ravishing smile. 'Moreover, it's late. Could you tell me the way to your altar? I should like to pray before we set forth again.'

'Pray to whom?' asked the Count of Argor.

'An altar devoted to any one of the First Ancestrals will suit me. No doubt he will carry my prayers to Eth'ril.'

'My wife also prayed to the Dragon of Dreams. I will open her chapel for you,' said Teogen, without showing the emotion he felt at the memory of his wife.

The young woman placed a hand upon her chest and bowed slightly.

'Thank you very much, count.'

Once they were alone, Teogen and Duncan remained silent for a moment. The count had risen to pour himself another glass of wine. He drained it in one gulp and, in a matter-of-fact tone, said:

'It's too late to prevent the cession of Angborn.'

'True,' admitted the Duke of Feln. 'So we need to prepare for the future. Even if the High Kingdom were at the height of its power and glory, the prospect of a war with Yrgaard should worry us, but in our present state… We'd better pray too, if we don't act…'

Count Teogen was not the sort of man who looked to the First Ancestrals for rescue. Or to anyone, for that matter.

'Pray!' he exclaimed.

'Yes, count. Let us pray that if the Black Dragon attacks, she attacks as late as possible. Let us pray that the tribute Yrgaard will pay suffices to replenish our treasury and, if not, let us pray that Vestfald continues to sell us grain on credit. Let us pray that the foreign bankers do not ask for an immediate reimbursement of the enormous sums they have loaned the Crown. Let us pray that the countryside is not set alight. Let us pray that the next winter is not too hard. And while we're at it, let us pray that the king is cured of the illness that ails him and that the queen recovers a semblance of good sense. Let us pray, count.'

Teogen heaved a sigh. He sat down, reflected for a moment, and then asked:

'What do you expect of me?'

The duke leaned forward and said:

'Queen Celyane takes advantage of the king's illness to exercise a regency that is not only disastrous but illegal. We have every reason to be opposed to her. If I stand against her, the great lords of the realm will follow me…'

'For the sole good of the High Kingdom, of course,' the Count of Argor commented ironically.

Duncan gave him a faint smile.

'It's true that some will only aspire to regain the titles and the honours that were theirs before the queen excluded them, just as she excluded you. But what do their motives matter? It's a question of saving the kingdom.'

'However, although the great lords will follow your lead, the lesser nobles of the sword will follow mine. And you would also like to be able to count on my wyverners. That's why you want me at your side.'

In all of the High Kingdom, there were no better wyvern riders than those of the Argor Mountains. And only Argorians knew the secret of training the winged reptiles for combat.

'Indeed,' agreed the duke. 'Except I do not want you at my side, but at our head.'

Teogen chuckled.

'At your head,' he said. 'Well, well…'

He marked a pause and, looking Duncan straight in the eye, said:

'So that my head will fall rather than yours if the little adventure you're proposing goes sour…?'

The duke stood up and protested:

'Count! You can't—'

But Teogen cut him short by bursting into loud laughter.

'I'm teasing you, Duncan. I'm teasing you… Sit down.'

But he meant every word, even so. Becoming serious again, he added:

'It remains the case that you are asking me to take up arms against the throne. It would mean plunging the kingdom into a civil war.'

'No. If you were leading our troops, I doubt very much that a single drop of blood would be shed or a single cannon fired. When she sees the entire kingdom has risen against her, the queen will have no choice but to give in to our demands.'

'Which are?'

'A regency, this one legitimate, until the king recovers.'

'If the king ever recovers. And who will exercise this regency?'

'The Council.'

'Where you will sit.'

'As will you.'

Thinking hard, Teogen nodded distractedly, his eyes lost in the distance.

'If the queen does not give in,' he said at last in a grave tone, 'then it shall be war. And it will be a bloody one.'

*

After his meeting with the count, Duncan of Feln found his daughter waiting for him in the courtyard with his horsemen. Wearing her great cloak, she was already in her saddle.

'Since when do you pray to the Dragon of Dreams?' asked the duke as he straddled his mount.

'Since I learned the late countess did.'

'Clever,' conceded Duncan with a smile.

He gave a slight kick of his heels and the troop moved off.

'So?' asked Eylinn before they picked up too much speed and the din of the ride drowned their words.

'So I gave him food for thought.'

'Only that?'

'It's what I was expecting. Teogen is a rock that can't be easily moved. But all the same, this meeting was not in vain. After all, even the highest tower begins with a single stone, doesn't it?'

With a satisfied cluck of his tongue, the Duke of Feln urged his horse into a gallop.

14

Lorn grimaced upon waking.

He was hurting, his body stiff and painful, a migraine boring into his temples and almost blinding him. He breathed with difficulty, his torso bound tightly to keep his ribs in place. He was lying in the room assigned to him within the prince's apartment at the governor's palace. How had he reached his bed? The drawn curtains maintained a gentle dimness in the room although it was sunny outside. Everything was quiet.

Father Domnis prayed in silence, kneeling at his bedside. When he saw Lorn was conscious, he removed the hood of his white robe and stood up.

'How are you feeling, my son?' he asked in a soft voice.

'Father?'

Lorn attempted to sit up and groaned.

'Try not to move, my son. Are you in pain?'

'I'm thirsty.'

'Of course.'

The priest brought him a glass of water to which he added a few drops of amber liquid. Then he helped him drink it by propping up his head gently. Lorn recognised the taste of kesh liqueur with satisfaction. There was nothing better to combat pain.

While Lorn closed his eyes again, waiting for the drug to take effect, Father Domnis went to open the door slightly and said a few words to the guard in the hallway. Then he quietly shut the door and returned to the bed.

Lorn felt his migraine diminish.

'What happened?' he asked, keeping his eyes closed.

His voice, weak and hoarse, was that of a man on the point of sinking into slumber.

'You don't remember anything?' asked the white priest.

'I'm… so… tired…'

'Then go back to sleep, my son. And let me pray for your soul…'

Later, Alan joined Father Domnis at Lorn's bedside. With all the waiting and vain searching, he had not slept a wink since his friend had disappeared.

'No one seems to know who the girl Lorn left with was,' he said quietly.

'Perhaps she had nothing to with this.'

'I doubt it…'

'You should rest, my son.'

Alan acted as though he had not heard and gazed bleakly at Lorn. Looking very pale, his face marked by blows, his friend was plunged into a sleep too deep to be reassuring. The priest wiped away a small drip of black bile that still leaked from between his closed lips

'What happened to him, father?'

'I fear he heard the Call of the Dark.'

'The Call of the Dark? What's that?'

'Lorn has spent a long time in close company with the Dark. Too long…'

'I know that.'

'But if he survived it, it's because… How should I put it?' The white priest hunted for the right word. 'It's because the Dark has… accepted him rather than seeking to destroy him. It has spared him and allowed him into its bosom, as the mark on his hand bears witness.'

'Spared him? You think so?'

'I'm not explaining this well… You know of the ravages the Dark can wreak upon bodies and upon souls. Your friend has not become a raving lunatic. Nor a stammering idiot. And his body has not been corrupted.'

'There is the matter of his eyes.'

'That's relatively minor, compared to the deformities suffered by some wretches…'

'That's true.'

'Lorn is strong. No doubt that's why the Dark has chosen him.'

'And now it's calling him.'

'In a sense. He's longing for it. At Dalroth, Lorn was exposed to an abundant source of the Dark. He became… habituated to it. And now, he misses it like…' Embarrassed, Father Domnis cleared his throat. 'Like…'

'Like I missed kesh. Don't trouble yourself on my account, father. I understand what you mean… Will he recover?'

'I don't know.'

'Answer me.'

'Nothing is impossible, my son. But…'

'What else?' Alan asked impatiently, trying not to raise his voice. 'Out with it!'

Father Domnis nevertheless took his time choosing the right words.

'Now there's no doubt that the Dark is within him.'

Lorn shifted restlessly in his sleep.

Alan took the white priest by the arm and drew him away from the bed.

'What are you trying to tell me, father? That there's no hope?'

'No! Lorn can purge himself of the Dark that is within him. But he has to want to.'

'Want to? But of course he will! How could he not want to?'

Father Domnis found it wiser not to contradict the prince on this point, for all that he knew the Dark could exercise an irresistible attraction. That for some, it was a terrible and lethal drug; one they could not do without despite the harm it caused them over time.

'It will be long and painful, my son.'

'Long?'

'An entire lifetime might not be enough.'

*

The morning came when, sitting up in his bed, Lorn could eat without assistance.

It was the first real meal he'd had since a patrol had found him in Bejofa and brought him, still unconscious, to the governor's palace.

'Now this is a pleasant sight,' said Alan as a servant took away the remains of the copious breakfast that Lorn had just wolfed down with appetite.

As the servant was young and pretty, Alan could not prevent himself from following her with his eyes. No fool, she gave him a coy smile before closing the door.

'How are you?' asked Alan.

'Much better, thank you.'

'Would you allow me to let a little sunshine in? It's a magnificent day outside and it's like a vigil for the dead in here.'

With the shutters half-closed, the room was plunged into dimness.

'I'd prefer it if you didn't,' Lorn said.

'Oh? You're not over that?'

Lorn shook his head.

His eyes were still sensitive to bright light. The right one, now a pale grey, hurt him in particular: very soon after being exposed, it was as if white-hot needles were being stuck into his skull.

Alan made the mattress tilt and Lorn, who was still careful when making the slightest gesture, grimaced with pain.

'I'm sorry,' said the prince, realising his clumsiness.

'It... It will be all right...' said Lorn, cautiously finding a comfortable position.

Alan tried not to move again.

'We were worried sick, do you know that?'

'We?' noted Lorn.

'All right. I was worried sick,' the prince corrected himself, emphasising the 'I'. 'But what got into you, disappearing like that?'

'I... I don't know...'

'I hunted for you everywhere, that night. As I had a very bad feeling, I ordered search parties. And it was only the following day that they found you. Unconscious. And in Bejofa! What the hell were you doing in Bejofa?'

'It's a long story.'

'Not a problem. I have all my time.'

'I'm tired, Alan.'

'No. You'll sleep once you've told me who put you in this state.'

The tone was friendly but firm.

Lorn knew Alan well enough to realise he would not rest until he obtained satisfaction. The prince's solicitude was as sincere as his worry and his questions. He wanted to know, and he would.

'There are witnesses who say they saw you leave the party in the company of a beautiful young brunette,' said the prince.

Lorn nodded.

He recounted his meeting with Elana and the trap into which she had lured him, up to the moment when he threw himself out the window. But he concealed his fit of violence when, convinced she had betrayed him, he'd tried to make her talk. And he did not mention Irelice.

'The house she took you to, could you find it again?' asked Alan.

'I think so, yes.'

'I'd be surprised if there was anyone waiting for us, but perhaps they left some clues behind. You really don't know what these people wanted from you?' Alan asked.

'To abduct me. But other than that...'

'Since you were seen leaving together, I made some enquiries about this Elana. No one knows who she is, exactly. And she wasn't on the guest list.'

'She's a bold one. She was chatting to you and the Yrgaardian ambassador when I joined you.'

'Yes, she must have been after you from the start. No doubt she thought the best way to reach you was through me.'

'And since you've never been able to resist a pretty woman...'

'That's an exaggeration,' Alan protested, on principle.

'You don't say.'

'And then?'

'It's... It's fairly cloudy in my mind. I remember falling into the river and I don't really know how I managed not to drown. After that...'

Lorn disguised the truth again.

He mentioned Delio but said nothing of the fit he underwent, nothing of the despair and the shame, nothing of the anguish and the suffering that had gripped him to the point of regretting that he was still alive. Did he really expect to fool Alan or was he lying to himself? He couldn't say. Perhaps he simply wanted to postpone the moment when he would have to face the events of that terrible night. But the main thing was that, due to the Dark and its hold over him, he found himself concealing the truth from his only friend.

But the prince was not so easily deceived.

'Why are you lying to me?' he asked sadly.

Lorn looked at him without being able to utter a word.

'I know,' Alan went on to say, 'that something else happened to you that night. Something terrible that Father Domnis names the Call...'

Since Lorn continued to remain silent, Alan finally stood up.

'The guards brought you back here in the same state as they found you in the street where you were lying. Half-dead. And covered in a black bile which you're still coughing up at times... That was enough for Father Domnis to understand what had happened to you.'

'I... I don't remember anything about that,' Lorn attempted to say.

'Stop it!' Alan said angrily, but without raising his voice. 'Just stop... Nothing obliges you to confide in me. You don't owe me a thing. You don't owe anything to anyone. But don't take me for an idiot. If you don't wish to talk about something, then say so and that will suffice.'

They stared at one another for a very long moment.

'I do not want to speak of that,' Lorn said at last, before averting his eyes.

'As you wish. But I can't help you against your will.'

'I haven't asked you for anything, Alan. Leave me alone.'

For the prince, it was a hard blow.

Lorn regained strength.

In the course of the days that followed, he was soon fit enough to walk in the gardens, with the help of a cane at first, and then without. He got better and forced himself to perform long and painful exercises. It was not simply a matter of healing from his wounds. He wanted to recover the vigour, speed and endurance he had possessed before Dalroth. Also, the efforts he made prevented him from brooding and, when night-time came, caused him to fall into a deep sleep. So he trained from morning till evening, spending long solitary hours in the fencing room wielding a sword and riding mounts borrowed from the stables until they were exhausted.

He and Alan did not return to the painful conversation they'd had. The prince waited for Lorn to express regret, if not offer an apology, while Lorn did not wish to ask for forgiveness now from anyone. So they acted as if nothing had happened, but their relations became cold and tense. When Father Domnis voiced concern about this, Alan explained what it was about. The priest had then pleaded Lorn's cause: it was no doubt the Dark that had spoken. Alan had understood that. But despite everything, Lorn's words still wounded him.

As he completed his convalescence, Lorn was forced to admit that if his body was healing, his eyes remained as sensitive as ever. It was painful for him to go outside in full sunlight without protection, a weakness he would henceforth have to deal with. At first, he decided to wear a patch over his right eye, but that interfered with his depth perception and dangerously reduced his field of vision. Then Father Domnis found the solution and had some rectangular spectacles made whose tinted glasses allowed Lorn to see without being dazzled. Lorn was not pleased at first: he was not yet thirty years old and, for him, spectacles were only worn by old men and scholars smelling of paper and ink. But he came to agree that these glasses did the job perfectly well.

Along with his black hair, his pallor, his silence, his mismatched eyes and the sombre outfits he liked to wear, the spectacles put the finishing touch to the aura that surrounded him.

Even without mentioning the seal on the back of his left hand, he had a dark and disturbing air about him. People bowed their heads when they passed him in the hallways, gave him sidelong glances and whispered about him behind his back. It did not bother him. On the contrary, he relished his solitude. He found a certain degree of comfort in it, between four walls of silence and oblivion.

15

One morning, Lorn announced to Alan he was leaving.

'When?'

'Today.'

The prince took in the news without blinking.

'I should be thinking of going home, too. I've received a letter from my mother: she is calling me back to Oriale.'

In fact, the letter had arrived a few days earlier. But Alan had not wished to reply to the queen's summons before Lorn was completely recovered. He thought of offering to accompany Lorn instead, but without a sincere reconciliation between them, a touch of pride prevented him from doing so: he did not wish to appear to be begging.

'The Duke of Feln is up to his usual mischief,' he said casually.

'The duke?'

'I'm talking about Duncan.'

Duncan of Feln.

Lorn felt his guts knotting up.

He gave no sign of it, however, and simply asked:

'Still up to his neck in intrigue, old Duncan?'

Alan stifled a small laugh.

'More than ever. Especially since my mother's authority is being questioned and those willing to lend the duke an ear are growing in number. But the lesser nobility of the sword are wary of him, and without them he will never manage to do anything against the throne.'

'So he's become a duke.'

'Yes. He's led the House of Feln since his elder brother's death. And will do so until his nephew comes of age.'

'Poor nephew. I doubt he'll live to see his bones grow old,' said Lorn.

The prince and he fell silent, embarrassed.

The few words they had just exchanged were mere social chit-chat, intended only to fill the silence and mask the lingering ill-feeling from their quarrel, and were unworthy of their friendship.

Unworthy of them.

Alan sighed.

'Where do you intend to go' he asked.

'To Sarme. I'm planning to ask for Enzio's hospitality for a while.'

The prince felt a stab of jealousy.

'If you're trying to see Alissia again...'

He did not finish his sentence, as a livid veil of sadness passed over his friend's face. Alan immediately regretted his words.

'I'm... I'm sorry, Lorn. I did not mean—'

'How is she?'

'Well.'

'Is she...?'

'Married? No, but—'

'I know, Alan. There's no need to spell it out for me. I know that I shall never wed her.'

Lorn tried to remain impassive, but the memory of Alissia had pierced his soul and his heart like a blade of icy fire. In his mind he saw her again, beautiful and fragile, as she was the day he had asked her father, the powerful Duke of Sarme and Vallence, for her hand. And he saw her again the night he left them, she and her brother Enzio, on a quay in the port of Alencia.

It was a torment.

The prince wanted to make amends and asked:

'What do you need?

Lorn shrugged.

'A good horse. Money. Supplies. A sword... Only the bare minimum.'

'Understood. But it's a long journey to Sarme.'

'I know.'

'Take an escort.'

'No.'

'Just a few men. You can pick them yourself.'

'No, Alan.'

'You were attacked on the very night of your return. What makes you think the people who wanted to make you disappear won't try again?'

'I'll be careful.'

'You know as well as I do that it's not always enough. Accept an escort, Lorn. You can send it back as soon as you're safe in Sarme.'

The prince was truly worried and Lorn understood that. But he remained obstinate and refused again: he wanted to travel alone, whatever the risks.

'As you will.'

'I'm going to get ready,' Lorn said.

He waited as the prince looked away in silence, both saddened and exasperated by his friend's attitude: Lorn, once again, was refusing his help.

Lorn moved off but halted before he left the room.

He hesitated, and then said:

'Thank you. For everything.'

Alan turned his back to him.

'Of course,' he replied in a cold voice.

An hour later, in the stables, Lorn was checking that his horse was in good health and correctly saddled when Father Domnis came to join him.

'I learned you are leaving, my son.'

'Indeed,' Lorn replied without ceasing what he was doing.

'The prince is worried about you.'

'So he sent you?'

'No. I share his concern, however.'

Lorn was silent as he lifted his mount's hooves one by one.

The white priest insisted:

'You could have another fit like the one... the one you had before.'

'I know.'

'If it happens, it would be best if you were not alone.'

'No doubt, yes.'

There was another silence, but this time it was Lorn who broke it:

'Listen, father. I know the nature of the illness I'm suffering. But the choice before me is quite simple. Either I live in fear of another Call that may occur whether I like it or not. Or I take the risk of living my life.'

'It's a risk you may be forcing others to take as well, my son,' said Father Domnis in an even tone.

Lorn looked at him and said:

'The Dark has already stolen so much from me.'

'I understand, my son. Nevertheless, you can't—'

'Goodbye, father.'

Lorn led his horse out and put one foot in the stirrup.

'Just a minute!' exclaimed the white priest. 'Take this, would you? Who knows if it might be of use to you?'

He held out a medallion bearing – in white enamel – the rune of Eyral, the White Dragon.

Lorn hesitated before taking the pendant and climbing onto his horse.

Then he kicked his heels.

Lorn left the governor's palace without looking back. He did not see Alan who, with a grave expression, watched him depart from a window. He only halted at the gates of the city, where he called out to a beggar and tossed him Father Domnis's medallion.

Seeing that the pendant and its chain were made of silver, the man broke into a toothless smile and shouted in delight:

'Thank you, my lord! May Eyral accompany you!'

Lorn was already trotting away.

16

'His ancestor was Erklant I, whose glorious name he bore. King of Langre, Erklant I, nicknamed 'the Ancient', had fought during the Last Shadows and led his kingdom to victory against the armies of Obscurity and Oblivion. He then vanquished the dragon Serk'Arn and, through a series of conquests and treaties, became the first High King. He died after living almost a century.'

Chronicles (The Book of Kings)

The gate was so tall that it seemed narrow, when twenty men abreast might have crossed it. The immense double doors shook. A luminous crack appeared between them and widened as they drew apart. Then they halted, barely opened. But it was more than enough to grant entry to a tiny silhouette, that of an old, ill king who advanced leaning on a cane.

The gap between the doors had traced a long, narrow carpet of light upon the floor. The High King followed it, walking straight ahead with a slow step, his back bent, preceded by his inordinately stretched-out shadow. The darkness was thick. But from the way it absorbed every sound, one easily sensed that the place was gigantic and cavernous: a hollow mountain.

King Erklant hobbled towards a stone platform, where four bowls of oil burned. They framed two thrones facing one another. One, with its back to the door, was empty. The other had an immobile occupant, sculpted from the same rock as the seats.

It was a king.

A warrior king, with his crown and boots, wearing a

hauberk, one hand on the armrest of his throne, the other gripping the hilt of a sword resting with its point on the floor.

The first of the High Kings.

The old king sat before his ancestor, whose name he bore. The resemblance between them was striking. They seemed to be of the same age and looked almost like brothers. The same clothing. The same wrinkles and hollow face. The same sharp cheekbones. The same jutting jaws. The same long straight hair. And the same deep eye sockets.

'Good evening,' said the High King.

He waited for the pains in his joints to diminish. He also needed to catch his breath.

'It has been a while since my last visit,' he said finally. 'Forgive me.'

He sighed.

'The news is bad. The city of Angborn is going to be ceded to Yrgaard...'

He was alone, yet the old king sensed a presence. A powerful and immense presence whose invisible aura was almost palpable.

'Yes,' he said as if in answer to a question. 'Ceded. Or rather sold.'

King Erklant became thoughtful. His gaze grew vague for an instant, and then his attention returned.

'Sold! Can you believe it?' He became agitated. 'And to the Black Dragon! To the Hydra of Yrgaard. And they dare to present this as a diplomatic success?'

He calmed down and his voice filled with sarcasm.

'For diplomatic relations will at last be established between Yrgaard and the High Kingdom, do you see? As if Yrgaard could ever become our ally...'

Gloomily, the High King fell silent, before murmuring to himself:

'I already made the mistake of believing that. Wasn't once enough?'

He shook his head and, directing his words at the invisible presence, added:

'But one has to admit that the queen has laid the groundwork well… Esteveris has been negotiating in secret with Yrgaard for months and now everything has been arranged. Or almost. Whether the other kingdoms like it or not. Or anyone else, for that matter…'

His voice died.

Despondent, the old king knew that Yrgaard would never be a loyal ally. A few years earlier, he had let himself be persuaded to attempt a rapprochement. To no avail. The hatred of the Black Dragon for the High Kingdom was too deep and too ancient. She had ruled Yrgaard since the Shadows and had a visceral enmity towards Eyral, the White Dragon of Knowledge and Light – the protector of the High Kingdom. Eyral was still worshipped here and his oracles continued to guide the High Kings.

'I don't know what Yrgaard has in mind,' confessed Erklant II. 'I only know that Angborn is being handed over to it cheaply and in complete contempt of the blood shed to liberate the Free Cities. But the final straw… The final straw is that we have almost as much to fear from an honest alliance with Yrgaard as from the Black Dragon's treachery. For the other kingdoms all have good reasons to worry at seeing the two most powerful realms of Imelor allied to one another. For the moment, they're putting on a brave face before the fait accompli. But how long before they react?'

The old king's shoulders slumped, but then he straightened up upon detecting a movement in the darkness.

'There remains one source of hope, however. Lorn will soon be here; did you know? I sent my guards to seek him… They will soon bring him back here… I raised him as my own son and I believed he betrayed me, but that was a mistake. In truth, he has always been loyal and the Guardians say that…'

A sound like the scraping of metal against stone interrupted him.

'Yes,' the High King resumed. 'He's returning from Dalroth and I know full well what that means… Three years. Might as well say an eternity. Yes, an eternity…'

His thoughts eluded him once again.

*

Once the old king went away, once the tall doors were closed again and the bowls extinguished, shadows massed around the stone thrones, a pair of red eyes opened and a dull roar rose from beneath the mountain.

17

'After the sacrifice of the Dragon-King and the cataclysm that followed, after the drowning of the province of Elarias and the birth of the Captive Sea, long after the end of the Last War of the Shadows, the Deadlands remained cursed and corrupted, subject to the Dark which impregnated the earth and the water and the stones and the wind.'

Chronicles (The Book of Elarias)

Upon leaving Samarande, Lorn did not travel up the Eirdre valley although it would have led him to the heart of the High Kingdom. Instead he rode west, following the coast of the Sea of the Free Cities for several days, and then turned south. His intention was to cross the province of Issern until he reached Brenvost. There he would embark on the first ship leaving for Loriand, from where he would travel to the duchies of Sarme and Vallence. It was not the shortest route, or the easiest one. But Lorn knew he was in danger and although he had refused the escort offered to him by Alan, it nevertheless seemed safer to take byroads. Moreover, his destination mattered less to him than the journey itself, which he hoped to put to good use reflecting on his situation. He was not even sure he would reach Sarme, and he did not care.

The king's illness, the queen's regency, the cession of Angborn and the intrigues of Yrgaard, all of that left him indifferent. As did Alan's doubts and worries. And Irelice. And even the Dark. Lorn was no longer the man he'd been. He no longer felt any obligation to the High Kingdom, or to the High King. He wanted to have no dealings with anyone. He only aspired to one thing: to be left alone. He wanted to travel for a long time on his own, incognito.

He wanted to forget.

To flee.

And, perhaps, to lose himself.

The province of Issern was hemmed in by wild mountains to the east and the Deadlands to the west. A few isolated farms were scattered across it. Its only real value was the royal road that linked the Free Cities to the coast and to Brenvost, one of the busiest and most prosperous ports on the Captive Sea. Merchants and merchandise travelled this road every day, despite the brigands who had been preying upon them since the High Kingdom had withdrawn the troops keeping watch over the region – due to its inability to maintain them. Now increasingly bold and audacious bands were robbing travellers before finding refuge in the nearby hills.

The only really safe places were the great inns built along the road. Completely self-sufficient, they were fortified and defended by mercenaries. One could eat and sleep there, but also change mounts, have one's horse shod or repair a cart wheel. All these services, however, commanded exorbitant prices. A pallet and a bowl of soup cost as much as a fowl. But the walls were high, the stones solid and the gates robust. Here, one could rest and relax with peace of mind between two anxious days on the road. And too bad for those who lacked the means to pay or preferred to save their money.

The first two nights, Lorn spent sleeping under an open sky. Each time, he moved away from the road and took care to find a discreet spot, where his fire could not be seen and his horse could not be heard. He had more than enough to pay for several nights at inns. Even so, he preferred solitude and never grew tired of observing the Great Nebula above him. He had missed this spectacle during his imprisonment at Dalroth. Moreover, with his eyes sensitive to the weakest glimmers, he could now appreciate details that others could not make out. Everything – the dimmest star, the faintest coil, the smallest milky cloud – appeared to him with perfect sharpness when he was not wearing his dark glasses. It almost seemed as though he was now, like some animals, better adapted to nocturnal life than to the daytime.

On the evening of the third day, however, Lorn decided to stop at one of the inns.

The idea of eating a cooked meal and sleeping in a proper bed was quite tempting. Perhaps he would even remain a day or two, provided he could occupy a quiet room on his own. His horse was also in need of rest, as well as a new shoe for his right front hoof: spending a little time in the stable would do him good.

Moreover, Lorn had suffered another mild fit while on the road, towards the end of the afternoon. It had started with pains in his hand and arm. Then came the trembling and the beginning of a fever. Luckily, Lorn had only needed to concentrate and take some long, deep breaths to bring himself under control. But he now dreaded the next outbreak, which he feared would be both imminent and more violent. And all things considered, he preferred to have it surprise him in a place where someone could come to his rescue and where he could receive care afterwards. He was not happy about the prospect. Coming to terms with these fits was admitting the Dark's hold on him. But he needed to deal with it. Hiding his head in the sand would be suicidal. The Dark was an adversary who would not be ignored.

Located at a slight remove from the road, the inn was built on a river whose current powered a waterwheel. Its thick walls protected not only the inn itself, but also a stable, a forge, a barn, an entire farmyard, a vegetable garden and an orchard, an oven, a mill and a chapel consecrated to the Dragon-King.

Having dismounted, Lorn entrusted his horse to the ostler, and then, as he sluiced his neck at the water trough, discreetly looked around the place. The inn was busy, pleasant and welcoming. And it must have been prospering because a new building, no doubt destined to house more guestrooms, was under construction. Upon the outer walls, sentinels kept watch over the surrounding area but also glanced towards the enclosed compound from time to time. Others guarded the gate. Lorn wondered what these men were worth. Times were troubled and anyone carrying a sword could call himself a mercenary. But it was enough if their presence dissuaded the brigands from attacking. After all, it was all that was required of them...

Lorn requested a room of his own, which did not please the proprietor, for – like all innkeepers – he did not rent rooms, but places in each bed. He had only one big bed left in a large chamber, a very comfortable one, as it happened, and he boasted of its merits. Lorn rented both the bed and the entire room. He paid cash on the nail, and that, added to his sinister air and the impassive gaze of his dark spectacles, convinced the proprietor to hand over the key without further discussion.

That evening, Lorn demanded a hot bath and chose to dine alone in his room. He only left it to make sure that his horse was in good hands, after which he blocked his door with a chair, closed his shutters, and fell into a haunted sleep. He was unaware that he had been recognised upon his arrival and that, just as he was falling asleep, a man was riding flat out to collect the rich reward he had been promised.

18

The following morning, as the Dark's mark still hurt and it seemed his right eye was even more sensitive to the light than usual, Lorn remained in the dimness of his room. He rested, drowsed, suffered in silence, and waited.

But nothing happened.

In fact, he felt better and, after midday, he decided to take some fresh air and have a short stroll. The bright sunshine made him blink as soon as he stuck his nose outside, obliging him to draw his hood above his dark glasses. He hesitated for an instant, working the joints of his marked hand, then made up his mind and descended into the courtyard.

Three families had just arrived and were negotiating the price of their stay with the innkeeper. The men, women and children seemed exhausted. They weren't rich and were only asking for a corner where they could spend the night and water for the mules harnessed to their wagons. The children would cost nothing: they would sleep in the same bed and eat from the same plates as their parents. But the proprietor remained inflexible. He refused to grant them a discount and voices were raised, an old woman appealing in vain to his generosity, a man reproaching him for profiting from their desperation and fixing unfair prices. Some mercenaries approached and lent support to the innkeeper, silent but menacing. Their presence sufficed. The families realised that further discussion was to no avail and after conferring, they regretfully clubbed together the necessary funds. Wary, the innkeeper insisted on being paid in advance. He counted his money while an infant cried in its mother's arms.

Lorn went on his way.

He returned to the stable to look after his horse, exchanged a few words with the ostler, then bought a bottle of wine and went to sip from it in a chair left in the shade of an oak tree, secluded in a quiet corner away from the bustling courtyard. He had removed his hood but kept his spectacles on, and was rubbing his left hand, immersed in his thoughts, when he perceived a presence beside him.

It was a little girl, three or four years in age, dirty and bare-foot, who was staring at him as she sucked the fingers of her right hand.

Lorn returned her gaze without saying a word and waited.

The little girl then raised the hand she was not devouring and pointed a chubby index finger at Lorn. He realised that she wasn't indicating him but his spectacles. No doubt she had never seen anything like them before. He removed them and held them out to her so that she could look at them closely.

The child hesitated.

This unsmiling man made her feel shy.

Lorn then held up the dark glasses in a sunbeam that broke through the branches. The little girl approached. She wanted to touch the spectacles, but Lorn shook his head. She restrained herself for a moment, looked Lorn in the eyes, and took another chance, advancing her hand very, very slowly.

Lorn smiled and put his spectacles back on.

'There you are!'

The little girl gave a start.

A young woman approached with a hurried step and one could read a great relief upon her face but also the vestiges of a worry too fresh to be easily erased. She was blonde, attractive and not yet thirty years old, although weariness had added to her apparent age. Lorn recognised her. She had arrived with the families who had tried to haggle over the price of their stay.

'You know how I hate it when you run away that, Idia! I always want to know where you are, do you hear me?'

To seek pardon, the little girl ran to her mother and hugged her legs.

The woman softened and, caressing her daughter's hair, reproached her gently.

'I was worried sick, I was.'

Whereupon she lifted her head and said to Lorn, who had not moved:

'Forgive her, sir.'

Lorn did not say a word.

'I hope she did not bother you…'

'No,' replied Lorn.

There was an embarrassed silence, the woman hesitating to take her leave without further ado. So she asked her daughter:

'Say goodbye, Idia.'

But the child, with her face in her mother's skirts, refused.

'I'm sorry,' said the woman. 'She's sometimes a little shy…'

Lorn nodded.

'Well, goodbye, sir… And once again, forgive Idia.'

Upon which, the woman was about to turn round when Lorn suddenly asked her:

'Where do you come from?'

Caught short, the woman stammered:

'Where…? Where do we…?'

'I saw you arriving, just now.'

'Yes, I remember. You… You were there.'

'You're from the Cities, aren't you?'

'Yes.'

'Angborn?'

The woman frowned.

'Yes. But how…?' And then she understood. 'Ah. My accent. You can hear it, can't you?'

'A little,' said Lorn with a friendly smile. 'And where are you going?'

'We're going to Brenvost.'

'For long?'

'Perhaps for always. We don't want to become Yrgaardians.'

This sentence, spoken with pride, caught Lorn's attention. It even aroused a trace of admiration in him.

'So you'd rather move…' he said.

'Move?' The woman smiled sadly. 'Our goods wouldn't fit in a wretched cart, if we were moving. We're not moving, sir. We fled.'

Lorn stood up.

'Fled? What do you mean?'

With a gesture he invited the woman to take his seat. She remained undecided for moment, then suddenly felt very tired and willingly agreed to sit for a few instants in the shade, with her daughter on her knee.

'You were saying you've fled Angborn, you and your husband?'

'Yes, sir.'

Answering Lorn's questions, she explained that for the last several months the inhabitants of Angborn had not been allowed to leave. The future Yrgaardian authorities feared a mass exodus before the cession, so definitive departures were forbidden and those leaving the city could not take more than they ordinarily would for a journey. It was even impossible to sell one's house or goods. If one decided to move elsewhere, one had to leave practically everything behind.

Lorn would have liked to learn more, but the woman's husband arrived and asked warily:

'Is everything all right?'

'Yes,' replied his wife. 'I was just resting a little, that's all.'

She rose as the man took their daughter in his arms.

'Goodbye,' said the woman.

'Goodbye,' said Lorn, after exchanging a plain nod with the husband.

Who was quick to lead his family away.

When evening came, Lorn went to take his supper in the common room.

Although he did nothing to cause it, his entrance drew notice. His sombre appearance was disturbing and his spectacles aroused curiosity, so that conversations faltered as he found an empty place on a bench.

They resumed when he ordered.

Lorn supped without saying a word, listening to the chatter around him. His neighbours alluded in low voices to the prices being charged by the innkeepers.

To complain about them, of course:

'It's theft. Theft, pure and simple.'

'You'd think they were feeding the chickens with grain made of gold.'

'And that their carrots were sown in silk!'

'You said it! You can bet they're making a fat profit…'

'If you think about it, the only choice is between being robbed in here or out there.'

'But here, at least, we don't run the risk of having our throats slit.'

'That remains to be seen.'

'How's that?'

The discussion took a new turn.

'The brigands are growing more and more numerous. And more and more bold. You'll see: one day, they'll attack an inn.'

'You think so?'

'I'm sure of it! Where do well-to-do travellers stop, if not in places such as this?'

'That's true.'

'And you think these brigands don't know that?'

'But all the same, there are the walls. And guards.'

'Walls can be climbed. And guards can be killed. Or paid off. You'll see that one night we'll go to bed believing we're safely tucked away, only to find ourselves with our throats cut in our slee—'

'That's enough,' said Lorn in a tone that brooked no argument.

The three traders who were conversing near him fell silent, and by way of explanation, Lorn pointed to little Idia.

As chance would have it, he was seated at the same table as the girl and her parents. Her father and mother, weary and too busy discussing how the meagre funds remaining to them would last until the end of their journey, had failed to perceive that the child was listening closely to the traders' talk with her eyes wide open in fright. Embarrassed, the men apologised and did not utter another word during the rest of their meal.

Lorn, however, was no longer much concerned by what Idia might have heard. The Dark's mark was hurting him and the pain was climbing his arm. He felt both hot and cold, and sweat was beading upon his brow. The fit he'd been dreading for several days now was imminent.

He stood up, walked out of the room as steadily as he could, and once he was out of sight from others, he took several deep breaths. Gripping a railing, he struggled to keep control of himself but knew that his efforts were to no avail. He needed to return to his room and lie down while he still had the strength to do so on his own. He wondered whether he would have done better to have warned the innkeeper he was ill and asked the man to keep an eye on him. Lorn's pride had prevented him from doing so and now it was too late.

The path to his room passed through a gallery open to the air on one side.

Lorn attempted to climb the stairway that led to it, leaning on the bannister, and once he reached the top he was one of the first – along with the mercenaries standing guard – to see the coach rapidly approaching on the road. Escorted by riders, it entered the courtyard with a great din of hooves, ironclad wheels and creaking axles. This sudden arrival caused an uproar at the inn and quickly drew everyone outside. Even Lorn remained where he was and, pricked by curiosity, watched from the gallery.

'Close the gates!' yelled the coachman, as he pulled on the reins to bring the coach to a halt. 'Close the gates! We were attacked!'

As the heavy gates were being shut, Lorn, who could see over the outer wall, scrutinised the surrounding area in the glimmering dusk. But his sight was blurred; it was like looking through a billowing veil. He gave up and focused instead on the coachman, who, in front of the inn, had jumped down from his seat and was recounting how bandits had ambushed them but they had managed to force a passage. Worried questions poured forth from his listeners. Where had the ambush taken place? How many bandits were there? Had they pursued the coach?

The coach.

Despite his difficulties in concentrating, Lorn observed that the person or persons whom the coachman had been driving had still not shown themselves. Then he noticed that the escort riders had dismounted but that only a handful of them remained by the coach they were supposed to protect. Most of them had already quietly slipped away while the coachman drew all the attention to himself.

Something was up.

Something that Lorn sensed was about to happen, without being able to identify it clearly.

He understood when he saw who finally left the coach.

Dark-haired, young, pretty.

She had claimed to be called Elana and, a few weeks earlier, she had tried to abduct him.

At first he thought he was delirious, that his fever and the Dark were playing tricks on him. But he recognised the young woman without a shred of doubt when she raised her head as if she knew exactly where to find him and he met her gaze.

She smiled at him.

Lorn cursed and rushed to his room, locking the door and jamming it with a chair. Anxious and fretful, he paced up and down trying to collect his wits. He needed to think. Quickly. He had no shortage of ideas, but they jostled about in his head, overlapping and cancelling one another, while the pain in his strained arm provoked a sort of dizziness in him.

They were there for him.

To abduct him. Irelice had missed its chance in Samarande but had not given up.

He was in no shape to fight.

He had to flee.

Starting by escaping this room in which he had trapped himself...

Lorn suddenly realised that screams of horror and the sounds of combat were rising from the courtyard. And just then, someone tried to open the door.

His combat instincts took over.

He snatched up his sword in its scabbard, passed his good arm through the strap of his bag, opened the room's window and threw his legs over the sill. The window was ten feet above the ground, behind the main building. Handicapped by his left arm, he fell rather than leapt out at the very moment when his door was kicked down. His landing hurt but caused no serious injury and, limping slightly, he went to the corner of the building and discreetly glanced around it.

It required an effort to clear his sight, as fat drops of sweat stung his eyes.

Chaos reigned within the fortified inn. In the light from torches and lanterns, the warriors who had been escorting Elana were fighting the mercenaries and had taken possession of the premises, striking at anyone who stood in their path, shoving aside men, women and children.

A man was leaning out from the window of Lorn's room.

'THERE HE IS!'

Lorn rushed into the melee, unsheathing his sword.

He struck a warrior who was taken by surprise, deflected the attack from a second by pure reflex, and riposted by slitting the man's throat.

'OVER THERE!'

Lorn turned round and sensed rather than actually saw Elana, who was calling and pointing at him from the gallery. A warrior rushed him and Lorn struck blindly. Once. Twice. And he struck again at another menacing figure, before feeling the spatter of warm blood upon his face. The world had become an appalling muddle of sounds, cries, tumbling shapes and brimming colours. Lorn lost all awareness of himself and once again became the terrified madman who had fled beneath the storm at Dalroth. It was a fall into an abyss of violence, screaming spectres, primitive fears and savage impulses. He no longer knew who he was attacking or whom he was defending himself against, warriors or mercenaries, or perhaps even innocent bystanders.

When he returned to his senses, he found himself on horseback, wounded, and holding the reins with the same hand that gripped his bloodied sword. His mount reared with a whinny, panic-stricken, before the gate in the outer wall. Had he forgotten that the mercenaries had closed it after the coach's arrival? Or had he simply not thought about it at all, caught up in a frenzy?

Whatever the case, the gate still stood tall and shut tight before him, and the walls meant to protect him had become a deadly trap.

Unless...

'Surrender!' Elana called. 'It's over!'

His mouth dry and his eyes sore, dazed by the migraine boring into his temples, Lorn tried to take stock of the situation.

Elana and her warriors had him cornered. Fighting had ceased in the corpse-strewn courtyard. The inn's clientele had taken refuge in the buildings and were peeping fearfully from the windows.

Lorn sheathed his sword...

Before spurring his horse with his heels.

Determined to risk all, he knocked over one warrior, forced several others to dive to one side. Continuing to gather speed he crossed the courtyard at a gallop, charging towards the new building under construction.

Elana understood what he intended to do.

'No!' she cried. 'You're going to—'

But she did not finish her sentence.

The workers had built a ramp in order to haul their materials up to the first floor, which was still a platform sprouting sections of wall and cluttered with tools, sacks, boards and piled bricks.

Lorn charged up the ramp without slowing.

It groaned, creaked and split with a crack, before finally collapsing in a cloud of dust. The horse leapt when the structure gave way beneath it and traversed the first floor like a cannon ball, following what would one day be a hallway ending at a window.

Frightened, foaming at the mouth, the steed launched itself into space and jumped over the compound's outer wall.

Lorn disappeared into the night.

19

Lorn woke in the morning and stretched in the grass, his horse's reins held in his left fist as the beast grazed peaceably nearby. He had difficulty moving, his body aching and a trickle of black bile staining his mouth and chin. He sat up, wiped his face clean and gradually pulled himself together.

Having escaped from the fortified inn, he had travelled as far and as fast as possible. Then, when his mount could no longer maintain this pace, he continued at a walk, struggling to remain conscious and wobbling in his saddle, before finally fainting and falling off like a sack. The fury of combat and his survival instinct had allowed him to hold on, but the Dark had finally got the better of him.

How could it have ended otherwise?

Lorn sighed.

He was still alive and he was free. That was something, at least.

But Irelice's men had no doubt been on his trail since first light. Lorn sincerely doubted Elana would abandon the hunt now, after all her previous efforts.

He had already wasted enough time.

Lorn stood up with a grimace, discovering a minor wound to his arm, and got back on his horse.

Taking several detours along rocky paths or streams to cover his tracks, Lorn continued southwards. He proceeded cautiously but was still trying to reach Brenvost on the Captive Sea. It was a big city. Besides, the other options open to him were unpromising. To the east, wild mountains blocked the horizon. If he gave up on reaching the coast, he was left with a choice between turning back towards the Free Cities or heading west, into the Deadlands.

Lorn rode for three days and thought he had shaken off his pursuers when, one evening, he noticed three horsemen upon a ridge. So they had picked up his trail. Or at least they were searching in the right direction. But how? The hypothesis of an expert tracker was sufficient explanation, but Lorn thought he found the true answer when, the following day, he spotted winged shapes flying beneath the clouds and barely had time to take cover.

Wyverns.

Wyverners were criss-crossing the sky and combing the region below. Had Irelice tasked them to assist Elana and her men in their search? Lorn had trouble believing it, but was forced to acknowledge the facts: whoever was seeking him was employing considerable means to find him.

He had a decision to make.

When evening came, Lorn looked after his horse and dined on a heel of bread and some dried meat. Then, at the edge of a copse of fir trees in which he had been forced to take refuge to escape detection by the wyverners, he sat facing the sunset. His gaze distant, he thought while he absently rubbed the palm and the back of his marked hand wrapped in its leather strap.

From now on, he would have to keep an eye on the sky as well as the horizon and travel by night as much as possible. But even so, the risk of being seen and captured was too great if he continued south. The riders had probably guessed that he was trying to reach Brenvost. If he wanted to escape them he would have to set out in another direction, but which one? There was no question of returning to the Free Cities: even if he managed it, they would be waiting for him there. East? The wyverners might spot him before he reached the mountains. So what to do?

Head into the Deadlands?

The region that spread to the west as far as the eye could see had been subjected to the Dark's corruption during the

Shadows. For a long time, nothing had survived on its poisoned water, air and soil. But nature had little by little regained its hold there, but without truly prevailing and sometimes giving rise to monstrosities. Now the Deadlands were an immense moorland, wild and austere. And these days, the Dark represented a real danger only in the most remote parts.

At least, Lorn hoped so.

Because the idea of venturing into the Deadlands was more and more tempting. Of course, it would not be free of risk. All the same, did he have a choice? He was convinced that a wyverner or a rider would find him sooner or later if he did not do something to catch his pursuers off guard. Moreover, it was not a question of journeying deep into the Deadlands, but simply of making a slight detour through them, in order to reach the Captive Sea unhindered. Perhaps he would make it to Brenvost, after all.

Furthermore

Furthermore, he had a hunch that he should go into the Deadlands. Without being able to explain it he felt that the journey he had undertaken was supposed to take that route. Something was waiting there for him, perhaps. Or someone. He sensed a need, together with a vague promise that he would find some comfort there.

Sitting still, with the fading dusk reflecting off the dark glasses of his spectacles, Lorn gave himself time to think matters over. He weighed up the pros and cons, and then looked at his horse. It was not the same mount on which he had arrived at the inn. He had probably stolen it from one of the riders who had been escorting the coach. This horse had rendered him good service. It had saved his life, but Lorn had nevertheless lost out in the exchange. This beast had neither the stamina nor the speed of the steed he had been forced to leave behind. The way they had been travelling, it would not last much longer.

His mind was soon made up.

Lorn checked his equipment one last time and took an inventory of his supplies. When night fell, he climbed back onto his weary horse. He rode off beneath the pale light of the

Great Nebula, towards the distant horizon of a windy, desolate moor, where, beneath an immense sky, big bluish rocks broke through expanses of rust-coloured lichen.

20

Lorn encountered the Dark on the third night.

He was surprised at first, but it was indeed a Dark mist that had risen and was spreading across the moor. Cautiously, he moved to a rocky hillock and stood in his stirrups to observe. The mist formed a red, vaporous sea before him. It seemed to pour from the entrails of the world and unfurled on either side of the old paved road along which he was travelling.

Lorn turned in his saddle.

The Dark stretched across the horizon behind him and was advancing, immense and unstoppable, covering the road. If he lingered too long, he would find himself isolated on this outcrop. And now there was no question of his turning back.

Perplexed, Lorn rubbed his marked hand, which prickled. He knew he should feel afraid, be terrified of the Dark that threatened to engulf him. And he was not merely seeing it. He could sense it. He felt its strength in his flesh. It was as if a slow shudder ran beneath his skin and formed a ball in his gut. But the arrival of the Dark aroused neither fear nor distress in him. On the contrary, it was a familiar, reassuring presence. It only sought to find him again, to envelope him, to gather him in as it had done at Dalroth.

It would be so easy.

All he had to do was abandon himself to it...

Lorn shivered when he realised what was happening to him. Father Domnis was right: Lorn had once again heard the Call. Yet the Dark was right there before him; this time it had not manifested as a painful fit, but in an attempt at seduction, an attraction, a bewitching that had taken on the appearance of a sensible decision.

Entering the Deadlands to escape his pursuers had been sheer folly. Lorn realised this now, but nevertheless, had he really ventured as far as all that?

It was impossible.

He could not have crossed the dozens of leagues that separated him from the regions where the Dark was likely to emerge with such virulence. Moreover, he was heading south, not west. Therefore, either the Dark's influence was stronger throughout the Deadlands than he had been led to believe, or something very unusual was taking place.

Lorn then raised his eyes to the night sky and swore at himself. Dark red spots were spreading over the grey moon like seas of blood, while the Nebula was turning purple and scarlet.

It was a Dark Night.

A night when the Dark gained added strength wherever it might be. Long ago, during the Shadows, all nights were Dark Nights and they still happened occasionally and unpredictably. As sinister and ominous as they were, they proved almost harmless where the Dark did not hold sway. But in places and beings where the Dark had already impregnated itself…

Suddenly nervous, his mount grew restless.

Lorn soon discovered why: creatures had appeared. They were still distant but approaching rapidly in the mist. Wolves. Large, dark and powerful. As tall and as heavy as wild boars, and they were hunting as a pack.

Lorn returned to the road and took off at a gallop.

Seeing their prey escaping, the wolves immediately changed course to cut across the moor. Out of the corner of his eye, Lorn saw the pack closing on him by taking the shortest route. Nevertheless, he did not want to risk leaving the road. Even if it meant exhausting his horse too quickly, he urged it on with his heels, forcing it to redouble its efforts and pass ahead of the wolves just as they reached the old paved road. One of them leapt and was cut down in the air by a sword stroke which gutted it. It failed to dissuade the others. With exposed fangs and glistening chops, their paws trailing diaphanous scarlet tatters, they did not slow and raced along the road in pursuit of the rider. Behind them, the closing mist swallowed the dying wolf.

Lorn rode flat out, his horse's shod hooves hammering upon the paving stones at a frantic rate. He knew it would weaken before the wolves did. He knew they would catch up in the end and bring it down, if it did not stumble first out of sheer exhaustion. These were no ordinary wolves. Their size and mass were enough to convince him of that and their gleaming eyes betrayed the Dark's hold over them. Had it perverted them or had they been born this way? It mattered little. Driven by a bloodthirsty rage, they would never give up.

So there was no salvation except to take flight.

But for how long?

Lorn felt his horse falter while the pack continued to gain ground. Two wolves were running level with him to either side of the road. They were no doubt waiting for another member of the pack to attack from behind and tumble both horse and rider. Lorn had not resheathed his sword, but it served no purpose. Now the wolves were careful to keep their distance.

Untiring.

Relentless.

Lorn was now merely waiting for his horse, mad with terror, to collapse beneath him; it would happen at any moment now. And he was not even hoping for a miracle when he saw the mound.

There were mounds scattered throughout the Deadlands. They housed ancient tombs. Always crowned by three sacred stones, they kept the Dark at bay. Lorn didn't know how or why. He did not even know if it was true and it scarcely mattered at this point. The mound was standing before him, at a slight remove from the road, and seemed to be destined for him. Like an island, it stood all alone, bathed in the red mist.

Lorn remained on the road for as long as he could. Then, when he saw that a wolf was catching up with him and threatening to leap upon the rump of his horse at any second, he abruptly turned off in the direction of the mound. Taken unawares, the pack had to turn before it could resume the pursuit. Lorn was already racing across the moor, cleaving through a thick mist that clung to the flanks of his foaming mount and tore away in shreds.

The wolves were just drawing level with him again when he reached the mound and discovered it was surrounded by a ring of bristling stakes. Charging at full gallop, his mount leapt. It was an impossible jump. The horse tore its belly open on a stake and fell as it landed. Thrown from the saddle, Lorn rolled over a short distance. His sword still in his fist, he stood up while his horse, unable to regain its feet, struggled on the ground, sliding over its own entrails at the bottom of the mound and breaking several stakes as it whinnied in pain and distress. Lorn had no time to worry about its fate. The wolves were already leaping out of the mist, over the ring. There were six of them. One of them impaled itself on a stake. Three others rushed forward to finish off the gutted horse. Two attacked Lorn.

He severed the throat of the first, spun round and struck the second at the very instant when it launched itself at him. He struck its shoulder, which failed to discourage the animal. It immediately repeated its assault. But Lorn dodged and delivered a terrible blow to the back of its neck, almost decapitating it. The beast fell, stone dead.

Lorn then turned towards the three wolves that had already finished with the horse and were now approaching him, growling. Lorn prepared himself, holding his sword in both hands, standing firmly planted on his legs. His gaze was steady and his breathing regular. Yet he doubted whether he could win this battle. His heart was beating furiously. But he was a warrior and warriors died in combat.

Seeing that the wolves, still as threatening as ever, were deploying themselves to encircle him, Lorn slowly retreated. One step after another, without ever taking his eyes off his adversaries, he climbed backwards up the mound… until he reached the great standing stones.

And there, with his back to the steles, he waited…

Snarling louder than ever, crouching down, the wolves hesitated, displaying their fangs, snapping at Lorn as he tried to keep all three in sight.

Suddenly, one of them bounded forward, signalling the attack.

Lorn managed to dispatch the quickest of the three. He broke its jaw with a kick of his boot, before bringing his sword down between its eyes and splitting its skull. Then he grabbed the throat of a second wolf that had risen up on its hind legs to attack him and drove his blade into its belly, up to the hilt. He got away with no more than a shoulder mauled by sharp claws, before breaking clear and raising his sword as the last wolf leapt at him. The beast impaled itself upon the steel blade. But despite the weapon planted in its chest, it succeeded in toppling Lorn as it fell heavily upon him and tried to bite his neck. His face speckled with bloody slaver, Lorn was forced to release his sword in order to seize the animal's maw with both hands and keep it at a distance. The two opponents struggled for a moment until the wolf finally weakened and Lorn was able to rise to his knees, straddling its body. With one forearm trapped by the monster's fangs, he fumbled around until he found the dagger tucked inside his boot and desperately stabbed at the wolf's flank, striking again and again.

At last, the wolf grew still…

Lorn rolled onto his back, exhausted and winded. He had lost a lot of blood and was at the end of his strength. After a moment, he managed to drag himself to the top of the mound and sat with his back against one of the standing stones. He needed to catch his breath. After which, grimacing with pain, he removed his doublet and tore off the sleeves of his shirt. He knotted one of them around his bloodied forearm and made a bandage with the other, which he pressed against his lacerated shoulder.

Dawn was near.

The mist was dissipating upon the moor.

Alone, wounded and now without a mount, Lorn fainted, just as it occurred to him that he would never find the strength to get up again.

Soon, the first carrion-eaters would arrive.

21

*'Almost nothing was known about them. Some claimed they lived
for centuries, as devoted servants of the Assembly of Ir'kans.'*
Chronicles (The Book of Secrets)

Lorn woke lying on a blanket with his head in shadow, a piece
of cloth knotted between two slanting makeshift posts protecting it from the sun. Which was high in the sky.

Lorn squinted painfully and discovered a weight upon his
chest. The weight was a cat who sat there watching him and
seemed to be waiting for something. It was ginger-coloured,
quiet and patient.

Lorn detected a sizzling sound and the smell of something
frying.

He rolled onto his side, obliging the cat to move. As far as
he could make out in the dazzling light that hurt his eyes, he
was still on the mound and there was someone crouched near
a campfire.

A man wearing a hood had his back to Lorn.

His thoughts still hazy, Lorn found his spectacles close by
and put them on. The dark glasses relieved his eyes, but did
nothing for his throbbing migraine.

He grimaced.

'How is your shoulder?' the stranger asked without turning
round.

Lorn's forearm and shoulder had both been carefully bandaged. They did not cause him pain. He only felt a faint itch:
the beneficent sting of the healing process accelerated by the
action of some exceptional balm. Indeed, despite the pain stabbing his temples, he didn't feel too bad. He flexed his shoulder

joint without too much difficulty and then balled his fist several times while turning his wrist.

'It's…' he began hoarsely.

He cleared his throat and then resumed in a more distinct voice:

'It's all right. Thank you.'

'Are you hungry?' the man enquired, before breaking three eggs into the pan where slices of bacon were already frying.

Lorn's mouth immediately watered. He was famished and thirsty.

'There's fresh water in the flask.'

Lorn looked down to see a goatskin bag placed on the ground near him. He drank greedily, despite lips parched by the sun, and wet the palm of his hand before rubbing his neck. Meanwhile, the stranger had finished preparing the eggs.

'It's ready,' he announced, turning towards Lorn to hand him the pan. 'Enjoy your meal.'

Lorn froze.

The face beneath the hood was not that of a human being. The stranger was a drac, a reptilian creature whose race had arisen in the realms of Obscurity and Oblivion during the Shadows. His scales were white and gleaming. His slit eyes were an intense turquoise in colour.

'Not hungry any more?' the drac asked in a quiet, even voice.

Lorn got a hold of himself.

'Yes!' he said, taking the pan and the wooden spoon held out to him.

'Some bread?'

Lorn nodded, his mouth full.

The drac drew a round loaf of bread from a travelling bag and cut off two thick slices. One for Lorn and one for himself, which he ate slowly while Lorn gulped down his meal, watching the stranger as he did. The drac wore a signet ring on the third finger of his left hand and another ring of black arcanium pierced the arch of one eyebrow. A long dagger hung from his finely crafted belt. His clothes, otherwise, were those of a traveller. It was impossible to guess his age, or even his sentiments.

Sated at last, Lorn put down the pan and wiped his mouth with the back of his hand.

'Thank you,' he said, looking the drac straight in the eye. 'For everything.'

The stranger accepted his thanks with a simple nod of the head.

'You're welcome, Lorn.'

Lorn stiffened, suddenly on the defensive.

'You know me?' he asked.

'Everyone knows you.'

'That's an overstatement, surely?'

'I'll grant you that. Let's just say that I know you. As do a few others.'

'Who are you?' asked Lorn.

'I'm an Emissary of the Grey Dragon.'

'The Dragon of Destiny. What's your name?'

'Is it not enough to know that I am an Emissary?'

'No.'

The Emissary pulled a face that seemed to say: *Well, why not?*

'I'm called Skeren.'

The ginger cat had remained in the shade, upon the blanket. It stood up, stretched, and came over to settle on Lorn's knees. Lorn allowed it to do so before gently caressing its back. The animal started to purr softly.

'It seems that before ordering my second trial, the High King was visited by an Emissary,' said Lorn in a casual tone. 'What was that one's name?'

The Emissary smiled.

'He was also called Skeren.'

'That's quite a coincidence.'

'Indeed.'

Lorn smiled in his turn and gave his full attention to the cat, still stroking it. Its eyelids half-closed, the cat pushed its head beneath his hand.

'I imagine I also owe you thanks for that,' acknowledged Lorn.

'You don't owe me anything. The High King makes his own decisions.'

'No doubt. But without you, would he have ordered a new trial?'

The Emissary gave no reply.

'What did you say to the High King?' asked Lorn.

'First of all, that you were innocent.'

Lorn chuckled.

'So what? If we started freeing all the innocent people in prison…'

'Then,' the white drac was saying imperturbably, 'we told him who you are…'

'Who I am?' Lorn asked in surprise.

But the Emissary did not elaborate and instead continued:

'Lastly, we told him what you were perhaps destined to accomplish. Because you have a destiny, Lorn. And that is not something given to everyone.'

'How lucky for me…'

Lorn scratched the cat's head. Then, neglecting the animal, he thought for a moment, his thumb rubbing, beneath the leather strap, the palm of his marked hand.

'I imagine that my destiny was not to rot away inside Dalroth,' he surmised.

'Of course not.'

'Then what is it?'

'I don't know.'

'But the Assembly of Ir'kans knows.'

'It knows enough, yes.'

The drac seemed to choose his words carefully and explained:

'You see, Destiny is always fulfilled in one way or another. If it's written that a king shall die beneath the dagger of an assassin, it will happen no matter what. The assassin may fail. Or die prematurely. Or follow an entirely different path. But in that case, another will take his place. Another whose steps will be guided by Destiny. And at the appointed hour, or thereabouts, the king will die. Perhaps he won't be stabbed by a dagger. Perhaps he'll be poisoned instead. But he will be assassinated. Inevitably… You understand?'

'Yes.'

'The Dragon of Destiny always fulfils its purpose,' concluded the Emissary.

'With the help, sometimes, of the Assembly of Ir'kans.'

'Sometimes, yes. But the Guardians only work to further the fulfilment of Destiny. Never anything else. When the stakes are high, they act so that everyone can achieve their destiny…'

'…in the interest of Destiny.'

'Yes. Exactly. What's written must come to pass.'

Lorn remained silent.

He reflected while he caressed the cat and then suddenly said:

'I don't give a damn about Destiny in general or my own destiny in particular. Find someone else to fulfil it, Emissary.'

The drac remained perfectly impassive.

'A royal wyverner has already spotted the smoke from our fire,' he said. 'Before evening, the Grey Guards searching for you will be here.'

Lorn could not help smiling to himself.

So, the wyverners he had seen before entering the Deadlands were looking for him, but on behalf of the Grey Guards that the High King had sent out after him.

'Their orders are to escort you to the Citadel,' continued the Emissary. 'Willingly or not. You'd best go along with them.'

And as Lorn gave no reply, he added:

'The High King is dying and awaits you.'

Lorn looked down at the cat, which was still purring beneath his caress.

'So what?'

His tone was meant to be ironic, but it lacked conviction.

Lorn became aware that some part of him remained in service to the High Kingdom. A part he was resisting with cynicism and rancour. A part of the person he'd once been, which had not completely vanished in Dalroth.

'Didn't you say that if I do not fulfil my destiny, someone else will do so in my place?'

'Yes,' conceded the drac. 'But that won't happen without a cost. Destiny always prefers the least difficult path. It won't give up readily, now that it has chosen you. And the entire High Kingdom will suffer from your decision, not to mention what awaits you personally…'

'Are you trying to scare me?'

'No. But I know where the byway you desire to take will lead. It goes to Sarme and makes you an assassin.'

Lorn raised an eyebrow.

'Whereas if you agree to speak to the High King…' added the Emissary, letting his sentence drag out, 'your destiny will be an extraordinary one. Believe me, if you embrace it, it will provide you with ample means to wreak your revenge.'

He rose upon uttering these words, as did Lorn. He gathered up his effects, stuffed them into a bag and mounted his horse waiting attached to one of the stakes in the circle surrounding the mound.

'Goodbye, Lorn. Make your destiny your ally. You will find none more powerful.'

Lorn saluted the Emissary gravely with a nod of the head, before realising that he still held the ginger cat in his arms.

'You forgot your cat!' he called out.

'Cats don't belong to anyone,' retorted the drac, who was already moving off. 'But that one seems to have adopted you. Keep it near you.'

'Does it have a name?'

'Almost certainly, but I don't know it.'

The Grey Guards arrived at nightfall and found Lorn waiting for them, sitting cross-legged with the cat rolled into a ball between his thighs as he poked distractedly at the embers of his campfire.

Raising his head, Lorn watched the troop approach.

It was composed of twenty horsemen in armour with crested helmets, five black crowns adorning their grey banners and shields. Lorn knew these signs and emblems only too well, having borne them himself before being accused, defamed and convicted. So, when he saw the pennants flapping in the wind amidst the rumble of a steady gallop, an unexpected emotion squeezed his throat.

147

He remembered the ceremony, conducted with great pomp, when he was admitted to the ranks of the Grey Guard. He remembered what an honour it had been to belong to this elite company, to which the king entrusted his life. He remembered his feeling of pride, and even more, his father's pride. And he remembered the moment when he was arrested. Only a few months had gone by between the moment when the captain of the Grey Guard had handed him the famous crested helmet in the king's presence and the moment when he'd demanded that Lorn give up his sword...

Lorn pulled himself together.

Holding the cat in his arms, he stood up and waited for their arrival.

22

'It is the hardiest, the rarest and perhaps the most beautiful flower of Imelor. No snows are cold enough to prevent it from blossoming in the springtime and enduring until the last days of autumn, no drought is cruel enough, no rain is violent enough, no hail is heavy enough. And it is said that even the Dark is powerless to tarnish its lustre or wither its beauty. As if immortal, it grows only on the eternal summits of Langre, of which it is the emblem and the pride. It bears an ancient name: Irelice.'

Chronicles (The Book of Symbols)

Eylinn of Feln enjoyed, alone, the delights of a hot, perfumed bath. Languid, her eyelids closed, she relaxed in the soft light. A few candles were burning. Her hair lifted into a loose chignon and her slender neck resting upon a cushion, the young woman breathed peacefully, a thin smile upon her lips.

She only opened one eye when her father entered. Duncan of Feln seemed irritated. Perhaps even angry. He let himself fall heavily into an armchair in the luxurious bathing room and heaved a sigh.

'What's the matter, father?'

With a sombre look, the duke stared at a point in front of him. His breathing wheezed and his jaw was clenched tight. He sat there silently containing his wrath, his muscles stretched to breaking point.

'The imbeciles!' he muttered to himself.

Eylinn knew her father rarely gave way to anger. He considered it a weakness whose consequences were always detrimental. An angry man thought poorly and made bad decisions. He allowed his emotions to govern him, rather than his intelligence and experience. But in politics – the domain in which Duncan of Feln excelled – allowing oneself to be ruled by sentiment was more than a mistake: it was a fault that might prove fatal.

'The imbeciles,' repeated the duke.

Eylinn turned away and pulled on a robe as she rose from her bath. She got out of the tub, dripping, and approached her father, placed a kiss upon his brow, and then went behind him to rub his shoulders.

Duncan gradually recovered his composure.

'They tried to abduct Lorn in Samarande,' he announced. 'And a second time on the road to Brenvost. And they probably would have tried again, if a troop of Grey Guards patrolling in the region hadn't forced them to give up...'

'Relax, father.'

'And now... And now, they have the nerve to come to me...'

The duke took a deep breath, before closing his eyes and exhaling slowly. He waited a moment for his daughter's skilful massage to take effect, and said:

'It's Hebart. He took advantage of our journey through Argor to organise this... idiocy. I imagine he had little trouble convincing the others. They've all been shitting themselves since they learned that Lorn was to be freed...'

'But Lorn only had dealings with you.'

'That's right.'

'So he has no knowledge of Irelice's other members, does he?'

'Of course not! But what can I say? They're afraid of their own shadows.'

The young woman pondered for a moment.

'What were they planning to do with Lorn once they'd abducted him?' she asked aloud.

'As for that!' Duncan chuckled. 'I'm not certain those cretins even knew themselves.'

'Who was in charge of carrying out this task?'

The duke shrugged.

'I don't know. I still don't know all the details of the affair. But I doubt Hebart dirtied his own hands... Be that as it may, the damage is done. And it's up to me to deal with it, now.'

Her hands paused on her father's shoulders, before Eylinn asked:

'What damage, exactly? Is it really so serious, father?'

'Who knows how Lorn will react? What if he decides to come after us?'

'Assuming he knows who tried to abduct him...'

'Who but Irelice would want to silence him? Who else would profit from having him disappear? If Lorn hasn't worked it out yet, he will soon enough.'

Eylinn took a few steps, thinking out loud.

'That's by no means certain. Lorn has no doubt many other enemies who are unlikely to be pleased by the news of his return. Besides, what can he do against us? Speak out? Why would he do that now, when so far he has kept silent?'

'Yes... Perhaps you're right... Nevertheless, we'll need to keep an eye on him.'

The young woman ceased pacing back and forth.

'Wasn't that your intention, in any event?'

'Yes,' admitted Duncan ruefully.

He remained pensive for a moment and then declared:

'I'm going to make sure Hebart regrets this blunder for a long time. I will make sure he toes the line and marches in step from now on. As for Lorn... I believe the best thing to do is to wait and see. I'm convinced that if the High King ordered his liberation, it was not simply to repair a...'

He hunted for the right word.

'An injustice?' suggested Eylinn.

The duke smiled.

'Yes,' he said. 'A terrible injustice.'

23

'Having found Lorn in the Deadlands, the Grey Guards sent after him by the High King escorted him to Elarian, where they embarked for Ryas. After a short crossing on the waters of the Captive Sea, they resumed their journey by road and, riding towards the Citadel, reached the Egides Mountains.'

Chronicles (The Book of the Knight with the Sword)

They made a stopover at the foot of the Egides range, at an old castle that defended the access to a steep-sided valley. The halt was a welcome one to all, and in particular to Lorn who had not yet recovered from his fight with the wolves in the Deadlands.

The Dark, moreover, continued to tax him.

During the short crossing by water to Ryas, he suffered withdrawal symptoms which he managed to keep secret. Alone in his cabin, lying huddled up on his bunk, trembling and feverish, with cramps in all his limbs, he had stifled his moans of pain. The crisis happily proved less acute than the first one and he was able to contain it. In the morning, he had discreetly poured overboard the black bile he had vomited into his chamber pot and the only proof of his illness left was his sheets, drenched in a sour sweat. Even so, he feared the next fit would surprise him without his being able to conceal it. He wanted to believe his need would diminish over time, that the fits would become less frequent and less violent. But would he ever be truly weaned from the Dark?

That evening, like every evening since the Grey Guards had been escorting him, Lorn ate a short distance apart from the troop, without anyone saying a word to him. Then he lit the end of a candle he'd kept in his pocket and opened a small stained, dog-eared book which he had purchased in the port before embarking for Ryas.

Indifferent to the conversations of the horsemen who were talking in low voices in the castle's vast refectory, he was absorbed in his reading and stroking the cat left to him by the Emissary, when the officer in command of the troop came and sat down by him. His name was Rilsen and, until now, he'd barely spoken to Lorn. Like his men, he had treated the knight with a cold respect, as if scrupulously fulfilling a duty against his will. Lorn asked for nothing more. Besides, the silence he was condemned to suited him very well, with the young ginger cat as his sole companion.

Rilsen said nothing for a moment and drank from the neck of a thin metallic flask which he kept about his person. Then, with an abrupt gesture that betrayed a certain embarrassment, he held it out to Lorn.

'The nights are always cold within these old stones,' he said.

It was an attempt to break the ice. Lorn pondered it for a moment, but saw no reason to reject the peace offering. He closed his book, took the flask and lifted it in a silent toast to the officer before taking a small gulp of brandy.

It tasted good.

'Thank you,' he said as he returned the flask.

Rilsen restoppered it before slipping it into his boot.

'What are you reading?' he asked.

'The *Chronicles*.'

'Which book?'

'*The First Kings of Langre.*'

The *Chronicles of the Kingdoms of Imelor* was an immense text comprising a hundred volumes gathered in books and divided into songs and verses. History and legend were mixed together, and scholars argued over whether such-and-such a book deserved to be included in the canon, if this song was really in its proper place or that verse shouldn't be interpreted differently. The debates were endless, all the more so because the books continued to be written and expanded year after year. Certain volumes were travel tales, others philosophical musings, collections of prayers, or mystical and prophetic texts. The origin of the most ancient books was a mystery, which did not prevent some of them from becoming founding documents in the High Kingdom and elsewhere.

The Book of the First Kings of Langre was one of them.

'That's one of my favourites,' said Rilsen.

'Mine too.'

'My father read *The First Kings* to me when I was a child. I learned my first letters with it.'

Lorn gave him a sad smile.

At Dalroth, he had often recited the passages he knew by heart. And when he grew tired of those, he reconstituted others from snippets he could recall. Sometimes, only the rhythm or flavour of a verse remained in his memory, while the actual words were missing. In that case, he invented new ones. All means were valid if they allowed him to escape in thought from his situation.

Rilsen saw the painful veil that clouded Lorn's gaze but did not know the cause. His eyes fell upon the cat, which had fallen asleep.

'What's its name?' he asked.

'I haven't the slightest idea.'

The reply left the officer perplexed.

The truth was that Lorn was still looking for a name. He hesitated because he was familiar with cats and knew one never really named them. When a name seemed to finally suit the animal, it was because the cat had chosen it.

There was a moment of silence, while Rilsen, having exhausted more innocent topics of conversation, felt obliged to come to the heart of matters.

'I wanted you to know I have no quarrel against you,' he said.

Lorn looked at him, thinking he had been just like this young officer once.

Three years earlier, he too had belonged to the Grey Guard and no one, back then, had doubted that he would one day command it. The High King was his godfather. He was the friend and confidant of Prince Alderan. He had covered himself in glory at the borders of Valmir and – despite his modest origins – he was going to marry the daughter of the powerful duke of Sarme and Vallence. Everything seemed to being going right for him.

'I joined the Grey Guard a year after your departure,' explained Rilsen.

'My departure...' noted Lorn bitterly.

'At the time, everyone believed you guilty. And the guards even refused to speak your name.'

Lorn was affected by that piece of news.

Perhaps he was less indifferent than he thought, after all. But hearing that the Grey Guard, of which he had been a proud member, had disowned him, wounded him more than he could admit.

'And now?' he asked.

'Now, they don't know what to think. Those who arrived after you, like me, are more sympathetic to your cause. They think nothing can be held against you now, since you were innocent of the charges brought against you. But the others...' The officer sighed. 'You need... You need to understand that all of them, including Captain Norfold, were under suspicion after you were convicted. And you know full well that mere suspicion is already a blight upon one's honour. Some of them could not bear it and quit the Guard rather than answer defamatory questions. And those that remained have trouble forgiving you. I know,' he hastened to add. 'I know... But for three years, you embodied everything they most despised: a traitor to his own honour and to his king, who besmirched the honour of the company of the Grey Guards. And now, all of a sudden... That's why they're giving you the cold shoulder. And I must confess that I don't entirely know what to do. Because even though the king demanded that your innocence be recognised—'

'Just a minute,' Lorn interrupted.

Fearing he'd heard correctly, he stood up, upsetting the cat.

'You said the king demanded that...'

He did not finish.

'That your innocence be recognised, that's right,' said the officer. 'Why?'

Lorn made no reply.

Up until now, he had thought that the High King had ordered a new trial at the end of which he had been absolved. At least, that's what Alan had said to him and what everyone seemed to believe. Yet Rilsen appeared to be saying that the High King had decreed his innocence. Had a second trial actually taken place? If it had, was it merely a formality whose outcome had been ordained in advance, in accord with the royal demands? It seemed to Lorn that the king had wanted him freed and used his power in order to make that happen. But why? Why now, after three long years? And had the High King acted on his own, or at the behest of the Assembly of Ir'kans?

After all, if the Emissary were to be believed, Lorn had a destiny…

'What's the matter?' asked Rilsen worriedly.

'Nothing,' lied Lorn. 'Nothing. I'm… I'm tired, that's all.'

And since Lorn now seemed preoccupied solely with caressing the head of his purring cat, Rilsen stood and went to rejoin his men.

They left the following morning.

They were obliged to follow several ravines and pass through increasingly steep-sided valleys and gorges. With each passing day, the air grew colder and sharper, the vegetation sparser. They endured sometimes biting winds which whistled and carried their moans as far as the bare summits. The Egides were an austere world of black and grey rocks, meagre grass, thorny bushes and stunted trees clinging to the stone. The riders spoke little, often travelling single file along the precipitous paths, halting for the night in the ruins of fortified towers, which, during the Shadows, had defended each pass on the route to the Citadel.

Protected by his hood and his dark spectacles, his cat resting upon his shoulders or tucked into one of his saddle bags, Lorn seemed to be surrounded by a black aura. This was partly due to his reserved air, his expressionless silences and the distance he kept between himself and the others. But it also stemmed from something deeper. Like the crew of the ship that had taken him from Dalroth, the guards avoided meeting his glance and spoke in low voices behind his back. He aroused both curiosity and concern. Without actually fearing him, the riders of his escort were wary and maintained an instinctive prudence. No doubt they sensed the presence of the Dark within him.

Lorn had all the time he desired to reflect.

He now regretted the way he had treated Alan before leaving Samarande. He felt guilty about having repeatedly spurned the helping hand his friend had offered him. But if he had accepted it, he would then have been obliged to open up, reveal himself and surrender to emotion. Dalroth had given him a thick skin, but beneath it the flesh was still raw. Lorn had no idea who he was now. How could he share his feelings, his doubts and his fears? He knew he was not completely free of Dalroth and that it would take time. But did he have that time? Would the Dark ever leave him in peace? He was afraid that it had welded itself to him so intimately that he could not be rid of it without amputating part of himself. Perhaps he had become a solitary, tormented soul who would never find repose. Perhaps he should simply admit it and adapt to this terrible truth. And perhaps he would be doing a favour, both to himself and to those who loved him and were trying to help him.

Only the Emissary's cat managed to soothe him.

So, stroking the animal who was purring with its eyes closed, Lorn lost himself in the contemplation of the landscape. The immensity of the mountains, the depth of the chasms and the height of the summits made him almost feel drunk. He had often crossed the Egides on his way to the Citadel. But the spectacle that spread before him was not of the kind one grew used to. And how many times had he dreamed of these mountains in the darkness of his cell. Today, the Egides range rose up at the borders of the High Kingdom. But once they had looked out over a vast wild region that had since vanished for the most part beneath the Captive Sea. Of the rest, now only the Deadlands remained. History had been written and legend forged here. During the Last War of the Shadows, it was in the Egides that King Erklant I, at the head of several thousand men, had fallen back to resist the triumphant armies of the Dragons of Obscurity and Oblivion. It was in the Egides that those heroes had built the Citadel where, cornered, they had courageously fought on until the sacrifice of the Dragon-King had provoked a cataclysm and opened the way to victory. And it was also in the Egides that Erklant I, alone, had vanquished the Dragon of Destruction and appropriated his power.

The history of the High Kingdom had been born here and it was here that Lorn had witnessed its zenith, its decline and its fall. He had faced his destiny in the shadow of these legendary mountains.

And now he was returning.

24

At last, after long days, they reached a valley tucked between abrupt ridges and walls. By means of an old paved road, they went past a town and continued to the end of the valley. This ended in a dark crevasse whose steep sides, pointing towards the sky, met in a cul-de-sac.

Here lodged the Citadel.

It was an immense fortress. Before reaching it, they needed to cross several walls barring the crevasse. Then they arrived at the foot of the first rampart. The Citadel never seemed as imposing as at this particular angle, where one waited, tiny and crushed, for the gates to open, the drawbridge to be lowered and the portcullis to be raised. Other ramparts lay behind it, in rising ranks, the tallest enclosing a castle whose keep and crenellated towers were partly dug into the cliff.

Lorn followed the escort to the castle, at a walk, in a reverential silence, the hooves of their horses clacking on the flagstones. The Citadel was a sacred place, impossible for a subject of the High King to enter without experiencing fear and respect, for the history and the legend of the High Kingdom were forged here. But Lorn felt a special emotion of his own. He had been born in the Citadel. He had been dubbed a knight and received honours here, and then imprisoned while his trial took place, until he was finally convicted. Memories returned to him, melancholy and often painful. Words spoken. Laughter and tears. Fleeting odours. And a maelstrom of contradictory feelings which threatened to overwhelm him…

Norfold, the captain of the Grey Guard, was waiting in the castle's upper courtyard. Behind him, soldiers in armour formed a guard of honour leading up to the keep's stairway. Lorn dismounted and handed the reins of his horse to a squire. Still mounted, Rilsen gave him a nod and moved off, followed by the horsemen he commanded.

Lorn looked at Norfold without saying a word.

His life had become a nightmare when the captain had arrested him, three years earlier. Lorn had been entrusted with the security for some highly confidential meetings taking place between the High Kingdom and Yrgaard. Those meetings were designed to lay the basis for a peace treaty and required the utmost secrecy. The High Kingdom and Yrgaard were hereditary enemies and the balance of alliances among the Imelorian kingdoms rested for a large part on this centuries-old antagonism. If their allies discovered that the High Kingdom and the Black Dragon were coming to a rapprochement behind their backs, it would set off a series of political and diplomatic crises that would be certain to ruin all their efforts. But if initial ground for agreement were found, other negotiations would ensue, perhaps putting an end to five centuries of open and covert warfare. Lorn knew the dramatic consequences that even the slightest leak would have on the outcome of these talks. Warned of the stakes, he was equally aware of the trust accorded to him by the High King and the honour shown him. And everything seemed to be proceeding smoothly, until the day Norfold, expressionless, had demanded his sword and placed him under arrest.

Facing Lorn, three years later, Norfold was just as stoic.

He'd barely changed at all. Tall and solidly built, he was about fifty years old and had an impeccably trimmed goatee. He remained silent, containing his anger, but his look was baleful and expressed everything he could not say aloud. He had not forgiven Lorn. He did not believe in his innocence. And although Norfold would fulfil his duty, scrupulously obeying the orders and the will of the High King, he left no doubt as to his own deep conviction. Lorn inspired nothing but anger, hatred and scorn in him. His place was in Dalroth, until he died.

Lorn, head held high, met him with a gaze that was just as eloquent.

A tranquil gaze, which said: *To hell with you.*

Norfold understood it and nodded almost imperceptibly, as if to signify he would lift up the gauntlet and respond to the challenge. Both men realised they were henceforth sworn enemies.

'Follow me,' said the captain after a moment.

'Is the king expecting me?'

'No. It's already late in the day. His Majesty will receive you tomorrow. You can go and rest.'

Together, they climbed the keep's great staircase between stiff, grim-looking soldiers who stared straight ahead. Evening was already falling upon the Citadel and torches were being lit.

Lorn made use of the castle's steam room, then retired to the chamber assigned to him in one of the towers. He found clean clothes waiting for him, pressed and folded. The walls were bare and the furnishings austere, but the bed was soft and after several days riding in the mountains and camping in bivouacs, Lorn fell into it with pleasure. And he was on the point of drifting into sleep when a meal was brought to him.

A second knock came at the door a little later, when he was finishing his dinner.

'Come in,' he called, after wiping his mouth.

The door opened and a tall, stern-looking fellow appeared. He towered over Lorn by a good foot, wore the black breastplate of the King's guards and sported a martial-looking moustache. He was thirty-five to forty years in age and it was easy to see that he had been a soldier his entire life. A scar in the form of a crescent moon marked his right cheek.

Lorn did not remember having seen him before.

'Yes?' he asked.

'I've received orders from Captain Norfold to present myself to you, my lord.'

'Why?'

'I have been charged with your protection.'

'My protection or my surveillance?'

'Only your protection was mentioned.'

The man's gaze was tranquil, almost indifferent. Lorn tried to size him up, but in vain.

'There's nothing I can do about it, is there?'

'I beg your pardon, my lord?'

'No matter what I say, you will remain at my side.'

'Orders are orders, my lord. They can be changed by those that give them, but not ignored by those who receive them.'

'And the one you've received thus came from the captain of the guard.'

'Yes.'

Lorn saw no reason to make a fuss.

'So be it,' he said. 'Your name?'

'Hurst.'

'Hurst. That's a name, is it?'

'It is when one is called Hurstvenskaren.'

'I see. Any first name?'

'Veskarstendir.'

Lorn wondered if the guard was having fun with him. He watched him attentively, but the other man seemed to be one of those people completely devoid of a sense of humour.

'Veskarstendir,' repeated Lorn.

'Yes.'

'Veskarstendir Hurstvenskaren.'

'Yes.'

Lorn made a big effort to keep a straight face.

'I could call you Veskar.'

'I prefer Hurst.'

'Then Hurst it shall be. Good night, Hurst.'

'Good night, my lord.'

And with that, Hurst closed the door behind him.

Lorn pondered why he'd been assigned a bodyguard. Who, upon reflection, was just as much his keeper. Norfold distrusted Lorn and probably wanted to show he had his eye on him. But perhaps the captain had learned that Lorn had been the target of an attempted abduction at Samarande. And his duty, however disagreeable, was to protect Lorn. If something happened to him, Norfold would no doubt have to answer to the High King. Because he knew him well, Lorn held his former captain in high esteem: there was no man more loyal, honest, or devoted. If the king gave him the order, he would give his life to save Lorn's.

It was sadly ironic…

His mood becoming sombre again, Lorn poured himself a glass of wine and went to lean a shoulder against the window frame.

Almost deserted at this hour, the Citadel was silent. One heard only the wind whistling outside, the flapping of banners and the ringing bells that marked the rhythms of military life. The Citadel had never been a joyful place, but Lorn had known it to be far busier when, as adolescents, he and Alan had spent summers with the High King. King Erklant had always preferred the Citadel to his other palaces. Because he was a warrior king. But also because from here he could frequently visit the tomb of his ancestor, Erklant I, whose name he bore and whose memory he venerated.

Erklant the Ancient.

The one who had triumphed during the Last War of the Shadows. The one who had founded the High Kingdom. The one who had defeated Serk'Arn, the Dragon of Destruction, and appropriated his power.

History and legend were so closely intertwined concerning him that it was difficult to believe he had been an actual being of flesh and blood, who had dwelled in this Citadel and fought against the armies of Obscurity and Oblivion in these mountains. But it was still more difficult to believe that his body rested close by, beneath a stone slab.

Lorn's wandering gaze was caught by the silhouette of a tower. It housed the prison where Lorn had awaited the outcome of his trial. He had not even been present during the proceedings. Accused of having breached the secrecy surrounding the negotiations, which he was supposed to ensure ran smoothly, he had been reduced to helpless silence while his judges, behind closed doors, heard testimony and examined documents that apparently established an overwhelming case against him. No one spoke in his defence. The trial was a summary affair and, less than a month after his arrest, Lorn embarked for

Dalroth. As for the negotiations between the High Kingdom and Yrgaard, they resumed two years later at the initiative of the queen's minister, Esteveris. And by some strange whim of Destiny, Lorn had returned at the very moment they would lead to the re-establishment of diplomatic relations between the two countries and, in the end, a peace treaty.

Feeling bitter, Lorn drank a gulp of wine without tasting it.

Exhausted, Lorn fell asleep and dreamed.

His nightmares sent him back to his private hell. He found himself wandering, lost and anguished, the corridors of a fortress which was both Dalroth and the Citadel. He heard cries, sobs and moans. His own, perhaps. The Emissary spoke to him, but his voice was muffled by the din of a storm whose purple lightning bolts dazzled him. Helpless, Lorn watched the Emissary walk away. Then he turned and, terrified, raised his eyes towards a polished dragon's skull. He screamed when the dragon's jaws opened and set his entire body alight with burning fire.

Lorn awoke with a start, his heart pounding and his lungs gasping for breath. The cat was sitting nearby and watching him, one paw placed upon his sweat-soaked chest.

25

Lorn was ready when they came to fetch him. He was waiting in the castle's hall, indifferent to the portraits of Langre's kings that adorned the walls. He was anxious. He had no idea what Erklant II wanted from him and only knew what the Emissary had told him: he had an extraordinary destiny before him and it started here, in the Citadel, in the form of an audience with a dying High King.

He was granted entry to the throne room.

It was long and high-ceilinged, punctuated by columns and plunged into darkness. Its narrow arched windows were all hidden behind thick black curtains. Large candelabra were positioned at regular intervals from the door, but the flickering flames of their candles permitted one to see only dimly.

Lorn advanced towards the throne set upon a dais, at the end of a long crimson carpet which muffled the sound of his footsteps. The silence was profound, but there was a sense of a vibrant presence beneath the stone arches. Lorn had indeed the feeling that he was walking towards his destiny. He held himself straight and tried to remain calm, his fist gripping the hilt of the Skandish sword which hung at his side.

The old King Erklant II waited unmoving on his throne of ebony and onyx. He was booted and wore grey chain mail and black leather. A dark veil, held in place by his crown, concealed his face. His right hand rested on the pommel of his sheathed sword as if it were a cane.

Lorn bowed when he reached the foot of the dais covered in a black-and-silver carpet. The platform was overlooked by a large skull that seemed to be made of polished stone: that of

Serk'Arn, the Dragon of Destruction slain by Erklant I at the end of the Shadows.

'Come. Approach so I can see you better,' said the High King in a hoarse voice.

Lorn climbed the steps to kiss the signet ring on the hand the king held out to him – a dry, bony hand. Then, backing away, Lorn returned to his place at the foot of the dais and knelt, his head bowed in a sign of respect and obedience.

'Rise, Lorn. Rise,' said Erklant, accompanying his words with a wave of his hand.

Lorn stood up to let the king observe him. He then noticed Norfold standing in the shadows two paces from the throne, never taking his eyes from the knight.

'Your eye,' said the High King after a moment. 'The right one. It's… It's changed, hasn't it?'

Lorn had not donned his dark glasses to appear before his king. Besides, they would have been useless in the dim light.

'Yes, sire.'

'The Dark?'

Lorn nodded.

'Show me your hand,' said the High King.

When Lorn hesitated, he insisted:

'Show me.'

Lorn slowly undid the leather strap wrapped around his left hand. Then he set one foot on the dais and leaned forward, his arm outstretched, so that the High King could see the stone seal embedded in his skin. The old king took his hand and examined the mark of Dalroth carefully.

'Does it hurt?' he asked.

'Sometimes.'

With slow, delicate gestures, those of a fragile old man, the king yielded Lorn's hand.

Then he sat up and asked:

'We have done you a grievous wrong, haven't we?'

As Lorn remained silent, the old king repeated as if to himself:

'Yes. A grievous wrong…'

He remained pensive for a moment, before declaring:

'I'm glad to see you again, son.'

Son.

The High King had always called him 'son' out of affection. To be sure, he had other godsons besides Lorn because he never refused that honour to the elder sons of his lords and knights. But in Lorn's case, the bond had been truly special. Lorn knew the king loved him like a father. He had never doubted that, at least, not until his trial and his sentence. Erklant had done nothing to save him, or even to defend him. He had not spared Lorn from Dalroth. He'd abandoned him.

For Lorn, the wound had been deep and it remained so.

'You... You did nothing,' he said, in a voice that quavered with emotion. 'You could have... One word from you and... and...'

He was unable to complete his sentence, feeling his guts tighten in anguish.

The High King did not reply, but his gleaming eyes continued to scrutinise Lorn from behind the black veil that hid his gaunt face.

After which, he nodded gravely.

'Help me,' he said.

He tried to stand, holding on to his throne with one hand and leaning on his sword with the other. Surprised, Lorn hesitated as Norfold came hurrying forward and assisted the High King to his feet.

'Thank you, Norfold,' said Erklant after catching his breath. 'But I believe... I believe Lorn is strong enough to lend me his arm.'

The captain understood and regretfully entrusted the king to Lorn. Taken aback, the latter had no choice and found himself supporting an old man who seemed fragile. He thought that it would take almost nothing for Erklant to break his neck and, meeting Norfold's gaze, read the terrible warning there.

'That way,' said the High King, indicating the tall black curtains.

There was a balcony behind them.

Lorn helped the king pass through them, and then accompanied him to the balustrade. From here, one had a view of

167

the entire valley. Dusk was falling. The cold shadows of the mountains stretched out, wide and unruffled. Pent up between its cliffs, the Citadel was already plunged into night.

The king held onto the railing, but Lorn sensed his legs were weak and did not release his elbow.

'At present,' said Erklant, after taking in the scenery, 'this is my entire kingdom…'

'Sire, you are still the High King.'

'I wear his crown, yes,' retorted the old king with immense weariness. 'But it's too heavy… I no longer have the strength to reign, to govern. My kingdom is ailing because of it. I have neglected it too long, Lorn. Far too long. And because of me, it is dying. As I am…'

Tired, he turned and, with a long wrinkled finger, pointed to an armchair on the balcony. Lorn eased him into it and, acting the role of a nurse, arranged the cushions as best he could.

Once he was seated comfortably, the High King heaved a profound sigh of relief.

'That's better,' he said. 'Thank you.'

Then he hunted around for something, seemed irritated and, as Lorn remained standing, called out:

'Have a chair brought out here for the knight!'

'No, sire. I assure you that—'

'A chair for the knight!'

Someone hurried to bring a stool to Norfold, who had stayed back, standing at the threshold of the balcony. The captain left it beside the king's chair and withdrew.

'Sit down,' said the king. Lorn obeyed. 'Closer, closer…'

Lorn drew the stool near enough so that the High King, leaning to one side, could speak in his ear. Erklant's breath was acrid and he wheezed whenever he took a breath.

'I could do nothing, you know that?' he confided. 'If I had intervened, interceded in your favour… I would have been accused of supplanting my own justice. Because you are my godson. And Alan's friend… Do you understand?'

No, Lorn did not understand.

For what the High King had refused to do back then in the name of his integrity, he had finally done three years later. Out of remorse or sense of duty. Or more likely still, at the behest of the Assembly of Ir'kans.

'And secrecy had to be maintained,' added the king. 'Secrecy as to the accusations brought against you and secrecy regarding your trial. All that to preserve another secret. A bigger secret. The secret of those damned negotiations with Yrgaard.' The king's eyes blazed behind the veil. 'With Yrgaard... Yrgaard! How did I let myself be persuaded that a rapprochement with Yrgaard was not only possible, but desirable? How?'

The king interrupted himself and, with a resigned air, recovered his composure.

'If I had defended you, it would have been a scandal,' he said. 'Word would have leaked out about how and why you were accused. And of what. Our... Our allies would have learned about our discussions with Yrgaard. Learned what we were preparing to do. Betraying our alliances. Reneging on our treaties. There... There would have been crises. Wars, perhaps...' He grew as heated as his meagre strength allowed. 'And the evidence, Lorn! The evidence against you! It... It left no room for doubt! I could not believe you were guilty, not you, who I loved like a son. But you were, Lorn! You were!'

He fell silent and between his bony fingers took the hand Lorn had placed upon the armrest of his seat.

'Forgive me,' begged the old king in a broken voice. 'Forgive me...'

Distraught, furious, Lorn did not know what to say or do.

As if caught in a shameful act, he glanced surreptitiously at Norfold, who remained expressionless but stood ready to intervene. He felt a desire to withdraw his hand, but King Erklant clung to it with the small tenacity that remained to him.

He hesitated.

And felt rising within him an emotion he was slow to recognise and which overwhelmed him...

Revolt.

No longer able to bear it, he stood up abruptly and drew back his hand as though the king's had suddenly become burning hot.

'No!' he exclaimed.

The High King instinctively cringed.

Norfold leapt forward, his hand on his sword and a few inches of steel already emerging from the scabbard as Lorn turned round and, shaking, leaned on the railing.

The old king halted his captain with a gesture and kept one arm stretched towards him in order to keep him back.

He waited.

Lorn got a hold on himself, still quivering with anger but his breathing easier. His eyes remained stormy, however. In the distance, the sky grew overcast just as night was falling and the thick clouds concealed the Nebula from view.

'It was the Assembly of Ir'kans who told me you were innocent, Lorn,' said the old king in a voice filled with emotion. 'I swear to you I did not know...'

Lorn did not react.

'The Guardians also said you have a destiny, and that destiny needs to be fulfilled.'

Realising the danger had been averted, Norfold relaxed and resheathed his sword, but did not step back.

'They also told me who you were,' added the High King.

That caused Lorn to raise an eyebrow.

'Who I was?'

'Who you are,' Erklant rectified. 'Who you have always been.'

Lorn recalled what the Emissary had confided to him in an offhand manner: 'We told him who you are.'

'Sire, I don't understand.'

The old king stood, brusquely refusing Norfold's help, and slowly, painfully, made the effort to walk over to Lorn.

'If the Guardians are right, you are more than you believe, Lorn. But sometimes, the Guardians are mistaken. Or they dissemble because they deem it necessary for the will of the Grey Dragon to be fulfilled... But if they are telling the truth, then you may well be the High Kingdom's last hope.'

No longer knowing what to think, Lorn could not help giving a cynical smile.

'The last hope,' he said mockingly. 'Me!'

And with the slowness of an anger he found difficult to

contain, he turned towards the old king and raised his left fist to show him the Dark's mark on the back of his hand.

'Me?' he repeated in an almost menacing tone.

None of this made any sense.

A fat white drop exploded on the armrest of the king's seat. Others followed and spattered on the balcony's flagstones, its balustrade and the rooftops nearby.

The High King raised his eyes towards the sky and smiled resignedly.

Lorn knew the white rains were said to be sent to the High Kingdom by Eyral, the White Dragon. In the draconic pantheon, he was the Dragon of Knowledge and Light. Bearing a pale ash that became dust as it dried, these rains were often an evil omen, warnings sent to the High King by Eyral from the Sacred Mountain.

'Let's go in,' said Erklant. 'I'm very tired.'

Lorn remained out in the rain.

'Tomorrow, I will pay my respects at the tomb of Erklant the Ancient,' said the old king as Norfold escorted him inside. 'Accompany me, Lorn. That's all I ask of you. Accompany me tomorrow...'

And he added:

'After that, you shall do as you like.'

26

Lorn again dined alone in his room, with Hurst standing guard at the door. He had barely any appetite and soon pushed his plate away, pensively stroking the ginger cat which had jumped into his lap. Added to the drumming of the rain upon the roofs, the cat's purring soothed him and helped him stem the tumultuous flow of thoughts, fears and questions.

The rain ceased, leaving pale white drip marks on the grey stones. Night was falling and the Citadel seemed deserted. Abandoned. Not a movement. Not a sound except that of the drops falling from the roofs into large white puddles.

A tomb.

At his window, Lorn recalled when the Citadel, albeit as austere as ever, had been a fortress full of life. It had always enjoyed the High King's preference. But it was isolated and not easily accessible, uncomfortable and inconvenient. It did not lend itself well to the exercise of power, to the point that Erklant II had resigned himself to residing there only during the hottest month of summer, when the heat was unbearable at Oriale, in the heart of Langre. It was the month when Alan and Lorn stayed with the High King before returning for the remainder of the year to the duke of Sarme and Vallence, who had been entrusted with the prince's education.

Lorn could not help from smiling at the memory of the happy days he and Alan had known in the shadow of these walls, which, back then, had not seemed so sinister to him. It was before the Citadel had become the final resting place of a very old king grown lonely and ill, awaiting death surrounded only by his personal guard and observing the decline of his kingdom from his now tottering ebony-and-onyx throne.

Lorn realised he would be unable to sleep.

Under the cat's watchful eye, he donned his baldrick and a hooded cloak before straddling the window sill. He knew the Citadel's rooftops by heart, having run over them all night long with Alan each summer when they were younger. For the thrill, for the pleasure of discovery and of transgressing the rules. But also to elude the vigilance of their guardians.

Just like today, Lorn said to himself, thinking of Hurst.

Nothing and no one could forbid him from going where he liked, but he wanted to go there on his own.

From rooftop to rooftop, taking care not to be seen by the sentries, Lorn left the Guards' district where he was lodged. Then, fearing he might slip on the damp tiles or take a bad fall in the darkness that had settled upon the fortress, he descended to the paved streets and made his way to the Weapons district.

The Citadel was divided into districts, which usually consisted of a courtyard and a few buildings. They were separated from one another by wall walks, watchtowers and crenellated ramparts, forming a mosaic. The King's district was the largest and best defended of them. Partly dug into the cliff, it overlooked all the others. But there was also the Stables district, the Arsenal district, the Ambassadors' district, the Temples district, the Schools district, the Hospital district and several others, modest or glorious, sometimes forgotten, making it almost impossible to count them all.

The portcullis of the Weapons district was raised.

The place seemed empty. The courtyard was deserted and the buildings around it were plunged into darkness.

Not a sound.

Lorn felt a lump in his throat.

Traditionally, the Weapons district was where the royal master-of-arms and the royal blacksmith lived. The first trained and instructed the High King, while the second forged weapons and armour for him. Each, in his fashion, was entrusted with the king's life. It was a prestigious but heavy responsibility, and one had to prove oneself worthy of it.

Lorn's father had been Erklant II's master-of-arms. He had

accompanied the High King on all the fields of battle, and once the time of wars had passed, remained at his side. Lorn had spent the first years of life here; been raised here by his mother and father; returned here each summer during his adolescence. It was here that he'd been trained in the harsh crafts of weaponry by his father, sweating blood alongside Alan, but never giving up despite fatigue or wounds.

Lastly, it was here that he had loved for the first time.

Her name was Naéris. She was the only, adored daughter of Reik Vahrd, the royal blacksmith. A true tomboy, she had shared in Lorn and Alan's games when they were children. When she became a winsome adolescent, both boys became besotted with her. Later, she would fall in love with Lorn, but he was looking elsewhere. But that particular summer, she preferred Alan, who was already adept at courting females. Over the years, Lorn became used to this state of affairs. Alan was silver-tongued, attractive, elegant and full of energy. There was something radiant about him. He enchanted people. And the same qualities that made the crowds adore him also meant that sooner or later women ended up in his arms. No one resisted him for long.

Alissia had been the only exception.

Lorn remained silent for a moment in front of his childhood home. In his eyes, it was his father's above all – the place where the master-of-arms, following the death of his wife, had grown old on his own until his death.

The shutters were closed.

Lorn tried to open the door. It was locked but wobbled on its hinges. Shoving against it with his shoulder, he forced it without too much trouble and let it swing open before him with a creak.

He hesitated for a moment on the threshold, an odour of mustiness and old dust filling his nostrils.

Then he went inside.

He could barely see in the darkness. However, the place was familiar to him and nothing seemed to have moved since...

Since as long as he could remember.

Or at least since the last visit he'd paid his father, upon his

174

return from Sarme and Vallence where he'd gone searching for Alan. Of course, he'd been unable to say anything about his mission, or about the hold that kesh had taken over a prince of the High Kingdom. Even to his father. Even to the royal master-of-arms.

Two days later, Norfold had demanded his sword and placed him under arrest.

'Who are you?' asked a voice at Lorn's back. 'And what are you doing here?'

Lorn turned round and was immediately dazzled by the light from a dark lantern. He raised his hand to protect his eyes and averted his head, while trying to catch a sideways glimpse of the other person.

'I warn you that if I call the Guard, it will be to collect your corpse!' threatened the young woman who stood in the doorway. 'So answer me!'

Wearing boots, breeches, shirt and doublet, she brandished her lantern in her left hand and held a sword in her right.

'Naé?' exclaimed Lorn. 'Naé, is it you?'

The young woman hesitated.

'L... Lorn?'

She raised her lantern, which illuminated her face while ceasing to blind Lorn with its glare. He had no difficulty recognised her large dark eyes and wilful air, the tender gleam in her glance and her left cheek marred by a nasty scar.

Naéris.

'It's me, Naé.'

'Lorn!'

She let go of both sword and lantern to throw herself into his arms and hug him tightly for a long moment, her slender, firm body pressed against him disconcertingly. He didn't know what to do with his hands, but finally put them round her.

Moved, the young woman struggled to find her words.

'It's... It's you, it's really you... I... I thought...'

'I was freed, Naé. Declared innocent...'

'But how?' she asked, taking a step back to look at his face; 'We didn't even know if you were...'

She smiled, tears in her eyes.

'I was recalled by the High King,' said Lorn. 'I—'

Naéris interrupted him.

'No, not here. Come,' she said, pulling him by the hand. 'You're going to tell us everything. Papa will be so glad to—'

She fell silent, suddenly grave.

'What's the matter?' asked Lorn anxiously.

'I... I'm sorry, Lorn... About your father.'

'Thank you, Naé.'

'It was Papa who found him, did you know? One morning. It... It was already too late...'

Naéris's eyes grew misty again, and these tears were no longer ones of joy.

'Go on, lad. Have another glass.'

Lorn had lost count, but did not have the heart to refuse. Besides, Reik Vahrd had started pouring without waiting for his assent and, seeing the bottle empty, turned towards his daughter.

'Bring us another, Naé.'

'Are you sure?'

'Of course I'm sure!'

'Don't you think you've drunk enough?'

The old blacksmith considered his daughter with a muddled gaze.

'You know that you're still young enough to get a spanking?'

'No I'm not, and I haven't been for some time. Furthermore, it would be the first you've ever given me.'

Shrugging, Reik leaned across the table to confide to Lorn:

'I think I botched my daughter's education...'

Lorn smiled and pushed his full glass towards Reik.

'She's your greatest success.'

'If you say so,' replied the blacksmith with a doubtful expression... before winking at his daughter seated at the end of the table, slightly apart from the two men.

With age, Reik's blond hair, gathered in a ponytail, had become mixed with silver, but he was still as tall and massively built as ever. His rolled-up sleeves revealed some of the blue tattoos that covered his arms, chest and back. Skandish tattoos, similar to the ones Lorn's mother had borne. Magical, they turned red and changed shape whenever the person they protected was swept up by a warrior's fury. Reik was both Skandish and a blacksmith so he knew how to work arcanium, allowing him to forge extraordinary weapons and armour.

'He fought to the very end, you know?' Reik said suddenly. 'Your father. He never believed the accusations against you. And when you were sentenced, he tried everything in his power to… But what could he do? Everyone turned their back on him. Even the High King, don't you see?'

He grumbled.

'Everyone, except you two,' objected Lorn.

The blacksmith exchanged a glance with his daughter and smiled at him.

'Yep. Except us,' he conceded bitterly. 'For what good it did… I should have liked to have done more for you, lad.'

Lorn nodded.

'I know.'

He knew that Reik was sincere. He was Skandish like his mother and in many ways Lorn had been the son he'd never had. His wife had died giving birth and he had never remarried. He adored his daughter, but she wasn't a son.

'Your father swore he would have your name cleared,' resumed the old blacksmith glaring into empty space. 'That he would obtain a second trial… He raged about it. He couldn't sleep. He knocked at every door. Every single one. In vain, and it wore him down. He found himself alone and exhausted, with neither friends nor money. But he never gave up…' Reik heaved a sigh. 'And then one morning, since he hadn't opened his shutters, I went to see him. The door was open. He was sitting there in his armchair, in front of the fireplace. Dead.'

Lorn was suddenly cold and felt his hands tremble. His mouth turned dry and a weight crushed his chest. At first, he thought another fit might be coming on. But it had nothing to do with the Dark. It was the anger and pain that invaded him like a burning poison running through his veins.

Staring into space, he had trouble holding back his tears.

'Where is he buried?' he asked after a moment.

'Here,' replied Naéris. 'In the small cemetery within the Weapons district.'

'What?' protested Lorn. 'Not the one in the King's district?'

'No,' said Reik. 'No.'

He drained Lorn's glass in a single gulp and stood up with less difficulty than one might have imagined, saying:

'Wait. Don't move.'

He stomped out of the kitchen where they had gathered, at the back of a large house that was now almost empty. He left the door ajar and vanished into the backyard.

'Where is he going?'

Naéris slid along the bench to sit closer to him. She emptied half of her glass into Lorn's and they each drank a mouthful of wine before she replied.

'His place.'

'What do you mean?'

'He sleeps above his forge,' she explained.

'And you?'

'Here. But in the attic.'

'Why?'

The young woman looked Lorn straight in the eye.

'Papa is no longer the royal blacksmith, Lorn. We've lost almost everything. And no one is willing to open their door to us… We shouldn't even be here any more but Papa won't leave the Citadel. So we're practically hiding out. Never knowing if someone will come to expel us tomorrow.'

'And the forge?'

'Extinguished,' Naéris said it as if she were announcing a death.

Reik Vahrd was no ordinary blacksmith.

He knew the secrets of Skandish warsmiths and how to work arcanium and steel to make the best weapons and armour anywhere. On becoming the royal blacksmith, he had sworn an oath forbidding him to forge for anyone other than the High King.

Lorn looked at the empty bottles upon the table and understood why Reik did not fear losing his touch by drinking more than was reasonable.

'All this happened because you supported my father, didn't it?'

'Yes. But don't say anything to Papa,' Naéris hastened to add on hearing her father returning. 'You know how proud he is. He—'

Reik entered, coming to sit back down and placing on the table, before Lorn, a sword in its scabbard.

'Here,' he said. 'It's yours.'

He took the sword, which he had recognised, and could not resist unsheathing it with a smile.

There was no possible doubt.

This sword was his, the one Norfold had demanded from him when he placed him under arrest. It had been given to him by his mother, who, like all Skandish women, had been a warrior. The sword was also Skandish, and excellently made: its blade was wide and heavy, sharp-edged on one side, and its basket guard enveloped his hand. A formidable weapon, but one that required skill to wield.

'In the end, that's all your father had left,' the old blacksmith explained. 'I do not know how he managed to obtain it.'

'Thank you,' said Lorn in a choked voice. 'Thank you.'

Later, after taking his leave of Reik and his daughter, Lorn found Hurst waiting for him at the gate to the Weapons quarter.

'How did you know where to find me?' he asked, as the Grey Guard fell into step with him.

'Your windows are guarded.'

'So you followed me and you've been watching me from the start.'

'I'm protecting you. But yes, from the start.'

'Why reveal your presence only now?'

'I thought you wanted to be alone.'

Lorn smiled.

'You follow a strange logic, Hurst.'

'No, my lord. I obey orders.'

'Did you know the High King's former blacksmith still lives here?'

'Yes. With his daughter. Everyone knows that. Or almost everyone.'

Lorn nodded thoughtfully.

He had already resolved to take revenge against those who had betrayed him.

To that list, he was going to add those who had abandoned his family and friends.

27

'Because he wanted rest for eternity in the place where he had first known glory, where he had faced and vanquished the dragon.'

Chronicles (The Book of Kings)

The valley was covered with a veil of pale ash when they left the City and followed a steep track until they reached a pass defended by an imposing fortified gate, a vestige of the Last Shadows.

Norfold led the troop, followed by six horsemen carrying grey banners, some of which depicted, in black thread, the five crowns of the High Kingdom, while others had the wolf's head which was the king's personal emblem. Lorn and the High King advanced behind them. Twenty riders brought up the rear, wearing helmets, dark leather and mail, their swords at their side and their shields hung on the rumps of their mounts.

Topped by his crown, the High King's face was concealed by an ebony mask encrusted with silver. He had donned a long cloak and thick gloves, so that not an inch of his wrinkled skin was exposed to the sun. Lorn was astonished to see him thus, but even more so to see him riding in the saddle, helped only by a squire. The knight had directed a questioning glance at Norfold, who remained expressionless.

'Let's be on our way,' the king had said in his hoarse voice, before spurring his mount forward.

After three hours, they arrived in a valley through which a capricious wind whistled, raising whirlwinds and sheets of greyish dust which slowly unravelled in the air. A single road crossed this sinister and desolate valley. It led to the temple built on the flank of highest mountain in the Egides range, which sheltered the mausoleum of Erklant I.

They passed some pilgrims, most of them poverty-stricken, who drew apart ahead of them and doffed their hats, saluting respectfully upon seeing the colours of the High Kingdom and its ruler. The escort thundered by at a full gallop. In its dust it left behind men and women who stood gaping and incredulous, unsure if they had caught an actual glimpse of their king, watching the riders move away in a deafening din of ironclad hooves, whinnying, clanking armour and banners flapping in the wind...

Like them, the High King was going to the temple, where, forewarned of his visit, tattooed priests with shaven heads awaited him. Dressed in grey robes, they belonged to an order solely devoted to honouring the memory of the first of the High Kings, tending his tomb and praying for his soul. All had pledged an oath of silence.

The horsemen dismounted in a courtyard shielded by a high red canopy. Exhausted, the king was stricken by a malaise that obliged Lorn and Norfold to seat him on a bench. Lorn then realised the cause for his surprising vigour: his breath was laced with the heady scent of kesh.

So the High King was drugging himself.

Removing his glove, the king snapped his fingers impatiently to draw Norfold's attention. The captain handed him a vial from which he drank a few small sips, lifting his ebony mask from below. Lorn watched a golden drop run down his king's bony chin.

'Sire,' he said, 'you shouldn't...'

But the dying king did not want his solicitude, and dismissed it with a vague gesture. When he finally felt better, he grasped Norfold to stand up.

'Come, son,' he said to Lorn in a sepulchral voice. 'We're almost there now.'

A vertical line of light appeared in the deep darkness. It widened, becoming a slit between the two panels of an immense door as it opened.

The king entered, leaning upon Lorn, and once the door closed behind them, they walked towards the stone platform, the two facing thrones and the flaming bowls burning in the shadows before them. Lorn matched the king's pace, supporting him without any idea what they had come here to do.

'Where are we?' he murmured.

The king gave no reply.

They climbed the steps of the platform, which used up the king's remaining strength. He collapsed on the empty throne and struggled to regain his breath.

Lorn knew nothing of this place.

He was familiar with the temple, the mausoleum and the immense funerary monument to the glory of Erklant I, before which he and Alan had been required to pay their respects each year when they were children, on the anniversary of the first High King's death. The pilgrims filed past this same monument in reverent silence, under the watchful eyes of the priests. For they believed the remains of the vanquisher of Serk'Arn lay within.

In fact, the real tomb was elsewhere, behind the colossal doors, in the dark, cold belly of the mountain. Plain but massive, it stood behind the stone throne upon which the effigy of Erklant I sat. Lorn could barely see it in the darkness, on a pedestal, the flames of the bowls reflecting on its black marble veined with arcanium, a frieze of ancient runes encircling its base.

Lorn wondered who else, besides the temple priests, was aware of this secret.

'Here he is,' said the old king. 'I brought him to you.'

Lorn turned back to the High King who had removed his ebony mask and seemed to be speaking to the statue of his ancestor sitting opposite him.

'Sire?'

But the king ignored him and added:

'Only you can tell me if he is who the Guardians claim he is.'

'Sire, you're not...'

The High King then turned towards Lorn.

'Come. Come here, next to me...'

Lorn hesitated but obeyed, standing on the king's right.

'Look,' the king said, pointing in front of them.

Lorn looked in the direction indicated, towards the statue of Erklant I and the tomb in the darkness beyond.

'We are ready,' announced the old man, straining to raise his hoarse voice. 'We await you! You can appear!'

Disturbed and worried, Lorn stared at the statue seated before him.

Its likeness to the current High King was stupefying, to the point that Lorn expected to see it move, shake off its mineral rigidity and come to life. It would start with a slight twitch. Perhaps a shudder that would crack the stone. Or a gleam in the depths of the eye sockets…

Suddenly, Lorn became aware of a presence in the immense shadows surrounding them. There was the heavy sound of chains being dragged. Then that of claws of steel and bone scraping rock. A movement in the air caused the fire in the bowls to flicker.

He was looking in the wrong place; the High King wasn't speaking to the ghost of his ancestor. A cold sweat running down his spine, Lorn raised his eyes towards the tomb just in time to see a leg set down upon it.

An immense scaly leg.

That of a dragon who, coming forward, slowly poked its head out of the darkness.

'*I am Serk'Arn*,' said the dragon in a powerful voice that resounded in Lorn's mind. '*Who are you?*'

Livid, Lorn drew his sword. A futile reflex. An inferno would swallow both him and his Skandish blade if the dragon belched fire.

'I'm not in any danger,' said the king, supposing that Lorn had meant to protect him. 'Nor are you, if you are who I believe you to be. Put away your sword. It's useless to you.'

Lorn wasn't listening.

Torn between fascination and horror, he could not take his eyes off Serk'Arn, the Dragon of Destruction whom, according to legend, the first High King had confronted and slain. And yet the dragon was right here before him.

It had come out of the shadows and it was looking at him.

Lorn felt his heart pounding madly.

The dragons had once ruled the world. They had been divine beings before the sacrifice of the Dragon-King had hastened their decline at the end of the Shadows. When Erklant the Ancient had faced Serk'Arn, it was no longer the immortal creature of former times. And no doubt it was even less powerful now, five centuries later. But there was a furnace growling in its throat. Its claws could rip through the best armour and its scales would blunt the best steel. Its jaws were wide enough to close around a man and its fangs were sharp enough to sever him in two.

And nothing would resist its breath.

Yet, the worst thing was probably the evil aura which emanated from him, an aura that terrified Lorn and covered him in an icy sweat. Because the inferno that burned in the entrails of this monster was not of this world, but was fed by the Dark.

The Dragon of Destruction advanced its head into the light from the bowls. Its red eyes glowed like two spheres filled with incandescent metal. Crossed by ivory horns, a membranous ruff surrounded the base of its skull. It almost hid the arcanium collar which tightly encircled its neck and was attached to long, heavy chains that, dragging on the stone, shackled its chest and legs.

Erklant I had not killed Serk'Arn. He had captured and enslaved him.

'It was subjugated by a spell to the kings of Langre and their descendants,' said the old king as he stood. 'Ever since, we have derived our power and our glory from it.'

Feeling stunned and disorientated, Lorn turned towards the High King, but the latter was addressing Serk'Arn:

'So, my old friend? What is your verdict?'

The humbled dragon stirred in its chains and roared. Nevertheless, it plunged its terrible gaze into that of Lorn and probed, hunting for something…

…which it found at last.

'*The Guardians did not lie to you,*' it announced regretfully. '*I can do nothing against him.*'

The High King's thin dry lips smiled. His pupils, reduced to little black dots, shone with hope and joy.

'Which means,' he said, 'that I am going to entrust you with the destiny of my kingdom. Because I am dying. In less than a year, I will no longer be here.'

Lorn turned and raised his gaze towards the dragon's blazing eyes. It felt as if Serk'Arn's powers could sweep him away and annihilate him at any moment.

It was...

'And if nothing is done, the High Kingdom will disappear with me,' the old king was saying.

It was like facing a silent storm, an invisible hurricane.

'I know this is a terrible thing to confess, Lorn. But I need you. The High Kingdom needs you.'

It was like being pierced by an incredible force, rising out of the entrails of the world and of time.

'Lorn, are you listening to me?'

But Lorn did not answer.

Or rather, he did not answer the king, because he was concentrating wholly on the words he was exchanging in thought with the dragon – words that they alone could hear.

A long moment passed in silence.

Late Spring 1547

1

'And so he left the Citadel and its grey stone ramparts. Except for the High King, none knew his destination. He rode the byroads, alone, with a sword at his side and a wolf's head ring on his finger. Finally, after long days, he left the plains of Langre and climbed the first foothills of the Argor Mountains. In his sleeve he carried a letter sealed with a black wax seal.'

Chronicles (The Book of the Knight with the Sword)

'Ma'am?'

Queen Celyane of the High Kingdom did not turn round.

She was alone, watching the rehearsal from an upper gallery, surrounded by an odour of sawdust, wood glue and fresh paint. The Palace's grand hall had been rearranged to match the layout of another hall, two hundred and fifty leagues away, where Angborn would be ceded to Yrgaard in the course of a long ceremony. Ropes stretched between poles divided the space and marked off the places where the attendees would sit. Around them, curtains closed off certain perspectives while opening others and provided the outlines of corridors. Drawn in chalk, a central aisle led to a wide dais on which mannequins sat in armchairs imitating thrones. On either side of this aisle, workmen were building terraces of seats. The racket of their hammer blows annoyed the master of ceremonies. Aided by his assistants, he was carefully choreographing a group of servants who had been requisitioned to embody the diplomats and other dignitaries who would be attending the event from the far corners of Imelor.

'I beg your pardon, ma'am.'

The queen still gave no reply.

It was as though a spectacle or a sumptuous theatre play was being prepared on a stage with a painted backdrop. One almost expected to see some pyrotechnical effects being tested. Yet in fact it was the signature of a historic treaty between the High Kingdom and Yrgaard that was being organised. The smallest details of the ceremony had to be meticulously worked out in accordance with the demands of protocol and etiquette. While taking into account the specific enmities and susceptibilities of each participant. One faux pas, the slightest delay or oversight, might spell disaster. The queen did not want any hitches. This treaty would mark the success of her foreign policy and would definitively impose her authority both within and without the borders of the High Kingdom. Nothing must be left to chance. Nothing must mar the day of her triumph.

Celyane stood there thinking for a moment, her eyes shining, a half-smile upon her lips. Then, growing irritated at the presence of her minister at her back, she asked:

'What is it, Esteveris?'

The man came forward but took care to remain in the shadows behind her.

'There is news from the Citadel, ma'am. The troop of Grey Guards heading towards Samarande did indeed have orders to escort Lorn Askarian to the fortress. Where the High King granted him a private audience.'

'Very well. And?'

The queen made no effort to hide her boredom.

'Who knows what the king told him?'

'What do you mean, who knows? And here I was, thinking that you would know.'

The minister's face clouded over. Ordinarily, he was very proud of the effectiveness of his vast network of informers, which he maintained at considerable expense.

Or at least considerable expense to the Crown...

The queen smiled.

She liked to score points over Esteveris, who she knew to be highly intelligent. Better still, she adored making him recognise his ignorance or impotence. Indeed, she took particular pleasure in humiliating this fat bald man, with his pink oily skin and small porcine eyes, who – in secret, he believed – lusted after her.

Esteveris was not the only one who had spies.

'No doubt, I will find out soon enough,' he said. 'However, there's something even more worrying…'

He left his sentence dangling.

But as Celyane remained silent and kept her back turned towards him, he had to continue:

'The king and Lorn went to visit the tomb of Erklant I the following day. Then the king appointed Lorn First Knight of the Realm.'

The queen raised an eyebrow at this and finally turned round.

'First…'

'…Knight of the Realm.'

She cast about in her mind. The title meant something, but what?

And then it came back to her.

There had once been an Onyx Guard. It had been founded during the Last War of the Shadows and served the kings of Langre until the advent of the High Kingdom. Erklant I had dissolved it. The title of Knight to the Ebony and Onyx Throne – or Onyx Knight – had then become purely honorific and, the current High King having bestowed it upon some of his first companions-in-arms, there were only a few ageing lords who still wore the black signet ring with the wolf's head.

The queen shrugged.

'That title doesn't represent much any more,' she said. 'Who still cares about it? And a ring in return for three years in Dalroth is not much of a reward, when you think about it…'

'The king has made several Onyx Knights, true. But he has just given Lorn the title of First Knight. That's not the same thing, ma'am. In fact, it's quite different.'

'Then explain it to me, Esteveris!' snapped the queen in a voice that betrayed both impatience and anger.

The minister bowed slightly by way of apology.

'The First Knight commanded the Onyx Guard, ma'am. No one has been named First Knight since it was dissolved.'

'So the king has appointed Lorn the head of a guard that has not existed for several centuries,' said Celyane ironically. 'Do you think he plans to re-establish it?'

'Who knows?'

'And with whom? And how? When? With what funds?'

'I don't know,' admitted Esteveris.

Celyane bared a superior smile…

…before frowning on seeing her minister's anxious expression. He was ambitious and devoted, devoid of scruples and cruel. He could err through excessive zeal and perhaps even out of pride. But he wasn't one to become easily alarmed.

The queen started to share his worry.

'What aren't you telling me, Esteveris?'

In the Palace hall, a great crash was heard, provoking cries of horror and pain. Built too hastily and poorly, a whole flight of terraced seats had just collapsed beneath the weight of the bit players who had taken their places, while the workmen were still working underneath. The queen leaned over the balustrade and looked down on the disaster. In the wreckage of broken planks, she saw grimacing faces, bleeding wounds and broken bones. People were already hurrying to help the victims, jostling one another in their efforts to extricate them.

But completely indifferent to the distress and suffering of the injured, Celyane was looking at something else, torn between stupor and fear.

In tumbling down, the terraces had pushed back the dais with the mannequins. The figure representing the queen had fallen from her seat and her false crown had rolled onto the floor.

Livid, with her back stiff and her features frozen, the queen turned slowly towards her minister. He had been her astrologer before becoming her counsellor. Being very superstitious, she continued to consult mages, seers and fortune-tellers. Esteveris knew that this accident, for her, was a frightening omen.

'What haven't you told me?' repeated the queen between clenched jaws.

Withstanding her gaze with difficulty, the minister said:

'I've consulted the texts, ma'am. Command of the Onyx Guard is not the First Knight's only prerogative...'

2

'Northern rampart of the High Kingdom, the feet of the Argor range are bathed by the Sea of Mists. It is a province of tall mountains, beautiful valleys and high pastures, blue granite, cloudy ridges, elevated peaks and eternal snows. The air is crisp there and the water clear, the nights are often cool and winter is never far away.'

Chronicles (The Book of the High Kingdom)

Lorn did not see the first man die.

But he'd heard the Gheltish war cries and knew what he would discover when he arrived at the crest of the ridge. He had prudently left his horse behind, tethered to a dead tree. Lying flat on his belly, he observed the soldiers taking refuge behind some rocks in the bed of a dried-up river below. Caught in a trap, they were being harassed by riders with dark brown skin and long black hair, wearing leather and bone armour, who circled them at a gallop, firing volleys of arrows.

Ghelts.

Lorn counted twenty to twenty-five of them, against only ten soldiers. Already wounded for the most part, the soldiers did not stand a chance of winning the fight and were preparing for a heroic final stand. Did they know this engagement would be their last? Did they know they could expect no mercy? Lorn was familiar with Ghelts, having fought them for a year in Dalatia. They were brave warriors, formidable and often honourable, but they gave no quarter. If no one came to rescue them, these soldiers were doomed.

Lorn studied the valley, the flanks of the surrounding mountains and the road that snaked its way into the distance and climbed towards a pass.

No one.

Having emptied their quivers, the Ghelts assembled into a mass and charged, screaming. Only a few of the soldiers were in any shape to fight. Covered in blood, exhausted, they confronted the riders who bore down on them before jumping from their saddles to engage their opponents in furious close quarters combat. The doomed soldiers fought with desperate energy, trying to protect their wounded comrades. It was a savage and murderous business. A massacre. Heads flew through the air. Opened bellies spilled their steaming guts. Blood spurted in great sprays of sticky crimson, accompanied by cries of agony and rage.

Lorn watched the soldiers fall one after another without feeling any real emotion. The last, staggering, bearing wounds all over his body, did not even have the strength to raise his weapon against the fatal blow.

The wide blade of a scimitar decapitated him.

The Ghelts looted the soldiers' bodies and took their horses. Lorn watched them ride away at a gallop, whooping victory cries.

Without hurry, he walked back to find his horse. His ginger cat – who he had finally named Yssaris – was sitting on the saddle, waiting for him. Lorn rubbed its head and allowed it to climb onto his shoulder while he mounted. Then he went over to the site of the carnage.

The bodies lay on the ground, mutilated and grimacing, while the air reeked with a warm odour of blood and guts. Lorn had not thought for a second of coming to the rescue of these men during the attack and he felt no remorse because of it. Their hour had come, and that was all.

Besides, he had a mission to fulfil.

He heard a moan.

Lorn dismounted again while Yssaris jumped from his shoulder, and he turned over a soldier he had believed dead like the others.

He practically was.

The man had a terrible wound to the skull and another,

more grievous still, in his side. With a mere glance, Lorn could tell he would die soon. The instants remaining to the man could only be used to find a certain peace.

Lorn gave a resigned look to Yssaris who was watching him, quietly seated a short distance away. After that, he wiped away the dust, the sweat and the blood staining the soldier's face. Then he lifted the man's head gently and brought the mouth of a water flask to his dried lips.

The soldier managed to drink a little.

He opened his eyes and gave thanks with a nod of the head.

'The Ghelts…' he murmured in a broken voice. 'We… We found them but they…'

'I know,' Lorn interrupted him. 'I saw.'

'Saw? You… were there? And… And you did… nothing?'

'It would have been just one more death.'

The soldier tried to rise but was so weak that Lorn merely had to place a hand on his shoulder to prevent him.

'We must… We must warn the castle!'

'No,' said Lorn. 'You'll be going nowhere.'

The man looked at him, and then understood.

The features of his face sagged and he let his head fall backwards. He was not yet thirty years old. No doubt he was a husband and a father.

'I'm going to die,' he said.

'Yes.'

'I… I'm not in much pain. Perhaps…'

'No. It's over.'

Lorn had accompanied enough dying men in their final moments to know that it was useless to either lie to them or say too much. The best thing was to be there, to be present. Nothing was worse than solitude in the last moments. Lorn waited until the soldier's breathing became regular and said:

'What's your name?'

'Sares.'

'Are you a believer?'

'Yes.'

'Then this is the moment to pray, Sares.'

With tears in his eyes, the soldier nodded weakly. He brought a filthy hand encrusted with blood to his chest and seized a pendant in the likeness of the Dragon-King: a crowned dragon with an upright body, its wings deployed horizontally.

Expressionless, Lorn took the dying man's other hand.

He stayed with him until the end.

When the soldier was dead, Lorn stood up. He looked for a long while at the contorted bodies lying all around him, which, in the heat, were starting to attract insects. Then he raised his eyes towards the ridge from which he had watched the battle.

A rider was there.

A Ghelt sitting straight and motionless in his saddle, pointedly watching Lorn, his silhouette clearly outlined in the raw sunlight.

A lookout. Or a straggler, thought Lorn.

Eyes squinting behind his dark glasses, he observed the warrior in turn, as Yssaris leapt into his arms. A long moment went by before the other man turned away and disappeared behind the ridge.

Lorn then climbed atop his own mount and left in the opposite direction.

3

Lorn found Calaryn in an uproar. Once he crossed the draw-bridge and double portcullis, he had to dismount in the court-yard and hold his horse by the reins.

Count Teogen's castle was in a state of full alert.

Soldiers came and went, marching in ranks or jostling past one another in a disorderly fashion, archers, crossbowmen and pikemen all mixed together. Their faces looked tense and wor-ried. Horses were champing at their bits. Hooves rang on the sonorous paving. Beneath an archway, men were struggling to hold on to the chains of a snorting wyvern. One needed to shout to be heard and use one's elbows to advance in the mob. Standing apart, a group of arquebusiers practised their manoeuvres. They charged, shouldered their weapons and aimed at mannequins swinging from poles in front of the ramparts. They opened fire without startling very many in the general racket, the salvo frightening only a murder of crows, who cawed as they flew off.

Lorn knew this fervour: it was the one that preceded battle.

Spotting a steward to whom everyone seemed to be directing their enquiries, he hitched his horse, leaving it under Yssaris's guard, and went to plant himself in front of the man. As he continued to deal with various matters, the steward glanced over several times at the stranger wearing a hood and dark glasses, who did not say a word.

Finally, he asked:

'What do you want? Be brief!'

'I have a letter. For the count.'

'Give it to me. I'll have it brought to him as soon as possible.'

'No. I must deliver it in person.'

The steward, busy consulting a register that had just been presented to him, grew impatient.

'Listen, I don't have time to waste. We're at war! The Ghelts have attacked three villages and taken captives. So either you give me the letter, or you—'

He interrupted himself when he raised his nose, because the stranger was already walking away.

He shrugged and returned to work as Lorn climbed a staircase leading to the ramparts.

Count Teogen of Argor had assembled the inner circle of his barons and knights at the top of a wide crenellated tower. Crowded around a table covered with maps, all of them were wearing armour, with swords at their side and gauntlets in their belts, their helmets tucked under their arms. Adjoining the main keep, the tower was used for launching wyverns. Scarlet banners flapping in the winds at the four corners of its wall walk, it loomed over the castle, its approaches and even the surrounding area, allowing one to see over considerable distances. From this position, it seemed that the entire province could be viewed, as far as the snowy peaks under a never-ending sky.

Teogen was holding a war council.

Placed upon the table, his famous fighting mace prevented the maps from rolling up while he discussed urgent measures to be carried out and pointed out a road to be taken, a bridge to be guarded, a mountain pass to be closed. It was a question of locating the Gheltish riders who had organised an incursion into the province and managed to pillage several villages and farms only a few leagues from the castle. The task was an arduous one because Argor was spread across countless valleys, hollows and glens. A maze. A maze protected by fortified towers, gates and bridges, to be sure. But any armour has its weakness and the Ghelts, who had been threatening the north-eastern border for months, had struck at the heart of the province. And they were elusive, vanishing immediately after each raid and appearing elsewhere unexpectedly.

The latest attack, however, had been one too many. It had

taken place just when Teogen was calling up his cavalry and assembling an army. The army was still not up to full strength, but the count now had enough horsemen to comb the northern part of his province, hunt down the Gheltish marauders and – with the help of the Red Dragon – run them through with steel.

'Time is of essence,' said Teogen of Argor.

Bent over his maps, he studied them with a baleful eye.

'The Ghelts have taken female captives,' he continued. 'If they haven't already had their way and killed them, it means that they are intending to cross back over the border soon, along with their prizes.'

'The Ghelts will escape us if they regain their territory,' said a knight with a gaunt face, white hair and leathery skin.

'That's true,' confirmed Teogen. 'We'd be unable to execute them for their crimes and we'd never see their prisoners again.'

'Why not cross the border? Why not pursue these Ghelts into their own territory?' asked a young baron. 'They have no scruples about doing the same to us!'

'Because it would be suicide,' replied Orwain. 'Even at the head of an army.'

'And it would start a war,' added Teogen.

'A war?' objected the young knight. 'But isn't that what we already have—?'

'No, Guilhem,' the count interrupted. 'If we were at war with the Ghelts, we would know it. And we would have greater worries than a band of marauders. All Argor would be a bloody battlefield.' His face darkened at the thought of another Gheltish war. 'I would rather believe we're dealing with warriors who, for one reason or another, have decided they no longer respect the treaties. Perhaps they belong to a clan that has splintered off. If they've just crowned a young king who's a little too ambitious…'

The Count of Argor, sighed, straightened up and looked round at his vassals with a grave face. Despite his years, he remained a formidable man and still wore the same breastplate that had protected him during Erklant II's early campaigns.

'I won't take the risk of starting a war,' he added. 'But there's no question of allowing these Ghelts' crimes to go unpunished.

We'll catch them before they regain their territory and we'll put them to the sword.'

Everyone nodded except Orwain, who said in a low voice, as if to himself:

'Executing these warriors may provoke the clans' anger. It would be better to capture them and hand them over to be judged and sentenced by their own kind.'

There were murmurs of disapproval in response to this, but he took no offence. He knew he was right, but he also knew that the voice of wisdom was rarely heeded in difficult times.

The Baron of Ortand spoke up.

His features drawn by fatigue and anger, he had been one of the first to answer the Count of Argor's call to arms. Some of the pillaging perpetrated by the Ghelts had taken place on his estate. He had witnessed impotent, tortured bodies hanging from the trees or burned in the still smoking ruins of buildings.

'These barbarians have looted, raped and killed. They have shed Argorian blood. They should pay the price on the end of an Argorian blade or rope.'

The others expressed their agreement.

Orwain exchanged a look with Teogen and realised that Teogen would have to satisfy his vassals on this point. Besides, it was not just a question of vengeance; no doubt they needed to teach the Ghelts that Argor's borders could not be violated with impunity and that the count would fight back.

'Have no fear, Ortand,' Teogen replied. 'Their heads will end up on our pikes.'

The baron nodded, mollified.

'But we still need to find them before we can eliminate them,' said a knight whose armour was decorated with black and scarlet patterns. 'These Ghelts did not come on a whim. They waited for the season when our wyverners cannot take to the skies and they seem to be familiar with the valleys they're passing through. Even with an army, hunting them down will be no easy task.'

Tall, slender, dark-eyed and sporting a well-trimmed beard, Dorian of Leister cut an imposing figure. At his side hung a sword whose pommel was adorned with a red opal. He would soon be thirty years old and seemed rich and cultivated, even refined. Needless to say, he stood out among the other rustic lords of Argor, even Teogen himself.

But he was nevertheless treated with respect.

And heeded.

'True,' said the count. 'But if the Ghelts are returning to their lands as I believe, then we can concentrate our searches in these regions.' He pointed with his index finger to three places on the largest and most detailed of the maps spread across the table. 'Because they will need to cross one or another of these passes, won't they?'

Orwain shared his opinion.

However, he did not need to study the map closely before raising an objection:

'Seven passes. Nine, if the Ghelts take the risk of crossing the Dark Vale or the Steel Falls. That's too many. Even if we left now, we could not watch them all.'

The count nodded in reluctant agreement.

'I'm well aware of that.'

'Some of our patrols haven't returned yet,' said Leister. 'The last should be back by tomorrow evening, let's wait for them. Perhaps they will bring us the intelligence we're still lacking.'

Teogen knew that this was the wisest course. Yet he fumed at the idea of delaying longer.

And longer...

'One of those patrols will not be returning,' announced Lorn.

All eyes turned towards him.

Lorn had resolved to find the Count of Argor by his own means and had succeeded without much difficulty. It had been enough to show the signet ring on his finger to each sentry he met. His confidence and natural air of authority did the rest. He was not one of those who found his way blocked for long.

'What are you doing here?' asked the Count of Argor.

'The High King sent me.'

'So, that's it, then? I'm finally being sent the help I've been demanding for months now, to guard the border?' he asked ironically, raising several smiles from the other lords. 'You've arrived in the nick of time, knight. But I was expecting more than one sword.' He looked down at Lorn's weapon. 'A Skandish blade, if I'm not mistaken…'

Staring at Lorn as he removed his hood but kept on his dark glasses, Teogen declared:

'I know you. You're Lorn, aren't you? The son of the master-of-arms.'

'That's me. Lorn Askarian.'

Fist over his heart, Lorn bowed to salute the Count of Argor. The latter was now recalling other details and, despite his outward lack of expression, Lorn read in the other man's eyes what he was thinking at that precise instant:

Dalroth.

Lorn drew a letter from his sleeve and stepped closer.

The High King has charged me—' he began to say.

But Leister interposed himself between Lorn and the table. Lorn challenged him wordlessly. A silent contest then ensued before the vassals, most of whom had placed their hands upon their swords. Orwain advanced prudently, with the intention of preventing an open quarrel.

It was Teogen, however, who disarmed the situation.

'You said that one of our patrols would not return. What do you know of that?' he asked.

Lorn turned towards him.

'They were massacred by the Ghelts,' he announced, provoking stunned silence. 'I watched the battle.'

'Watched, hmm?' said Leister.

Lorn ignored him. He reckoned he owed no accounting to anyone, unless it were the count.

'I kept a soldier company during his final instants,' he said. 'His name was Sares.'

Teogen consulted Orwain with a glance.

The old knight nodded gravely: Sares was indeed the name of a soldier who had left on patrol that very morning.

'When did this happen?' Orwain asked.

'A few hours ago.'

'Where?' demanded Teogen. 'Show me.'

Lorn waited for Leister to step aside and advanced to the

table, bent over the map presented to him, hunted... and pointed to a valley.

'Here,' he said.

The count and his vassals seemed puzzled.

'Are you sure?' asked one of them.

'Yes.'

'That can't be,' said another.

'I know how to read a map,' said Lorn in an unfriendly tone.

Looking worried and perplexed, Teogen pored over the map, thinking aloud:

'That makes no sense at all...'

'Why?' asked Lorn without addressing anyone in particular. 'What's wrong?'

'If you're not mistaken...' Orwain began to explain.

'I'm not.'

'If you're not mistaken, then the Ghelts aren't returning to their territory as we believed. It makes no sense because they've taken captives who can only be slowing them down... How many of them were there attacking the patrol?'

'A little more than twenty riders.'

'Then they weren't all there.'

'More than twenty Gheltish warriors against a patrol!' protested Guilhem, the youngest knight present. 'And you did nothing?'

'There was nothing a single man could do,' retorted Orwain, pre-empting any response by Lorn.

And turning to Lorn again, he asked:

'Did you see any prisoners?'

'None.'

'Then they were with the other Ghelts...'

'Or they were already dead.'

Orwain stared at Lorn.

He reminded the old knight of certain veterans in whom the experience of war had erased any trace of humanity. They made excellent fighters. But although such men could win victories and change destinies, although they made formidable adversaries and precious allies on the battlefield, they were lost souls who would founder sooner or later.

'Unless…'

Teogen did not finish his sentence.

Hurriedly, he pushed aside his mace to retrieve a packet of maps which he pawed through roughly, until he found one – the oldest and most ragged of the lot – showing some ridges, passes and valleys in detail. Having unfolded it, he consulted it briefly and displayed a smile.

'That's it!' he said.

'What?' asked Orwain.

'Don't you see?'

The landless knight studied the map, but it was Leister who found the solution first.

'The Twin Passes!' he said.

'Yes,' said the count, straightening up his massive body. 'The Twin Passes. The Ghelts are trying to return to their territory, but they're not taking the shortest route.'

'Or the most obvious one,' observed Orwain, 'We would never have gone looking for them out there. Or only too late, after finding that patrol…'

Teogen turned towards Lorn with a grateful look.

'Thank you, knight. Your help has been invaluable.'

And addressing his vassals, he declared:

'My lords, tomorrow we leave on an expedition from which not all of us shall return. Choose your best blades, your best men and your best horses. Go! You know what to do.'

Everyone nodded and, with a clatter of armour and ironclad heels, they went off to issue their orders. Lorn remained alone with the Count of Argor and Orwain. Evening was approaching and night would fall quickly, as it always did in the mountains. A north wind rose, cold and sharp.

Without saying a word, Teogen held out his hand.

Lorn gave him the High King's letter and waited. The count broke open the seal before perusing it. Then he refolded it carefully and slipped it into his sleeve with slow gestures, giving himself time for thought.

Then he gave Lorn a long searching look as if he hoped to find in him all the answers he was seeking. His gaze lingered particularly on the hand wrapped in leather, which was also the one on which Lorn wore an onyx ring adorned with a silver wolf's head set against two crossed swords. Teogen wore one that was almost identical, except that it did not bear a royal crown. As far as he knew, there was only one of its kind, and he had always seen it on the High King's ring finger.

'The king has made you First Knight of the Realm,' he said in a cold matter-of-fact tone.

'Yes,' Lorn replied.

'Do you know the content of this letter?'

Lorn shook his head.

He did not know what the count was trying to learn, what questions the royal missive had aroused in him. He had no idea what it said, but he guessed that it posed a problem for the count and that he, Lorn, was somehow involved in it.

Teogen stood up abruptly and, as he started to walk away with a brisk step, said in a firm tone:

'You will dine at my table this evening, knight. You will then remain for as long as you desire beneath my roof. Unfortunately, as you know, it will be impossible for me to keep you company.'

'I'm not staying,' said Lorn.

Teogen halted.

'You've made a long journey from the Citadel. You should rest.'

'I'm riding out with you tomorrow.'

The count hesitated.

'I know your history,' he said, thinking of Dalroth, the Dark and the ordeals Lorn had endured.

'Then you know I have fought the Ghelts before and that my help could be precious to you. Besides, can you really afford to turn down an extra sword? Are you hoping that reinforcements will come from the High Kingdom? You made a jest about it just now, but as far as reinforcements are concerned, it's just me. And it was the High King who sent me.'

4

'Erklant's first feat of glory was to liberate the provinces of the High Kingdom that had been invaded by Yrgaard. The second was to avenge his father whose life had been stolen by the Dragon's Sword. The third was the conquest of the Free Cities, for the High King did not content himself with retaking the lands that were his. He captured the Cities, driving out the armies of the Black Hydra who returned to Yrgaard, beyond the Sea of Mists and its bleak shores.'

Chronicles (The Book of Kings)

That morning, the High King had not found the strength to rise. He kept to his bed in his chamber draped in black and grey, refusing all food, wanting only to wet his lips with a glass of honeyed wine. The servants washed him as they would have washed a dead man.

In the evening, he called for Norfold.

'Any news of Lorn?' he asked.

The air was heavy with scents meant to mask the morbid odour of his dying body.

'None,' replied the captain of the royal guard.

He was dressed in armour. His sword at his side, he wore the famous grey breastplate and carried his crested helmet under his arm.

'Do you think he's already arrived in Argor?'

If he had indeed taken the road to Argor, thought Norfold.

'No doubt,' he replied.

'Then he has met the count. And given him the letter.'

The High King grew thoughtful and added:

'Good. Yes, good… Good…'

And then gathering his wits, he said:

'When he opens the letter, Teogen will understand. I know him. He will understand. And he will do what needs to be done…'

Looking even graver than usual, Norfold said nothing. He was a soldier. He knew when to remain silent and keep his feelings to himself.

But the old king knew him well enough to read his thoughts.

'You don't approve of my choice, Norfold.'

'Sire, it is not for me to—'

'I know what you're thinking!'

And as the High King seemed to be waiting for him to explain, the captain hesitated, and then said:

'You have made him First Knight of the Realm, sire.'

'You don't believe him worthy of it? Yet I remember when you wanted him to succeed you one day at the head of the Grey Guard…'

Norfold nodded and said in a vibrant voice:

'He committed treason. He abandoned all honour and duty.'

'He was unjustly accused. It was a plot. He was innocent.'

Norfold made no reply, wondering which of the two of them the High King was trying to convince.

'You did not like Lorn. You never liked him. And now… And now, you're jealous of him…'

'I assure you that's not so, sire.'

'It is,' insisted the old king in a slurring voice. 'Jealous. Jealous…'

'But you have made him your representative,' continued Norfold. 'And with that signet ring on his finger, he is… He is you! He speaks and acts in your name.'

'I know.'

'And what if he decides to disobey you, sire? What if he abuses the power you have entrusted him with, and—?'

'I know!'

The High King resembled a mummified corpse: wrinkled skin, withered limbs, bony chest, hollow cheeks, prominent cheekbones, sunken eyes and invisible lips. But it was like a fire had been lit within him.

Growing excited, he declared:

'I need a champion, Norfold! A knight who will be my arm, my eyes and my voice! One who can save the High Kingdom. Protect it from its enemies. From Yrgaard! From the queen! Who can even protect it from the Dark!'

In his passionate outburst, he had sat up in his bed, eyes ablaze. Now, abruptly drained of energy, he fell back against his pillows and said:

'Lorn is the one! He... He always has been.'

A fit of coughing overcame him.

Norfold called out and did his best to help him before the servants took charge, plumping the High King's pillows, making him drink a little water and wiping his mouth.

The captain stepped back.

He felt out of place and underfoot here. He hated seeing the suffering of this king whom he loved and towards whom he was unable to show his affection other than in the rough manner of an old soldier. He had confronted death several times, but faced with illness and inexorable decline he felt completely at a loss, both hesitant and clumsy.

'You'll see,' said the High King, shaking a skeletal finger at him. 'Lorn will prove himself worthy of my confidence. But above all, he will prove himself worthy of his destiny.'

This was said with such hope that Norfold could not help but nod and give a falsely reassuring smile. At that instant he wanted nothing but the well-being and tranquillity of his king, even at the price of a white lie.

'And then, he's of my own blood,' added the High King as his strength left him and he began to sink into sleep. 'That counts for something, doesn't it? Of my own blood... That... counts for... something...'

'Led by Count Teogen, they rode for days, nights, and still more days. Their hunt took them far into mountains, through wild valleys and lofty passes, towards the high ridges where the wyverns nested. Their supplies ran out but they were driven by a fierce determination and their horses were tough beasts accustomed to the rigours of the Argor Mountains. They did not falter, despite their aches, despite their fatigue, despite the threatening sky.'

Chronicles (The Book of the Knight with the Sword)

They had set up their bivouac on a mountainside, at the entrance to a wide cavern that would shelter them, and, above all, hide their fires. The danger was not so much the light being seen by the Ghelts they were pursuing, but by the wyverns that hunted at night. It was, in the heart of summer, the moment of the year when the young attempted their first flights. In the day, the mothers watched over their fledglings that constituted easy prey for the large solitary males. As a result they couldn't go off in search of food until night fell, and then, both famished and anxious, they were particularly aggressive. This season of First Flight was moreover the reason why Teogen could not make use of his wyverners to locate and pursue the Ghelts who were pillaging his lands. Between the males lying in wait and the females that attacked on sight, flying over the high valleys of the Argor was suicidal.

Sword in his fist, Lorn had been charged with exploring the rear of the cavern at the head of a few men. They came back without having flushed out any bears or mountain lions, while the rest of the troop was finishing taking care of the horses and erecting the camp. Like all the members of the expedition, Lorn was exhausted but did not allow it to show. Teogen's resolve had overcome all weakness: tireless, he was a force that nothing deterred and one could only follow his example. Even so, Lorn wondered if they would catch the Ghelts before they regained their territory. Doubt was starting to show on faces and the other men were certainly asking themselves the same question. But like Lorn, they said nothing.

He was counting on enjoying a moment of rest when Dorian of Leister said curtly:

'The count is asking for you.'

There had been immediate enmity between the two men and they had almost crossed swords at their very first encounter. Since then, Leister had obviously been keeping a close eye on Lorn, who for his part pretended to ignore him. They did not speak more than was necessary, but their mutual hostility required only glances and silences to express itself. Besides, Teogen would not have tolerated anything more.

'What does he want?'

Leister did not reply.

Lorn turned towards the count who was sitting at the entrance to the cavern, facing the dusk, apart from the sentries who were studying the sky and the winged silhouettes in the distance. Lorn went to join him, feeling Leister's gaze on the back of his neck, and paused for an instant before announcing his presence.

'Count?'

His drawn features and the dark circles under his eyes betraying his weariness, Teogen made no response, lost in his thoughts. It had already been several days since they had lost sight of the fires in the towers guarding Argor. Yet, every evening, the count still looked out in their direction, as if his eyes could see through the mountains separating him from his castle.

And from his wife's grave.

'Do you think this expedition makes any sense?' asked Teogen, his gaze fixed on the setting sun.

Lorn was not given time to think of a reply.

'We all know the women these Ghelts have abducted are probably dead by now,' the count continued. 'Killing them will not bring back those they have slaughtered and will not erase the evil they have done. And in order to make them pay for the crimes, more of us – you, me, Orwain, who knows? – will die…' He turned towards Lorn. 'So I ask you, knight. Does all this make any sense to you?'

In his turn, Lorn contemplated the dusk whose fires were reflected on his dark spectacles, and said:

'You have failed to protect your province, your subjects and your vassals, count. What choice remains to you, but to bring back some heads?'

His eyes full of fury, Teogen gazed at Lorn's expressionless profile for a long moment. Then his anger faded. Lorn was right. As cynical and disillusioned as his judgement might seem, he was right and Teogen was forced to admit it.

'You told me you were unaware of the contents of the letter you brought me, didn't you?' the count remarked.

'It's the truth,' said Lorn.

'Here.'

The count handed him the letter from the High King. Lorn recognised the black seal and took it without understanding.

'Open it,' the count urged him.

'Count, I don't know if…'

'Open it, knight.'

Lorn hesitated. Then he opened the letter and immediately thought it was a jest whose meaning escaped him.

It was blank.

He raised his eyes and addressed a silent question at Teogen. The latter gave him an amused and derisive little smile. Lorn then remembered how calmly the count himself had opened and looked over the High King's letter. At the time, he had not shown the slightest surprise or sign of ill humour, although he was said to be irritable and readily angered. No doubt he was. But no doubt he also knew how to hide his feelings.

'What does—?' Lorn started to ask.

'Astonishing, isn't it?'

'I don't understand.'

Teogen smiled.

'You don't understand? Well, I see two possible explanations.

212

The first is that the king has lost his mind, as some claim. That he has gone mad, to the point of sending blank pages to his last allies. Or to the point of naming you First Knight of the Realm,' he added.

The barb sank home.

A gleam lit up in Lorn's eyes. He clenched his jaw but said nothing. The hand on which he bore the signet ring with the wolf's head was also the one, wrapped in leather, which bore the mark of the Dark.

'Here they are,' announced Teogen, rising to his feet.

His train of thought interrupted, Lorn followed the count's gaze and saw who he was referring to: the scouts were returning at last. Armed with bows and long daggers, they wore light armour and approached at a walk upon tired mounts.

Orwain was at their head.

'They bear news,' surmised Teogen, going out to meet them.

'The Ghelts are going to split up,' announced Orwain.

The Count of Argor had gathered his knights around a fire, away from the rest of the troop. They numbered less than a dozen, including Lorn, and were listening to Orwain. Of all of them, this veteran was the one most familiar with the remote areas in the mountains into which they were heading, and the one whom Teogen trusted most.

'We followed their tracks as far as here,' he said, pointing to a spot on the map he had drawn roughly upon the ground with his dagger. 'They turned off here and took this valley eastward.'

'Eastward?' asked Leister in surprise. 'They're going east now?'

'How much of a lead do they have on us?' asked Teogen.

'A day,' replied Orwain. 'A day and a half, perhaps. But not much more than that.'

'We'll catch them. Good.'

'But why are they going east?' insisted Leister. 'It's absurd!'

'Since we're gaining ground, perhaps they hope to shake us off,' suggested Guilhem.

'Or draw us into a trap,' said Ortand. 'It's been three days now that the Ghelts have been travelling north. Three days that they've been heading towards the Savage Mountains and their territories. So why this change in direction? Lester's right. It doesn't make any sense.'

'I'm not so sure,' said Orwain.

'Have you guessed what they're up to?' asked the count.

'I think so. My lord Guilhem has made a good point: the Ghelts know we'll catch up with them and that worries them.'

Flattered, the young man gave an embarrassed smile. He was not yet twenty years old and was the son of a powerful vassal and friend of the Count of Argor. Upon the sudden death of his father, a few months earlier, he had succeeded to his title without being truly prepared for it. Since then, he tried to demonstrate that he was equal to the task and he had been one of the first to respond to Teogen's call to arms. Despite everything, his youth and inexperience meant that he had to struggle to assert himself and he hesitated at times to express his views.

'But the Ghelts aren't seeking to shake us off,' the old knight continued. 'In my opinion, they're going here.'

His dagger pointed to a new place on the map traced in the dirt.

'To Erm's Fork?'

'Yes, count. And there, they will split up.'

'Why?' asked Ortand.

'To oblige us to divide our own forces,' said Lorn. 'Or else give up the chance to catch half of them.'

'How do you know that?' asked Leister.

Lorn gave him a black look.

'I fought the Ghelts for a year in the border regions of Valmir. I know them.'

'Besides,' intervened Orwain, 'two small groups of riders will travel more quickly than one big one.'

Teogen spoke up:

'If you're not mistaken about their intentions and they have about a day's advance on us, it means they'll camp at the Fork this evening. And split up tomorrow.'

'One group will go north and the other will continue eastwards,' confirmed Orwain.

'But we won't know for certain until tomorrow evening, when we arrive at the Fork,' remarked Ortand.

'In fact,' said Teogen, squinting at the map drawn on the ground, 'we'll perhaps know a little sooner than that.'

He was looking at a little pass which, despite seeming insignificant, his old companion in arms had taken care to include in his sketch. And now he realised why.

'This pass,' explained Orwain, 'the Ghelts did not take. Either because they were unaware it exists, or because they had already passed it when they decided to head for Erm's Fork. But we still have time. And it will gain us a few precious hours.'

The Count of Argor straightened up with a wide grin on his face.

'My lords,' he said with satisfaction, 'we have the upper hand at last.'

Later, despite his fatigue, Lorn had difficulty finding sleep. He'd left Yssaris behind at Argor castle and, since the beginning of the expedition, it had been clear each evening how much the animal's presence had soothed him. It was as if the ginger cat drove away his anxieties and his demons. Without it, the nightmares, the cold sweats, the doubts and the remorse all returned as soon as he fell asleep.

When he managed to sleep at all.

He was drowsing when the crackle of a log in the fire awoke in him the echo of a lightning bolt ripping the sky above Dalroth. Lorn started and, his breath cut short, he remained sitting up in his bedding for a moment, as if in a daze, before becoming alert. His marked hand was painful and he was worried someone might find him in this state. But fortunately, everyone in the cavern seemed to be asleep.

But Lorn realised he would not be rejoining them in slumber. He sighed and got up, grimacing due to the back pains from days of hard riding. Taking his sword, he signalled discreetly to the sentries on duty and went outside.

Standing in front of the entrance to the cavern, Lorn granted himself a moment to enjoy the surrounding quiet and – the summer days being hot – the coolness of the wind at this altitude. The night was clear and the moon was high. The pale constellations of the Great Nebula spread towards a horizon of black ridges. Visibility was good and it was a relief for Lorn not to have to protect his eyes from the bite of the sun.

He let himself be filled by the calmness of the wild Argor Mountains and smiled…

…before spotting two men standing a short distance from the cavern and conversing in low voices, so that no one could hear what they were saying.

Lorn had no trouble distinguishing the count's massive silhouette. But he had to wait until the other man turned his face before recognising Guilhem. He hesitated an instant about whether he should approach noiselessly, but preferred to observe them from a distance.

Teogen displayed affectionate, paternal gestures towards the young man. No doubt he had watched him grow up since his earliest childhood, and was advising him and reassuring him before the forthcoming combat with the Ghelts they had been tracking for days. Guilhem was listening, nodding, visibly trying to make a good impression, wanting to demonstrate his valour.

After a moment, Teogen gave him a hug intended to dissipate his remaining doubts and buck up his courage. After that, they separated. Plunged into his dark thoughts, Guilhem returned towards the cavern without seeing Lorn, who was seated on a large flat rock. The count, however, spotted him and came over to sit down next to him, heaving a tired sigh.

'Did you hear that?'

'No, but I understood.'

'He's afraid.'

'What could be more normal? We're increasingly vulnerable the further we travel into these mountains. Our horses are worn out and our supplies will soon be running out. The men are starting to have doubts. And tomorrow we'll have to divide our forces to continue the hunt.'

'We'll catch up with the Ghelts soon. Tomorrow. Or the day after.'

'And then men will die. Guilhem is right to be afraid.'

'He's not frightened of dying.'

'Then he's mistaken.'

Intrigued, Teogen turned towards Lorn.

What could this man have in common with the young knight he had once been? Lorn had been Guilhem's age when the count had met him for the first time at the court of the High Kingdom. Several years later, he had come back covered in glory from the border conflicts in Valmir, had joined the Grey Guard and was going to marry the splendid Alissia de Laurens, daughter of the powerful Duke of Sarme and Vallence. Fortune seemed to be smiling upon him. Like his happiness, his success was insolent.

'You're not sleeping, either,' observed Teogen.

Lorn smiled resignedly.

'But I'm not afraid. My fears died at Dalroth.'

'They died there? Or do they remain imprisoned there? If that's the case, I don't envy you. And man is never more than the sum of his fears and his courage, knight. If your fears are still there, that means you've lost a part of yourself. I won't commit the insult of feeling sorry for you, however.'

Now it was Lorn who turned towards the count. They exchanged a long glance, Lorn wondering to what extent Teogen might be right. Then he looked out again at the night's horizon.

Without really seeing it, however.

From a small bag that hung from his belt, Teogen drew forth a tin flask. He uncorked it, drank from its neck and offered it to Lorn. Lorn accepted it readily and took a gulp of flavoured brandy that flowed down his gullet like molten metal. He swallowed with difficulty, grimacing, and almost choked.

'It's a little strong,' the count conceded, taking back the flask.

'A... A little?' said Lorn in a hoarse voice.

He cleared his throat before adding:

'What is that?'

'A recipe from my mountains. Not bad, is it?'

'It's... memorable.'

'Want some more?' proposed Teogen, holding out the flask.

And when Lorn refused, he shrugged and drank again.

'You don't like Dorian much, do you?' he asked, after a period of silence.

Lorn hesitated, before noting that the count was smiling and that his smile was not only conciliatory, but understanding. Evidently, he knew how matters stood with Dorian of Leister. Lorn must not have been the first to have problems with him.

'No,' he said. 'But it seems to be mutual.'

'Leister is wary of you, knight. And frankly...' Teogen paused and waited until he had caught Lorn's eye. 'Well, can you truly blame him?' he asked in a tone of friendly reproach.

Lorn did not reply.

Then he lowered his eyes towards his marked hand, working his knuckles. He thought about who he was, what people knew or thought they knew about him, his appearance and his manner. Whereupon he raised his eyes and met the count's friendly and amused gaze.

'Dorian is a pain in the arse, but he's loyal, fair and valiant,' said Teogen. 'Unfortunately, for some reason, he's angry with the world and with himself. You'll see. You'll end up getting along, the two of you...'

Slapping both hands against his thighs, the count stood up, stretched his wide shoulders, and added:

'I should try to get a few hours' sleep. You should do the same, knight. I'm sure that tomorrow Orwain will wake us even earlier than usual. Good night.'

'Good night, count.'

Teogen walked towards the cavern, but Lorn called him back.

'Count!'

Teogen turned round.

'Yes?'

'Earlier, before the scouts returned, you didn't tell me what the other explanation might be. If the High King isn't mad, why did he give me a blank letter for you, do you think?'

Teogen planted himself firmly on both his legs, crossed his arms, and waited, convinced that Lorn already knew the answer.

'I'm not the messenger, am I?' said Lorn. 'I'm the message.'

The Count of Argor nodded.

'You, and that signet ring on your finger. By sending you to me, the High King has made his intentions plain. He's letting me know he hasn't given up, that he's ready to get back into the game, and that you are the trump card he's planning to play. The High King has named you his representative. He has made you his arm, his sword.'

At that instant, Teogen's expression became grave, severe and, in the dark, almost threatening.

'Why he has done so, I do not know,' he concluded. 'All that matters to me now is to find out whether you are worthy.'

6

They broke camp just before dawn, crossed over the pass that won them precious hours and reached Erm's Fork at midday. Prudently, Teogen dismounted and sent Orwain ahead with some scouts. Sentries were designated. The men hitched the horses and gathered in small groups, in the shade, to lunch on a slice of dried meat and a piece of hard bread. They had been rationing themselves for three days already and hunger was beginning to gnaw at them painfully.

'Luckily, there's plenty of water,' said Guilhem, coming back from filling his flask.

Born of the lively, clear waters of a high glacier, a torrent ran not far away between mossy rocks.

'Perhaps we should devote an hour or two to hunting,' said a knight with a braided beard.

Squat with broad shoulders, a battle-axe tucked into a ring upon his belt, his arms were covered with tribal tattoos. His name was Garalt and he spoke with a Skandish accent easily recognised by Lorn – it was the same as his mother's.

'The scouts may return at any moment,' replied the Count of Argor. 'We would then need to wait for the men we sent out hunting. And perhaps in vain, if they come back empty-handed. We won't let ourselves die of hunger, but we'll hunt on the return journey, once we've accomplished our mission.'

A hoarse, bestial cry then tore the silence of the summits. It was not the first such cry Lorn had heard that morning, but none had been so close. He raised his head and examined the sky.

'A male wyvern,' Teogen indicated to him. 'A challenge. It shouldn't be long before we hear a—'

He could not finish his sentence.

A second cry rang out, before the echo of the previous one had died in the distance.

'There!' said Leister, pointing.

Two wyverns had just appeared above a rocky ridge. Two young males who circled one another in a furious ballet. They snapped at one another and struck with their claws, aiming to bite the neck or gut their adversary.

'Two males fighting it out,' said the Baron of Ortand.

He squinted, using one hand as a visor against the sun.

'We're approaching an area where the wyverns reproduce and build their nests,' Teogen explained to Lorn. 'We're going to bypass it. The Ghelts won't take the risk of crossing it and neither will we.'

'Those two are just playing,' said Leister.

He had barely glanced at the wyverns and, sitting on a big rock, made a show of being interested only in the piece of cheese he was eating with his knife.

'Are you sure?' asked Ortand in surprise.

'Certain of it.'

Not knowing much about wild wyverns, Lorn was unable to say whether he was watching a real combat or a mock duel.

The baron turned towards Teogen.

'Count? What do you think?'

'I would have said the same as you…'

'Ah!' exclaimed Ortand triumphantly. 'Did you hear that, Leister?'

'I heard.'

'But knowing Leister, I would defer to his opinion,' the count continued.

'Really? Well, I still maintain that I am right,' said Ortand.

'I would not wager on it, if I were you.'

'A wager? Now, that's an idea!'

Lorn exchanged a knowing look with Teogen. The count had deliberately slipped in the idea of a wager and was glad that his knights, for a while at least, did not have their minds on the Ghelts.

'What would you say to a wager, Leister?' asked the baron.

'That it's easy money.'

The reply amused Ortand.

'Twenty-five silver langres?' he proposed.

'Fifty?'

'Done. Fifty.'

'You're wrong, Ortand,' said Garalt. 'You should have listened to the count.'

'We'll see about that. Do you accept, Leister?'

Leister carefully wrapped up the piece of cheese in his rag and wiped his knife upon his thigh. He could not appear more sure of himself, but without a hint of arrogance or jubilation. He simply displayed the tranquil certainty of being right.

'I accept,' he said. 'Baron, you owe me fifty silver langres.'

And as if to support his claim, the wyverns ceased fighting at that precise instant. They flew off, playfully chasing one another.

There was some laughter, and even some mockery, which Ortand accepted with a good-natured smile.

'Brothers, no doubt,' he said. 'True male rivals would have torn one another to pieces.'

'I did warn you,' said Teogen gleefully. 'Leister knows more than any of us about wyverns.'

'My word, it's true… Leister, I shall pay you your fifty silver langres upon our return.'

Dorian of Leister stood up and turned towards the baron.

'I don't want them. Give them to the wretches who have lost everything because of the Ghelts instead.'

'Understood. But in that case, I'll double the amount.'

The two men exchanged a handshake before being congratulated by the others on their generosity. Teogen had a paternal smile upon his lips, a smile of mixed joy and pride.

But it soon faded.

The scouts were returning.

'They've split up,' said Orwain as he jumped down from his saddle.

He drank from the water bag offered to him, giving thanks with a glance, and added:

'At Erm's Fork, just as I thought. Two groups. One is headed towards the north pass and the other towards the east. The traces they've left are clear.'

'How far ahead of us?' asked Garalt.

'Barely a half-day,' said Orwain with satisfaction.

'We have them!' cried the Count of Argor, balling a vengeful fist.

They resumed their pursuit.

It had been agreed that the Count of Argor would take half of the troop towards the east pass, while the Baron of Ortand would lead the other half towards the north pass, which was further away. The two columns soon separated, each of them taking a large horn and an equal share of provisions. Despite the prospect of catching the Ghelts and confronting them at last, the men were in a sombre mood. In addition to their fatigue, they did not know when they would see one another next, or even if they would ever meet again.

Along with Orwain, Lorn and Leister were among those who accompanied Teogen. Garalt, Guilhem and others followed Ortand, each column comprising twenty to twenty-five riders. Lorn regretfully gave a parting nod to Garalt, who appeared to be a valiant combatant. The warrior with the braided beard and tattooed arms responded gravely to his salute. They had barely had the chance to speak and to become acquainted, but they instinctively felt a mutual esteem. Garalt, moreover, was aware that Skandish blood ran in Lorn's veins.

Before they lost sight of one another, the two troops halted. Turning round, Teogen ordered the horn to be blown by way of a farewell. Ortand did the same and the count watched as the baron's column moved away in good order up the valley. He was worried. An evil premonition nagged at him, but he did not let it show.

Or at least so he believed, until he saw Lorn watching him.

They exchanged a glance and the count realised that Lorn had guessed his feelings. How, Teogen did not know. The knight sent to him by the High King seemed to watch everything attentively from beneath his hood and behind his dark glasses. Perhaps they shared the same apprehension.

And perhaps for the same reason.

Instinct.

Teogen having given the departure signal, Lorn urged his horse forward with a cluck of his tongue.

They started off on a path that snaked its way along a rocky wall and climbed towards jagged ridges. They were aiming for an elevated pass that led to a high valley surrounded by three mountains whose peaks were invisible among the clouds. The riders formed a long file that progressed slowly along the edge of the precipice until the track became so narrow that prudence dictated they should continue on foot. The horses snorted nervously. They had to be held firmly by the bit to prevent them from taking a fatal sidestep when the rocks slipped beneath their hooves or when a sudden gust of wind spooked them by howling past their ears.

Orwain took the lead. He walked four or five switchbacks ahead of the others and often halted to read the traces left by the Ghelts, observing the surroundings and listening carefully. He had traded his light armour for chain mail and solid spaulders, but he was without a helmet, his white hair floating in the wind. The Count of Argor advanced at the head of the column, followed by Lorn. Leister closed the march, far behind them.

The afternoon was drawing to a close when the landslide surprised them.

Orwain gave the alert too late.

He saw the first boulders go by, which dislodged others, and then still more, lifting billows of dust, causing waves of rocks and pebbles to race down the slope, and mowing down the members of the column. Lorn dived for cover beneath a slight overhang, crouched down and protected his head between his elbows. Less lucky, other knights, soldiers and mounts were engulfed, broken, crushed, swept away and pushed out into thin air. The roar of the landslide drowned their cries. Struggling to breathe, debris raining down upon his shoulders, Lorn closed his eyes and waited.

Waited for the deafening din to cease.

Waited for the rolling hell that carried everything before it to finally halt...

And the landslide came to an end, almost suddenly.

His ears ringing, Lorn straightened up cautiously, still hesitant to raise his head above his shoulders. He coughed and spat, trying to see through the particles that were falling gently all around, while pebbles still came tumbling past. He could make out a massive silhouette, that of the Count of Argor, who, covered in dust, with a cut on his brow, came towards him.

'All right?'

Lorn nodded and followed Teogen towards the heap of stones and dirt that covered the path behind them. They heard moans and plaintive whinnying coming from within. Blood flowed from between the blocks, forming red rivulets. The landslide had decimated the troop. Only those at the head and tail of the column had been spared.

And Orwain.

He arrived at a gallop as Teogen, Lorn and some others were already searching for survivors.

'The Ghelts!' he exclaimed, jumping down from the saddle. 'They—'

'Later!' thundered the count. 'Help us!'

Lorn, Leister and he were trying to lift a boulder that had trapped the leg of one poor fellow. Orwain lent them his strength but could not help saying, in an afflicted tone:

'I saw them moving out. Not more than ten of them. It was a trap. A trap. The Ghelts... The Ghelts planned the whole thing. The detour, the Fork, the two paths, everything. And I led us into—'

He did not complete his sentence.

Like all the others, he grew still upon hearing a sound that froze his blood.

The sound of a horn blowing in the distance, mournful and lonely, carried by the echo.

'Ortand!' cried Teogen.

'They're under attack,' said Lorn.

7

They arrived at the spot where the fighting had taken place after nightfall.

There were no more than a handful left with Teogen of Argor.

They were dirty, exhausted, demoralised, some wounded, and riding horses which were spent from fatigue. And still they considered themselves lucky not to have been attacked following the landslide. None would have survived, but that was not part of the Ghelts' plan. Contrary to what their tracks indicated, contrary to what Orwain and the scouts had believed, they hadn't divided into two equal groups. After reaching the Fork, only ten of them had gone east to prepare the landslide, while all the others had gone to set up the ambush.

Carefully organised, Ortand and his men had no chance against this ambush. The baron had fallen beneath the first volley of arrows, his throat pierced. After that, some thirty warriors had charged the disorganised horsemen struggling to steady their panicked mounts.

Lorn knew what an ambush was like.

He knew what it was like to set one and what it was like to fall victim to one. He had even experienced, a few years earlier, a Gheltish ambush. The Ghelts he was fighting back then had been threatening the borders of Valmir, three thousand leagues from the Argor Mountains. But it was the same group of nomad tribes. Arriving at the site of the massacre, among the scattered fires, the aligned corpses and the distraught wounded, Lorn recalled the showers of barbed arrows, the battle cries, the warriors who appeared out of nowhere like screaming spectres and, after furious combat, promptly vanished again.

Despite his wounds, Garalt was one of the few still standing. A sentry having spotted them, he advanced towards Teogen and the others, dismayed to see there were only seven of them, including one injured man.

They dismounted in silence.

Lorn and Orwain helped the rider whose ankle had been broken by a boulder to slide down from his saddle. And as the Count of Argor remained silent, taking in the sad spectacle before him, Leister said:

'The Ghelts were waiting for us. They started a landslide as we were climbing towards the pass.'

Garalt nodded.

He did not have much need to explain the ambush.

'How many survivors?' Teogen asked.

'Seven with me. All wounded.'

'Ortand?'

'Dead.'

The count greeted this news with a clenched jaw. Ortand had been his friend and a worthy man.

A soldier with his arm in a sling and a bandaged shoulder came over and murmured a word in Garalt's ear.

'It's Guilhem,' the Skandish warrior said gravely. 'He doesn't have long to live.'

The young knight was stretched out beneath a dead tree, his head resting upon a saddle bag. Livid with pain, he was grimacing and pressing both hands against the improvised bandage that was holding in his entrails. He was shivering next to a fire. Someone had just added wood, but it did no good.

Upon seeing Teogen, Guilhem wanted to sit up.

'Lie still, son. Lie still.'

The count unhooked his fighting mace from his belt, handed it to Leister, and crouched by the dying man. Lorn remained a few steps back. All that could be seen of his face beneath his hood were the flames reflecting off his dark spectacles.

Teogen took one of the young man's bloodied hands in his own, huge and filthy.

'Be brave, son.'

Guilhem nodded painfully.

'It... It was my first... battle...'

'Garalt says you were valiant. I'm proud of you. As your father would have been.'

'You... You think so?'

The count smiled, moved. Tears sprang to his eyes.

'I'm quite sure of it!' he exclaimed, exaggerating to conceal his distress.

A faint smile appeared on Guilhem's lips. He struggled not to close his eyelids. His respiration weakened.

'You'll... avenge me, won't you? Me, and... all the others?'

'I give you my oath.'

Leister turned round to give Lorn a look of surprise and worry.

'And I would like... also... for...'

'What is it?' asked Teogen. 'Tell me.'

But Guilhem's head had already fallen to one side.

He had just exhaled his last breath.

Garalt had established the camp in a spot sheltered from the wind, not far from the site of the ambush, at the foot of a big pile of rocks from where a single man could easily keep a lookout all around. He considered it unlikely that the Ghelts would return, for if they had wanted to eliminate any survivors, they would have done so. But caution was required as the Argor Mountains presented other dangers: from various points in the distance, a wild beast or a solitary wyvern screamed in the night. The wounded who could not stand were laid out as comfortably as possible, close to the fires. The others rested, drowsing a little, but most of them unable to sleep. Off to one side, Teogen, Garalt and Leister were conferring in low voices.

Orwain had volunteered to stand watch.

When his turn came, at midnight, Lorn went to relieve the old knight and found him sitting perfectly still, his wrists resting upon his knees and his gaze lost in the distance. A small stone rolled beneath Lorn's boot, startling Orwain who spun round, hand upon his sword.

'It's me,' said Lorn.

His face growing expressionless, Orwain resumed his previous position, eyes fixed on the line of black ridges beneath the milky constellations of the Great Nebula. But did he actually see them?

'I'll take your turn on watch,' he said. 'And the others after that, until dawn.'

Lorn hesitated, then sat down next to the old man. He removed his hood and, with his glasses pushed up onto his brow, looked off in the same direction as the veteran, keeping silent, his mismatched eyes barely blinking.

A moment went by.

Then Orwain said:

'It was my fault all these men died. Ortand, Guilhem, all of them. I failed. I thought I was cleverer than the Ghelts and I led us straight into the trap they laid for us. I'll never forgive myself.'

He shook his head disconsolately and repeated:

'Never.'

He fell silent.

'How did they know the region so well?' asked Lorn.

'What's that?'

'The Ghelts. These aren't their mountains, are they? They're in enemy territory. So how is it they know them so well?'

Orwain frowned.

'I... I don't know,' he admitted.

'The trap they laid for us was an elaborate one. They knew you would guess they were heading for the Fork. They foresaw we would take that little-known pass to gain half a day and grow overconfident, believing we had the jump on them. It was very well thought out. But it also proves they knew...'

'...the pass existed,' Orwain concluded.

'Exactly. But how? Do they have maps?'

'Of this region? I doubt another exists, besides the one Teogen possesses.'

'Then they had a guide. An Argorian guide.'

'A renegade,' spat Orwain, his eyes sparkling with hatred.

Lorn stood.

He walked away without turning round and rejoined

Teogen who still conversing with Leister and Garalt. He sat on his blanket, at a slight remove, and listened.

'Count, it's madness,' the Skand was saying, trying not to speak too loudly.

'We can't abandon these women to their fate.'

'We only have eight riders now,' said Leister. 'All of them wounded, three seriously. The other five will be hard-pressed just to bring them home.'

'Meaning,' added Garalt, 'It's just you, me, Leister, Orwain and... Lorn?'

He turned towards Lorn to verify that. The latter nodded.

'Five men,' resumed Leister. 'Against thirty, at least.'

'Thirty who won't expect us,' stressed Teogen. 'Thirty who believe they're safe and sound... Besides, I'm not talking about taking them all on. But setting free their prisoners and escaping with them.'

The Skand did not know what else to say.

Leister sighed and tried to make Teogen listen to reason one last time.

'Count, you know that Garalt and I will follow you and obey you whatever happens. And I know the promise you made to Guilhem... But the Ghelts now have a full day's lead on us. And we're all at the end of our strength. We'll never catch up with them.'

The argument hit home.

Teogen was no imbecile. He knew that Leister was right. Setting off in pursuit of thirty Gheltish warriors did not frighten him. But he was pragmatic, a realist. What good would it do, if they had no chance of catching up with the Ghelts?

It was at this point when Orwain chose to advance into the light.

He had heard everything and said:

'If you still have any faith in me, I think I have the solution.'

8

'There were no better wyverners than the Argorians and no better wyverns than the ones they rode. They were born in the most remote mountains. Black-scaled, they could not be tamed by any save the sons of Argor. And not only could the Argorians alone train them, but only Argorian wyverns could be used in war, unfrightened by fire, by steel, or by the noise of exploding powder. Once bridled and harnessed, the great black wyverns were proud and formidable mounts. In the wild, they were the most ferocious and relentless beasts imaginable.'

Chronicles (The Book of the Glories and Defeats of Argor)

They left before dawn and rode for a full day, almost without a halt.

They were now only five.

Five men who out of honour, courage, duty, folly, or loyalty – had not wanted to give up. Their chances of success were meagre. They were exhausted and would have to fight at odds of six or seven to one.

Laes's Fault was a deep, jagged wound which split a broad plateau surrounded by high ridges. Travelling through it from one end to another entailed a walk of two to three hours between bare, abrupt cliffs, from which entire sheets of the rock face were flaking off. But these rock falls were not what made crossing the Fault in this season utter madness. It was the wyverns who nested in the cracks of the walls and would attack on sight in order to protect their young.

'By way of Laes's Fault,' Orwain had said, 'we can reach the Gorlas valley in two days. Perhaps even arrive there before the Ghelts themselves.'

'But why wouldn't the Ghelts take this route, too?' Lorn had asked.

The terse reply came from Leister:

'Because it's suicide.'

'The wyverns make their nests in the Fault,' Garalt had explained. 'And it's the season of First Flight, so the females are more aggressive and more dangerous than cornered lionesses. In the daytime, they may drowse but still remain particularly vigilant. The slightest sound, the smallest movement alarms them and they pounce upon the intruder… A big troop would have no chance of passing without waking them and being torn to pieces.'

'But a handful of men might, is that it?' Lorn had asked.

Teogen had turned towards Orwain, who'd simply nodded.

'Laes's Fault,' said Teogen. 'It's been a long time since I last saw it.'

They had halted at an overlook point as they were descending from a pass. They sat in their saddles, observing the plateau that Laes's Fault cut in two and the steep ridges surrounding it, punctuated by elevated peaks and needles. Wyverns were gliding above, coming and going with slow beats of their wings, disappearing within the rift. From time to time, one of them would scream. Its cry, both hoarse and high-pitched, ripped through the silence and prompted a response from one or more other creatures, their echoes mixing and being carried off into the distance, like warnings.

'We'll be there tomorrow at noon.'

'Perfect,' said Leister glumly.

As evening was approaching, they decided to camp there. They did not build a fire, drank from the same flask and shared some small game that Garalt had killed a short while before, eating it raw. The night was cold, the wind blowing from the north.

They arrived at the entrance to the Fault the following day, shortly after noon. It made a breach in the rocky wall and opened up into a gigantic crack with vertical walls.

Roars and complaints could be heard within, echoing in a sinister and menacing fashion.

Teogen did not insult his knights by asking them whether they were still ready to follow him. He did, however, give Lorn a questioning glance.

The latter nodded.

They tore up their blankets to make rags which they wrapped around the hooves of their mounts and tightened every strap, checked every loop of their kit. They removed their breastplates, spaulders and tassets that risked clanking against one another and only kept on mail or leather. It was no sacrifice on their part. Inside the Fault, the heat would be sweltering.

Teogen entered first.

Followed by Orwain, Lorn, Leister, and Garalt, who closed the march. The crevice was almost always wide enough for them to advance two or three abreast, but they decided to proceed in single file, separated from one another by a few lengths. They feared rock falls and did not want one of their horses annoying or spooking another. All it took was one whinny – or even a loud snort – to alert the wyverns.

They advanced at a walk, in a silence disturbed only by the sinister cries of the wyverns and small falls of stones and dust that ran down the walls in brief, thin cataracts. They did not speak. They were anxious. They pricked up their ears and kept an eye on the heights, watching for the slightest movement. But they soon had difficulty seeing, dazzled by the sunlight and with sweat stinging their eyes. For Lorn, the ordeal was terrible. He squinted behind his dark spectacles and was obliged to put his hood up, beneath which it was stifling. The sun, which had barely begun to descend from its zenith, pounded the rift with its light and heat, turning it into a blinding furnace, a static burning hell in which the air cooked.

It was not by chance, however, that they had decided to cross the Fault at this hour of the day. They inflicted this torment upon themselves for a simple reason: the heat numbed, almost stunned, the wyverns who drowsed at the top of the cliffs. Their vigilance was reduced and they were slow to react. They might not check the origin of a noise if it did not repeat itself.

As punishing as this heat was for the men and their mounts, it was their ally. It protected them.

Or at least they hoped so.

His bald head shining with perspiration, Teogen halted after an hour and waited for the others to join him. The rift here was narrow and falling sections of the cliff had obstructed it. They would have to climb their way through the jumbled blocks.

The riders dismounted.

'I'll go first,' Orwain said in a low voice.

The Count of Argor nodded.

Leading his mount by the bridle, Orwain ventured among the sometimes precariously balanced rocks. He did so in careful fashion, taking the time to see where he placed his feet. He succeeded in passing and showed the way for the rest of the party.

The others followed him, one after another.

First Teogen.

Then Leister.

Lorn.

And finally Garalt.

Each of them held their breath, fearful of slipping, of falling, of feeling a rock tip beneath their feet or that of their horse. Those who waited their turn were no less nervous. They raised worried gazes towards the glaring sky each time a stone rolled or a block scraped. The walls looming over them seemed particularly fragile. Entire blocks, from which rivulets of dust spilled each time the wind blew a little harder, seemed to be on the point of giving way at any moment.

None of that happened and all of them felt a great relief when Garalt crossed the rubble pile. His mount only needed to step down from a flat rock. Which it did quite easily…

But in doing so it dislodged a stone, from beneath which a serpent darted forth to bite it in the hock.

The horse reared, whinnying in fear as much as pain. Garalt almost let go of the reins. He had to leap to catch hold of the bridle and somehow managed to calm the beast.

Too late?

The others had frozen, listening for a sound, for a movement, almost afraid to look up. Time was suspended and for a few prolonged seconds they heard only the wind.

After which, a winged form launched itself into space at the top of the cliff.

'THERE!' exclaimed Lorn.

Then a second, and a third.

'INTO YOUR SADDLES!' ordered Teogen. 'FLEE!'

All five straddled their mounts and took off at a gallop. The Fault was waking, emerging from its torpor. It filled with strident cries and beating wings. Added to the hooves that beat a furious charge over the dusty ground, the noise was deafening. The horsemen rode flat out, jumping obstacles without slowing down or turning to look back. Their only safety lay in flight. Their worst fear had just come to pass and there was nothing they could do but run. Escape. Exit the Fault before they were caught inside.

And pray that the wyverns, having driven the intruders from their territory, would not pursue them further...

But Lorn was not praying.

Concentrating, he pushed his mount to the limit of its strength. At that instant, it mattered little to him whether it died after it carried him out of this screaming hell, just so long as did. There would be time for regrets, second thoughts and other considerations later. Right now, Lorn was focused on living.

On surviving.

Teogen and Orwain were up ahead. Garalt was level with him. He did not see Leister: so he must be following. Or else he had fallen. It was impossible to distinguish the sound of one gallop from another in the midst of this chaos. But above all, Lorn could hear only too well the piercing screams and the beating of leathery wings approaching. Memories came back to him. Memories of nightmares in a universe of torments and spectres that haunted him night after night, without respite. The commotion of the pursuit became that of an eternal storm whose peals of thunder shook a cursed citadel.

He was afraid.

He felt a pain in his belly.

A cold sweat drenched his back.

The sky filled with winged silhouettes. More and more wyverns emerged from their sleep and took flight, the first ones alarming the neighbours, who in turn woke others and with their cries provoked a contagious hysteria. Instinctively, most of them rose above the Fault: they sought the source of the danger that threatened their colony, failed to find it and – furious, frustrated, worried – challenged one another, quarrelled and sometimes fought. Only a few of them spotted the horsemen at the bottom of the gorge and dived towards them. There were about a dozen chasing them, including one old female whose wingspan was so great that the tips seemed to touch the walls of the crevice when it started to narrow.

Lorn saw Garalt pass him. He spurred his mount mercilessly but it was no use: the horse was slowing, exhausted. Luckily, the end of the rift was in sight. It presented itself, up ahead, at the very extremity of the walls speeding past him, as a breach of dazzling light that led to safety.

Lorn still had a chance.

Despite his faltering horse, despite the wyverns who were gaining ground, he knew he could hope to escape. It would be tight. Very tight, even. But if his mount and his luck both held…

He risked a backward glance.

Leister was still in his saddle but trailed by a few lengths. Behind him, the wyverns skimmed the ground and the cliffs with great, powerful beats of their wings, their maws open and fangs exposed, eyes ablaze.

Suddenly, a shadow fell over Lorn.

He ducked just in time: a wyvern had swept down at him from the heights. It straightened its flight at the last moment and its talons closed on empty space. It screamed in frustration and flew off, wings deployed, carried away by its momentum.

Teogen and Orwain left Laes's Fault.

Garalt emerged next.

Followed shortly by Lorn.

Then Leister.

They did not halt. They galloped on without slowing down

or turning back, only too happy to have escaped from the furnace heat, the screeching noise, the deadly trap of the rift. Most of the wyverns gave up the chase as they rode away from the Fault and the nests, eggs and fledglings it sheltered. They had succeeded, or at least they were starting to believe they had, when the great female wyvern, the last one still pursuing them, struck Leister and pushed him off his mount. Lorn heard his yell and saw him rolling in the dust as the others continued to ride straight ahead.

Lorn made his decision in a fraction of a second.

He called out and, pulling on his reins, forced his horse to rear and pivot on its hind hooves in order to go back in the direction they had come from.

Towards Leister who was drawing his sword and staggering like a drunk.

And towards the old female wyvern who was already coming back.

It made a second pass. Still dazed, Leister saw it at the last instant and could not protect himself. It knocked him over before banking into a tight turn. Leister picked himself up as best as he could. He bravely faced his adversary despite his blurred vision. The world seemed to reel around him. The mountains wavered and he was just barely able to make out the silhouette of the creature as it dived towards him with a scream.

This third pass would be the last.

Leister would not rise again and he knew it. He decided to put all his remaining strength into the only blow he could hope to land against the old female. He could not kill it, but at least he would leave it with a very bad memory of their encounter…

He adopted a defensive stance.

Lorn appeared just as the wyvern was swooping upon Leister, talons first. His horse launched itself into a prodigious leap and passed beneath the reptile's outstretched neck. Reins held between his teeth, Lorn was brandishing his sword with both hands. He struck. The Skandish steel sparkled and cut deeply. The wyvern screamed. The horse whinnied as it stumbled. Blood gushed forth and Lorn was thrown from his saddle.

The great wyvern brushed Leister and crashed into the earth

behind him. Its head bounced to the ground a little further away.

And rolled...

Until it came to a standstill against a rock.

Lorn struggled to his feet, sword in his fist.

Dazed, dusty, bearing a cut on his brow, he gathered his spectacles from the ground and waited for his eyes to adjust.

Leister seemed to be in one piece.

Then Lorn became concerned for his mount. He looked around and saw it: the horse also seemed to be all right. He walked towards it, scrutinising the heights to set his mind at rest.

But the sky was empty.

Alerted by Lorn's call, Teogen, Orwain and Garalt had taken longer to turn round. They soon arrived. Orwain and the Skand remained next to Leister, while Teogen urged his horse towards Lorn.

The latter was coming back without haste, pulling his tired and slightly lame mount by the bridle. He halted when he saw the count approaching at a trot.

And waited.

Teogen halted in turn before him and remained in his saddle. They looked at one another in silence and then the count said:

'Thank you.'

Lorn nodded.

And starting to walk again, he said:

'We'll need at least five men for the task awaiting us.'

9

They crossed a pass that led them into the Gorlas valley and they continued onwards when evening came. With night falling, their vigilance waned and they found themselves nodding off dangerously, on spent horses that threatened to collapse under them at any moment. But they needed to move forward at all costs, as much as they could. They did not know whether they had arrived ahead of the Ghelts or not. Only one thing was certain: they couldn't be very far.

In the black of night, with the Great Nebula particularly pale and the moon absent from the sky, Teogen judged it wise to call a halt in the shelter of a copse of pine trees upon a hill. Once again, they camped without a fire. And they fasted, despite being famished and exhausted. They knew they could not go on much longer in this fashion, without food or any real rest. Just as they knew they would soon have no hope of catching the Ghelts they were chasing. It would be tomorrow, or never. After that, the Ghelts would reach their own territory and the poor hostages they had captured – if they were still alive – would be lost for ever.

It was Leister who first caught sight of the fires in the distance.

Lorn slit the first sentry's throat.

The young Ghelt had been drowsing where he sat. Lorn pressed one hand against his mouth and held him during his brief death throes. Then he laid the warrior out gently on the ground and, all his senses on alert, carefully looked all around. It was the first grey hour of dawn and the Ghelts' camp was still asleep.

But for how long?

They had crossed the valley and came as close as they could on horseback. Then they had left their mounts, hidden from view in the steeply embanked bed of a dried-up stream. They had rid themselves of anything on their person that might make noise or draw the eye. Their faces blacked, they had then proceeded taking great silent strides, bent down, making use of the darkness and the slightest relief in the terrain, waiting if necessary for clouds to pass over before venturing across open ground.

They had agreed to eliminate the sentries first, and then counted on finding the prisoners before the alarm was raised and fighting broke out. But daylight was almost upon them. The Ghelts would soon be waking to resume their trek.

Unless...

Intrigued by an odour, Lorn picked up a wooden goblet that had fallen beside the body and sniffed it. He smelled brandy. The sentry had been sleeping at his post because he was inebriated. So the Ghelts had been drinking and the fires they had lit that night must have been joyful bonfires. Why be so imprudent? Perhaps they were celebrating in advance the success of their raiding party, but it mattered little.

The Ghelts were camped at the foot of a cliff, beneath a wide overhang shaped like an eyelid, at the top of a fairly steep slope. Lorn had spotted three sentries halfway up this slope. He turned to the right and saw Leister signalling him that everything was all right. Then he moved to the left, circling round a big boulder, and saw Garalt stealthily approaching the third sentry. This one was wide awake, but was busy urinating and swaying slightly on his feet.

A noise drew Lorn's attention.

He looked to the top of the slope and saw a warrior emerging from a tent made of sewn hides. It was the only tent in the camp. Most of the Ghelts were sleeping under the stars, on blankets thrown down wherever their drunken state had left them. The warrior who had just appeared yawned and stretched. Tall and well muscled, with skin the colour of mahogany, he was wearing only a pair of breeches. Lorn thought he had the bearing of a chief. His skull was shaven, except at the back where a long braid of black hair with red tints fell between his shoulder blades.

Lorn felt himself breaking out in a cold sweat.

The tall warrior was going to spot him, or spot Garalt, and there was nothing he could do about it. The Skand had not perceived the danger. He leapt upon the sentry, immobilised him and cut his throat. He made no noise but the sudden movement was enough. The Ghelt by the tent turned and opened his eyes wide. Lorn's heart skipped a beat. He rushed forward but it was too late. The warrior was already yelling a battle cry.

As he was charging up the slope to attack the Ghelts' camp, Lorn heard Teogen and Orwain screaming as they launched their assault too. He had no difficulty gutting one dazed and disarmed warrior, but had to dodge the blows of a second. He riposted, deflecting his adversary's blade, struck him in the belly with his knee, grabbed him by the hair and planted his sword in the man's throat. Lorn kept an eye out for the prisoners, but the camp was already the scene of a furious melee. A knife hissed past his ears, that of Orwain stabbing a Ghelt in the chest as he was about to strike Lorn from behind. Lorn barely had time to give the old knight a grateful look: a warrior armed with two long bloody daggers was leaping upon him. Lorn ducked, threw the Ghelt over his shoulder and sent him rolling in the dust. But the other man picked himself up immediately to counterattack. Enraged, his eyes flashing and lips curled back, he was filled with a murderous frenzy that forced Lorn to retreat and parry, parry, and parry yet again. Finally he sidestepped, severed his adversary's right wrist and, spinning all the way round, decapitated him with a backhand stroke.

Making the most of the brief respite, Lorn halted and took stock of the situation.

They were still outnumbered, but the element of surprise had served them well. Ten Gheltish warriors, already, were lying dead or wounded, and the others had still not managed to organise themselves. Perhaps they would carry this off, after all, as far as Lorn could judge within the chaos of cries, hatred and violence that surrounded him. Teogen had taken on the chief who had given the alarm; Leister, one arm bloodied, disarmed a Ghelt and broke his skull with the man's own club; Garalt gutted a warrior with an axe blow before severing the arm from the shoulder of another; Orwain neatly finished off an opponent who had fallen to his knees. Blood ran, spurted, spattered faces and soaked the earth. In the din of battle, the moans of the wounded blended with the rattling breath of the dying.

And then Lorn saw them, behind the crush of fighting men.

Against the cliff, five women with dirty hair, wearing torn clothing, were tied by the wrists to stakes driven into the ground. Taking advantage of the fact that no one was watching them, they were straining at the leather bonds until they cut into their skin.

Striking to the left, striking to the right, throwing a Ghelt off balance with a punch before cutting his throat with a back-handed blade, Lorn headed for the prisoners. He eliminated another adversary who tried to stop him, but did not see the scarified Ghelt who pounced from behind and toppled him. They grappled, rolling in the dust. Lorn's head struck a round rock. Pain exploded in his skull with a dazzling flash. He regained his feet as best he could, tottering for a moment, his vision clouded and his hearing filled with a loud buzzing. His opponent was also struggling to rise and Lorn charged at him. He crashed into the man's shoulder, lifting him off the ground and letting him drop under his full weight. The impact left the Ghelt panting, but the effort had exhausted Lorn. Beset by dizziness, he took a few clumsy steps backwards and managed to find a precarious balance. Scarcely better off, the Ghelt stood and unsheathed a knife. He squinted as if trying to see through a thick fog, then his gaze fell upon Lorn and he rushed forward with a scream.

Lorn was waiting for him.

He succeeded in seizing the Ghelt's wrist and in giving him one, two, three great blows of the knee to his belly and ribs. But his opponent barely slowed and headbutted him in the face. Lorn fell backwards against a rock. He pulled the warrior with him and found himself with his back arched to the point of breaking, crushed between the stone and his adversary. He blocked the knife blade just a few inches from his face. The Ghelt was pressing with his entire weight behind his weapon which he held in both hands. Lorn could neither push it back nor deflect it. Worse still, he felt himself weakening. Slowly, inexorably, the blade crept forward. Lorn grimaced, sweating, resisting with all his might. Big drops of perspiration were obscuring his vision, but not enough to prevent him from seeing the trembling blade pointed at his pale eye.

Lorn scratched his eyelid against it when he blinked.

And suddenly, the Ghelt ceased fighting. He froze and then collapsed, as if struck by lightning.

Lorn saw the person standing behind the warrior, holding a big blood-stained stone.

It was one of the captives.

Barefoot. Filthy. With drawn features and a crazed look in her eyes. Leather straps dangled from her bruised wrists. She was wearing the tatters of a dress. She was young. With big light blue eyes. Her tangled hair fell in heavy black curls.

She seemed lost, broken.

Lorn thought she was beautiful.

An hour later, in the peaceful glow of the early morning, all of the Ghelts who had not fled were dead. Without flinching, Orwain and Garalt took charge of finishing off the wounded, while Leister saw to the captives and Lorn went to fetch the horses. They only took one prisoner: the renegade who had guided the Ghelts through the Argor Mountains, who Teogen wanted to stand trial. He'd been captured by Orwain, who had almost beaten him to death, blinded by rage. The man was in a poor state, to the point that it was doubtful whether he would survive the return journey. With his broken teeth and fractured jaw, he was in no fit shape to answer questions. They did not even know his name.

Besides their mounts, the Ghelts had left food and weapons – and even part of the loot they had collected in Argor. As there was no lack of horses to serve as pack beasts, Teogen ordered them to take everything. They soon broke camp, leaving the bodies to the carrion-eaters.

10

During the first days of the return journey, they worried about being followed. But it seemed that the Ghelts had indeed fled and would not be returning. So they slowed their pace, camped for longer periods, avoided the dangerous passes and took the less difficult paths. They showed consideration towards the freed prisoners but did not ask them about their ordeal and let the stronger women take care of the more fragile and worst off.

Lorn noticed, however, that one of them remained apart from the others. It was the young woman with the light blue eyes who had saved his life. The others did not speak to her much, avoided her and did not assign her with any tasks, but they never neglected to bring her meals. One evening, in camp, Lorn sat down beside Orwain and asked him if he knew who she was and why she was being treated in this manner.

Her name was Mairenn.

'A witch,' the old knight explained, before spitting between his feet to ward off ill fortune.

Lorn asked no more about it.

Yet, intrigued, he felt more and more drawn to the young woman as the days went by. Her beauty did not explain the attraction. Nor her mystery. There was something else, an affinity both deep and physical which she perhaps shared and seemed to understand better than he did. Often she caught him observing her and she held his gaze with a strange calmness.

The calmness of one who knows and waits.

One night, Lorn awoke with a start and saw Mairenn kneeling beside him and staring down at him, one side of her face lit by the flames from the fire, the other plunged into shadow.

'It's about to start,' she told him, in the same sort of tone that Lorn had used to tell to the wounded soldier, encountered upon arriving in Argor, that he was going to die.

He noticed then that he felt hot, very hot, much more than he should have despite the heat from the campfire nearby. His sweat, on the other hand, was icy. And he was trembling.

He realised at the same moment that a pain was shooting up his left arm, originating from his mark.

The Dark.

Lorn's moans and convulsions quickly roused the rest of the camp and caused a stir. Feverish, his muscles aching and his guts on fire, he could make out the silhouettes that had gathered round and were leaning over him.

Their voices ran together.

'What's going on?'

'Is he ill?'

'What's wrong with him?'

'Lorn! Lorn!'

In the confusion, one voice stood out, clear and serene, that of Mairenn:

'It's the Dark.'

That prompted much consternation.

'The Dark!'

'He's under the Dark's hold!'

'But Lorn! Look!'

'Is he going to die?'

They were spectres bending over him now. Spectres come from Dalroth, attentive and cruel. They watched him struggle against the invisible bonds that burned his limbs, and revelled in his madness.

A man forced his way through them.

'No!' said Teogen. 'He's not going to die. Leave off, I know what it is.'

'Then help me, count,' said Mairenn.

'Orwain! Lend us a hand here. And you others, stand back! Stand back! This isn't a show!'

Lorn felt cool hands grip him firmly. Unthinkingly, he struggled against them, wanting to free himself.

But to no avail.

Chanting, the witch placed a hand upon his brow. It felt as though molten lead passed through his skull and ran down his spine. He screamed like a demented man. Kicked out. Arched his back. And despite everything, he heard prayers, those of the women who fell to their knees, calling on the protection of the Dragon-King.

'Make them be quiet!' exclaimed Mairenn, before resuming her incantations, her hand still pressed to Lorn's burning brow.

'Silence, women!' ordered Teogen. 'Silence!'

And suddenly it was over.

Lorn lost consciousness at the same moment as a fragment of the Dark left him. He did not see Mairenn reel back as if she had received a blow to the face, nor Teogen supporting her as, exhausted, she went to cough up a big clot of black bile into the crackling fire.

The following day, the sun was already high in the sky when Lorn woke. His mind felt rested but his body ached, as if it had received a beating the previous night. Still sitting in the same place nearby, Mairenn watched over him.

'Good morning,' she said, upon seeing him open his eyes.

'Good morning.' He sat up with a grimace. 'How am I doing?'

The young woman smiled.

'Better. At least I think so. Here, drink this.'

She handed him a goblet which he drained in one gulp. He immediately regretted it. The concoction tasted of earth and bitter herbs.

'What was it?' he asked, fighting an urge to be sick.

'Perhaps you should have asked before drinking it, no?

'You have a point.'

Squinting in the dazzling sunlight, Lorn watched the men and women going about their business in the camp. He noticed they were looking at him out of the corner of their eyes and conversing in low voices. They hesitated to approach him.

He decided not to pay any attention.

'Thank you,' he said, returning the goblet to Mairenn. 'For that. And for last night.'

'You're welcome.'

'How did you know I was about to have a fit? You knew, didn't you?'

The young woman lifted her long hair behind her right ear to reveal, embedded in her pale skin, a seal similar to the one on the back of Lorn's hand. It was smaller, however, and the stone was grey.

'I was born with it.'

So, thought Lorn, that's why he'd felt an affinity with Mairenn.

The Dark had recognised the Dark.

'You'll feel better for a few days,' she said. 'But don't go thinking you're cured. I've only relieved the symptoms.'

Lorn nodded.

'Thank you just the same.'

Teogen came over.

'Well, knight? How are you feeling?' he asked briskly. 'Better? Good!'

Mairenn stood up.

'I'll leave you.'

'I'm not driving you away, am I?'

'No. I have things to do.'

The Count of Argor watched the young woman walk away, and said:

'Pretty girl...'

Then he crouched to place himself at the same height as Lorn and, with a grave expression, asked in a murmur:

'How are you, knight? Really.'

'I'm fine.'

'Can you climb back into your saddle today?'

'Yes.'

'You frightened everyone, last night. You should have warned me that...' He hunted for the right words and could not find them. 'Well, you know.'

'The fits are becoming less frequent,' Lorn said.

'Good! Good... I'm familiar with this, you know.'

When Lorn frowned, Teogen realised he had the wrong idea.

'No!' he explained. 'Not me. But my wife. She… She died of it.'

Surprised by this revelation, Lorn did not know what to say. 'Sorry,' he finally said.

The count was pensive and melancholy for an instant, his gaze distant. Then he pulled himself together and suddenly stood up, full of drive once again.

'Have a bite to eat and prepare your things. We'll be breaking camp in an hour.'

The last days of the journey passed by without incident, Lorn and Mairenn usually riding side by side without speaking. Then, one evening, they saw the fires of the towers of Argor and realised they were safe. The night was joyful for all, except Mairenn. Lorn did not understand why, but asked no questions.

The following morning, she had already left when Lorn and the others awoke.

'No one knows who she is, exactly,' explained Teogen. 'She was passing by chance through one of the villages when the Ghelts attacked. She'd gone there to sell potions. It seems she deliberately drew the Ghelts' attention in order to allow a mother and two daughters to hide.'

Lorn turned towards the count, who added:

'You'll see her again if the Grey Dragon wills it, knight. Let's be on our way.'

11

After a week's rest at Calaryn, the Count of Argor's castle, Lorn deemed the time had come for him to depart. He had recovered from his fatigue and his wounds, had slept more peacefully at night thanks to Yssaris, and felt fit enough to pursue the mission assigned to him by the High King. Making himself known to Teogen was only a beginning. Now he needed to go to Oriale, the High Kingdom's capital.

Besides, he was growing bored and he disturbed people.

Like Teogen and the others, he'd been welcomed as a hero upon their return with the freed captives. Like them, he had suffered and braved death. Like them, he had risked everything to rescue women doomed to slavery, women to whom he owed nothing. They had feted him. The count had invited him to stay as long as he liked at Calaryn, where he would always be welcome:

'My door will never be closed to you, knight.'

But little by little...

Lorn did not seek company or anyone's gratitude. He did not respond to the displays of friendship and respect. He did not care whether he pleased or displeased others. Nor did he care whether he was admired. Gloomy, he spoke little and did not smile. He spent most of his days reading, training, or going for long rides in the valley, with his cat as his sole companion.

His attitude bothered people and was taken for aloofness. And rumours grew about him, as people learned that the king had made him his First Knight, but also that he had been locked away for three years at Dalroth – and only recently released. For what crime, exactly? No one knew for certain, although some spoke of high treason. But it must have been serious, very serious indeed.

Lorn started to arouse distrust and rejection. The castle's residents avoided him and no longer spoke to him, except at the count's table. And if his left hand still drew looks, it was not only to see the famous onyx signet ring, but also to guess at what the ochre stone seal hidden beneath the leather strap looked like. People wondered why the High King had elevated Lorn to the rank of First Knight of the Realm. They spoke of the Dark and how it corrupted souls. All souls. They discussed the fit he'd suffered during the return journey and the details were exaggerated by hearsay. Some came to ask themselves whether there wasn't too strong a shadowy part within him and whether his presence wasn't harmful. And around Calaryn it started to be said that Lorn, perhaps, had brought ill fortune down on the expedition led by Teogen...

'Good evening.'

It was the eve of his departure.

Night was falling and Lorn was leaning out of a wide window to enjoy the cool evening air on his own. Behind his dark spectacles, he was staring at a molten sun that was sinking into an immense gap between two distant peaks.

Lorn turned towards the woman who approached him.

He recognised her, but did not know who she was. He had noticed her during dinner, seated at Teogen's right and conversing in a familiar fashion with him. She had just arrived that day at the castle. She was tall, slender and endowed with a rare beauty and distinction. Since everyone showed her considerable respect, Lorn gathered that she belonged to the high nobility of Argor. Nevertheless, he did not recall having seen her at the court of the High Kingdom or elsewhere.

The unknown woman smiled, wearing the white and grey dress that he'd seen her in at dinner – a simple dress with a perfect elegance that enhanced her figure. In her arms, Yssaris allowed its neck to be scratched, purring contentedly.

'He's yours, isn't he?'

Lorn looked at her.

Still smiling, she handed him the young cat. He took the animal, which immediately climbed onto his shoulders.

'What's he called?' asked the woman.

'Yssaris.'

'A fine name... It means "soul" in Skandian. Your mother was Skandish, wasn't she? And a warrior queen.'

Lorn did not reply.

He waited, and then asked:

'Who are you?'

'Dame Meryll. May it please you.'

Lorn raised an eyebrow.

The woman extended a slim hand and, on seeing her wrist, his suspicions were confirmed. The symbolic patterns tattooed in red, yellow and blue extended towards the back of her hand and disappeared beneath her sleeve. Lorn knew they ran up to her shoulder and no doubt went even further.

Dame Meryll was a Lily.

'Lorn Askarian.'

'I've already heard much about you, knight.'

By way of explanation, she glanced pointedly at Lorn's marked hand. But was she alluding to his signet ring or the stone seal? Both, most likely.

Turning to the window, Lorn set Yssaris down and contemplated the light from the setting sun outlining the black silhouettes of the mountain ridges. Dame Meryll came to stand beside him and they remained silent for a moment, long enough for him to notice that the Lily's presence was not unpleasant. That was hardly astonishing: Lilies knew how to please men just as assassins knew how to kill them.

'Try not to hold it against them.'

Lorn frowned.

'I beg your pardon?'

'I've seen how the people here in the castle treat you. And I also know what you have done. Try not to hold it against them. Forgive them for their ingratitude.'

'It's all the same to me.'

'Truly?'

'I did not do what I did to please them.'

'Then why did you?'

Lorn thought about it.

'Someone had to,' he said. 'Besides, I wasn't alone.'

'That doesn't diminish your merits.'

'Think rather of the merits of those who fell.'

And brusquely, he asked:

'What do you want from me?'

The Lilies had initially been an order of elite courtesans. They still were, but their missions had become diversified over time. Beautiful, intelligent and cultured, travelling frequently and with access to private bedchambers, they were also employed as messengers, spies, intermediaries and negotiators. Discreet and influential, respected, they served wealthy employers and knew the secrets of the powerful. They never forgot, however, to protect their own interests.

Dame Meryll's placid smile did not falter.

'I only wanted to pay my respects, knight. Count Teogen speaks very highly of you. And it's not every day that one meets a First Knight.'

'Nor a former inmate of Dalroth, am I right?'

The Lily did not blink.

One might think at first sight that she was thirty to thirty-five years of age, but Lorn surmised she was ten years older than that. He reckoned she was in her — very beautiful — forties. It was a matter of her self-assurance and the depth of her gaze. As well as the small wrinkles at the corner of her lips. And a certain serenity that did not come with youth. It was also a matter of the respect shown to her, a respect that must corres-pond with her rank within the order. Most Lilies retired once their beauty faded. The ones who remained were those who desired — and were able — to rise within the hierarchy.

Only the best remained.

'It seems to me you were declared innocent, knight.'

Lorn shrugged.

'It's like a scar on one's face. It doesn't matter whether the wound was deserved or not. It doesn't matter whether he who inflicted it regrets his gesture or not...'

'The king has nevertheless bestowed on you the signet ring

of the First Knight of the Realm. That is a measure of the confidence he accords you.'

Lorn looked down at the onyx and silver ring on his left hand. He knew some of the reasons that had prompted the High King to appoint him First Knight. Not all of them were good ones and no doubt there were others he was unaware of. But he was sure of one thing: this signet ring was going to arouse curiosity, anxiety and envy.

'What do you want from me?' he repeated.

He was now on his guard, convinced that the Lily was hiding her true intentions.

'I simply wanted to convey my sympathies, knight. Do you find that so odious?'

Lorn felt Yssaris place a velvet paw on his marked hand. He drew in a breath and calmed himself.

'No,' he confessed.

The power of this woman verged on magic, on enchantment. But he felt no desire to fight it.

'I also wanted to assure you that we are pursuing the same goal,' said the Lily in a softer tone. 'You and me. Or rather, you and us.'

She smiled again.

'And what goal is that?'

'The good of the High Kingdom, of course.'

Lorn stared at her for a long time, without her appearing to grow upset.

Then he gave her an odd smile and, carrying Yssaris, walked away.

'Good evening, madam.'

'Good evening, knight. Until we meet again.'

The following morning, very early, Lorn saddled his mount himself. With Yssaris resting upon one shoulder, he led the horse by the bridle from the stable as the castle began to stir in the first light of dawn. He crossed the courtyard and found Teogen at the portcullis of the inner wall.

Lorn was surprised because he had bade the count farewell the previous evening, at the end of a private audience during which he had explained the details of the mission the High King had entrusted him with. But there Teogen was, waiting for him, wearing boots and a long vest of padded leather, cinched by a wide belt.

'Good morning, knight.'

'Good morning, count.'

'I wanted to wish you a safe journey. And to thank you again.'

'There's no need.'

The light being still dim, Lorn was not wearing his spectacles, or his hood. Teogen could thus look directly into his mismatched eyes.

He read nothing there.

'Come,' he said, after a brief hesitation.

With a gesture, he invited Lorn to follow him.

Lorn placed Yssaris upon the saddle of his horse and the two men walked a few paces together, watched by the young cat.

'The king's plan has every chance of failing,' said the count. 'As for this idea of reconstituting the Onyx Guard...' He shook his head sceptically. 'But the venture is worth attempting and you may count on my help.'

'The king will no doubt soon be enlisting you. And your wyverners.'

'I am and I remain at the High King's service.'

Lorn nodded.

'But you, knight, will be quite alone,' continued Teogen. 'You will need to find other allies besides myself. And ones much closer to hand. That signet ring elevates you and protects you, but it also exposes you and does not make you invulnerable. Trust no one and beware of daggers in the night. And be sure to see Sibellus. I told you about him yesterday: he will be of great assistance to you. He's an old friend. I vouch for him.'

'I will be sure to call upon him.'

The count remained silent for a moment, while they returned to Lorn's horse. Then he said:

'I still don't understand what motivates you, Lorn. But you are preparing to accomplish the impossible in the name of the High King and for that sole reason...'

He did not complete the sentence, but simply exchanged a firm handshake with Lorn.

'Some victories start off as lost causes, don't they?'

Teogen rejoined Dame Meryll on a rampart of the outer wall. Wrapped in a grey cloak that fluttered in the wind, she watched as Lorn rode away towards the morning sun.

'Well?'

'I really don't know what to make of this Lorn,' the count confessed. 'He's brave, intelligent, determined and one of the best fighters I've ever met, but...'

He left his sentence dangling and shook his head, helpless.

'Do you think he might succeed?' asked the Lily. 'Do you think the king has made the right choice?'

'I don't know,' admitted Teogen. 'And the king has committed numerous errors as his reign draws to a close. But if this man returned from hell is the last chance that remains for the High Kingdom, then we must put him to the test.'

Summer 1547

'Within the Assembly of Ir'kans, the Seventh Guardian was the one who, before his peers, had demanded and defended the liberation of the Knight with the Sword, so that his destiny might be fulfilled. Contrary opinions were voiced and the Assembly debated and decided in favour of the Seventh despite the opposition of the Third Guardian and others. An Emissary was named and the Knight with the Sword was rescued from the Citadel of the Shadows and the torments of the Dark. So the Knight's star shone once again in the firmament of the Grey Dragon, but with a sinister gleam. And all doubted whether they had acted rightly.'

Chronicles (The Book of Secrets)

Evening was approaching.

The white drac had lit a campfire in the clearing. His horse hitched not far away, he was sitting on a fallen tree trunk and watching a hare he had killed that afternoon, on his way, cook in the flames. He was wearing plain, sturdy clothing, without armour, but with a long dagger at his belt. His scales were white. A ring of black arcanium pierced his right eyebrow. His slit eyes were an intense turquoise.

Skeren saw the smoke rising from his fire twist in the air, as if shaped by invisible hands. They sculpted a bust, a head, a face hidden by an ample hood. A thick darkness fell all around. There was silence, then the ghost apparition grew animated and the Seventh Guardian said:

'We, the Grey Council, require your aid.'

'It is yours,' replied the drac in an even tone.

'Do you know the Ancient Tongue?'

'I understand it and I speak it.'

These were ritual formulas. The Emissary and the Guardian punctuated them with solemn bows of the head, before continuing their conversation in a language forgotten by men.

'We have seen the star of the Knight with the Sword grow dim.'

'He almost perished, trying to escape his destiny,' explained Skeren.

'Did you save him?'

'Yes.'

'And what became of him?'

'The Knight spoke with the High King in the Citadel and he was brought before the dragon Serk'Arn. Then he travelled to Argor, where he distinguished himself and won Count Teogen's esteem.'

'That will be useful to him. Do you believe him worthy of his destiny?'

'I don't know,' admitted the white drac, weighing his words carefully. 'His soul is... troubled.'

'His star shines with a sombre gleam that darkens that of the prince. Perhaps... Perhaps we were mistaken...'

The confession disturbed Skeren, but he tried to remain calm and waited.

'But what we have done cannot be undone,' the Guardian continued.

The drac nodded.

Because he was the Seventh Guardian's favoured Emissary, he knew much about his intrigues and secrets. He had carried out many missions on his behalf, over a very long period of time. He had always served him loyally, even when he had been obliged to use byways in order to succeed without running afoul of the Assembly. The Seventh Guardian was something of a maverick. He was a strong, proud and independent spirit who often acted on his own initiative and presented his peers with a fait accompli. In his eyes, the end justified the means as long as the end sought was the will of the Grey Dragon: nothing must stand in the way of Destiny. It had sometimes led him to make questionable decisions and, despite the attempts by the Assembly to bring him to heel, to exceed his prerogatives. So he had not hesitated to resort to ruses and lies in order to hasten the liberation of the individual whose star was now surrounded by a troubling aura.

'Where is the Knight, at present?'

'He's on his way to Oriale.'

'Good.'

The Seventh Guardian bowed his head a second time and abandoned the dragons' tongue.

'Serve us well,' he said.

'I shall be the Emissary of the Dragon of Destiny,' replied the white dragon.

These were more ritual exchanges, marking the end of the interview.

Skeren blinked when the apparition vanished into the coils of smoke. Around him, the thick shadows lifted and gave way to an ordinary darkness. The forest filled with sounds, and the Nebula started to emerge in the night sky.

2

'Oriale was the capital of Langre before it became that of the High Kingdom, and since time immemorial even before that, it had been the heart of the Imelorian Empire, when the Divine Dragons ruled over the lands, the seas, the skies and the destiny of Men. There was no city more glorious and sacred, or more vast and populous. The ravages of the Wars of the Shadows had not spared it and on one occasion the Dark had completely overwhelmed it. But the protection of Eyral, the White Dragon, had preserved it from absolute destruction.'

Chronicles (The Book of Cities)

With Yssaris on his shoulder, Lorn arrived on horseback in the Redstone district. It was a poor, lower-class neighbourhood that stank and whose old houses leaned upon one another, forming a tangled skein of streets, alleys, courtyards and narrow passages. Oriale had once been a city paved in white. It still was in some places, where its splendour remained intact. But elsewhere, its wooden paving blocks had turned grey or a dirty brown. Except in the Redstone district. Here the paving blocks were made of stone the colour of dried blood, so it was impossible not to know where one was when setting foot on them.

It was sunny at the end of this afternoon. Lorn wore his spectacles beneath his hood and was dressed in grey and black, his Skandish sword at his side. He rode at a walk, without looking to right or left. In Redstone, everyone knew one another and strangers were rare.

Lorn was noticed. He was intriguing.

And worrying.

That was just as he'd hoped…

He took Yssaris in his arms and, passing one leg over the horse's withers, slid down from the saddle in front of an abandoned and partially collapsed black tower. He stood for a moment considering it, aware of the suspicious glances he was attracting. Protected by a high wall, the keep was almost a ruin. Long ago, there had been one like it at the top of each of the nine hills on which Oriale was built.

This one was the last still standing.

A moat had defended the wall. Now there only remained a muddy ditch partly filled with rubbish and not much broader than the drawbridge allowing passage over it. A drawbridge that was raised, as it happened. And did not seem about to be lowered any time soon.

Continuing to ignore the curious onlookers gazing at him more or less discreetly and speaking in low voices to one another behind his back, Lorn approached a small door adjoining the main entrance. He tried to open it but only managed to push it a little way: its lock had been forced but a chain still barred the way.

Lorn eventually opened it with a great blow of his boot, in plain sight of everyone. He calmly entered, tugging his horse by the reins, preceded by Yssaris who went off on an initial inspection tour. The keep stood in the middle of a narrow courtyard, surrounded by a few buildings backed by the rampart, beneath the wall walk. These buildings were in no better state than the keep itself but Lorn easily recognised their functions: barracks, stable, stockrooms, forge and others. There was also a well into which Lorn dropped a stone. He heard it splash into water and, satisfied, turned back towards the keep whose shadow covered him and whose hulking silhouette was outlined against the bright sky.

A coat of arms and an inscription were carved in stone above the door. The coat of arms – a wolf's head over two crossed swords – was that of the Onyx Guard. And the inscription was its motto.

The High King we serve.
The High King we defend.

263

Lorn had not been alive when nine identical Black Towers rose over Oriale. That dated back to the reign of Erklant I, five centuries earlier, when the Onyx Guard was at the height of its power and glory. Back then, perfectly maintained, they had housed dozens of horsemen and symbolised the protection provided by the Guard to the city and its inhabitants, but above all to the High King. The nine hills of Oriale in fact surrounded a tenth, which was covered entirely by the Royal Palace. The Black Towers were thus like sentries standing guard around the king, their dark stone contrasting with the white Watchtowers which rose at regular intervals along the capital's outer ramparts, defending it against the Dark.

The Watchtowers were still there, even though the Shadows had long since ended. The Black Towers, on the other hand, no longer existed. After the Onyx Guard had been dissolved, they had all been abandoned, looted, knocked down, or dismantled stone by stone.

Except for this one.

More relaxed than he had been for a long while, Lorn drew in a deep breath. He had sensed the salutary influence of the Watchtowers long before he saw them emerge over the horizon. He knew that as long as he remained under their protection, as long as he did not leave Oriale, he need not fear having another fit. Within the city, the Dark was atrophied. The Watchtowers prevented the Dark from approaching, like a dyke containing the tide. But they also prevented it from sprouting, from expressing itself, from developing where it was already present. It was a relief, accompanied by the feeling of breathing more easily, seeing more clearly, of being lighter, more optimistic and more bold…

Hands on his hips, Lorn was looking at the Black Tower with satisfaction when he heard people coming through the small door he had kicked open. Glancing discreetly over his shoulder, he saw a patrol of the neighbourhood militia arriving. Someone had clearly decided to alert the authorities to his presence.

The militiamen deployed themselves cautiously. Hesitant,

they did not know what to make of this intruder who made no effort to hide.

Lorn was one step ahead of them. His hands still on his hips, leaning back slightly, he had the air of a property owner admiring a recent acquisition and, without turning round, he announced:

'My name is Lorn Askarian. First Knight of the Realm. I'm taking possession of this tower.'

3

That very evening, Esteveris received a visit from Yorgast the prefect. In Oriale, each district was administered by a prefect whose authority was unquestioned as long as ordered reigned and taxes were collected. That was the case in the Redstone district, where Talinn Yorgast was in charge.

Despite the late hour, Esteveris was still working at his desk, in his private apartment. Since he just taken his third and final daily bath, beneath his silk and brocade dressing gown he wore only a gauzy cotton shirt that clung to the bulges and folds of his obese body. His smooth skull shone with the pomade that a servant had patiently applied and whose purported virtue was to soothe the terrible migraines from which the minister suffered. As usual, his stubby fingers were heavily laden with rings and gemstones. His lips were greasy from the pastries into which he bit as he read a worrisome report.

The prefect's unexpected call did not enchant him, but he allowed the man to be shown in. Yorgast was about thirty years old, svelte and carefully groomed.

Esteveris rose to greet him.

'Good evening, Talinn.'

'Good evening, Uncle. Thank you for receiving me.'

'Unfortunately, I can only grant you a few moments.' He indicated his desk crowded with papers, maps, reports and dossiers bound with leather laces. 'As you can see, my days are long and full.'

Yorgast was the minister's nephew by marriage, which explained his appointment as prefect. Esteveris had never had cause to regret it. He knew Yorgast was dishonest, ambitious, greedy for gold, and corrupt, but he was loyal and his district was firmly in his grip.

Esteveris sat back down and offered a seat to his nephew. He would have liked to offer him a pastry as well, but saw there were none left intact on the plate. The minister had acquired a taste for these confections made with honey and orange blossom during a journey outside Imelor, when he still a cleric of the Church of the Sacrificed Dragon-King. He now had a plateful served in his room every evening after dinner. He dipped into it distractedly as he worked, replacing the pastry that he had just chewed, and then, his mouthful consumed, reached out his hand to retrieve the bitten morsel… or another.

'So, Talinn, what can I do for you?' he asked in a friendly voice.

The prefect squirmed upon his chair.

'To tell you the truth, Uncle, something happened today in Redstone. Something I just learned of, that will no doubt be of interest to you.'

Esteveris made a show of licking away the sugar that remained stuck to his fingers.

'I'm listening.'

'Well… A man arrived today. He goes by the name of Lorn Askarian and claims to be First Knight of the Realm. I know it's impossible, but he has a signet ring that seems to prove it. And he's taken possession of the Black Tower.'

The minister already knew all that. He had learned of Lorn's arrival a few hours earlier, thanks to the extraordinary network of spies and informers he maintained at all levels of society, from the slums of Bejofa to the queen's antechamber. He preferred, however, not to tell his nephew that. One useful way of winning people's loyalty was to let them believe they were useful, even indispensable. After greed, there was no shorter or stronger leash than vanity.

'I did not wish to intervene,' Yorgast continued. 'Not without having informed you and consulted with you beforehand, Uncle.'

'You did well.'

For form's sake, Esteveris asked a few questions which the prefect answered eagerly. Following which, Yorgast asked:

'But what does this mean? Who is this man? Is the signet ring on his finger authentic?'

'It is, unfortunately.'

'So you know who he is?'

'A man the High King has recalled to his service.'

'The High King!' exclaimed the prefect. 'But that—'

'Don't be alarmed,' his uncle interrupted him. 'There's nothing to be concerned about.'

'Truly?'

'I assure you.'

Yorgast hardly seemed convinced.

He kept his district firmly under his thumb. He had crushed it with taxes, taking more than his share and even using his position to engage in some profitable trafficking. The idea that a representative of the king was going to install himself right in the middle of Redstone was not at all to his liking.

'Don't worry,' insisted the minister, rising from his armchair with a smile he meant to be soothing.

Realising the interview was over, the prefect also rose. He continued to wear a sombre expression.

'But what does he want, this… this Lorn?'

Esteveris took his nephew by the elbow in order to see him out.

'I don't know…' he said with a shrug. 'Perhaps to recreate the Onyx Guard all on his own!' he added.

Yorgast open his eyes wide.

'You think so?'

The minister burst out laughing.

'I'm jesting, Talinn! I'm jesting! Come now, get a grip on yourself!'

Anxious not to leave a bad impression, Yorgast forced himself to cheer up and laugh in turn.

'All the same,' Esteveris added, 'you would do well to keep me informed of all this. You're vigilant, that's good. So continue to be, all right? Keep a discreet eye on this man and report to me regularly about his deeds and gestures.'

It was an unnecessary precaution, as the minister already had the new occupant of the Black Tower under surveillance.

'Understood, Uncle.'

'After all, what harm can one man do?'

'None,' the prefect acknowledged.

But he didn't sound very convinced.

Once Yorgast had left, Esteveris sat back down at his desk. Preoccupied, he swallowed several pastries in a row as he reflected. He did not know what Lorn was doing in Oriale. He only knew that Lorn was the High King's key piece and had just been pushed to the middle of the board. The opening moves complete, the match was at last truly starting.

Esteveris sighed.

As if he needed this! As if he didn't have enough worries, enough problems to solve, with the cession of Angborn approaching! Did the High King really have to choose this moment to start acting up from his citadel? Couldn't he simply die there, retired from the world?

Esteveris realised he'd finished off the plate of pastries and reproached himself. With a sudden grimace of disgust, he pushed it away in a fit of ill temper and let it fall upon the wooden floor, where the porcelain broke into several pieces.

The noise drew Draniss, the minister's private valet. Mute as usual, the black drac passed his head through the door and gave his master an enquiring look.

Esteveris waved him away with an irritated gesture.

Then he changed his mind and called him back.

'Draniss!'

The drac returned.

'Is Dalk still here?'

Draniss nodded.

'Send him in.'

Nodding again, the drac left.

When Sorr Dalk entered, Esteveris was waiting on the balcony.

Announced by the rapping of his heels and the jingling of

his spurs, he joined the minister but waited to be asked before saying anything. The night was warm, clear and peaceful.

And Dalk was not an impatient man.

He bided his time, with a thumb stuck in the buckle of his belt and a hand resting on the pommel of his sword.

'I read your report,' Esteveris said at last. 'Is there really cause for concern?'

Dalk had returned from Angborn.

'I think so.'

'And who is this Cael...'

'Cael Dorsian. A very minor and very dubious member of the nobility of the sword. He has gathered around him all the opponents of the cession of Angborn to Yrgaard. He speaks of treason, of dishonour. He does not recognise the queen's right to govern. He says he only owes obedience to the High King. People are listening to him.'

'Can he be reasoned with?'

'No.'

'Can he be bought?'

'Again, no.'

'Silenced, then?' Esteveris asked angrily, turning towards his henchman.

Dalk did not blink.

'That would be ill-advised,' he said.

The minister cursed and took a moment to calm down.

'I know that,' he said. 'It's never a good idea to create a martyr to a cause... What about arresting him? Hasn't this baron already done something illegal?'

'Nothing. Nothing we can prove, at least. For the moment.'

'What do you mean?'

Dalk explained that, for some time now, a band of brigands had been active in Angborn. They only stole from wealthy Yrgaardians, or from merchants, bankers and shipowners favourable to Yrgaard. Cargoes had been stolen, houses burgled, warehouses emptied, stockrooms burned. All of it with such minimal violence that up until now there had only been some cuts and bruises. But for how much longer?

The brigands signed their misdeeds with printed leaflets

which they left behind at the scene or posted at night on the city's walls. Very popular, they claimed to be loyal subjects of the High King. They condemned the queen's illegal regency, which was leading the High Kingdom to its ruin. They rejected the cession of Angborn and promised to continue the struggle when the city was handed over to the Yrgaardians. They were fighters, preparing to wage a legitimate war by seizing funds from the enemy that would soon be needed for their cause.

'And according to you, Dorsian is the leader of this band,' said Esteveris.

'Dorsian denies it. But he says the same sort of thing as they do. Moreover, he's a man of action. And he has all the qualities needed to gather about him a handful of brave and determined volunteers.'

Troubled, the minister mulled this over.

The actions of these brigands risked compromising the good relations that were being established between the High Kingdom and Yrgaard. They needed to be stopped as quickly as possible, before they did any further harm and attracted more supporters. The idea that they might try to strike a daring blow during the treaty signature caused Esteveris's temples to break out into a cold sweat. The queen, who wanted that day to be her triumph, would never forgive such an insult.

Or anyone responsible.

'Return to Angborn, Dalk. Leave tomorrow.'

'Understood.'

'Do as you see fit. Use any means necessary and spend whatever you have to. But I want these criminals dead or behind bars as soon as possible. And guilty or not, I want Dorsian silenced. Is that clear?'

Dalk bowed and withdrew.

Sensing a migraine coming on due to anxiety, Esteveris called out:

'Draniss!'

The black drac appeared.

'Some wine,' demanded the minister. He hesitated. 'And pastries.'

4

The following day, very early, when the city was barely waking, Sibellus found someone waiting for him in the street in front of the Royal Archives. He was astonished at first. Then he wondered who this man was, dressed in grey linen and leathers... before noticing the dark glasses that hid his eyes in the gentle morning light.

Then he understood.

Lorn was sitting on a stone bench, leaning forward with his elbows resting on his knees. Looking thoughtful, he raised his nose when he heard the archivist take out his keys, and he straightened up.

'I am Lorn Askarian. The Count of Argor advised me to come and see you.'

Sibellus nodded.

'The count warned me of your visit by letter. But come in.'

He opened three locks with three different keys and pushed open the heavy door carved with the arms of the High Kingdom. Lorn followed him inside and as he shut the door, remarked:

'No guard? No one to watch the place at night? What if a fire broke out?'

The archivist gave a small resigned laugh.

'No, there's no one. And if a fire broke out, there would be some parties who'd rejoice at seeing this place go up in smoke.'

'Some parties?'

'At the Palace. There are certain people who find that all this old paper is quite expensive to preserve. They are perhaps not entirely wrong... It's this way.'

Lorn trailed Sibellus through corridors and a series of rooms where chests and shelves overspilled with bound books and scrolls of parchment. Everywhere there was the same dust, the same odour of wood and ink, the same impression of neglect. The floor creaked beneath the soles of the knight's boots. Paint was peeling from the walls and slabs of plaster threatened to fall from the ceilings.

'You came quickly,' said the archivist as he showed the way. 'The count's letter arrived by wyverner only a few days ago. How long have you been in Oriale?'

'Since yesterday.'

'If you don't have somewhere to sleep, I will gladly put you up until you find—'

'Thank you. But I've already taken possession of the Black Tower.'

Sibellus halted and turned towards Lorn.

'Already?' he asked in surprise. 'You have every right, but...'

He let his sentence go unfinished.

'Why wait?' asked Lorn.

The archivist thought for a moment, then shrugged his shoulders with an uncertain expression.

'After all...' he said, and then resumed walking.

He invited Lorn to enter his private study, at the top of a rickety wooden staircase. Without knowing exactly why, Lorn expected to see a room crammed with papers, piles of documents and pyramids of scrolls. Instead it was tidy, although dust motes danced in the light, here as elsewhere. Hanging from a stretched cord, a curtain separated a small cot from the rest of the space.

'Sometimes I'm too tired to go home,' explained Sibellus, seeing Lorn's gaze. 'Old age.'

He seemed to be sixty to sixty-five years old. Of medium height, he was slightly stooped from the weight of time, but his eyes remained alert and no doubt his mind likewise. Very modestly dressed, he boasted a perfectly trimmed collar of beard which was joined at the temples to a crown of short white hair. The fingers of his right hand were stained with ink. A knife was tucked into a sheath that hung from his belt on two small chains.

'I must give you something.'

He turned towards an iron cupboard, opened it with a key tied around his neck and took out a small round purse which he handed to Lorn.

'For you,' he said.

Lorn took the purse while the archivist closed up the cupboard – which did not seem to contain much besides some documents sealed with black wax. The purse, on the other hand, was full of gold langres.

A small fortune.

'From the Count of Argor,' Sibellus explained. 'He asks only that you make good use of it.'

'I'll see to it.'

Lorn slipped the purse into the inner pocket of his doublet. And as he was removing his spectacles, they heard, coming from a nearby room, the sound of many books falling from a considerable height.

The archivist sighed, excused himself with a glance, and went to open the door to his study slightly.

'Is that you, Daril?' he called.

'It's me,' a youthful voice answered him. 'It's all right, master. I'm unharmed.'

Sibellus sighed again.

'Put it all back in its proper order, will you?'

'That's what I was doing when—'

'Just be careful. Have the others arrived?'

'The others, master?'

'Who do you think I'm talking about? Cam and Lerd.'

'Umm… I don't know.'

The archivist shut the door.

'That,' he said in a murmur, 'means "no". But Daril isn't one to rat on the others.' Another sigh. 'Why is the only one who is punctual also the clumsiest of the lot?'

He sat down and invited Lorn to do the same.

'"Master"?' enquired Lorn.

Sibellus nodded.

'I'm the master archivist,' he said.

'And to help you, you only have—?'

'Two archivists and an apprentice, yes.'

'For the entire Royal Archives?'

'Two years ago there were twenty of us. But you see, my funds have melted away like snow in the sun. And without money... That doesn't stop documents, laws, decrees, treaties and whatnot from continuing to pour in here. And since we can't deal with it all, it accumulates. In ever-growing piles, which will end up burying poor Daril one day,' added Sibellus with a smile. 'But what can I say? The kingdom is on the verge of ruin and no one knows what tomorrow holds. So who has the time to be interested in the past? And isn't that what we are, here? The past?'

Lorn did not reply. He simply looked calmly at the archivist with his mismatched eyes. Sibellus returned his gaze, wondering what to make of this man who seemed both attentive and strangely detached from everything. The archivist knew his story from Teogen. He knew that Lorn had lost everything and spent three years in the dungeons of Dalroth for a crime he had not committed. What had he endured there? And how had he survived?

Summoning his wits, Sibellus said:

'So, you're a man of means now. Is there anything else I can do for you?'

'The count said I could rely on you.'

'It all depends for what.'

'I have come to restore the High King's authority.'

Dumbfounded, the archivist fell silent and stared for a long moment at Lorn, who did not blink.

Restore the king's authority?

When the queen had seized all power and excluded, bought, broke, or eliminated anyone who resisted her? When the king, stricken by his mysterious illness, had locked himself away and was dying in a distant citadel? When he was said to be mad? Or at least guilty of having abandoned the High Kingdom and its people? With the exception of a few who struggled in secret at risk to their lives, Erklant's last supporters remained silent and in hiding.

But perhaps they were just waiting for a man who would stand up and guide them.

Could Lorn Askarian be that man?

Teogen seemed to believe so, thought Sibellus.

He granted himself a few more instants of reflection beneath Lorn's impassive gaze, and then said:

'For that, yes, you can rely on me.'

Lorn nodded gravely.

They did not swear an oath. They did not even exchange a handshake. But from that moment, a pact united them and Sibellus felt a curious shiver of excitement and hope run up his spine.

'I want to know everything about the rights conferred by this ring,' said Lorn, showing him his onyx signet ring. 'Rights and duties, according to the law. But also according to custom.'

'Very well.'

'Find me all the documents. The most minor decree. The slightest decision. The most obscure ruling rendered by the High King's justice.'

'I understand.'

'I also want to know everything about the Onyx Guard. Its history. Its organisation. Its prerogatives.

'So be it. But you know what means are at my disposal. It will take a while.'

'I will read everything as and when you find it. Send the documents to me at the Black Tower. Fear not, I'll take good care of them and return them to you as soon as I have studied them.'

Sibellus flinched inside at the idea of some of his most precious documents leaving these walls. Two years earlier, such a release of rare documents would have been impossible. Or it would have been difficult and certainly drawn attention. But at present... The master archivist told himself that since practically no one cared what might become of the High Kingdom's memory, he was free to do with it as he pleased.

As long as it remained intact.

'Where do you want me to start?'

'With the rights and duties of the First Knights of the

Realm. I must learn them in order to remain above reproach, unimpeachable. Or at least know when I'm overstepping the bounds, as the case may be.'

Sibellus raised an eyebrow.

'As the case may be?'

Lorn looked him straight in the eyes.

'I am going to accomplish the mission assigned to me by the High King. Whatever the cost. But you don't need to concern yourself with that.'

The archivist felt trepidation rising within him, but said nothing. All he could utter was:

'Be... careful, knight.'

After Lorn's departure, Sibellus ordered that he not be disturbed and spent a long moment thinking.

Then he called out:

'Daril!'

An adolescent of sixteen years soon poked his head through the half-opened door.

'Yes, master?'

'Come in, Daril. And close the door. I'm going to be needing you.'

Upon returning from his meeting with Sibellus, Lorn immediately set to work. He started to clear the debris and the filth from the ground floor of the tower, as well as the earth and the weeds and the brush that obstructed it. He spent the day doing this, without making much headway. Of course, Teogen's gold would have allowed him to hire workers and no doubt he would do so for the structural repairs. But he needed to toil alone, even if it meant being taken for a madman. And he also needed his efforts to be seen.

When evening came, Lorn decided he had sweated enough.

Without even washing, he went into the first inn he found and bought bread, wine, pâté, cheese and grapes, ignoring the deep silence that fell upon those present when they saw him arrive. He paid, promised to bring the basket back and returned to the tower at a brisk pace. He installed himself inside the keep, straddling a bench, his victuals placed before him, while Yssaris chased a mouse on the floors above.

And he was about to tuck into his supper when someone cleared their throat on the doorstep. He was a rather scrawny adolescent, with tangled hair and protruding ears, who was carrying a small chest and seemed not to know what to do with it.

Lorn looked at him and waited.

The boy swallowed and did not dare to speak.

And the longer Lorn waited, the shyer the boy became. A mouse in his jaws, Yssaris came to see and sat down on a step at the top of a stairway.

'Well?' asked Lorn, losing patience.

The boy gave a start.

'My name is Daril,' he said. 'I was sent by Master Sibellus. I've brought some documents for you. At least...'

He hesitated to continue.

'Yes?' Lorn prompted.

'You are the knight Lorn Askarian, aren't you?'

As far as knights went, Daril found himself facing a dirty man in shirtsleeves, with his hair full of dust and a disagreeable expression, who was grabbing a quick bite and drinking from the neck of a bottle inside a ruin.

'That's me,' said Lorn.

'Then these documents are for you,' said the boy with visible relief.

'Put them where you like. Thank you.'

Daril searched around for a likely spot to deposit the chest, did not find one, and finally put it down at his feet. Lorn then thought he could dine in peace, but the boy did not seem in any hurry to leave. He stood there, idly gaping about at the place, the disorder, the old furniture, the tattered tapestries, the exposed timbers and the wrecked floors.

He seemed fascinated.

'Anything else?' asked Lorn.

'No, no,' answered the boy.

But still he did not leave.

His attitude intrigued Lorn, who turned towards Yssaris.

The cat had let go of its dead prey but remained on the highest step of the stone stairway that climbed along one wall. It waited, curious to see what would happen.

Lorn hesitated, and surprised himself:

'Are you hungry?'

Daril was one of those gangly adolescents who were always hungry.

'I'll say...'

With a wave of his hand, Lorn invited Daril to join him. The boy did not wait to be asked twice. He hurried over to straddle the bench and drew a penknife from his pocket. His eyes shining and full of gratitude, he then displayed a ferocious and joyful appetite. He was too busy eating to speak, but smiled cheerfully between mouthfuls. Lorn dined with less enthusiasm, but could not help grinning too.

At last full, Daril wiped his knife on his thigh, folded it and stood up.

'Thank you, my lord. But I'd best be going now.'

And as Lorn simply looked at him while finishing the cheese, he added:

'Master Sibellus said that you would be returning the documents.'

'Since that was what we agreed, yes.'

'Because I could come back to fetch them, if you like...'

Lorn considered the boy with a mixture of stupefaction and amusement.

'Good night, Daril.'

'Good night, my lord.'

Daril started leave, reluctantly, but turned back just before he passed the tower's threshold.

'My lord?'

'What?' asked Lorn, forcing himself to recall that patience was a virtue much prized by philosophers.

'If I were you, I wouldn't place much trust in these timbers.'

Lorn looked at the beams overhead.

'Because in my opinion,' the boy continued, 'if they don't kill you by collapsing beneath you, it will be because they have already fallen on top of you... If I may say so myself, my lord.'

'They don't look to me to be in such a bad state as all that…'

'The master beam is warped. And those joists over there, on the right, are about to give way. You need to reinforce them but it would be simpler to tear it all down.'

Lorn asked in surprised:

'Are you an expert, then?'

'A little bit. My father is a carpenter. He wanted to teach me the trade and it seems I have a good eye but, well… It was thanks to a cousin that they found me a place in the archives. It's boring but I prefer it to carpentry.'

'And what is it you dislike so much about carpentry?'

'Splinters,' the boy answered, without hesitation.

Lorn looked at Daril, then at the tower's timbers, then at Daril again.

He smiled.

5

Days went by, during which Lorn continued to clear out the tower. He worked alone, sometimes sweating blood, but never giving up. He knew he was being watched and that the rumours about him were growing. In fact, he made sure they did. Although he spoke little, explained nothing to anyone and allowed free rein to interpretations of all kinds, he willingly made a show of himself. He noted with satisfaction the curious faces at the windows of the neighbouring houses and left open the small door he had kicked in when he arrived. It would have been ideal if he could have lowered the drawbridge to allow passers-by to have a look into the courtyard, but the mechanism was jammed with rust and dirt.

Nevertheless, the news that the Black Tower had a new occupant and that the occupant was exerting himself to restore it did not take long to spread beyond the Redstone district. Indeed, Lorn was counting on it soon becoming common knowledge throughout the city. And he did not doubt for a second that word had already reached the Palace.

One evening, Lorn went to the inn where he had adopted the habit of ordering his meals. But instead of paying and leaving with the basket of victuals that was waiting for him, he sat down at a table and called for a pitcher of beer. A thick silence fell, everyone watching the mysterious occupant of the Black Tower from the corner of their eyes. But since he said nothing and did nothing except drink his beer in the shadows, there were merely some awkward clearings of throats before conversations resumed and the inn regained its usual atmosphere.

They forgot about him. Or almost.

After a moment, two men took up places at a neighbouring table without noticing Lorn's presence. One was a tall bearded man, a former soldier by the look of him, and the other a workman with calloused hands and hair whitened by plaster. They had barely sat down when they were joined by a young man, as badly dressed as he was badly nourished, who worked as a public scribe. They ordered drink and, very soon, the conversation turned to the topic of Lorn.

And more specifically, of his signet ring, the focus of every sort of speculation.

'It's made of onyx,' said the scribe. 'With a wolf's head upon crossed swords. And a crown over it. And all of that in silver.'

'Where did you hear that?' asked the workman.

'I heard it from the woman who came to see me this morning for a promissory note. Wife of one of the militiamen the knight showed his ring to, the day he arrived.'

'The wife of a militiaman. You have dealings with those sorts of people, do you?'

Lorn had already had occasion to observe that the militiamen in Redstone were hated and feared by the population.

The young man shrugged by way of excusing himself.

'What would you have me do? A man has to make a living.'

'The crown and the wolf's head are the personal emblems of King Erklant,' said the former soldier pensively. 'The wolf's head and the crossed swords were those of the Onyx Guard. But there only exists one ring that bears both the king's coat of arms and that of the Onyx Guard.'

'Which is?' asked the scribe.

'That of the First Knight of the Realm,' said a man, listening to the conversation.

It was Cadfeld, an old white-haired man whose thick drooping moustache was dark grey. He was also an inhabitant of the neighbourhood and a regular at the inn. Dressed in filthy rags, he lived off public charity and the little he earned from selling second-, third- or even fourth-hand books. Lorn had seen him walking the district's streets, a bag full of tattered dog-eared volumes over his shoulder.

'The First Knight is both the captain of the Onyx Guard

and the representative of the High King,' explained Cadfeld. 'That's why he bears both coats of arms. But he must renounce his own and those of his family.'

'For good?' asked the workman in surprise.

'Yes,' said the former soldier. 'Until his death.'

'For as long as he remains the High King's representative,' corrected the seller of old books.

He took his glass and, leaving the small table where he'd been sitting on his own, went over to join the trio. His glass was empty. He filled it from their jug of wine and said:

'In the beginning, the kings of Langre only named a First Knight on special occasions. A tourney, for example. Or a duel in an affair that obliged the king to defend his honour, weapons in hand – something he could not do, since he was the king. It was an immense honour to represent the king, but a fleeting one. After the tourney or the duel, the king withdrew the title and the First Knight went back to being... himself. Because we say, for convenience's sake, that the First Knight is the representative of the king. But it's actually much more than that. He *is* the king. He embodies him. He becomes his physical person.'

'Really?' said the scribe.

'Consult the legal texts,' said Cadfeld. 'What the First Knight does, the king does. What he says, the king says. And what happens to him, happens to the king. The only power the king does not abandon to his First Knight is that of reigning. But everything else...'

He drained his glass, poured himself another, and then added in a conspiratorial tone:

'You need more convincing? Then listen to this...' The three other men leaned forward over the table, silent and attentive. 'There's mention in the *Chronicles* of a king who was wounded in the course of a hunt. This king was named... No. I forget his name, but it doesn't matter... That same evening, a ball was to be given at the Palace and the queen was eager to dance there. Something which the king was incapable of doing, because of his injury. On learning this, the queen grew angry, cried, threw a tantrum and made impossible demands. But in vain. A queen

283

of Langre is only allowed to dance with her spouse, so she would not dance at all that evening...' Cadfeld had a gulp of wine before resuming his tale. 'Who was it who had the idea of naming a First Knight for the duration of the ball? Some say it was the king, in order to please his wife. Others say it was the queen, and that she herself chose the knight. In any case, the king named a First Knight of the Realm. So the queen had a partner. And she could dance as much as she pleased. But the story does not end there...'

Cadfeld paused at a carefully calculated point.

Lorn, who was taking care to go unnoticed without missing the smallest scrap of the story, could not help smiling.

'For during the ball, the king retired to his apartment to rest for a while and fell asleep. Fatigued by his wound, no doubt. Or perhaps it was the remedies the queen had given him against the pain... Be that as it may, at the end of the ball, the First Knight was still First Knight. And he remained so the following morning, when he was caught discreetly leaving the queen's chamber...'

There was another pause and another draught of wine. The bookseller wiped his mouth on his sleeve and continued:

'The affair was hushed up to avoid scandal. But the First Knight was never brought to justice, although he lost the king's trust and was exiled at the first opportunity. Yet, neither the queen nor he had done anything reprehensible. She had slept with her husband and he had slept with his wife. That night, in the eyes of the law, the queen had received the king in her bed. Little did it matter that the king, at that very instant, was sleeping in his own...'

Quite proud of himself, Cadfeld punctuated his anecdote with a last quaff and sat up. The others straightened up in turn, smiling. The old man had drained their jug of wine, but his story had been worth it.

There was a silence, which the scribe broke:

'So the rumour is true,' he said. 'The High King has indeed named a First Knight.'

Lorn winced. He had not been aware that this particular detail had spread.

'And he's here,' said the former soldier. 'In Oriale.'

'That's what I have the most trouble believing. I don't know who this man is who has taken possession of the Black Tower. But I cannot believe his signet ring is authentic, or if it is, that he did not steal it… The king has named a First Knight. Very well. But what would he be doing here?'

'The Black Towers belonged to the Onyx Guard. The one in Redstone is the last one standing. What would be more normal than for him to return there?'

'In that ruin, Liam? When he could lodge at the Palace?'

The veteran had no answer to that. He shrugged.

'And a First Knight of the Realm would break his back rebuilding a tower, alone, with his own two hands?' insisted the workman.

There again, the former soldier had no answer.

Yet, he had the feeling that all this had a meaning. Like most people, he'd felt abandoned when the king had retired to the Citadel and left the government of the kingdom to the queen and her ministers. The High Kingdom, at that point, was already doing poorly. But since then, the situation had only grown worse, especially for the people. Liam, the veteran, was one of those who only asked to believe, who still hoped that the High King had not totally forgotten them.

'During his first campaigns,' said Cadfeld, 'the king saddled his own horse. And he let no one else furbish his weapons. He slept in a tent or under the stars, among his knights and his squires.'

'That's true,' said Liam. 'And the men with whom the king surrounded himself were made of different stuff than… the ones the queen coddles. They knew what sweat and blood were. They knew what effort was and they did not hesitate to strain themselves, up to their knees in the mud, if necessary…'

'Those men cannot have all disappeared,' observed the scribe.

'No. But it seems their era is over.'

Their era was also that of the former soldier. He seemed so bleak that Cadfeld tried to comfort him with a friendly hand on his shoulder.

Lorn stood up.

The four men noticed him then and fell silent. It was obvious he'd heard everything. The workman turned pale. The scribe froze. Liam and Cadfeld, for their part, looked at Lorn and waited.

Expressionless, he walked towards the exit, passing their table.

But then he halted.

Changed his mind, and went back to them.

'The cuckolded king,' he said to Cadfeld, 'was Galandir IV.'

Whereupon he tossed a coin to the innkeeper and declared: 'They're my guests.'

And then he left, taking his basket with him, followed by the eyes of everyone at the table except for the bookseller.

His back to the door, Cadfeld did not even give any sign of wanting to turn round. He remained pensive, his eyes lost in a blurred distance.

'He's right,' he said at the end of a long silence. 'It was indeed Galandir IV.'

Upon his return to the Black Tower, Lorn found Daril and his father the carpenter waiting for him in the courtyard. The boy made the introductions and, after a handshake, the man said to Lorn:

'So you have a problem with the timbers?'

Lorn's gaze passed between father and son, halted for a moment upon the son, and then returned to the father. Tall, massive and paunchy, the carpenter seemed to be a fine fellow. His handshake was firm and his palm calloused.

'It seems so, yes.'

'I can take a look, if you like.'

'All right,' said Lorn, after a moment's thought. 'Follow me.'

The carpenter entered the tower at his side, followed by Daril, grinning from ear to ear.

6

One evening, having brought back some documents to Sibellus and spent a long while conferring with him, Lorn was returning alone from the Royal Archives when, passing before an alley, he heard a stifled moan. He halted, listened carefully, examined the alley in the light of the Great Nebula, and noticed, lying on the ground, an old leather bag which he immediately recognised: it was Cadfeld's. He picked it up. The strap was broken and books in a very piteous state were strewn all over the paving stones.

Without thinking about it, Lorn stuffed the books back in the bag. Then he pursued his investigations a little further and, in a back courtyard at the end of the alley where they had dragged him, he came upon some militiamen who were beating the old bookseller. They were taking their time and aiming their blows carefully, out of playful cruelty.

The vision of another poor wretch being brutalised, one festive night behind a tavern in Samarande, struck Lorn like a slap in the face. The memory of his own cowardice resurfaced too. A cold anger seized him.

'Leave him alone.'

Surprised, the militiamen turned round. Since it was night, Lorn was not wearing his spectacles. They did not recognise him beneath his hood.

'Clear off.'

'I said: leave him alone.'

'Clear off, or you'll regret it.'

Lorn did not move an inch.

'Leave him. And sod off yourselves.'

The militiamen spread out, snickering, while Cadfeld painfully stood up.

There were four of them, wielding heavy lead-filled clubs.

Lorn was alone and unarmed. He did have a knife on his belt but, Oriale being a fairly safe city, he had not taken his sword with him to the Archives.

On the other hand...

The bag full of books whirled round at the end of its strap and caught one of the militiamen beneath the chin. The man toppled over, stunned, while the split bag flew free, spilling the books in a cloud of printed pages. Another militiaman was already attacking. Lorn parried the blow with the bag's strap, held horizontally. He stepped back, pivoted, gave a shove with his shoulder and then looped the strap around the wrist of the third militiaman... whom he sent stumbling over the one lying unconscious on the ground. Before the fourth man even realised what was happening, with a feint and two swift moves Lorn had forced him to his knees, then passed behind him and choked him with the strap.

The militiaman whose blow Lorn had blocked was preparing to attack again. And the one who had fallen over the body of his stunned companion was getting back up, rubbing his wrist with an evil expression.

But Lorn announced threateningly:

'One move, and I'll break his neck.'

To show that he meant business, he tightened the strap a little more. Scarlet-faced, his prisoner squealed, drooling, and his eyes rolled upwards.

The two militiamen hesitated.

'Throw down your clubs. Now!'

They let go of their weapons as if they had suddenly grown red-hot.

'Daggers too.'

They obeyed.

Lorn felt his prisoner starting to weaken: the man slumped forward and was clawing less vigorously at the leather choking him.

It was time to end this.

Lorn freed the man and pushed him roughly forward in the same movement. One of his companions helped him rise to his feet as he coughed, spat and struggled to catch his breath.

Lorn picked up a weighted club and pointed to the other militiaman still stretched out on the ground.

'Take him and piss off.'

He did not need to repeat himself. The militiamen lifted their colleague and fled, shamefaced. It was not until they were about to vanish around the corner of the alley that one of them threatened:

'We'll be seeing you!'

'Yes,' Lorn replied to himself. 'I'm sure of that.'

Lorn waited to be certain that the militiamen were not coming back before worrying about Cadfeld. The bookseller had not managed to stand up. He'd dragged himself over to a wall and was sitting with his back against it, his nose and mouth bloody, and his face swollen with bruises.

Dropping the club he'd picked up, Lorn crouched down near him and leaned over to briefly examine his wounds.

'Are you all right?'

'Not really.'

'Where do you hurt?'

'My head. My ribs. My belly. Just about everywhere, in fact.'

'I think your nose is broken.'

'I'd be surprised if it weren't. Do you think the ladies will still find me attractive?'

Lorn felt the old man's flanks through his rags. Cadfeld grimaced and moaned.

'They also broke two of your ribs.'

'They know their job and are fairly skilled at it. But one always performs best when one enjoys the work, don't you think?'

Lorn straightened up but remained crouching.

'Why were they beating you?'

The bookseller could not refrain from giving a pained smile.

'It seems I haven't paid my taxes.'

'How's that?'

'I'm a shopkeeper, according to them. So I must pay tax.'

As far as shops went, he had a small shack made of rickety boards, tightly squeezed between two houses, where he slept and kept his meagre belongings.

'By the way,' added Cadfeld. 'Thanks. Without you…'

'Can you walk?' Lorn asked.

'Not on my own.'

'I'll help you.'

'Why don't we ask that fellow over there to lend us a hand?'

Lorn turned round and saw Daril who was standing in the alley, looking embarrassed and awkward, not knowing where to put his hands.

'What are you doing here?'

'I… I was following you and…'

And changing tone abruptly, the boy exclaimed, eyes gleaming:

'Bloody hell, my lord! I saw the whole thing! There were four of them, with clubs. And you, you were on your own, and you—'

'Are you finished?' Lorn interrupted him.

'Pardon me?'

'Because if you're finished, I could use your help over here.'

Daril hurried over and between the two of them they eventually managed to get Cadfeld on his feet. He was heavy and, legs feeble, was in a great deal of pain. He nevertheless managed to put one foot in front of another, supported by Lorn and Daril.

When they emerged from the alley, they hesitated over which way to go.

'A doctor should examine you,' said Lorn.

'A doctor,' Cadfeld asked mockingly. 'In Redstone? You're in the wrong neighbourhood, my lord…'

'There's Father Eldrim,' suggested Daril.

'I don't care much for priests,' the old man grumbled.

Lorn ignored him.

'Father Eldrim, you say?'

'He runs a little dispensary for the ill and the destitute,' the boy explained.

'Is it far?'

'It's in Elm Square.'

'Perfect.'

'Couldn't you take me home instead?' asked Cadfeld.

'You need care,' Lorn replied. 'Besides, nobody asked for your opinion.'

Lorn knocked several times on the door.

Despite the late hour, a nun came to open it and, upon seeing the state Cadfeld was in, raised no objections to letting them enter. Lorn and Daril carried the old man inside the dispensary and to a room with ten beds adjoining one another, all of them occupied by two or three patients. A small cot had to be unfolded for Cadfeld.

Following which, Lorn and Daril were asked to wait in a very pleasant little courtyard. Ivy climbed the walls and the columns of an arcade. Benches and lawn chairs were set out here and there, beneath the night sky and the Nebula's pale constellations. The air was warm and the silence soothing.

Tired from hauling Cadfeld practically on his own, despite Daril's well-meaning efforts to assist, Lorn let himself drop into a lawn chair. He asked only for some relief to his aching back and, heaving a sigh, closed his eyes. His breathing grew very regular, to the point that the boy – who for his part had trouble remaining still – thought he'd fallen asleep.

But Lorn, without stirring, his hood over his eyes, said suddenly:

'So, you were following me.'

Daril trembled.

'P… Pardon me?'

'Before, in the alley. You said you were following me.'

'Yes. I mean, no… Well, yes!'

Lorn removed his hood.

He slowly turned his head towards the boy and waited.

Daril swallowed.

'I… I wasn't following you really. But I was going to the same place as you. To your place. We were taking the same route, is all.'

'And what were you going to do at my place?'

'To see you, by gum! But…' He hesitated. 'But I don't think it's the right moment to tell you… to tell you what I want to tell you.'

Intrigued, Lorn turned on his side, propped up on one elbow.

'I'm listening, Daril.'

'Here? Really? Are you sure?'

'You have something better to do?'

'No, no.'

The boy, standing, tugged on the cloth of his tunic and, his back very straight, announced:

'I'm bored at the Archives. Nothing ever happens there. The others, they like it there, but not me. And I spoke to Master Sibellus about it and he's agreeable to letting me enter your service.'

Lorn refrained from smiling.

'My service. Nothing less than that.'

'Yes, my lord. As a valet. Or a squire, since you're a knight. You are a knight, aren't you?'

'I am. And Sibellus has given you leave?'

'He said my only virtue, as an archivist, was punctuality. And all that meant was he knew what time the catastrophes would commence. But he also said I would probably make a good valet.'

'Or a good squire.'

'You need someone in your service, my lord. To take care of your horse and your weapons. To clean the house. Run errands. To do a little of everything in fact…'

'And your father, what does he think?'

Daril looked down.

'To tell you the truth, I was hoping you would be there when I told him. And that you might say it was your idea…'

Lorn gazed at him, unable to explain the affection he felt towards this young man who seemed to have grown up too fast, as if expelled from childhood by an excess of impatience.

'I'll think about it,' said Lorn.

'Really?'

'I haven't said "yes"! But there is a task you could carry out right now.'

'Anything you say, my lord!'

'Do you know where Cadfeld's cabin is?'

'I'm from Redstone, my lord.'

'In the future, whenever possible, answer with a "yes" or a "no".'

'Then, yes. I know.'

'Go there and bring back everything Cadfeld might need. Or anything that might have a little value. I'd be surprised if there's a lock on the door.'

'Understood, my lord.'

And Daril hurried off, almost jostling Father Eldrim who was coming out into the courtyard.

'Pardon me, father!'

Lorn stood up.

Tall, thin and with a stiff bearing, Father Eldrim was about thirty but seemed younger. He was wearing a black robe, for like all the priests of the Church of the Sacrificed Dragon-King, he was in mourning for the deceased deity. The Church of the Dragon-King had supplanted the worship of the other Divine Dragons almost everywhere. In Oriale, as in the rest of the High Kingdom, only the Church of Eyral, the Dragon of Knowledge and Light, could still compete with it.

'Good evening, father.'

'Good evening, my son.'

'I am—'

'I know who you are: people in the neighbourhood talk about nothing except you, these days. I was planning to come and visit you soon. But more importantly, I know what you did this evening for poor Cadfeld, and I thank you.'

Lorn wondered what the black priest's motive might have been for a visit. A courtesy call?

Not likely.

'How is Cadfeld?'

'He's sleeping. I made him drink a potion for the pain and I've bandaged his ribs.'

'Will he recover?'

'He's no longer a young man but he's still sound enough.

Let's hope that a good long rest will be enough. Other than that, we can only pray. It's up to the Sacrificed One to decide.'

Father Eldrim signed himself by brushing the effigy of the Dragon-King that adorned his chest with his index finger: a vertical line from the head to the tip of the tail, then a horizontal line linking the extremities of the spread wings. The Dragon-King had been the wisest and most powerful of the Divine Ones. By sacrificing his own life, he had put an end to the Shadows and allowed victory over the armies of Obscurity and Oblivion – which had in turn sealed the decline of the Ancestrals. But according to the black priests, he had also purified the souls of men, who since that time could aspire to eternal salvation.

Lorn did not believe his soul was eternal. And still less that there was salvation in store for it.

'According to Cadfeld,' he said, 'the militiamen were demanding that he pay a tax. What's going on here?'

The priest sighed and indicated that Lorn should take a seat.

'What's going on,' he replied once they were seated, 'is that our district prefect is greedy and corrupt.'

'Aren't they all?'

Father Eldrim gave a faint, resigned smile.

'More or less, yes. Especially since they are no longer designated by the city council, but appointed by the queen. Our prefect, Talinn Yorgast, excels in his category. He is crushing Redstone with the weight of taxes, skimming off an enormous share for himself and enriching himself still further through various forms of trafficking.'

'Can nothing be done against him?'

'He is the nephew of Esteveris, the queen's minister. Which means he's untouchable.'

Lorn raised an eyebrow.

Taking on the nephew might be a good way of reaching the uncle. Perhaps there was a card there to be played...

'And if anyone takes a mind to protest,' the black priest continued, 'Yorgast has the militia on his payroll.'

'I thought members of the militia were chosen from the inhabitants of the district. And by them.'

'As far as militias go, Redstone's is only one by name. Yorgast has turned it into his own private guard by recruiting thugs – sometimes taking them out of prisons – whose cruelty you witnessed this evening. And at their head, he appointed the worst of the lot: Andara. He's the one responsible for imposing terror on the streets around here.'

'Who is he?'

'No one knows. No doubt a former mercenary. But if you allow me to give you some advice, knight, I'd stay well clear of that monster.'

Lorn remained unperturbed.

'And you? Have you had any problems with Yorgast and his clique?'

'They don't like me because I do what I can to help the needy and give them hope. I think Andara sees me as an opponent to his rule. An adversary.'

Lorn wondered if Andara was entirely mistaken on that score.

The influence of the Church of the Dragon-King had indeed spread, winning new converts each day. Among the powerful, to be sure. But above all, among the less well off, to whom it provided assistance. In these troubled times, it gained popularity by standing for justice, order and hope. As well as by feeding and caring for the poor. All the same, the black priests' charity was not disinterested: it formed part of a strategy of conquest.

'They'll never dare come after me,' added Father Eldrim. 'The Unique protects me.'

He made the sign again.

'You can count on my help,' said Lorn. 'Don't hesitate to call on me if necessary. In the meantime, please allow me to pay for old Cadfeld's care.'

He handed over a small purse. The priest took it, opened it, and said:

'That's far more than necessary.'

'Devote the excess to the most destitute of your flock, father.'

'For them, I thank you.'

Father Eldrim had just pocketed the purse when they heard a drumming on the dispensary door. They exchanged a puzzled look, stood up, and saw Daril, who burst into the courtyard, pursued by two or three nuns he'd charged past.

Red-faced, out of breath, the boy barely managed to enunciate:

'Quickly! My lord... You need... You need to come right away!'

A great fire was blazing in the darkness, at the centre of the square, visible to all.

Dragged out of bed by the militia, the district's inhabitants had gathered in the warm night. Hastily dressed, barefoot in some cases, they kept a safe distance from the glowing inferno without saying a word, fearful and vaguely incredulous, forced to watch an obscene spectacle. There were plenty of dishevelled heads at the windows and curious gawkers arriving by the streets, drawn by the uproar.

Someone was burning the life of a good man.

The flames were tall. Kindled by some flasks of alcohol, they devoured worm-eaten boards, a stool, a crate that had served as a table, a pallet and a blanket, some shabby carpet, torn books whose pages fluttered in the air as they took flame and were lifted by the warm air, and a whole series of odds-and-ends accumulated over time. Indeed, the militiamen were still feeding the bonfire with what remained of the paltry treasures – a stuffed bird that had served as a faithful and patient confidant, a small chipped box decorated with mother-of-pearl patterns, a collection of small empty bottles – that Cadfeld's shack had contained before it was destroyed. It had only offered a feeble resistance. Two or three well-placed kicks had been enough to knock down its loose boards in a cloud of dust.

Andara smiled, satisfied, arms crossed upon his chest while his men finished tossing into the fire the little that a harmless old man had ever possessed. He was convinced the lesson would bear its fruits. This was what it cost to oppose the militia, to oppose him. By attacking his militiamen, someone had directly contested his authority. Like everyone else in the Redstone district, the person in question would learn there were consequences.

7

That night, in the square, Lorn chose not to intervene.

There was nothing that could be done to save Cadfeld's cabin and a public confrontation with Andara would have been premature. So Lorn remained at a distance and kept Daril close to him, while Father Eldrim, for his part, briskly made his way through the crowd. The priest's courage surprised Lorn, not hesitating to take Andara to task, accusing him of cruelty and cowardice.

He impressed Lorn all the more as he had little liking for the black priests or their dogma, which denied the divine nature of the Dragon with the exception of the Dragon-King, whom they called the 'Unique'. According to them, the other Ancestrals were just emanations or incarnations of the Dragon-King. To venerate them was a heresy to be combated by words and preaching, but also by fire and the sword if necessary. In Lorn's view, the Church of the Sacrificed Dragon-King embodied a faith he detested: intolerant, often blind, and sometimes fanatical.

Was it his faith that gave Father Eldrim the guts to stand up to Andara in front of everyone? And to insult him? Perhaps. But he seethed with an anger Lorn believed was genuine. He was clearly outraged and could remain silent no longer. Whatever the risks. Had he even thought about it before acting? Lorn somehow doubted it and observed Andara's reaction.

Immense, massively built, the leader of the militiamen towered over the priest by a head. He withstood the diatribe without flinching. Then he leaned over and, in the midst of a deadly silence, the entire group of onlookers holding their breath, he said a few words in the priest's ear, which Lorn learned of afterwards:

'Go away, father. Go away before it's too late and someone else pays the price for you this evening.'

Then he had added:

'We'll settle this little dispute later…'

Furious but impotent, fearful that innocent victims would suffer Andara's wrath because of him, Father Eldrim had given up and retreated.

'A curse be upon your head!'

'Come now, father. Where's that compassion inspired by the Unique's love for us all?'

Andara had then ordered his men to clear the square.

The militia members unceremoniously drove the crowd away while the fire died. The inhabitants of Redstone went home docilely. Lorn was one of the last to leave, once he was certain that Andara had seen him. They exchanged a glance, each of them recognising in the other a mortal enemy.

Daril did not understand why Lorn had stood by without intervening. But he said nothing about it and, Lorn having taken him into his service with the blessing of his father and Sibellus, he carried out his tasks with zeal during the days that followed.

The boy soon became a familiar figure in the neighbourhood. He was the valet of the knight in the Black Tower and everyone sought his good graces in the hope of finding out a little more about his master. Daril knew better than to say anything, made all the easier since Lorn told him nothing of his projects. Besides, he scarcely had time to enjoy his sudden popularity, Lorn preferring to keep him within the walls surrounding the tower. Lorn was convinced the militia would not let matters lie. He was afraid that Andara would single out Daril to reach him and thus deemed it prudent that the boy not venture out into Redstone too frequently. So he only occasionally entrusted him with running errands or gathering news of Cadfeld, as well as of Father Eldrim, who Lorn was sure was now in danger.

One morning, shortly before noon, Lorn returned from

a printer with some small posters he had ordered two days earlier. He gave them to Daril and told him to put them up in the district, but to keep an eye open and not stray too far from the tower. Daril read one of the leaflets and his eyes opened wide in astonishment. But as Lorn was looking at him and waiting, he dared not ask any questions and went off.

An hour later, he was back.

The rubble and debris that Lorn had cleared formed a pile in the courtyard. It had to be carried away and work started on restoring the tower, which Lorn could not do, even with the help of Daril – who proved to be more dangerous with a hammer than an oil lamp in a powder magazine. Lorn now needed competent workers and a master builder capable of organising the work and supervising the construction site.

The whole Black Tower was threatening to come down and its collapsed roofing had smashed through the upper floors. The simplest thing, no doubt, would have been to demolish it and rebuild. But even if it meant using up all the money given to him by the Count of Argor, Lorn was determined to establish himself in the last Black Tower in Oriale for the same reason he had done as much as possible without assistance: as a symbol.

But there was still one last task he needed to perform on his own, a task he had already postponed for far too long.

'Daril, fetch me the big sledgehammer.'

The drawbridge had remained blocked, and with construction work soon to begin, mules, handcarts and wagons would need to go in and out. Lorn had identified the defective parts in the mechanism, those that – after centuries of disuse – were stopping the chains from unwinding. He had tried to clean them, to remove them, to gently force them. To no avail. They were caught in the rust and sedimentary dust and now formed a single, solid, lump.

It had gone on long enough.

So it was with a heavy mallet on his shoulder that Lorn, in shirtsleeves, crossed the courtyard broiling in the sun that day. After spitting into his palms, he struck and struck again with great steady blows...

…until he could keep it up no longer and, arms stiff and shoulders aching, went to drink some water from the well.

He had exhausted himself for an hour to no avail. The mechanism seemed irreparably stuck in an accretion as solid as granite and Lorn was starting to seriously consider freeing the drawbridge by cutting the chains, something he had resisted doing since the beginning.

He has just poured water on his head from a bucket that Daril had hauled up when, his face still dripping with cool water, he squinted on seeing someone enter the courtyard. He put his spectacles back on and recognised the veteran who had been to conversing with Cadfeld and two others at the inn.

'Go and find something to do, Daril.'

The boy nodded and went off without arguing.

The veteran didn't seem to have a clear idea of how to proceed or where to go. He finally approached Lorn who, expressionless, did not take his eyes off him.

'Good day.'

Lorn replied with a nod of the head.

'Are you thirsty?' he asked.

The man nodded and drank from the bucket.

'It's fresh,' he said, wiping his mouth with his sleeve. 'Thanks.'

Lorn examined him.

He was taller than Lorn, with enormous hands, a thick beard and a gentle gaze. A cross-shaped scar split his right cheekbone. His clothing was humble, patched and worn, but clean. He had old rope sandals on his feet and carried a carefully wrapped sword upon his back.

'I saw the posters,' he explained. 'Is it true, what they say?'

'It's true.'

The former soldier took some time to absorb the news.

For he was a former soldier, Lorn was certain of it, even if he still did not know his name.

'You were at the battle of Urdel?' he asked.

'Yes.'

'What company?'

'Langre-Azure.'

'I was in Langre-Silver,' Lorn declared.

The mutual esteem between the two soldiers was immediate. They sized one another up, until Lorn said:

'There will be some hard knocks and we'll need to get our hands dirty at times. But we'll have a chance to make a difference. For the High King. And for the High Kingdom.'

'That suits me.'

'You don't want to know about the pay?'

'No.'

'What's your name?'

'Liam.'

Lorn held out his hand to the veteran.

'Welcome to the Onyx Guard, Liam.'

They hadn't finished shaking hands when they heard the noise a metallic mass might make striking a rock.

There was a very long creak.

Then a sharp crack and, with a furious clicking of great chains unwinding, the drawbridge lowered with a thud onto the street paving, lifting a thick cloud of dust.

After a moment which stretched into a long silence, Daril appeared.

Dumbfounded but delighted, he was holding the mallet.

Just as Lorn had asked him, he'd found something to do, and one blow had been enough.

8

Talinn Yorgast looked up from the poster that Andara had brought him. It bore the Black Tower's silhouette and the following inscription: 'The Onyx Guard is recruiting.'

'Well?'

'Did you recognise the seal?'

There was a red wax seal fixed to the bottom of the poster. To make it out, Yorgast had to approach one of the torches that illuminated the terrace of his summer garden that evening.

A wolf's head on two crossed swords.

And a crown.

Yorgast recalled the ironic manner in which his uncle had dismissed the idea that the High King's knight might try to reconstitute the Onyx Guard on his own. The calm evinced by the minister had impressed him and he wanted to instil the same effect now.

'The Onyx Guard will not be reborn with a few posters,' he said with a disdainful shrug. 'Is this why you're pestering me, Andara?'

'The Onyx Guard or another, it makes no difference to me,' replied his henchman.

Which disturbed the prefect of the Redstone district.

'Pardon?'

'The troubling thing is that he's recruiting,' explained Andara. 'First, the man takes possession of the Black Tower. Then he gives four of my men a hiding and becomes thick with that blasted priest. Now, he's recruiting.'

'So what?'

'Believe me, this man is dangerous.'

'I know what you're thinking, Andara. There's no question of that.'

'He would disappear. No one would ever know what became of him.'

'No!' snapped Yorgast.

Andara waited for a moment and said calmly:

'He's becoming popular. Soon it will be too late. Sometimes all it takes is for just one man to rise—'

'I know, I know...' the prefect interrupted him.

The situation worried him more than he wanted to let on. He wasn't keen on anyone – and certainly not a royal representative – doing as they pleased in the Redstone district. But Esteveris had been absolutely clear: it was out of the question to touch a single hair on the head of this Lorn Askarian. The signet ring on his finger protected him.

'Keep an eye on him,' said Yorgast. 'But I forbid you to go after him.'

'Understood.'

Andara left, leaving the poster behind.

Talinn Yorgast could say and order what he liked, but he did not know what really went on in Redstone. Andara did and he had a lot more to lose than the prefect if the district slipped from his grasp and its inhabitants started to grow restless. He had done the right thing by burning down that old fool's shack in full view of everyone.

But now, he would have to strike harder.

And higher.

9

Reik Vahrd crossed the Black Tower's drawbridge one morning, at the reins of an old creaking wagon that transported the royal blacksmith's most precious possession: his anvil.

'Our forge may be in ruins, but it does still have an anvil, didn't you know that?' jested Lorn, coming up as Vahrd stepped down from his seat.

'Not like this one.'

'You mean ours isn't as hard as that old head of yours?'

'Not half.'

Happily, they exchanged a warm and virile embrace, the sort that cut off breath, crushed ribs and cracked shoulder blades. Vahrd didn't know any other kind.

'I'm truly glad to see you,' said Lorn.

'Me too.'

'Did you have a good trip?'

'It's a long road from the Citadel...'

'But you came alone? And Naé? Didn't she accompany you?'

The old blacksmith scowled.

'No. I'll explain later.'

Lorn sensed a problem but did not insist. Besides, Vahrd was already changing the subject, looking about him, his hands on his hips.

'So you're really gone and installed yourself in this ruin,' he observed.

Lorn had informed him of his intentions before leaving the Citadel, the same evening he proposed that Vahrd join the Onyx Guard and help him accomplish the mission the king had set for him. Vahrd had asked for a night to think it over before agreeing – and then only on condition that the High King freed him from his service.

Which made him the first man that Lorn had recruited.

The first Onyx Guard.

In the courtyard flooded with sunshine, Lorn saw Liam coming out on the keep's porch, squinting in the dazzling light. He had been working inside when he heard the wagon arrive and had emerged to see what was going on. He was in his shirtsleeves, grey with dust, his brow shining and his armpits darkened by sweat.

Lorn signalled for him to join them.

'Who's that?' asked Vahrd.

'Liam. My first recruit. That is, after you.'

Lorn made the introductions and Liam could not hide his emotion on learning who the other man was. Reik Vahrd was not simply the High King's blacksmith, the person who forged his weapons and armour, the person – to a large extent – on whom Erklant II's life had depended in battle. He had also been the king's companion in arms during several wars both heroic and glorious, at the beginning of Erklant's reign.

Sensing what was going through Liam's mind, Vahrd gave him a friendly, knowing wink.

'That's fine,' he said with a frank smile. 'Glad to make your acquaintance.'

'It's... It's an honour.'

'That will pass after a few drinks... And that one? Another recruit?'

Vahrd pointed to Daril who was approaching, beaming and curious, Yssaris held in his arms.

'In a manner of speaking,' replied Lorn. 'He's been keeping me company for the last few weeks, and I have no cause for complaint. The other one is Daril, my... squire.'

'Hello, Daril.'

'Good morning, my lord.'

Escaping from the boy, the ginger cat went to have a look at the newly arrived cart and the horse that pulled it.

Lorn took Vahrd by the arm.

'Come. I'll show you the forge. Or rather, what's left of it.'

They went for a walk.

Built against the outer wall, the forge had been abandoned, like the rest of the Black Tower. There scarcely remained anything beyond the walls and a few wooden crossbeams, the roof having long since collapsed.

Arms crossed, one shoulder leaning against the doorframe, Lorn watched as Vahrd toured the place, stepping over brush and debris, and examined the forge itself, whose chimney still rose bravely into the air. Lorn used the time to inform the blacksmith of essential matters. He spoke to him of Sibellus, Andara, the prefect Yorgast, and what he had discovered about life in the Redstone district. Vahrd listened in silence, attentively but without interrupting his inspection of the premises. His glance finally landed scornfully on the anvil covered with rust and ivy that stood in the middle of the rubble.

Lorn waited a moment, and then asked:

'So? Naé? Did she decide to stay behind?'

Vahrd shrugged. The gesture did not indicate ignorance, however, but rather embarrassment over how to reply.

'As a matter of fact, she left the Citadel shortly after you did.'

'To go where?'

'I'm not sure. We... We had something of a quarrel.'

'About what?'

Another awkward shrug of the shoulders.

'She didn't like my accepting your offer to join the Onyx Guard at my age. But more than that, she...' Fearing to say too much, Vahrd chose his words carefully. 'She made a decision I did not approve of.'

The old blacksmith's precaution puzzled Lorn.

'Why all this mystery?' he asked.

'It was her choice...' Vahrd blurted out.

Lorn decided not to persist, but Vahrd continued:

'I raised her to be independent and make up her own mind. I wasn't going to stop her doing what she wanted just because it displeased me, was I?'

He seemed be seeking reassurance, some answer Lorn did not possess. Then, abruptly ashamed of having given way to a moment of weakness, the old blacksmith looked down, and Lorn had no idea how to assuage a father's fears.

There was a prolonged silence.

Then Lorn came to a decision that relieved both of them, and acted as if nothing had happened.

The old blacksmith looked over the ruined forge one last time before giving an appreciative nod and saying:

'My anvil will soon be singing in here.'

After Vahrd, others came.

They turned up as summer progressed and scaffolding rose around the Black Tower. Most of them were drawn by rumour. Andara had the posters torn down almost as quickly as they were put up but soon it was no longer necessary to replace them. Word of mouth worked perfectly well, especially among soldiers by trade and veterans nostalgic for the lost glory of the High Kingdom. It was said there was a new First Knight of the Realm and that he was recruiting for the Onyx Guard. A madman, perhaps. But this madman had Reik Vahrd with him, one of the High King's last remaining stalwarts...

So each week new candidates turned up.

Lorn received them in the presence of Vahrd, whom he looked to whenever he felt hesitant. Often, however, a mere glance sufficed to reject a volunteer. Lorn wanted men capable of fighting and riding a horse. But who would also obey orders, and endure pain and fatigue. Above all, he was looking for men obsessed by an ideal, men of honour and duty who had lost everything just as he had and yet preserved within them a secret flame.

A sacred flame.

Lorn recruited only four men in all those weeks.

Dwain, a red-headed colossus with a back striped by scars, who had been a farrier in the army of Ansgarn before being sent to the galleys. Yeras, a scout who – with a slit throat and an arrowhead in his left eye – had been left for dead at the end of a suicide mission in the Grey Steppes. Eriad, a young and attractive blond-headed man who dreamed of great deeds and heroic victories.

And Logan.

The latter showed up one evening with a sword at his side and its twin upon his back. Taciturn, he seemed wary of everyone and barely responded to Lorn's questions. The interview went badly, to the point that the man was already turning to leave when Vahrd called him back.

'Just a minute!'

Rather satisfied to see Logan departing, Lorn stared at the old blacksmith in surprise.

'Mercenary?' asked Vahrd.

'Yes.'

'How long?'

'Almost as long as I can remember.'

'You respect the Code?'

Logan lifted his sleeve and displayed the mark, branded by red-hot iron upon his wrist, borne by all mercenaries who swore to exercise their trade according to the commandments about courage and loyalty set out in the Iron Code.

Vahrd pretended to mull matters over, and then said:

'The two swords, are they merely for show?'

The question was deliberately provocative but Logan didn't rise to it.

'No.'

Another man might have drawn the weapons to put on a demonstration, performed a few practice strokes supposed to demonstrate his skill.

Not Logan.

Vahrd, then, smiled. And without consulting Lorn, he said:

'Be here tomorrow at dawn.'

The mercenary nodded and went off without uttering either a word of thanks or farewell.

'Are you sure?' asked Lorn, watching Logan leave the courtyard.

'Certain,' replied Vahrd.

He had recognised a suffering in the mercenary's eye that was only too familiar to him. The man was in search of redemption.

'On the other hand,' he added, 'I don't care much for Eriad.'

Lorn pulled a face.

'Bah! He dreams of glory a little too much, but so what? He's still young.'

'He's only five years younger than you.'

'I dreamed of glory five years ago.'

Lorn's face grew dark, thinking of who he had once been and could never be again.

The old blacksmith muttered a little more.

But embarrassed at having indirectly – and not at all deliberately – awoken bad memories in his friend, he finally cleared his throat and said:

'Well, let's just say I allow you Eriad and you allow me Logan...'

Lorn nodded.

'What do you make of the others?'

Vahrd thought briefly before replying:

'I like Dwain. I'd rely on him. I'm less sure about Yeras. Even with just the one eye, I reckon he's seen death up too close.'

'And Liam?'

'With him, don't worry. Make him your lieutenant.'

10

Life became more organised over the next few days at the Black Tower.

The first Onyx Guards fraternised and got to know one another, except for Logan who often preferred to remain apart. In the evening, when everyone gathered round a campfire at the end of a hard day's work, he remained silent and ducked away after saluting the company with a brief nod of the head. Their meals together were, however, friendly and often joyful affairs at the foot of the keep, beneath the stars. Sitting on pieces of beams or sacks of plaster, Lorn and his men ate, drank and spoke as people do when making acquaintance, alternating their own stories with questions aimed at others, and giving up some of their own half-secrets.

Daril listened to the talk, delighted, his face heated by the fire, and often he nearly burned the meat he was supposed to be watching. His admiration for Lorn remained as strong as ever, but he positively worshipped Vahrd whose hilarious anecdotes and epic tales enthralled him: in his eyes, the old blacksmith was a sort of demigod stepped out of heroic times. Indeed, the others felt almost the same way about him, impressed by his stature and his experience, but also comforted by his gruff modesty and natural frankness. They nicknamed him 'the Old Man' with a mixture of respect and affection. It rather pleased Vahrd and he allowed them to get away with it, so much that even Lorn sometimes found himself calling him that.

The Old Man enjoyed a special status no one disputed: that of Lorn's close confidant. But following Vahrd's advice, Liam became Lorn's right-hand man. It was a wise choice. The veteran was rigorous and precise, dependable and effective. If

he gave his opinion, it was never more than once and thereafter he carried out orders without further discussion. Discreet
and thorough, he was capable of taking initiatives. Moreover,
he kept his eye on everything and reported to Lorn what he
needed to know; which meant he did not report everything. A
perfect lieutenant.

One of his duties was overseeing the restoration work.

As it was time to tackle the structural repairs in the keep,
Lorn was determined to hire trained workmen and artisans.
For the timbers, he had called upon Daril's father, Elbor Sarne,
and asked him to recommend a capable overseer. Sarne recom-
mended several men for whom he had worked or knew by
reputation, but all of them refused the contract or desisted very
quickly. It could not be a coincidence. Was the prefect Yorgast
pulling strings? Or was Andara making threats? Whatever the
case, the result was plain: no one seemed willing to take charge
of the repair work in the Black Tower.

Except for Sarne himself, whom Lorn finally asked without
concealing the risks involved:

'The news won't please Andara at all.'

'Andara has laid down the law in Redstone long enough,'
Daril's father replied after a moment's reflection.

So the two men sealed their agreement with a handshake.

Lorn did not regret his decision.

Sarne proved to be competent. He had spent enough time
on building sites to be able to direct one himself. He had the
experience and authority required, and enjoyed the respect
and trust of the artisans he hired because he belonged to the
local building trade, like them. He hired the best. The keep
was furnished with scaffolding inside and out, and Lorn and
his men worked without protest, sweating and toiling in the
sunshine like simple manual labourers. The evening found
them tired but glad to be taking part in the rebirth of Oriale's
last Black Tower.

It became their tower.

The one they were building and would defend if necessary.

The first days of labour, however, were terrible for Eriad.

Lorn and Vahrd watched him exhaust himself, while his tender hands that had never seen hard toil were worked bloody. But he did not give up and never complained. His self-sacrifice earned him the esteem of the other Onyx Guards, who until then had regarded him with a wariness tinged by scorn. Even Vahrd acknowledged that he had perhaps been mistaken and recruited Eriad to help him, along with Dwain, restore the forge.

The work was proceeding well, accompanied by the blows of hammers, the singing of saws, the squeaking of pulleys and the comings and goings of carts. The scaffolding climbed higher and higher about the keep. The barracks were made habitable. The forge gained a roof. No incident disturbed the progress of the building site, but Lorn remained on edge.

The Black Tower's forge was working only two weeks after Vahrd's arrival. The royal blacksmith could then repair the equipment and tools used by the workmen engaged in restoring the tower, but also make the kit that the new Onyx Guard needed.

First of all, Lorn asked Vahrd to forge the armour and reinforced hoods that would allow them to be recognised in public. He wanted them to wear black leather lined with chain mail, in order to combine suppleness and sturdiness. And he wanted hoods rather than helmets, which restricted the field of vision too much. The blacksmith produced several models which Lorn tried on one after another, requesting an adjustment here, an improvement there. And each time, Vahrd carried out the modifications. Often, the hammer rang against his anvil until well into the night.

Finally, one evening after dinner, Daril came seeking Lorn. 'Your armour is ready, my lord.'

Lorn followed the boy across the courtyard. Night had fallen and, with the workmen gone, the Black Tower seemed deserted. A peaceful silence reigned beneath the Nebula. Only Logan was still on watch.

Vahrd was waiting on the forge's threshold, his broad silhouette outlined by red-orange light. He bade Lorn to enter and presented him with the armour he had just finished. Lorn immediately tried it on. He admired its lightness and made a few movements to test its flexibility.

'Well?' the blacksmith enquired.

'It feels like this is finally right.'

'I was inspired by a type of armour I saw a long time ago. The man who wore it said he took it from a Drakhen knight. I didn't believe it, but the armour was handsome. A little heavier than this, perhaps.'

'It's perfect.'

Lorn took two swords from a rack, threw one to Vahrd, adopted a guard stance, and the two men sparred within the forge, much to Daril's delight. It wasn't a matter of winning, but rather of testing attacks, parries and feints, all of the sequences likely to be carried out in mortal combat. The duel looked like the real thing, except that Lorn and the blacksmith were smiling and at times exaggerating their gestures. The boy did not miss the slightest move, even miming a sidestep or a riposte on occasion.

'Bravo,' said Lorn when the bout was over.

'Thank you.'

Vahrd was out of breath, but his arm hadn't weakened, as Lorn had seen for himself.

'You weren't just testing the armour, were you?' the old royal blacksmith asked him.

'No,' admitted Lorn. 'Sorry.'

'Don't be. I quite understand.'

A silence settled in the forge as Daril helped Lorn remove the armour. The knight could easily have managed on his own, but the boy took his duties as squire very seriously. And squires helped knights remove their armour, didn't they? Lorn and Vahrd exchanged a glance and tried not to smile.

At last, Daril headed off carrying the armour, with instructions to grease it in order to make the leather more supple and to protect the steel mail.

'The next armour you make will be your own,' said Lorn to the blacksmith from the forge's doorstep. 'The others will come and see you after that so you can take their measurements…'

'Understood.'

'We may need that armour soon, Vahrd.'

'I know.'

Like Lorn, Vahrd had a hunch that Andara would not stand idly by for long without moving against them. For the moment, he contented himself with keeping a watch on the Black Tower and its occupants, while his militiamen made their presence felt more than ever in Redstone and imposed a silent menace on the district.

'Are you planning to go and see Sibellus, this evening?'

Lorn nodded.

'I'm already late.'

At first, after dinner, he had tried to study the documents the master archivist had sent him on his own. But being very tired, he had often fallen asleep over a legal text or a commentary on a little-known excerpt from the *Chronicles*. So he'd adopted the habit of visiting Sibellus to ask him to read and explain the most important texts. Lorn thus assured himself of the legality of his prerogatives as First Knight of the Realm and discovered what the Onyx Guard had once been. Created and then dissolved by Erklant I, it had entered into legend and seemed to belong to an unreal, heroic past. But the duties and attributions of this elite troop were by no means imaginary.

'Be careful,' Vahrd advised him.

'I'll be back before midnight.'

'Ask Logan to go with you. In any case, he never sleeps, that one.'

'As you like. But I don't believe Andara will attack me directly.'

'Even so, keep an eye out.'

'I promise.'

Lorn went off with a smile.

'And take Logan with you!' Vahrd reminded him from within the forge.

11

Their troubles started one morning when Sarne arrived late, halted the building work and asked to speak with Lorn alone.

'What's wrong?' asked Daril in alarm, seeing his father's grave expression.

But Sarne did not explain and followed Lorn into the keep, where they shut themselves in.

'Things will turn out fine, lad,' Vahrd murmured to Daril.

All eyes were now turned towards the keep's door, an odd silence falling over the Black Tower.

The interview did not last long.

The two men came back out. Lorn assembled his guards while Sarne went to explain to the bemused artisans and workmen that they would be paid for the week but should go home and were free to accept other contracts. Work on the tower would not resume until further notice.

'Blast it, Lorn! What's going on?' Vahrd demanded to know impatiently as Sarne talked things over with his employees.

'He was threatened,' said Lorn. 'Last night some men broke into his home and ordered him to abandon the building site. Three of his master artisans received the same visit.'

'The bastards,' Liam swore softly.

'Andara?' asked Yeras for form's sake.

'Definitely,' said Lorn. 'Although Sarne said he did not recognise the men who terrorised his wife and him.' He turned to Daril. 'Your mother's all right, Daril. But no doubt she needs you by her side. Go to her.'

Looking very pale, the boy stammered his thanks and left. Vahrd then signalled Logan to follow him. The mercenary nodded and obeyed.

'We need to stop these filthy swine!' said Dwain.

'Without proof of their crimes, there's not much we can do,' objected Liam.

'Doesn't matter,' retorted Yeras. 'We know full well the Redstone militia is behind this. We just have to corner a few one evening and have a little talk with them…'

'Then we would be behaving just like them,' protested Eriad.

Yeras turned towards the young man, looked him straight in the eye and, very calmly, asked:

'So?'

Vahrd spoke up:

'Sarne is perhaps lying when he says he didn't recognise the men who threatened him. To avoid retaliation. If he agreed to testify—'

'No,' said Lorn. 'He's already done enough.'

They fell silent and turned towards the artisans and workmen who were putting away their things, packing up their tools and one by one leaving the site. Some of them addressed discreet but friendly farewells to the guards. Most of them left with a slow step and bowed heads, like a defeated garrison delivering a stronghold to the enemy.

'They're ashamed to be leaving,' Liam remarked.

'They know they were doing more than just rebuilding a tower,' said Lorn.

It was, in some sense, a small victory.

'Then don't let them go,' said Vahrd. 'Detain them. Or at least, propose that they continue work on the project. Some of them will accept. Maybe others will come.'

'Without a master builder?'

'We'll find another—'

'Really? Where? And when?' The blacksmith wanted to reply but Lorn did not give him time. 'And even if we restarted the site? How long do you think it would be before Andara killed someone? They're not messing about.'

'And that's precisely why we need to strike back hard! Believe me, Andara belongs to a race of men who only know one law: might makes right.'

Lorn looked round at his guards. All of them, except Liam,

agreed with the Old Man and he felt their disappointment when he said:

'I'll find a solution. But for now, we do nothing.'

'Damn it, Lorn!' protested Vahrd. 'You can't—'

'Yes, I can!' snapped Lorn. 'And I will! Do I have to remind you who commands here?'

Fuming, Vahrd balled his fists but succeeded in restraining himself.

'I...' he started to say. 'I don't understand how you can declare yourself defeated so quickly.'

'Who says I'm declaring defeat?'

'That's what it looks like, at any rate.'

With those words, the blacksmith turned on his heels and walked off.

'Where are you going?' asked Lorn.

'To have a drink,' replied the other man without looking back.

He crossed the courtyard on the double and left the Black Tower muttering darkly.

Liam gave Lorn a questioning look.

'Leave him,' said Lorn. 'He'll be back once he's calmed down.'

At the end of the afternoon, unable to concentrate, Lorn closed the heavy legal volume he was trying to read and called for Liam who arrived almost right away.

'Yes?'

'Has the Ol—' Lorn caught himself. 'Has Vahrd returned?'

'No.'

Lorn sighed, beginning to feel a knot of worry. And as he put on his black armour, he said:

'Go and find him. He shouldn't be far. You'll probably locate him in the first tavern you come across.' Then, thinking it over, he added: 'Or perhaps in that inn, where he usually goes...'

'The Griffin?'

'Yes, that's the one. Start there.' He put on the belt with his Skandish sword. 'As for me, I'll be at the Royal Archives for an hour or two.'

Liam nodded.

The Black Tower was now very calm and silent. Preoccupied and dissatisfied, Lorn welcomed seeing the bustling streets again and walked briskly to the Archives, crossing the Redstone district without worrying about who he might run into or – possibly – who might be following him.

When it came down to it, Vahrd was right. The Onyx Guard could not stand by and do nothing. They had to strike back at Andara, or else lose the small degree of credibility they had just started to gain with the local people. The Black Tower had given rebirth to a fragile hope among Redstone's inhabitants, that royal authority and justice would be restored. But now that his building work was interrupted, it could become an unfulfilled promise and bolster the case of the cynics and the resigned, imprisoned in its scaffolding like a lame leg in its splint.

Sibellus gave Lorn a warm welcome and listened as the knight told him about the interruption of the building work and his quarrel with Vahrd. The master archivist confirmed that he was right not to confront Andara immediately, a misstep the militia leader was no doubt trying to provoke.

'You are First Knight of the Realm. You know as well as I do that your title protects you. I would not be surprised to learn that the prefect Yorgast has forbidden Andara from attacking you. On the other hand, Andara probably believes he's authorised to defend himself and no doubt he's just waiting for you to strike the first blow. If you attack him, you must do so cleverly enough that he has no legitimate grounds to retaliate.'

'Or else hard enough that he does not get back up off the ground.'

Worried by the determination he saw in Lorn's eyes, Sibellus nodded glumly and conceded:

'Of course, of course...' Then, reconsidering, he said: 'Wait, I want to show you something...'

The master archivist rose, leaving Lorn in his study, and came back with a very old notebook whose thick leather cover was worn, dog-eared, scratched and even burned in places.

'Here, have a look at this.'

The notebook was open to a double page covered with a drawing representing a fortified gate. It was accompanied by spidery handwritten annotations.

'It looks like a travel journal, but one that might have been written by a madman,' explained Sibellus. 'I came across it by accident and only the Grey Dragon knows how it found its way here. Some pages have been torn out. Some are indecipherable and others make no sense. But my attention was caught by this drawing, which seems to be a faithful rendering. Read the inscription on the pediment above the gate. It seems as though someone tried to erase it with a chisel, but the drawing is precise enough to allow you to recognise the coat of arms and make out a few of the words...'

Lorn squinted and indeed recognised the coat of arms. The head of a wolf or dog, and two crossed swords: it was certainly that of the Onyx Guard.

But as for the text...

'It's in Old Imelorian,' said Lorn. 'But this is the motto of the Onyx Guard, isn't it?'

'It says: "The High Kingdom we serve. The High Kingdom we defend."'

Lorn looked up.

A shiver of excitement had run through him, as if he'd discovered the first element in a mystery unknown to him until now, but whose importance he sensed.

'Where was this drawing made?' he asked. 'What does it represent? What is that place?'

'I don't know. It's said to be a desolate site the notebook's author supposedly discovered after days and days of wandering... But that isn't the main thing. This notebook is ancient and I surmise that the inscription copied by its author is even older. So this motto that certain parties wanted to erase was no doubt the Onyx Guard's first...'

Lorn then thought about the inscription above the gate of the Black Tower and realised what the master archivist was driving at. There was only one word different between the

Onyx Guard's two successive mottoes, but it changed everything.

' "The High Kingdom we serve. The High Kingdom we defend." The High Kingdom, Lorn. Not the High King. Before becoming the High King's protectors, the Onyx Guards were originally protectors of the High Kingdom...'

Lorn returned to the Black Tower at dusk.

As he made his way, he thought about the strange travel journal tucked inside his armour. According to Sibellus, nothing permitted one to guess who the author was, but various clues led one to believe that he or she had lived about a century before. Other questions, however, excited Lorn's curiosity. What was this place the fortified gate defended? Had it really existed? And if it wasn't born of the demented imagination of some lunatic, did it still exist? And where? Lorn hoped very much to decipher the pages filled with spidery writing that Sibellus had failed to read. The text, he'd seen, was often absurd. But perhaps it concealed a hidden meaning.

And then there was the mystery of the Onyx Guard's motto.

Why had it changed? Was this modification as significant as Lorn surmised? Had it long preceded the disbanding of the Onyx Guard, during the reign of Erklant I? Were these two events linked in some manner or another?

Lost in his speculations, Lorn had almost forgotten about the rest. But reality came rushing back when he found the Black Tower in an uproar, with several dozen onlookers gathered before its drawbridge. He pushed his way through the crowd to enter and, in the courtyard, saw Liam and Logan keeping an eye on things.

'I was about to send someone for you,' said Liam.

'What's going on?'

'We found Vahrd. He's in the forge.'

Lorn hastened to the blacksmith's workplace, where Yeras was guarding the door.

Inside, Vahrd was stretched out on his cot, with Dwain and Eriad keeping him company. The old blacksmith had received several blows to the face and a blood-stained bandage was wrapped around his right hand. Numbed by alcohol, his eyes glassy, he was mumbling and complaining to himself.

'He fought with the militiamen,' explained Eriad. 'We arrived too late.'

'His hand?'

'They nailed it to a table before leaving. To make an example.'

Drawing Dwain aside, Lorn sat down at Vahrd's bedside.

'How are you?' he asked with compassion.

The old blacksmith recognised him through the fog of drink and grumbled:

'You're not going to be pleased...'

'Why don't you tell me about it?'

Vahrd groaned.

'As you wish. I was drinking. Peacefully... And then these... these blokes came in. Militiamen. They hadn't seen me. They wanted money in exchange for their... protection. But the innkeeper couldn't pay them so they started to... And there were five of them but I gave them a nasty thrashing before they overpowered me.' Vahrd grew heated. 'Bloody hell, Lorn! Would you have let them have their way, if you'd been there?'

'No,' Lorn acknowledged.

He stood up, looked at Vahrd from a moment, and then, his mind made up, he said with a smile:

'You win, you old fool. We're going to wage war against them. But we'll do it my way.'

'Glad to hear it. But be careful. Andara's men may be cowards that only attack when they have the numbers, but above all they're killers. Being First Knight won't protect you from a well-aimed dagger thrust.'

'He's right,' Dwain intervened. 'You might have a bad run-in with someone. Have an unfortunate accident.'

'And we'd find your body the next morning, stripped of that signet ring,' said Vahrd. 'Believe me, that worries Esteveris far more than it does scum like Andara...'

Dwain nodded.

Lorn shrugged but Vahrd seized him by the sleeve with his bandaged hand.

'Promise me, Lorn. Look what they did to me.'

Lorn received an official summons to the Royal Palace the following morning.

12

'In the middle of Oriale's nine hills there was a tenth, taller and vaster than the rest. It was occupied by the Palace, which had once been that of the kings of Langre and before them, of the Great White Dragon of Knowledge and Light. Ringed by gates and ramparts raised with the help of magic against the powers and influences of the Dark, the Hill of the High Kings was like an island with a palace containing countless courtyards and terraces, temples and private residences, towers and gardens, orchards, a wood, a river, ponds, ancient ruins and a port bathed by the waters of the Eirdre. It was said that one could live an entire life there and it would not be enough to explore all of it.'

Chronicles (The Book of Oriale)

Lorn passed through the Bronze Lions Gate and presented himself at the guard post. A palace usher was waiting for him. The functionary greeted Lorn with considerable respect and bade him to follow. The knight having nodded his assent, a small escort of halberdiers fell into step behind them.

Lorn grew tense.

The summons had arrived that very morning, brought by a royal messenger on horseback who did not go unnoticed in the Redstone district. He was trailed by several curious onlookers who had halted before the Black Tower while he crossed the drawbridge, which remained lowered, and entered the courtyard. Greatly impressed by the rider's livery, Daril had hurried to find Lorn. The latter had descended from the scaffolding, in shirtsleeves and covered in perspiration, his hair full of dust.

'What is it?' Liam had enquired after the messenger left.

The Onyx Guards were continuing restoration work on the

building as best they could in the absence of Sarme and his team of skilled artisans, when Lorn did not assign them other missions. That morning, only Yeras was absent. The others followed Lorn and Liam into the forge, where they now usually held their meetings, beyond earshot of any eavesdroppers.

'I've been summoned to the Palace at noon,' Lorn had announced after reading the message.

'By whom?' Dwain had asked.

'It doesn't say. But the seal on the bottom of the page is that of the High Kingdom.'

'A royal summons,' Liam had observed.

'Beware,' was Vahrd's only comment, working the joints of his wounded hand.

Lorn thought about the blacksmith's warning as he followed the usher through the Palace corridors, with six halberdiers at his back. How many arbitrary arrests had begun this way since Queen Celyane had been in power? How many had answered a summons before being imprisoned for a month, six months, a year? And how many had disappeared for good? It was difficult to separate rumour from fact. Because she was hated, the most far-fetched gossip circulated about the queen. But her cruelty and brutality, especially when she was angry, were by no means mere legend. As for Esteveris, he had waited for no one to start practising political assassination.

Lorn was convinced he would be meeting the minister, as was bound to happen eventually. He knew Esteveris had been keeping watch on him since his arrival in Oriale. Thanks to his spies, the minister had certainly been informed of his every deed and gesture. But the things Esteveris still did not know must intrigue him all the more. And perhaps even alarm him. What goal was Lorn really pursuing? Did he obey the king or himself? And to what end? Esteveris was too able a politician not to worry about the appearance of a new piece on the chessboard of the High Kingdom.

Lorn noticed that the usher was walking slower and taking more time than necessary to open certain doors. The man presented an expressionless face but his hands shook slightly, which aroused Lorn's wariness fully. All his senses on alert, he made ready to draw his sword and paid particular attention to the movements of the halberdiers at his back. They did not pass many people in the corridors and were walking through a part of the Palace Lorn did not know well. He had not really worried about this at first, thinking that Esteveris wanted to receive him in complete privacy. But these almost deserted hallways were also perfect for an ambush: a dagger thrust; the assassin who escaped as easily as he struck and would never be caught; the halberdiers who chased him and came back empty-handed, but not before Lorn bled out his life.

Lorn felt vulnerable.

Had he been mistaken in refusing to allow Liam to accompany him? A witness was always embarrassing and two swords were always better than one...

The usher left him in a cloister where climbing roses decorated the columns and arches. The halberdiers remained, watchful and impassive sentinels.

Troubled, Lorn wondered again who had summoned him to the Palace. Esteveris? It had to be someone authorised to use the High Kingdom's seal.

The queen? It was unlikely. And besides, why would she receive him here?

Prince Yrdel, then, the king's elder son and first heir to the throne? But like everyone in Oriale, Lorn knew he was in Angborn, charged with making preparations for the queen's arrival there.

Or else...

In the cloister's garden, where the central lanes of yellow earth crossed among the flowerbeds, the shrubbery and arbours, Lorn saw a sword planted in the ground.

He approached it.

The sword was a Sarmian rapier and something was hooked to its guard.

A mask in black leather.

Smiling, Lorn took off his doublet, rolled up his shirtsleeves, undid his belt, rid himself of his heavy Skandish weapon, removed his spectacles and put on the mask.

Then, he seized the rapier and looked carefully around him.

Two men soon appeared, each of them arriving from opposing points of the cloister. They too were in shirtsleeves. They too held rapiers identical to the one Lorn was holding.

And they were wearing masks.

One white. The other red.

They attacked Lorn together and combat was engaged. Rapid, skilful combat, but also joyful: the combat of three complicit fencers who knew one another perfectly.

The combat of three friends.

They fought one another two against one, but as the single fighter weakened, one of the two others immediately turned against his momentary ally. Through betrayal and turnaround, the combat was constantly switching assailants and defenders. Sometimes, each of the three fought only for himself and they attacked, parried and riposted in every direction. The steel rang, hissed and cleaved the air at the height of heads and bellies. Although no blood was shed, the fencers nevertheless did not spare one another. There were shoulder blows, elbow shoves and nasty trips. And with every feint, every ruse that worked, there came a burst of happy, mocking laughter.

At last, they could keep it up no longer.

Out of breath but delighted, they removed their fencing masks before falling into one another's arms with great smiles filled with emotion;

As they had when they were adolescents and trained together, Alan wore the white mask and Enzio wore the red one.

As for Lorn, he had always preferred the black.

An hour later, without leaving the Palace, they ended up having lunch on the grass by a pond, in the shade of some weeping willows. They were full, a little tipsy and idly watching the carp stirring the surface of the clear water.

'Hi have ha hoose hooth,' said Enzio, pushing one of his molars with the tip of his tongue.

'What's that?' asked Alan, whose cheekbone bore a handsome bruise.

'Hi haid… I said I have a loose tooth.'

Lorn smiled.

'It's going to take a while before I feel sorry for you.'

In addition to a split lip, Lorn himself had taken a blow to the ribs that still ached. Despite that, he felt good and more relaxed than he had since his liberation from Dalroth. The wine certainly played a part. Along with the enchanting, peaceful setting, the radiant sun, the warm, perfumed air. But above all, he was reunited with his two friends.

Elenzio de Laurens was the son of the powerful Duke of Sarme and Vallence, in whose home Lorn and Alan had grown up. It was traditional for princes of the High Kingdom to be educated by their godfather. Ordinarily, the godfather of a prince was chosen among the high nobility of the realm, but for his third son, King Erklant had preferred to honour a foreign ruler who enjoyed his full esteem and trust. At the age of twelve, therefore, Alan was sent to Sarme. Lorn accompanied him there and they both benefited from the same excellent education as Enzio, with whom they soon formed a deep, sincere friendship that would prove lasting.

Enzio's gaze was caught by Lorn's signet ring.

'First Knight of the Realm,' he said. 'Nothing less than that... Does that mean I must call you "sire"?'

Lorn chuckled.

'You cretin. It would serve you right if I made you.'

Enzio eyes widened.

'You could? Really?'

'In principle, yes. Except in the presence of the High King.'

'Oh?'

'Stop pulling Enzio's leg, sire. You don't want me to start calling you "father", do you?' Alan asked ironically.

'I find you've been leading a rather dissipated life, son.'

They burst out laughing.

Enzio picked up a bottle which passed from hand to hand, and then the prince said:

'Tell us instead about your Onyx Guard, Lorn.'

'It's not *my* Onyx Guard: it's *the* Onyx Guard. The king wanted me to re-establish it.'

'To what end?' asked Enzio.

'That of restoring his authority over the High Kingdom.'

'Do you have money?' enquired Alan.

'A little.'

'Men?'

'Some.'

'That's not much.'

'No. But it's a start.'

Enzio intervened:

'Is that why the High King made you First Knight?'

'I believe so.'

'You deserve it, Lorn. You've always deserved it,' said the Sarmian heir, patting his friend's shoulder.

'Thank you.

'I second that,' said Alan, lifting the bottle. 'To the First Knight of the Realm!'

And each of them drank another gulp of wine.

'All the same,' the prince continued. 'You might have told us when you returned to Oriale. Or even before.'

'I didn't know you were at the Palace.'

'Did you even bother to find out?'

'No, that's true. But I had a lot to do.'

'And why don't you take up residence here in the Palace? With Enzio here, it would be like the good old times.'

'The Black Tower is almost rebuilt. I'm better off there.'

'So that everyone understands that you have nothing to do with the powers-that-be, is that it?' Enzio suggested.

Lorn turned to him.

'Yes. Something like that.'

Elenzio de Laurens had always been the most able and the most wily of the three of them. He had inherited it. A talent for intrigue and a taste for plotting ran in the de Laurens family.

Enzio knew the impact of symbols in politics.

'There's much talk of you here in the Palace,' said Alan.

'And what do people say?'

'They're wondering about you, mostly. And it appears you've been making life difficult for Redstone's militia. Yorgast must be unhappy.'

'Who's Yorgast?'

'The prefect of the Redstone district,' explained Lorn. 'The militia there is in his pocket. He's ambitious and venal. Corrupt.'

'And Esteveris's nephew!' Alan added.

'That's right,' acknowledged Lorn. 'And Esteveris's nephew.'

That detail was of some importance and Enzio understood it. He looked Lorn in the eye with a faint knowing smile. His friend had definitely not chosen the Redstone district by accident.

'But tell me, what brings you to Oriale?' asked Lorn, pulling a plate of cheese closer.

'An ambassadorial mission,' replied Enzio. 'My father has charged me with representing him for the cession of Angborn.'

Lorn greeted this news with an appreciative expression.

It was a handsome honour that Enzio's father had bestowed on him. But it also meant that the duke, the High King's old friend and companion in arms, did not wish to witness in person the triumph of a policy that he condemned. But nor did he want to risk provoking a diplomatic crisis with the High Kingdom. The duke having fallen ill to a highly opportune fever, the duchies of Sarme and Vallence would be represented officially and with dignity by the eldest son in place of the father.

'The royal cortege leaves in two weeks,' said Alan.

'Are you going?'

'Everyone is! My mother, my brother, Esteveris. Me. And all the ambassadors and foreign representatives in attendance here at the Palace.'

'But before we leave, I'm giving a dinner,' announced Enzio. 'You're invited, of course.'

Lorn grimaced.

'Liss will be there,' Enzio informed him.

Lorn fell silent and his face slightly paled.

'I don't think that's such a good idea...'

'I believe she would love to see you again. You could talk to one another.'

'I'll think about it.'

'That's all I ask of you, Lorn. But I can assure you that she's missed you. My sister hasn't forgotten you.'

*

A little later, Alan showed Lorn the way out of the Palace.

'Are you all right?' he asked. 'I saw the mention of Alissia shook you just now. You still love her, don't you?'

'I don't know. I really don't know.'

'And other than that. How are you?'

'I'm fine. The High King has given me a purpose. That helps to keep me upright.'

'There's no shame in leaning on a friend's shoulder sometimes.'

They had arrived in the last courtyard of the royal apartments, where it was agreed Lorn would leave Alan.

They exchanged a hug.

'It would be good if you could send news without forcing me send you another summons,' said the prince.

'I promise.'

'Do you need anything at all? For your tower, for your guard, for yourself? If it's in my power, you only need to ask.'

Lorn thought about it and said:

'Horses. Good ones.'

'Done.'

'Thank you.'

'See you soon, Lorn. Take care of yourself.'

'See you soon, Alan.'

Lorn went straight back to the Black Tower.

That evening, ten magnificent steeds arrived from the Palace.

13

One morning, Lorn lined up his men for inspection in the courtyard of the Black Tower.

For the first time, all of them were wearing the black leather and chain mail armour the blacksmith had designed, with the emblem of the Onyx Guard – a wolf's head and two crossed swords – over the heart. They were grave-faced, dignified and proud. Eriad tried to make a good impression alongside the others. Vahrd's hand was still bandaged and his face marked by the blows he had suffered, but he stood up straight and his gaze was more determined than ever. Logan, impassive and gloved, was armed with his twin blades. Dwain held, resting upon his shoulder, a warhammer that an ordinary man would have found difficult to lift with both hands. Wearing a leather patch over his left eye, Yeras had a sword at his side and a Gheltish dagger in his boot. Liam bore upon his back the big sword that was his only possession.

Satisfied, Lorn turned to Daril who was approaching. The boy carried in his hand a bucket of paint in which a brush was soaking and a large piece of cardboard under his arm.

'Are you ready?' Lorn asked him.

'Yes, my lord.'

'Keep an eye open and don't stray from us, all right? And if things really turn nasty, take refuge inside the dispensary.'

'Understood.'

'I promised Sibellus that nothing would happen to you if I took you into my service. Don't make me a liar.'

They mounted the splendid steeds sent to them by Alan and crossed the lowered drawbridge, Lorn leading the way and Daril discreetly trailing, on foot, a few paces to the rear. Indeed, he was barely noticeable. Lorn and his escort of black riders attracted every gaze.

The armour and stern expressions of those wearing it were having the desired effect.

When they arrived, a crowd had already assembled in Elm Square, in front of Father Eldrim's dispensary. It consisted of inhabitants of the district alerted by word of mouth. But Andara and ten of his militiamen were also present, standing back in the shadows beneath the elm trees that gave the square its name.

Lorn dismounted and knocked on the dispensary door.

While waiting for it to open, he turned towards the crowd and wondered how many of them were there out of sympathy for Cadfeld and how many had come to watch a new act play out in what looked to be a tragedy. For there had been several incidents in recent days between the militia and the Black Tower, and no one doubted that Andara would strike. The only question was where and when.

Aware of the danger Lorn was risking by exposing himself in this manner, his men remained particularly vigilant. Still in their saddles, Dwain, Eriad and Logan guarded the access to the porch. A few steps up, Yeras scanned the crowd with a slow gaze, a crossbow armed and ready in his hand. As watchful as the others, Liam and Vahrd were only a leap away from Lorn.

The door opened and Father Eldrim appeared, followed by Cadfeld on the arm of a nun. The old man was still a sorry sight despite the care he'd received and the time that had passed since he was beaten up. He had grown thin. His face was bruised and he walked with small footsteps, leaning on a cane. He seemed very fragile and all those who saw him were moved.

Cadfeld stood still for a moment on the porch, in full view of everyone, looking dazed and hesitant.

At that moment, in the midst of a great silence, someone applauded.

And then another.

And a third, a fourth, and a fifth.

And as the militiamen did not intervene, the applause

spread, becoming stronger and more rapturous. Of course, it was for Cadfeld. But it also marked a longing for freedom, the stirrings of revolt. Not everyone clapped, but those that did so congratulated themselves on their daring; proud of their newfound boldness, they were sending a message to the militia.

Lorn knew it as well as Andara.

From on top of the steps, he exchanged stares with the leader of the militia over the heads of the noisy crowd that separated them. Andara could not see Lorn's eyes. Just two dark rectangles that reflected the sunshine. However, he did not doubt that they were filled with a look of challenge. He clenched his jaw and balled his fists, trying to remain impassive.

Without taking his eyes off Andara, Lorn leaned to the side towards Father Eldrim.

'Are you still determined to do this, father?'

'I am.'

'You can still back down.'

'I know. Let's do it.'

Lorn then gave a nod to Daril who was waiting at the bottom of the steps. The boy joined them on the porch and placed the sheet of cardboard he was carrying on the dispensary door. It was a stencil which he daubed with black paint in a few brushstrokes.

Curious, the crowd quietened down and soon saw the dripping drawing that remained on the door: two crossed swords whose meaning was obvious.

The Onyx Guard protected this house and those who dwelled in it.

Lorn spread his arms to demand silence.

'Residents of Redstone! I am Lorn Askarian, First Knight of the Realm. Starting from today, in the name of the High King and by virtue of the powers he conferred on me, I offer you the protection of the Onyx Guard! All you need is to want it and to show that by tracing this emblem upon your door! These swords are ours! They will protect you and I defy anyone to oppose them!'

A shiver ran through his audience.

In a state of uncertainty, everyone turned towards Andara.

Jostling elbows, craning necks, standing on tiptoe to see how he was going to react.

Standing completely still, the leader of the militia said nothing, his eyes flashing with anger. Then he gave a curt order and spun on his heels to stalk away, followed by his men.

The crowd watched him leave in humiliation without really believing it, before breaking out into sudden joy. There were shouts, bravos, laughter and cheers.

'There,' said Lorn with a grave expression. 'War has been declared.'

'I hope you know what you're doing, my son.'

'Andara will not dare to come after me. But be wary, father. He could come after you.'

'The Unique will protect me.'

Once again, Lorn wondered how much of the absolute confidence shown by the black priest in the face of danger was due to true courage and how much to blind faith.

'But don't be fooled yourself,' Father Eldrim continued. 'These people are applauding and cheering now. They're here in numbers and feel strong. They're intoxicated by the moment. It's giving them courage because it's making them reckless. But then they're going to return home. Alone. And they're going to reflect. They will think of everything they have to lose and become afraid once more. They will tell themselves that you can't protect them all, and they'll be right.'

As Lorn said nothing, the priest turned towards him and insisted:

'Won't they?'

'There's no war without casualties, father.'

The noise in the square was so loud they could barely hear one another, to the point that Father Eldrim believed he'd misunderstood.

'What did you say?'

'I said you're right, father. I can't protect all these people from the militia. Or their families. Or their houses. Or their shops.'

'Some of them are going to pay the price for their audacity today.'

'Yes. Sooner or later, Andara will wreak revenge for the humiliation he just suffered.'

Containing a growing anger, the black priest stared at Lorn, who for his part stood watching the crowd.

'And that doesn't bother you?'

'It's inevitable. So I accept it.'

'You accept it, but that doesn't cost you much,' the priest reproached him. 'And it's just too bad if innocent victims pay for your ambition. Because nothing matters more than the Black Tower, does it?'

Lorn forced himself to stay calm. He took in a deep slow breath and, after a silence, said:

'Some priests, black priests like you, came to Dalroth once. They prayed a lot, said a few masses and heard the prisoners' confessions. I remember one of them. An old man who had been a chaplain. He'd accompanied armies on campaign and was familiar with all the world's horrors. Since he was asking me to confess my sins, I told him that the biggest sinners, at Dalroth, weren't the prisoners, no matter what they may have done. Because I did not deserve to suffer what I endured there, every day and every night, father. And do you know what that old man told me?'

'No.'

'He told me that the sufferings and misfortunes inflicted upon us in this world did not matter at all. All that mattered was the salvation of my eternal soul.'

Lorn fell silent.

'And... so?' Father Eldrim asked hesitantly.

'Take care of their souls,' Lorn said, indicating the crowd with his chin. And turning to the priest, he lowered his spectacles slightly so that the other man could not fail to see the icy fire blazing in Lorn's mismatched eyes. 'Take care of their souls, and leave the rest.'

With Lorn at their head, the Onyx Guards escorted Cadfeld to the Black Tower, where it was agreed the bookseller would complete his convalescence. They installed him in an old shed they had fixed up and which Daril had furnished and prepared as best he could. There was a bed, a table, a chair, some books and a roof over four walls. It wasn't much but Cadfeld could not hide his emotion when he entered.

'Thank you,' he said in a choked voice.

'You're at home here,' replied Lorn, as Dwain helped the old man stretch out on the bed. 'Naturally, you're free to go wherever you like, but I advise you against leaving the Black Tower. It wouldn't be prudent.'

Cadfeld grimaced in pain as he sat up while Daril slipped two pillows behind his back.

'Believe me, knight, I'm in no hurry to face Andara's men again. And I promise you I'll resist the temptation to twirl about at the top of your scaffolding...'

Lorn smiled.

'I was going to forbid precisely that,' he said, standing back to allow Dwain to leave.

He thanked him with a nod.

'A useless precaution,' Cadfeld remarked ironically. 'All you needed to do was take away my crutches...'

'Good idea,' said Lorn in all seriousness. 'Daril, take Sir Cadfeld's crutches and don't give them back until I give the order.'

Dumbfounded, the boy turned towards Lorn with wide eyes.

'Really, my lord?'

After a moment of silence the two men burst out laughing at the same time. Embarrassed but good-natured, Daril realised he'd been the butt of their joke and smiled.

'Sorry,' he said.

'Off with you,' Lorn said affectionately. 'But come by regularly to see if anything's needed here, understood?'

'Yes, my lord.'

'I thank you.'

'You'll soon be on your feet,' Lorn promised the bookseller. 'And then I can tell Daril to take away your crutches without you missing them.'

'I hope so...' said Cadfeld.

But it was clear that he did not believe he would recover any time soon, or completely. Lorn could see that and chose not to insult his intelligence by insisting otherwise.

'Those crossed swords on the dispensary door,' said Cadfeld. 'Do you really believe that's a good idea?'

'It will be when more painted swords appear on other doors.'

'If that ever happens.'

Lorn shrugged.

'We'll see. But I believe the people of Redstone are weary of the militia's violent methods. With those crossed swords, I am giving them a way to say just that, without exposing themselves too much.'

'As far as Andara is concerned, it's a declaration of war.'

'I know.'

'You have six men under your command, knight. Andara has six times as many. At least.'

'Yes, but I have this,' retorted Lorn, displaying his signet ring. 'And I have this tower and everything it represents.' He smiled, sure of himself. 'Besides, I doubt that Andara's men will stand up to mine. Even at odds of six to one.'

Lorn saw a shadow pass over Cadfeld's face.

'What is it?'

The old man hesitated.

'I... I'm not sure. But I think there is something you should know about Andara...'

That evening, Andara remained awake.

The day's events had taken him aback. He knew that people would come out to support Cadfeld when he left the dispensary. Thanks to his informers, he'd also known that the Onyx Guards would be waiting for the bookseller to escort him and had therefore suspected that Lorn would use the occasion to put on a bold face. But he hadn't foreseen the business of the painted swords and was forced to recognise the idea was a good one, in particular now that bloody priest had clearly shown himself to be on the First Knight's side. That was going to give some people courage and a desire to rebel, no doubt about it...

Nevertheless, Andara wasn't worried. Annoyed? Perhaps. And furious at having been publicly defied by Lorn, of course.

But he held a trump card which he had not yet played and, upon reflection, it wasn't such a bad thing if Lorn believed he was calling the tune. The killing blow that Andara would deliver when the moment came would be all the more formidable. He just had to wait for the right opportunity. Until then, he only needed to mete out a few punishments to dissuade people in the district from painting swords upon their doors. Lorn believed in symbols. Andara believed in brutality and fear.

Since he had an hour to kill that evening, Andara agreed to receive the young woman who presented herself at the inn where he had established his headquarters, and where he and his men relaxed and conducted their affairs. It was the wife of Redstone's public scribe. And business was poor at the moment. The couple needed money and she had come to beg Andara for a loan her husband was too proud to ask for. Andara in fact made considerable profits from his moneylending and pawnbroking activities. Since the scribe's wife was as pretty as she was shy and docile, he would derive pleasure from giving her the money she needed and content himself, this time, with coming in her mouth, despite her tears.

The young woman was still on her knees sobbing when Andara left her and went out of the inn. He smiled, his vanity swollen by having humiliated and subjected another 'conquest' to his will – and like the others, she would have to come back to pay off the interest. Lorn could never allow himself to do such a thing, nor could anyone else in Redstone. The militia chief alone enjoyed that power and as long as that remained the case, he had no cause for worry. The rest was merely speeches and handwaving.

Midnight was chiming when Andara arrived at his meeting place, a small public garden left neglected. He was punctual, but his contact was already there.

'I don't have much time,' said Eriad, stepping out of the shadows.

338

14

Two days later, in the morning, Father Eldrim appeared at the gate of the Black Tower and wanted to speak to Lorn in private.

'What's happened, father?' asked Lorn.

'It's a rather delicate matter, knight. I need your help, but your discretion, with regard to certain aspects, would also be indispensable.'

'Very well.'

'Then meet me at the dispensary in an hour, if you will.'

'You can't tell me anything more?'

'I cannot tell you anything I learned through confession. I can only encourage the one who spoke to me to confide in others, if they can be of more help than I can.'

Lorn nodded.

'I'll be there in an hour, father.'

'Thank you.'

An hour later, in a garden at the dispensary, Lorn found himself in the presence of Father Eldrim and the tearful young woman he was trying to comfort. Lorn did not know who she was and doubted he'd ever met her before. She was quite young and rather pretty, modestly dressed. More curled up than sitting, she was trying to contain her tears, her eyes reddened and her features haggard from worry.

Lorn sat facing her, took off his spectacles, leaned forward, and said:

'Talk to me.'

The young woman addressed a silent question to Father Eldrim who, with a sympathetic smile, urged her to speak.

'It's... It's my husband... He's... disappeared.'

'When?'

'Since... We had an argument, yesterday evening... He left and... and he hasn't come back.'

She burst into sobs.

Lorn stood up and shot a stern glance at the priest. Had his help been enlisted merely to find a husband who stayed out all night after a domestic dispute?

'Perhaps you should explain from the beginning,' said Father Eldrim to the young woman. 'Start by telling him who you are and who your husband is...'

She nodded and pulled herself together.

'Yes, pardon me... My... My name is Mahaut. Mahaut Veren. I am the wife of Loah Veren.'

'Veren,' said Lorn. 'The public scribe?'

'Yes. That's him.'

Lorn recalled the young man in the tavern, who had been talking with others over a drink when Cadfeld had joined them.

'I don't know him personally,' said Lorn. 'But I've already run into him. I know who he is.'

The priest took the young woman's hands in his and murmured to her:

'You can tell the knight everything, Mahaut. Everything. I vouch for him. Besides, he can help you.'

Mahaut then explained how the small amount her husband earned did not permit them to make ends meet and, their debts mounting, how she had resolved to go ask Andara for a loan. Of course, she had done so in secret. Firstly, because Veren had too much honour and pride to owe money to such a hateful being. And secondly because Mahaut knew what the leader of the militia would demand of her. She'd been right about that, but at least she had brought back the money needed to meet their most pressing bills.

'I... I thought I did the right thing... We needed that money, you understand? Really needed it!'

Lorn nodded.

'But your husband found out?'

'Yes. He learned that I'd paid some of our debts and he wanted to know how. I… I couldn't lie to him. I begged him to forgive me but he became enraged. He… He insulted me. I even thought he was going to beat me, but he left instead. That was last night. And since then…'

Lorn had heard quite enough.

But noticing a bruise on the young woman's cheekbone, he asked:

'Who did this to you, then?'

'Andara. I know that Loah went to see him last night. I'm sure of it. So…'

'So you went back to see that brute?'

'Yes.'

Mahaut broke into tears again.

Upon returning to the Black Tower, Lorn assembled his men and explained the matter to them. Out of respect to Mahaut, he did not mention the favours that Andara had demanded of her, but no one was taken in.

'Vahrd, Dwain and Yeras, go and ask around quietly in the neighbourhood. Try to find out what Veren did after leaving his wife and if he was mad enough to confront Andara… The rest of you, stand ready: you never know.'

An hour later, Vahrd returned with a version of the facts which Dwain and Yeras later confirmed, give or take a few minor details. Andara and his men were so sure of their impunity that they hardly sought to conceal their misdeeds. But the Onyx Guards – and Vahrd more particularly – now enjoyed a certain amount of respect in Redstone. Tongues had loosened. As long as their anonymity was assured, witnesses had spoken up, only too happy to have someone to turn to.

'Veren started by drinking,' explained Vahrd. 'And then he went to knock on the shutters of the Broken Sword in the middle of the night. Dead drunk. Shouting insults at Andara at the top of his lungs. So he woke up the entire street and everyone saw what happened next…'

Lorn feared the worst. The Broken Sword served as the Redstone militia's headquarters.

'Andara did not show his face,' continued Vahrd. 'Maybe he was at home, that late at night. But five or six of his men came out. According to those who witnessed the scene, at first they just wanted to chase Veren away and pushed him into the mud. But he got back up and managed to land a punch on one of them. And that set them off…'

Vahrd paused to drink a gulp of wine and Lorn gave him a questioning look.

'Yes,' he replied. 'Beaten to death. I even know where the body is…'

The militiamen had their habits, which included getting rid of cumbersome dead bodies in a waste ground at the edge of Redstone. The spot was so well known that, sooner or later, anyone missing a person close to them, and who had troubles with the militia, went to look there.

The Onyx Guards, who had come out in full strength, searched the site and soon found Veren's body in a muddy ditch. They dragged him out with some difficulty. The scribe was almost unrecognisable and, seeing Father Eldrim arriving with Mahaut, Lorn ordered that a cloth be laid over his ruined face.

The young woman emitted a harrowing cry upon seeing the body of her husband. Rushing over, she embraced it and moaned:

'Forgive… Forgive me… I didn't want to… Forgive me…'

The guards tried to remain grave and impassive, but Mahaut's pain gripped them. They waited, not knowing what to do. It was finally Father Eldrim who took the young woman by the shoulders and found the words to make her relinquish her husband's corpse.

Vahrd sighed.

'And now, Lorn? What do we—?'

But Lorn was no longer there.

'Lorn?'

Already some distance away, he was walking briskly towards a group of militiamen who were watching the scene with mocking expressions on their faces. There were four of them and they realised too late the danger Lorn represented.

'Does this amuse you?'

He did not even give them time to reply.

He struck down one with a headbutt right in the face, broke the front teeth of the second with an elbow blow and doubled the third over with a vicious thrust of his knee. The fourth brought his hand to his short sword but Lorn stopped him.

'You draw that and you die.'

The militiaman's hand froze and his face paled, seeing the Onyx Guards hastening to join their captain.

'Go and find Andara,' Lorn said to him in an icy voice. 'Go and find Andara and tell him that…' He hesitated, sighed, and then said: 'Shit. Tell him this.'

Grasping the militiaman by the collar with one hand, Lorn sent the fist of the other crashing into his face, stunning him, followed by one, two, three more blows that broke his nose and caused blood to spurt forth. Vahrd had to grab hold of the knight to prevent him from killing the man with his bare hands.

That same evening, at the Black Tower, Lorn spoke to Vahrd behind closed doors for an hour before asking Dwain to gather the others. He spoke to them on the ground floor of the keep, beneath the timbers and the floors under repair inside the almost emptied building.

'I've decided we'll attack tonight. Andara will want to avenge his men and save face. I don't want to give him the time to do so.'

All eyes turned towards Vahrd who, standing back, held his peace but clearly disapproved of this decision.

'If we must act tonight,' said Yeras, 'that doesn't leave us much time.'

Indeed, night was already falling.

'I know. But we'll benefit from the element of surprise.'

The former scout seemed scarcely convinced but kept silent. He had once almost lost his life in a poorly prepared operation.

'We still need to pick a target,' said Vahrd.

Lorn nodded.

'We have a choice,' he said. 'First, we could attack the Broken Sword.'

'The militia's headquarters?' remarked Logan. 'Risky.'

'But it would make an impression,' said Yeras.

'On both the militiamen, and the population,' Lorn added.

'We'd run into strong resistance,' said Liam. 'Too strong, no doubt.'

Eriad nodded his head in agreement with this.

'Say we take the inn by force,' said Vahrd. 'What then? Do we set fire to the place? Kill everyone inside?'

'I wouldn't mind splitting the skulls of some of these scum,' said Dwain.

'We're not at war,' objected the blacksmith. 'Redstone district isn't the border region of Valmir and the Broken Sword isn't some Gheltish outpost.'

The argument hit home and a thoughtful silence settled within the keep.

'Then we could go after Andara alone,' said Lorn after a moment.

The Onyx Guards listened closely.

'Cadfeld told me about a house that Andara possesses,' explained Lorn. 'Officially, it belongs to a front man, but it's actually where Andara lives. It's surrounded by a large garden and protected by a wall. It's hidden by trees.'

'That would be perfect,' noted Yeras. 'No one to see us or hear us.'

'And who knows what we would find inside!' said Logan. 'That must be where Andara hides his loot.'

'At any rate, we'll find Andara there,' said Dwain, balling his fists.

'And only a few sentries, if we're lucky,' said Liam.

'That's what Cadfeld said,' indicated Lorn.

He looked at his men, who all seemed in agreement. Only Vahrd remained outside his field of vision and he refrained from looking back at him.

'So it's decided,' he decreed. 'We attack Andara's house tonight. But to avoid any nasty surprises, one of you will have to go and keep watch on the place now, while the others make ready. A volunteer?'

Yeras wanted to step forward but Eriad beat him to it.

'Me.'

Lorn hesitated briefly. He appeared to think about it, and then said:

'All right. But don't let yourself be seen. If Andara or one of his men spots you, they'll know something's up and—'

'I'll stay under cover,' the young man promised.

Surprised at having been rejected, Yeras remained quiet and aimed a questioning look at Vahrd. The blacksmith made no reply, while Lorn gave Liam a slight nod of the head instructing him to bring the meeting to a close.

'Gentlemen,' the veteran said, 'it's time to get ready.'

The Onyx Guards retired, except for Yeras whom Vahrd discreetly detained.

'I know you were expecting Lorn to choose you rather than Eriad,' the blacksmith said. 'But we have something else in mind for you...'

Less than an hour later, Andara was in a foul mood when Eriad presented himself at the Broken Sword. The militia chief had been drinking alone in his office and was still simmering with rage over the beating Lorn had given four of his men.

'What brings you here?' he said in an unfriendly tone. 'I've heard enough about the Onyx Guards for one day...'

'Exactly. And you'll be able to rid yourself of them tonight.'

15

Eriad returned after night had fallen, knowing that everything was ready. He had warned Andara, who upon learning of Lorn's plans had immediately called up his militiamen and a few extra thugs: an opportunity like this to eliminate the Onyx Guard would not happen twice. The trap was laid and only needed to be sprung.

Thirty armed and determined men were waiting for Lorn and the others. Andara wanted no survivors. He had deployed his troops in his house, the garden and the surrounding area. Their orders were to wait until the Onyx Guards had crossed the outer wall before attacking. For two reasons. The first was to place Andara in a situation of legitimate defence: he would be the victim of aggression, his property invaded in the middle of the night, and no one – neither the prefect Yorgast, nor royal justice – could reproach him for protecting his goods and his life. The second reason was that Andara wanted the combat to take place out of sight because it would be combat in name only: he was planning a massacre. At odds of six to one, Lorn and his men stood no chance of escaping the ambush.

Eriad knew that Andara wanted no prisoners and had even promised a bonus to the man who brought him Lorn's head. The young man told himself he could be the one. After all, wasn't he the best placed to deliver a fatal blow to the First Knight? Yorgast would perhaps be interested to learn who had killed Lorn. And who could say, perhaps his name would even one day reach the ears of Esteveris? For Eriad was ambitious as well as being a handsome lad. He had the face of an angel, but an unscrupulous one, incapable of feeling the slightest remorse.

It had almost been too easy fooling Lorn and his clique.

And it was almost as easy to draw them into the wolf's jaws.

Eriad was smiling at this idea as he entered the Black Tower's courtyard, but his smile was replaced by a puzzled expression when he found the Onyx Guards about to leave in two wagons.

'Something's come up,' Lorn told on. 'Climb up, we'll explain to you on the way.'

Caught short, the young man could not refuse the hand that Dwain stretched out to him.

Andara was waiting at the rear of a porch with two of his militiamen when a third came running up to them and identified himself.

'It's me,' he said, halting at the porch's entrance. 'Are you there?'

Andara took a step forward from the shadows.

'Obviously!' he snapped in annoyance. 'Don't just stand there, you cretin!'

Breathless, the man darted a last look behind him before obeying. He had come from the Black Tower, which Andara had ordered him to watch until the Onyx Guards' departure.

'It's on,' he said. 'They left.'

'Was Eriad with them?'

'Yes.'

'When will they be here?'

'In about half an hour, I think.'

Andara raised an eyebrow.

'That's seems a little long to me,' he said. 'Are you sure?'

'They're coming in wagons, that's why.'

'Wag—' Andara started to say. 'What?'

'Two of them,' the man stated.

Perplexed, the militia leader scratched his cheek.

'But why wagons?' he wondered in a murmur.

Bah! They'd see, soon enough...

Turning to the two militiamen he'd been waiting with, Andara said:

'Go and warn the others. Tell everyone to be ready.'

*

347

The Onyx Guards halted the wagons in an out-of the-way alley and waited for Yeras, who'd gone ahead as a scout, to find them.

'Only three sentries,' he announced in a low voice. 'One at the gate and two on patrol. No movement inside.'

'Perfect,' said Lorn.

The neighbourhood was very quiet, with few residents about. For the most part, it was made up of warehouses, silos, building sites, workshops and waste ground. In the sky, the Great Nebula dispensed a wan light.

Lorn addressed his men.

'Vahrd and Eriad, you stay here with the wagons and wait for our signal. The rest of you, with me. Ready?'

Everyone nodded.

'Then here we go.'

'Be careful,' said Vahrd.

Hand on the pommel of his sword, Lorn went off, taking long silent and graceful strides, followed by Dwain, Logan, Liam and Yeras. The old blacksmith watched them go, then, tranquilly, he turned towards Eriad and asked:

'You wouldn't happen to have a pair of dice on you, would you?'

In concealment along with fifteen other men scattered throughout the garden surrounding his house, Andara raised his eyes towards the sky and cursed. More than an hour had passed since the Onyx Guards had left the Black Tower and they still hadn't arrived. Had they been delayed? Had they given up at the last moment? Had Lorn smelled a trap?

What if Eriad had been unmasked?

Andara tried to reason with his fears.

An opportunity like this to get rid of Lorn would probably never repeat itself. It was well worth being a little patient. It would really be too stupid to miss their chance, just because they hadn't waited an extra fifteen minutes.

Lorn and his men would be coming over that wall before long, Andara was sure of it.

*

Hoisted up by Dwain, Lorn climbed over the outer wall and straddled it. Next, he helped Yeras up beside him, and then it was the others' turn. Dwain came last, requiring both Logan and Liam give him a lift up.

Lorn let himself drop quietly to the far side and drew his sword, all his senses alert. His men joined him, their weapons also in their fists. They knew what they had to do and were only waiting for a sign from their captain.

Lorn gave it to them before setting off to the right, Dwain at his heels. Liam and Logan went to the left, in order to circle around the immense warehouse that, dark and silent, stood before them. Meanwhile, Yeras began to climb the building without making a sound.

Eriad let nothing show, but his guts were knotted by a mixture of frustration, anger and anxiety. Liam had explained to him in the gently rocking wagon that their objective has changed. It was no longer a question of attacking Andara's house, but of emptying a warehouse in the port.

Being aware of Andara's business, Eriad had immediately guessed which warehouse was the target. Nevertheless, he listened as Vahrd explained it to him and confirmed his fears.

To spare Oriale from famine, the city council had been buying up poor quality wheat and transforming it into flour, which it resold, at very low prices, in the poorest districts. The operation was costly but necessary according to the civic leaders: it was designed to prevent rioting in the High Kingdom's capital. The district prefects were charged with distributing the subsidised flour, permitting Yorgast to enrich himself by diverting part of the stocks. This ill-gotten flour was hidden in a warehouse, waiting to be sold for a handsome price.

According to Vahrd, Lorn had decided to strip this warehouse at the last moment, based on an anonymous tip. It would no doubt be less well defended than Andara's residence and the blow they would strike would be just as damaging. The blacksmith, at any rate, seemed to prefer this option.

'And what are we going to do with all this wheat?' asked Eriad in surprise.

'Give it away, lad. Give it away…'

In the alley where Vahrd and he were guarding the wagons, Eriad could only think of Andara who was waiting in vain and would be outraged when he found out what had happened. It wasn't the young man's fault but he knew Andara well enough to understand that someone would be made to feel his anger. That someone might very well be him, Eriad. Or another. Andara would not tolerate this failure, not to mention the loss of earnings. And the worst thing was, he had removed most of the sentries from the warehouse in order to reassign them to his ambush…

But was this really by chance?

Eriad was not an imbecile and, as time crept by, his suspicions grew. What if he had been unmasked? What if Lorn had charged him with scouting Andara's residence before the attack in order to give him a chance to warn the militia leader? What if they had been planning to rob the warehouse all along?

More and more worried, Eriad told himself that the Onyx Guards knew and had set him up. Besides, wouldn't Yeras have been the logical choice to watch Andara's residence? Wasn't he the band's scout and lookout? Of course, Eriad had volunteered first, in order to tip off Andara. But why had Lorn picked him?

Feeling a nervous sweat beading his brow, Eriad realised that Lorn knew. He wanted to give him freedom of movement so he would contact Andara. Lorn knew he would step forward and was even counting on it.

Eriad had been manipulated from beginning to end.

It mattered little how he had been unmasked. Perhaps he had given himself away, after all. He needed to flee before it was too late. Lorn was no doubt waiting for the end of this mission to settle accounts with him, or worse let him leave while spreading word that he had betrayed Andara. That would be signing his death sentence. There was no question of letting that happen. Perhaps Eriad still had a chance to explain things to Andara, but he needed to escape now.

Starting by eliminating Vahrd.

He slowly unsheathed his dagger and turned towards the

350

blacksmith, who had been waiting until now at the entrance to the alley.

But he was no longer in sight.

Eriad sensed the presence behind him too late. He never saw the blow that knocked him out cold.

Vahrd looked scornfully at the body stretched out by his feet and spat on it.

'Traitor.'

Lorn and Dwain had no trouble getting rid of the two sentries who were patrolling the warehouse. Lorn knocked out his target with a blow to the back of the neck. Dwain lifted his from behind and choked the man until he lost consciousness, indifferent to the frenetic scrabbling of his legs.

Liam and Logan joined them after circling the warehouse.

'Nobody,' said Liam.

At the same moment, Vahrd arrived driving one of the wagons. The man guarding the gate stepped forward to force him to halt and ask him his business, but Yeras cut him down with his crossbow, from on top of the roof. The bolt had a small bag of sand instead of a point. Hit in the head, the man would have an aching skull when he woke.

The Onyx Guards hurried to open the gate for Vahrd. They hid the sentry and Logan went to find the other wagon, while Dwain and Liam pushed open the large doors of the warehouse.

Inside, sacks of flour were piled in neat rows.

'We load everything we can,' said Lorn.

'And him?' asked Liam.

He was pointing at Eriad, lying unconscious and bound in the back of the wagon.

Lorn hesitated.

'I'll take care of him when we've finished,' said Vahrd gloomily.

They set to work.

Andara found his spy early the next morning, legs and hands bound together, hanging by the neck from the sign in front of

351

the Broken Sword, with just enough rope to touch the ground on the tips of his toes. Eriad was alive, his eyes bulging and full of tears. A bloody rag stifled his desperate moans.

Exasperated, Andara ordered that his gag be removed first.

'You idiot,' he said. 'It really didn't take them long to find you out...'

But the young man did not reply.

Making a vile sound, Eric coughed up clots of black blood along with the tongue of a stray dog he'd been forced to keep in his mouth all night long, at the risk of choking to death. Several of the militiamen present retched violently.

One of them vomited.

'Talk,' said Andara, lifting the young man's head by the hair.

He was livid with anger, but this was nothing compared to the rage that came over him when he saw the warehouse where nothing remained but a few burst sacks of flour. He took out his frustration on a sentry whom he almost beat to death, then roared with his bloodied fists in the air, pacing back and forth like a wild beast caught in a trap.

For Yorgast, the lost revenue would be significant but he was rich enough already, so Andara already knew the prefect would not lift a finger. For the militia leader, on the other hand, the setback was severe. The financial loss was enormous, especially as the lost money was not just destined for his pocket, but also to pay or corrupt his henchmen, informers and other collaborators who only served him out of self-interest. But there was also the affront, the public insult which just been heaped upon him.

Because everyone would soon know or guess who had committed the deed and there was nothing he could do about it. The news was probably already spreading throughout the district like wildfire and Lorn Askarian, up in his accursed tower, could simply let people gossip and celebrate, the inhabitants of Redstone laughing at the daring, clever blow that he and his men had just struck against the militia. They had stolen from thieves, seizing contraband goods whose loss could not be reported. Unless he carried out justice himself, the militia leader would be forced to remain silent and grit his teeth.

And if there were still those who doubted whether the Onyx Guards were behind the theft, they all received blatant confirmation that afternoon, when the Black Tower hosted the first of a series of free distributions of flour.

With the compliments of the First Knight of the Realm.

After that, painted crossed swords began to appear on doors throughout the district.

16

Days went by without Andara appearing in public, while his militiamen kept their heads down: they continued to walk the streets of Redstone but they avoided making any trouble and even did people some honest services.

But it did not bode well.

Certain that Andara would not stand idly by and watch the crossed swords spread, Lorn had urged Father Eldrim not to go out alone. He had also charged Yeras with a special mission, secret from all except Liam, and he still forbade Daril from venturing out in the neighbourhood on his own for long. Lorn was convinced that Andara would not come after him, but instead attack a member of his entourage, or even innocent parties uninvolved in their conflict. Nevertheless, all he could do right now was wait for the militia chief to make his move.

So Lorn had his mind on other matters.

When he was not exhausting himself in building work, he could not stop thinking of Alissia, Enzio's sister whom he had loved so much. They had fallen in love during the years Lorn had spent in Sarme. Despite Enzio's prickly vigilance, they had kept company and promised themselves to one another. Unfortunately, Lorn's modest origins were an obstacle. For although his father was a former companion in arms of King Erklant II, his family belonged to the very minor nobility of the sword. Lorn's mother had been a hostage offered by a Skandish ruler to the High King, along with a golden shield and two steeds, during the signature of a peace treaty. Yet, aged sixteen, Lorn had found the courage to confess to Alissia's father the feelings he had for his daughter. He loved her. She loved him. He wanted to marry her. The duke asked for time to reflect on the matter, and then said he would approve the union when the time came, on two conditions. That Lorn respect his daughter until their wedding day. And that he become worthy of her through his merits. It was more than Lorn could have hoped for: he promised everything that was demanded of him.

And kept his word.

Several years later, he was fight Dalatian barbarians at the border of Valmir and found glory at the battle of Urdel, where he saved a city from destruction by his courage. Wounded, he returned to the High Kingdom and was welcomed as a hero. He became the darling of the entire court. King Erklant bestowed honours upon him, gave him lands and made him an officer in the royal guard.

So one fine autumn day, with a grey-crested helmet tucked under his arm, Lorn presented himself again before the duke of Sarme and Vallence. He was now a man marked by war, but his love for Alissia had not weakened. She was waiting for him, beautiful and delicate, with white flowers in her hair. The duke called him 'my son' before giving him a paternal embrace. It was agreed that the marriage would take place the following spring, after Lorn carried out a mission the High King had just entrusted him with.

The dream was very swiftly broken.

That day, at the end of the afternoon, Lorn returned from the Royal Archives only to find the Black Tower was plunged in an unusual state of excitement.

'What's going on?' he asked, handing the reins of his horse to Daril.

'We've made a discovery, my lord.'

Seen from the outside, despite the scaffolding which still surrounded it, the keep seemed almost completely rebuilt. But there was still considerable work to be done within and, urged on by Vahrd who could not bear to remain idle, the guards had decided to tackle it. Indeed, from below, one merely needed to raise one's eyes to see right through the timbers and broken boards almost to the top of the keep. Only the last floor was, if not habitable, at least relatively sound. As soon as the roofing was repaired, Lorn had installed himself in austere comfort there.

He entered the tower, where all of the guards were gathered.

'We've found a chapel,' announced Vahrd on seeing him.

The keep was flanked by three crenellated corner turrets as tall as it was. One of them had a spiral staircase that served all the floors. The two others housed bare round rooms illuminated by arrow slits in the shape of a cross. On the ground floor, one of these rooms had been walled up. No one had really paid much notice to it until Dwain knocked down the barrier of bricks and mortar blocking access.

And discovered a former chapel behind it.

Apparently it was consecrated to one of the Divine Dragons, but the statue overlooking the altar with deployed wings had been mutilated beyond recognition. Similarly, all of the bas-reliefs and all the wall paintings had been destroyed with hammers and chisels.

Yssaris was sitting on the stone altar and seemed to be waiting.

Lorn pondered the matter as he stepped over the rubble obstructing the threshold. He did not know the Onyx Guards had once prayed to a member of the Divine and wondered which one it might have been. But if they had, had they later abandoned their worship? And why? And why wall this room up rather than refurbish it for another purpose? Why disfigure the statue? Was it an act of hatred? Of fear? Had it been committed before or after the Onyx Guard was disbanded?

'That's not all,' said Logan, who was already exploring the room. 'Look at this.'

Lorn joined the former mercenary behind the altar and saw, on the floor, a broad carved flagstone. He crouched. The inscriptions had been scratched and rendered illegible, but one corner of the stone was missing and allowed a glimpse of a dark cavity beneath.

Lorn bent down, removing his spectacles...

And suppressed a shiver.

He had just felt something he had not experienced for a while: the presence of the Dark. It was like the whistling of a furious wind, a high-pitched howling beneath the immense vaults, the moans of tormented souls. An icy cold invaded him.

He stood up and, as Yssaris leapt into his arms, he said to Liam:

'Don't let anyone touch this slab. And seal off this room again.'

Liam nodded.

Managing to mask his turmoil thanks to Yssaris, who soothed him, Lorn had spoken in a calm and even voice. Nevertheless, the others were looking at him in surprise. Lorn could have chosen to say nothing, he still would have been obeyed. But he wanted to avoid arousing suspicions.

'We'll have time to explore all this later,' he said. 'Right now, we have more urgent things to do.'

The explanation seemed to satisfy everyone. Only Vahrd frowned.

'Explore what?' asked someone in a clear voice.

Lorn recognised Alan's voice and turned while the guards froze as if struck by stupor. Except for the knight, all of them abruptly got down on one knee and bowed their heads.

The prince did not seem to notice any of this and entered the chapel in a very natural fashion.

'What is this place?' he asked.

'A former chapel,' replied Lorn. 'We just discovered it and don't even know who it was consecrated to. And it seems there's a crypt beneath our feet.'

Alan looked around him with astonishment.

'I didn't know the Onyx Guard built chapels...'

'Nor did I. This might be the only one.'

Lorn made a mental note to question Sibellus on the subject.

'I've come to fetch you,' announced Alan.

'Me? To go where?'

'Enzio's dinner,' said the prince, leading Lorn out of the chapel. 'Enzio. You remember Enzio, don't you? Tall, dark-haired fellow? Thinks he's more handsome than either of us, but with only half the justification?'

They came out into the courtyard.

The sun was setting but Lorn, who still had Yssaris in his arms, had to put on his tinted spectacles.

Two saddled horses were waiting for them.

'Are you planning to bring him along?' asked Alan, pointing to the cat.

Sibellus left the Royal Archives at a later hour than usual.

He called out before shutting the heavy door, making sure he was the last to leave. It was a useless precaution. Since Daril had entered Lorn's service, the master archivist no longer ran much risk of locking anyone inside. Not that the boy had tended to work long hours. But on occasion he had fallen asleep while working and woken up in the middle of the night, alone except for the mice that teemed in the cupboards and two owls nesting in the attic.

Sibellus smiled.

He was forced to admit that he missed Daril. His former apprentice was one of the least gifted he had ever trained. But at least he was willing enough, unlike the other two employees the master archivist had under his orders, who did practically nothing to earn their salary. A very meagre salary, it had to be said. Which probably explained their lack of enthusiasm.

Sibellus, who had arrived at an age when the number of winters remaining to him were counted, often wondered what would become of his beloved archives when he took his retirement, or, as seemed more likely, he gave up the ghost among his registers, binders, scrolls and parchments. He feared that none of this would ever truly survive him. What was not thrown away would be destroyed, and what was not destroyed would be forgotten. If the Royal Archives were the memory of the High Kingdom, Sibellus was the last guardian of a patient doomed to amnesia.

Night was falling and he still had some distance to travel before he reached the small house where since his wife's death nothing had really changed. But the air was warm and Sibellus enjoyed the walk which, for him, was an opportunity to breathe in something other than centuries-old dust.

And to reflect.

Lost in his thoughts, he did not notice the man who had been following him for several days now, any more than he noticed the others who had flattened themselves against the wall at the corner of an alley, deserted at this time of night. If he had lived in Redstone, perhaps he would have recognised them as Andara's henchmen. He thought he was dealing with thieves instead, and said:

'I... I don't have much. Here. Take it all.'

But they weren't after his money.

He did not see the first blow coming.

17

As it was a private dinner, only twenty guests were expected. Among them were a prince of the blood and the minister Esteveris, who had apologised in advance for not staying long. The dinner would take place at the Palace, in the large salons of the residence of Sarme and Vallence. Among the residences within the Palace precinct assigned to foreign embassies, this was one of the most luxurious and refined. It stood in the middle of a magnificent garden whose terraces scattered with ponds offered a unique view of Oriale.

Lorn had been reluctant to attend but Alan would not hear otherwise. Lorn had never had a taste for social gatherings and since his return he had only really been at ease when on his own or in the company of a few close associates. The truth, however, was that he dreaded meeting Alissia again. He had loved her madly, convinced she was the woman of his life, the one with whom he would live happily until the end of his days. In his ardour, there was nothing he would not have done or sacrificed for her. And during his years of suffering at Dalroth, his memories of her had been a source of great comfort.

Yet Lorn was convinced that seeing her again would be painful.

Did she still love him, despite the years and sufferings? And what did he feel exactly? Did he love her or was it nostalgia for their past, for the man he had been before? Was he still capable of loving?

Rubbing the palm of his marked hand distractedly, Lorn pondered this, standing alone on a balcony, when he heard several people coming out of the salons. He turned round, blinking in the light from the big chandeliers, and saw a plump man matching the description of Esteveris, surrounded by several counsellors.

Night had just fallen. It was warm outside and the Great Nebula was almost absent from the sky.

'Knight Askarian isn't it?' said the minister, approaching.

Lorn bowed, respectful but silent as Esteveris turned to those accompanying him.

'Gentlemen, I present Lorn Askarian, First Knight of the Realm.'

Lorn and the counsellors greeted one another briefly, at a distance, whereupon the minister said, with every sign of sincerity:

'I was not aware you would be here this evening, knight.'

'I wasn't either.'

'Chance has done well then in bringing us together. I've been meaning to meet you for some time now, but... The affairs of the kingdom, you understand?'

'Of course.'

'But walk with me, would you?' The minister took Lorn by the elbow and drew him away from listening ears. 'Let us use this opportunity given us to speak a little.'

They went to sit on a stone bench lit by torches.

'I have learned,' said Esteveris, 'of the excellent work you are accomplishing in Redstone.'

'Really?'

'Oh yes, indeed... Your efforts to re-establish justice there, your good relations with Father Eldrim and, of course, the work you've undertaken to restore the Black Tower to its original state. As far as that goes, I hope you will soon find another master builder. I can recommend some excellent ones, if you like.'

'Thank you. I'm sure that won't be necessary.'

Lorn remained cold and distant but Esteveris continued to smile in a friendly fashion, as if he hadn't noticed anything amiss.

'You know, knight, I've always thought that this tower, since it is the last remaining Black Tower, should be preserved. That it should be saved, to keep the memory alive... But I must I confess I kept putting the matter off. There was always something more urgent, and funds are scarce. And so the days fly by...' He sighed, and then appeared to find his wits. 'But I digress.'

He placed a hand bedecked with rings upon Lorn's shoulder.

'Knight, I'm convinced the queen will insist on receiving you soon. Be assured that Her Majesty and I rejoice in knowing that the High Kingdom has a First Knight once again. And even more, that the Onyx Guard has been reborn. I have no doubt that, commanded by you, it shall render the kingdom great services and recover its former glory.'

With these words, his hands joined before his chest, Esteveris saluted him with a smile, stood up and rejoined his waiting counsellors. Lorn watched him walk away with the feeling of having just encountered a clever, cruel and patient serpent. He remained seated on the bench for a moment, thinking.

Until Alan came and found him.

'What are you doing out here on your own? Come on, everyone's in there. And take off those spectacles, will you? You're frightening people and it's deep night out here.'

Lorn obeyed, before following the prince back across the balcony.

'I was speaking with Esteveris.'

'No one speaks with Esteveris. One has the impression of speaking with Esteveris and later realises that one has merely been listening.'

Lorn smiled faintly and had to admit Alan had a point.

'And what did the good minister want?'

'To let me know he has his eye on me, I believe.'

'That sounds like him. Does he seem like a lizard to you?'

'Somewhat, yes.'

'I really don't understand how my mother puts up with him, all day long...'

They went into the salons and Lorn blinked in the bright candlelight reflecting off the mirrors and the gilt inside the room. Dazzled, he had to wait a little before he could see clearly. And then he froze in place.

Alissia was there.

362

She had arrived while he was meeting with Esteveris and was now happily conversing with someone.

Who was it?

Lorn could not care less. He had eyes for Alissia alone. She seemed more beautiful than ever. Her red-blonde hair was lifted above her exposed nape in a refined chignon held in place with combs adorned by emeralds. She was wearing a pale green dress whose embroidery, in a darker shade, highlighted her elegant curves. Her lips were only slightly rouged. Enhanced by golden glitter, her brown eyes shone. She was smiling and holding in her gloved hand an ivory fan encrusted with jade.

She noticed him in turn and looked troubled, nodding distractedly at the person she was talking to. As if all alone in the world, she and Lorn exchanged a long glance. She smiled at him. Tenderly. Moved. Sincere. And he did not know what to do, as warm lava ran through his icy veins. Then it was if a slow, silent lightning bolt split his chest apart.

He loved her.

And was stricken by the pain born of this henceforth impossible love.

'She's beautiful, isn't she?' observed a feminine voice.

Lorn did not react right away.

'Lorn,' said Alan, 'I'm pleased to introduce Eylinn of Feln.'

Alissia directed her attention once again to the person in front of her who had not ceased speaking. Lorn turned to see who had broken the spell and discovered a young woman of delicate beauty, very pale, with a crimson mouth and sparkling eyes.

'Delighted,' said Lorn, making an effort to be polite. 'I'm—'

'Everyone knows who you are, knight,' Eylinn interrupted gaily.

'Eylinn and Alissia have become inseparable,' said Alan by way of completing the introductions. 'Be good,' he added, before ducking away.

Lorn watching the departing prince shake hands and distribute smiles to the other guests.

'Don't worry,' Eylinn murmured to him, 'I won't hurt you…'

It was meant as a gentle jest.

Lorn accorded her a good-natured smile but remained on his guard. He knew who he was dealing with: Eylinn was the daughter of Duke Duncan of Feln, one of the High Kingdom's most powerful lords and a notorious plotter. And the daughter, it seemed, was just as talented as the father when it came to ruses and intrigue. Perhaps she even surpassed him, as she had two weapons the duke lacked: an air of innocence and a disturbing beauty.

'And what if you offered me something to drink?' the young woman suggested in a bantering tone.

'I was just thinking of that.'

'Liar.'

Charmingly, Eylinn took Lorn by the arm and led him to a buffet overspilling with food. The duchies of Sarme and Vallence were warm lands where one dined and went to bed late in order to take advantage of the cool evenings. In accordance with this custom, dinner would not be served until a little later, but there well-stocked buffets to help natives of the High Kingdom wait patiently.

Lorn did not wait for a servant to attend him. He filled two glasses of wine and he and Eylinn clinked them together.

'Were it not for the cession of Angborn,' said Eylinn, 'you would be the only topic of conversation here at the Palace.'

'Really?'

'You weren't aware of that?'

'I don't frequent the Palace much.'

'Which makes you all the more interesting, over there in your tower. How is the High King?'

Lorn raised an eyebrow.

'Why ask me that?'

'Because you are the only person I know who has met him in the past year. Perhaps even two or three years, if I don't count Prince Alderan.'

'The prince met the High King recently?'

'I think so, yes. Before he went to find you at Dalroth, if I remember rightly.'

Lorn nodded but was silent, distracted.

Eylinn caught him darting another glance towards Alissia.

At the other end of the room, she was now talking to her brother Elenzio and to Esteveris, who was wishing them farewell before he left.

'It might be difficult this evening,' said Eylinn, 'but I can arrange a meeting.'

'Pardon?' blurted Lorn in surprise.

The young woman smiled, amused by the ease with which she had suddenly captured Lorn's complete attention.

'Alissia wishes to meet you, knight, but discreetly. She wants to speak with you. I believe she... she has many things to say to you. And you have much to say too, no doubt. No?'

Lorn stared at Eylinn.

He did not know what to say or to do. He told himself, however, that the woman had deliberately caught him out and that the abruptness of her proposition was intended to provoke him.

To measure the sincerity of his feelings.

Or perhaps it was all just a game to Eylinn, who was watching him over the lip of her glass with a mischievous smile.

But Lorn did not have time to ponder this for long.

A sound caused him to prick up his ears.

'Did you hear that?' he asked.

It was the ringing of a distant bell.

Without waiting for a reply, he left Eylinn and hurried out to the balcony. Other guests had preceded him, also drawn by the far-off but clear echo of the tocsin.

And it was indeed the tocsin, ringing out over the city.

'Fire!' Lorn murmured.

He elbowed his way to the balustrade, but unlike the others, he did not have to search about before looking in the right direction.

He already knew what he was going to see.

A fire had broken out in the Redstone district.

18

Lorn arrived at a gallop but was forced to dismount when he reached Elm Square. A fire was ravaging Father Eldrim's dispensary. Immense flames were erupting from its roofs and its windows, licking the walls and raising whirlwinds of incandescent ashes. The heat was so intense that it forced people to keep a safe distance.

By the time Lorn reached the scene it was too late to do anything, except hope that the blaze would not spread. Luckily, the dispensary was surrounded by streets isolating it from other buildings. And the roofs of the neighbouring houses were being hosed with water, in order to douse the smallest flame or hot coal carried by the wind. But the dispensary itself would be nothing but smoking ashes by morning. And as for the unfortunate wretches who might still be within…

As soon as the fire had been detected, the nuns had tried to evacuate the establishment. Neighbours had offered their help spontaneously and the Onyx Guards had come running as soon as they'd heard the tocsin. But those first on the scene had discovered chains keeping the exits closed. With bars protecting the windows, tools had to be found to cut the chains while panic mounted among the people imprisoned within. Some had taken refuge on the roofs… and been forced to jump when they were cornered by the flames. Under Vahrd's leadership, the guards had not dawdled but had broken down the main doors with their axes and maces. Some had fought the fire while others, risking their lives, helped volunteers bring the bedridden patients out of the burning building. The tanks of mobile pumps were soon drained and the buckets of water transferred by human relays to the inferno proved woefully inadequate. The blaze devoured everything. Nothing could contain it and the battle was finally abandoned.

The huge, furious flames consuming the dispensary lit the gathered crowd, the corpses in rows on the paving stones, the wounded who were being treated as best as could be managed, and the more fortunate souls who had only suffered from smoke inhalation but who remained devastated, frightened and impossible to comfort, their faces blackened and eyes reddened. The dispensary sheltered the destitute as well as the sick. Fathers and mothers sought loved ones, a husband, a son, or a daughter within the crush of people, and called out for them in choked voices before, sometimes, emitting a harrowing cry and falling to their knees in front of a dead body.

Lorn could see no sign of Father Eldrim. On the other hand, he recognised Vahrd, with singed hair and a scarlet face, sitting on a bollard while a woman bandaged his calf.

'All right?' asked Lorn, straining his voice.

The roaring, crackling and hissing of the blaze were so loud he almost had to shout to be heard.

The old blacksmith nodded.

'I'm alive. But I won't be frisking about right away.'

'Is it serious?'

'No.'

'And the others?'

'Alive too, I believe.'

Liam and Logan joined them. They frowned on seeing Vahrd injured, but he reassured them with a tranquil snort.

'It looks like the fire was started in several places at once,' said Liam. 'And there were chains on the doors.'

Like everyone else, Lorn knew what that meant.

'Where's Yeras?'

'He stayed at the Black Tower,' said Liam.

'A problem?'

'Sibellus. Andara's men beat him up tonight.'

So Andara had attacked the master archivist on the same night as he burned down the dispensary. He had wanted to strike hard, and perhaps was not finished yet.

'I don't see Father Eldrim.'

'The last time I saw him, he was going back inside,' said Logan.

'A long time ago?'

'No.'

'And he's still in there?'

'I think so.'

'Lorn!' exclaimed Vahrd. 'No!'

But Lorn was already rushing away.

'WITH ME!'

The blacksmith cursed when he saw Liam and Logan following their captain without hesitation. Firstly, because they were launching themselves headfirst into an inferno. And secondly, because he couldn't do the same.

Lorn tore off one of his shirtsleeves and made a mask from it before entering the dispensary. The flames dazzled him and the heat was astonishing. The air seemed to baking.

'THAT WAY!' yelled Logan, pointing to the stairs. 'AFTER THAT, I DON'T KNOW.'

With Lorn at their head, they climbed the stone stairway whose railing was burning hot. They were in the main part of the dispensary. On the floor above, flames covered the walls of the hallways and crept across the ceiling.

Almost blinded, Lorn shouted:

'FATHER ELDRIM! FATHER ELDRIM!'

In vain.

'SEARCH!' he ordered the others.

A thick smoke poisoning the air, they ventured into the blaze, pushing open doors that liberated balls of fire, inspecting rooms where tall and powerful flames were devouring everything in a deafening din and an unbearable heat.

They stepped over some corpses and then Liam cried out:

'HERE!'

He had found Father Eldrim who, having succumbed to the heat, regained consciousness and coughed when they turned him over.

'He'll live,' said Logan.

'Quickly! Get him out of here!' ordered Lorn.

But Father Eldrim resisted when Liam and Lorn lifted him under the shoulders to carry him.

'No,' he moaned. 'No… There…'

'What did he say?'

'There… Next…'

'IT'S ALL ABOUT TO COLLAPSE!' warned Liam.

The dispensary was cracking and moaning within the roaring of the flames and entire sections of the building were starting to tumble down.

The black priest succeeded in lifting a hand to point at a closed door.

'N… Next…'

'Take care of him!' said Lorn to Logan, before going to see.

He pushed open the door and found a room full of flames. Two bodies were lying there: that of a girl and that of a man. The father must have been trying to save his daughter when the ceiling had come down. He was stretched out, unconscious, both legs broken beneath a heavy beam.

'LIAM!' yelled Lorn. 'TAKE THE PRIEST! LOGAN! HELP ME!'

'But I—' Liam started to say.

'DON'T ARGUE! SAVE THE PRIEST! COME BACK IF YOU CAN!'

Liam obeyed, although he realised there would be no chance of helping Lorn and Logan, even if he managed to get Father Eldrim out of this hell.

Lorn slipped under a tangle of beams, boards and slabs of plaster to catch hold of the little girl, dragged her towards him and then out in the corridor. Logan examined her; she had only fainted from breathing smoke. Relieved, he said:

'Alive.'

'The father, now.'

Between the two of them, they tried to lift the beam pinning the man. But it was heavy and blocked by other rubble. They failed a first time.

'Again!' said Lorn. 'On three! One… two… three!'

They combined their strength, struggling, and shifted the beam shift slightly, but nothing more. They had failed a second time.

'Impossible!' cried Logan. 'We have to give up!'

'No!'

'The child will die if we stay any longer!'

'Take her! I'm going to try again. I think if—'

'No! You'll never manage on your own! You—'

The mercenary coughed.

They could barely see due to the smoke and the tears filling their stinging eyes. A few yards from them, several feet of hallway burst into flames.

'Then help me!' said Lorn. 'One last time!'

Logan nodded reluctantly.

Once again, they gripped the beam.

Once again, they tried to budge it, grimacing, their muscles bulging and straining. And they were just about to give up when it suddenly lifted as if it weighed nothing.

Lorn saw that Dwain had joined them.

'QUICKLY!' said the red-headed colossus, holding the beam a few inches above the legs it had hitherto been crushing.

He had lifted the enormous weight alone, and could not hold it much longer.

Outside, in front of the lethal inferno which used to be the dispensary, the crowd was now silent, unmoving and as if stunned by the beauty of the terrifying spectacle.

Vahrd had to hold Liam back. The veteran had passed Dwain on the stairs and told his companion where to find Lorn and Logan. Now that Father Eldrim was safe, he wanted to go back inside the building.

'No!' ordered Vahrd. 'It's too late.'

And upon these words, the roof of the main building collapsed in the middle as if a giant's fist had struck it a mighty blow. A cloud of flames, embers, ashes and sparks shot up into the night, mixing ephemeral flecks of red and gold with the pale, unmoving coils of the Great Nebula. What remained of the dispensary shook, right down to its foundations, and the floors fell in one after another, starting from the attic, in a deafening conflagration.

Everyone held their breath, incapable of accepting what had just happened. Like all the others, Vahrd and Liam could not tear their eyes away from the façade where one could only make out the outlines and the dark openings within the storm of flames.

Father Eldrim fell to his knees and prayed, soon imitated by the members of his flock.

Then...

'THERE!' cried someone.

A surge of hope caused those watching to quiver. Everyone wanted to see. People stood on tiptoe. They craned their necks and jostled one another slightly. They were afraid but they wanted to believe...

'Yes! There! I see them!'

And everyone, then, glimpsed the silhouettes emerging from the flames. Staggering, they seemed fragile and wavery against the fire, their backs bowed and heads hunched between their shoulders.

It was Dwain and Logan carrying the injured man.

His breath cut short by anxiety, Vahrd sought to catch sight of Lorn.

'Dragon-King,' he murmured. 'Save...'

But he was not given the time to complete his prayer.

There were cries of joy and bravos.

Lorn was following the two others, holding the little girl, safe and sound, wrapped up in his doublet.

19

Dawn was breaking.

It would be daylight in less than an hour, but by that time Andara would be far away. He had needed more time than he liked to gather the fortune filling the two heavy saddle bags he was carrying over his shoulder. It wasn't everything; he'd been forced to abandon things that were dear to him. But he was in a hurry.

A big hurry.

The first part of his plan for revenge had succeeded beautifully: the priest's dispensary had gone up in smoke. But the men he had charged with abducting the master archivist had failed.

The imbeciles!

And yet their mission had been simple: overpower one old man and take him without killing him. A team of four. But no, even that was too difficult for the stupid brutes. And without the archivist, Andara had no leverage with Lorn. Nothing that would protect him from the wrath of the Onyx Guard. And to crown it all, he had learned of his men's failure far too late, when the dispensary was already on fire and he only had a few hours to make his arrangements.

For Andara was sure of one thing: Lorn would strike back, and he would be merciless.

He quickened his step upon hearing the bell for first prayers ringing in the churches of the Sacrificed Dragon-King. But the staging post wasn't much further. He soon arrived there and, after closely inspecting the vicinity, pushed open the doors to the stable.

He called out for the ostler, who ordinarily slept at his workplace.

To no avail.

Andara cursed but he didn't have time to wait. Too bad, he would saddle the horse himself...

He took the first blow of the pitchfork handle right in the face, another in the belly which doubled him over, and a third upon his back which laid him out on the ground scattered with straw. His nose bloodied, he tried to rise but a series of meticulous kicks broke several of his ribs. He rolled onto his back, dazed, nauseous and blinded by pain. And then he choked when the two tines of the pitchfork planted themselves on either side of his neck and immobilised him.

Pinned down, his throat crushed, he saw Lorn bending over him.

'Did you really think you could escape? That I don't know where you live? Which taverns you frequent? Where you stable your horse? Did you really think I wouldn't have you watched, as you did with me? And did you really think I wouldn't protect my people?'

Furious, Lorn stamped on Andara's groin with his ironclad heel. The militia chief gave out a long scream and placed his hands on his lower belly, lifting his knees. He would have liked to curl up on his side, but the pitchfork prevented him from moving.

He started to sob, his lips stained with pink saliva.

'You really never understood who you were dealing with, did you?' Lorn continued. 'Arsehole.' The insult was punctuated by another kick. 'You thought that not playing by the rules would give you an advantage. But I don't play by the rules, either. Or rather, I don't play by them any longer...'

Lorn drew up a stool and straddled it, his elbows resting upon his thighs.

'What... What are you going to do with me?' asked Andara.

'Shut up.'

'We can find a—'

'I said: shut up!' cried Lorn.

Andara fell silent.

'You know, we're alike, you and I. You're the worst sort

of filth, but I'm not much better. There is something in me, something that comes from... Wait, I'll show you.'

As if removing a bandage from a painful limb, Lorn slowly unwound the leather strap that wrapped round his marked hand. Then, balling his fist, he showed the seal embedded in his flesh. The skin had blackened around the ochre stone.

'Do you see this mark? Take a good look. It tells you what I have become, what I am, and what no one else seems to see. But the truth is there, in this stone seal. I'm stronger now. Stronger than I ever was. More decisive. More determined. And unfortunately for you, more pitiless.'

Lorn stood up.

'No! Wait!' pleaded Andara.

'You shouldn't have stood in my way, Andara. You shouldn't have attacked my people... And the true irony is that you did me a favour, in the end. I needed an adversary, a dragon to slay for the common good, a noble cause to defend... So I have to admit that if you hadn't attacked us, I would have come looking for you. Now, thanks to you, the Onyx Guards are loved and respected. And it only took a few weeks...'

A cruel smile on his lips, Lorn pressed down with both hands on the upright pitchfork handle.

'Wait!' said Andara. 'We can still reach an understanding. I have my entire fortune in these bags. Gold, silver, precious stones, deeds to properties. If you are like me, take half of it. And let me leave.'

Lorn looked at the heavy bags and thought about it.

Then he said:

'Since I am like you, why shouldn't I take all of it?'

And with a blow of his heel, he drove the tines of the pitchfork deep into the ground.

Logan discreetly kept watch on the stable to make sure no one entered. Carrying Andara's bags over his shoulder, Lorn joined him and, without a word or a backward look, they returned to the Black Tower as the sun was rising. There they found Liam, Dwain and Yeras guarding Sibellus's door.

'Is he all right?' asked Lorn.

'Yes.'

Fearing that Andara would attack the master archivist, Lorn had him followed day and night by Yeras. Sibellus hadn't known, so he was the most surprised of all when the one-eyed scout had emerged out of nowhere and eliminated the militiamen who were assaulting him. The first blow, the one Sibellus hadn't seen coming, had been delivered by Yeras. After which everything happened very quickly...

Lorn knocked and entered the room where the master archivist was being guarded.

Sibellus wasn't sleeping, but he looked tired. In contrast, Daril, who was supposed to be keeping him company, was slumbering soundly.

'How are you feeling, Sibellus?'

'Fine. Thanks to you and your men. I'm much obliged, knight... Do you know what those men wanted with me?'

Lorn pulled a face.

'To beat you and leave you lying on the paving stones as a message to me. Perhaps to kill you. Or to abduct you in order to put pressure on me... Whatever their plans were, don't thank me. It's my fault you were in danger to begin with.'

'I knew the risks entailed by associating with you. I wasn't in danger because I took your side, but because I took the side of the High King.'

Lorn decided not to disabuse Sibellus on this point. He had deliberately sought this whole conflict with Andara. He had stirred up the coals because it served his own interests, knowing that others would burn in his stead. The master archivist had come out of it with a severe fright, but Father Eldrim's dispensary was reduced to ashes and the fire had taken a tragic toll.

'You can go home, Sibellus.'

'Today?'

'Now, if you like. You're no longer in any danger.'

'Andara?'

'Dead.'

'And his men?'

'They'll flee as soon as they find out. And those that don't run fast enough risk being stoned or beaten or hung from a signpost.'

'So it's over.'

'Yes.'

'Thank you, knight. If you can do for Oriale what you have done for Redstone...'

'For now, it's a matter of restoring hope. But what we've done for Redstone, we will do for the High Kingdom. And soon.'

Sibellus nodded.

'If there's any way I can help...' he said.

Lorn hesitated. Was this the right time to ask the master archivist for the information he really wanted?

No doubt.

'I'd like the minutes of my trial,' he said. 'I know they were placed under seal. But I also know that you, the Master Archivist of the High Kingdom, have them in your safe keeping.'

Sibellus stared at Lorn for a long while before answering. Somehow, he had always known it would come to this.

'If I give you those minutes, I'll be guilty of perjury and high treason...'

Lorn did not blink.

'I know.'

After leaving Sibellus to his rest, Lorn found Vahrd waiting for him with a sombre air.

'A problem?' asked Lorn.

'You could have killed Andara weeks ago.'

'Yes.'

'And you knew you end up killing him. But you waited.'

'He had to commit an unforgivable crime. Redstone needed to rise from fear and resignation to anger.'

'People died in that fire, Lorn. Women and children. Innocent victims.'

'I know.'

'That doesn't seem to concern you.'

'I'm waging a war. All wars cause innocent vict—'

'Don't sing me that song!' the old blacksmith exploded. 'I've heard it too many times. Always to justify the worst possible deeds.'

Lorn fell silent, thinking that sometimes the worst had to come to pass before things improved. The man he had once been might have done the same thing, but he would have felt terrible remorse. He recalled having once been forced, while fighting on the border of Valmir, to abandon soldiers under his command – thereby condemning them to certain death. The decision had been the right one. It had ultimately saved numerous lives, and despite that, he had lost sleep over it for weeks.

Not now...

'I have a mission to accomplish,' he said.

Vahrd nodded gravely.

'All the same, I wanted to ask you a question. When you rushed into the burning dispensary, did you want to save lives, or merely demonstrate your courage and rally people to your cause?'

Lorn couldn't reply, because he didn't know the answer.

Lorn returned to his room exhausted.

Andara was dead, his militia would not survive him and, if he wasn't a fool, the district prefect would either lie low or else hasten to publicly rejoice at the turn taken by events: he would announce the formation of a new militia and allow the people to elect its leader. In the meantime, the Onyx Guards would maintain order, helped by a few volunteers appointed by Lorn.

But that could wait until tomorrow.

Lorn let himself fall upon the bed, still dressed, heaving a sigh of relief. Then he rolled on his back as Yssaris came and purred against his side. Lorn stroked the cat absentmindedly, already drowsing.

He had not looked in detail at the contents of Andara's bags, but he guessed they held a fortune. He intended to make use of it, starting by financing a dispensary in the name of the High King. Next he would redress some injustices and help the most deserving, which would solidify his popularity. Very soon, the Redstone district would only be too happy to enjoy the protection of the Black Tower. Other poor districts would envy it and word would spread in Oriale that life was better where the king's justice had been restored...

Lorn stretched and found the strength to sit up on the edge of his bed to remove his boots and his doublet. Whereupon he lay down again and, fingers entwined behind his neck, stared at the ceiling for a moment.

He fell asleep thinking of all he still had to accomplish.

Two days later, a wyverner arrived from the Citadel with a heavy leather bag containing the orders and decrees that Lorn needed.

20

Queen Celyane was holding her last Council before her departure for Angborn when an usher entered by a hidden door, approached with muffled footsteps and slipped a note to Esteveris. Without interrupting the debate, the queen observed Draniss who was waiting behind the door. She realised it was he who had given the note to the usher and her gaze darkened. She did not like dracs and detested this one in particular, no doubt because she had never succeeded in corrupting it. The only loyalties the queen tolerated were those directed towards her. Loyalty towards others aroused her jealousy, followed quickly and inevitably by suspicion and hatred.

Esteveris unfolded the paper beneath the table without delay. He was waiting for news from Sorr Dalk, to whom he had granted unlimited funds to wipe out the partisans opposed to the cession of Angborn. He had hoped that the matter would be settled soon, but weeks had gone by without word from Dalk and the royal cortege was about to depart for the Free Cities. Had Dalk succeeded or failed? Had he met with unforeseen difficulties? Had he been unmasked or eliminated? The minister was scarcely concerned about the fate of his agent. But he was anxious for this thorn to be removed from his foot: the outcome of the negotiations he'd been engaged in for months with Yrgaard depended on it.

Esteveris was disappointed when he discovered the contents of the note: it dealt neither with Dalk nor Angborn. But what he read astonished him nevertheless. Ordinarily, in such circumstances, he would have glanced over the message then refolded it discreetly and returned his full attention to the Council's discussions. This time, he read the note several times and looked perplexed for an instant, which in turn puzzled and annoyed the queen.

'Bad news, Prime Minister?' she asked curtly.

Esteveris raised his head.

'Forgive me, ma'am. No, not bad news. At least, I don't believe so...'

'Then what is it that troubles you so? Perhaps you will deign to share it with the gentlemen of the Council and myself?'

The ministers maintained a prudent silence and avoided moving, even breathing.

Esteveris was seated to the right of the queen, who presided at the end of the table. He leaned forward and, in private, told her:

'The knight Lorn Askarian requests an audience.'

'Lorn Aska—?'

'The First Knight appointed by the High King, ma'am.'

'I know who he is!' the queen snapped. 'What does he want?'

'I don't know, ma'am.'

The queen calmed herself and thought quickly.

'I will receive him upon my return from Angborn. Arrange that, would you? Right now we have enough to do.'

Esteveris quietly cleared his throat.

'Ma'am, as it happens, the knight is waiting at the door...'

The queen shrugged and, loudly enough for her Council to hear, declared:

'So? He doesn't intend to force his way in here, does he? He's at the door? Well, let him remain there.'

She provoked a few polite smiles, but Esteveris's embarrassment only grew.

'Ma'am,' he said in a low voice. 'If you please...'

As the minister's gaze became imploring, the queen deigned to lean forward so that he could speak in her ear.

'Ma'am, the First Knight of the Realm is the High King's representative. It is out of pure courtesy that he requests an audience. If he wished, he could enter without being announced...'

The queen stared disdainfully at Esteveris as if he were responsible for this situation.

'Ma'am...' the minister insisted.

Queen Celyane realised she must 'grant' this audience if she wished to save face. Furious, she pinched her lips but contained herself. She sat up, placed her hands upon the armrests of her chair, and nodded.

The doors opened and Lorn entered the room.

Gloved and booted, his hair tied back with a leather lace, he was wearing the dark armour of the Onyx Guard and bore his sword at his side. Expressionless, he advanced with a firm step and halted before the Council table. He was separated from the queen by its entire length. Her ministers and counsellors having withdrawn, only Esteveris remained.

Lorn bowed.

'I have come, ma'am, to convey the greetings of the High King your husband.'

'Thank you, knight.'

'He assures you of his affection and hopes to return to your side soon. And while awaiting that happy day, he is grateful to you for taking charge of the kingdom's affairs so ably.'

The queen gave a faint, noncommittal smile.

'Through my voice, the High King presents you with a request,' continued Lorn. 'He has no doubt that you will willingly grant it and thanks you in advance.'

The queen and Esteveris, who was standing beside her, exchanged a brief glance. They had both understood the same thing: that the High King's request was in fact a demand and he expected it to be obeyed. With all due respect to the queen, his orders could not be questioned.

'What request, knight?' the minister asked.

Lorn drew forth a letter from his doublet and showed it to them.

Esteveris stepped forward, took the royal missive, and brought it back to the queen. But she signalled him to open it. He hesitated, then broke the black wax seal and unfolded the letter. He read it and turned a worried face towards the queen. Growing impatient, she almost wrenched the paper out of his hands.

She read it in turn.

And paled slightly before addressing Lorn:

'It shall be done according to the will of the High King,' she said in a toneless voice.

IV

Autumn 1547

1

'Of all the Divine Dragons who once ruled and whose abrupt decline was brought about by the death of the Dragon-King, only one still sat, centuries after the Shadows and their ravages, upon the throne of an Imelorian kingdom. She was named Orsak'yr, the Hydra of Yrguard. And she was also known as the Great Black Dragon, who had once commanded Night and Death.'

Chronicles (The Book of Dragons)

In Dorvarsen, the capital of Yrgaard, the rider trotted through the first formal courtyards of the royal fortress before gracefully dismounting and racing up a gigantic staircase, wide enough to allow thirty men to climb it abreast. He entered the building and, still moving straight ahead, passed through several halls and corridors at a brisk pace. His spurs jingled in time with his footsteps, the doors ahead of him opening beneath the impassive gaze of scarlet suits of armour, whose wearers, if any, were completely invisible. Finally, he came to a halt before a pair of stone doors which seemed to have been carved out from a single colossal block of white marble.

The line dividing them could scarcely be discerned and yet the doors soon slowly drew apart without disturbing the total silence that reigned in this place. The man crossed the threshold before they finished opening and trod upon a long blood-red carpet. Stamped with a sinister black rune, very similar to that of the Dark, cloth hangings decorated the columns which supported the breathtakingly high vaulted ceiling above. These hangings marked with the sign of the Black Dragon were the same shade as the carpet. Other figures in scarlet armour stood guard, all of them carrying a large shield and a long spear.

They looked like dwarves against the pedestals of the huge columns, while distant silhouettes fluttered beneath the vaults as if it were a stone sky.

The man continued to advance with a more measured, respectful step.

Yet it was not simply the scale of the hall that intimidated him.

Nor the silence that crushed him.

Tall, slender and athletic-looking, the man was dressed in black and red, the colours of Yrgaard. He wore riding boots, heavy articulated gauntlets and an embossed breastplate. A cape hung from his shoulders. He had an imposing but haughty bearing, full of arrogance – that of a selfish, pitiless and cruel being, to whom the world was peopled by inferior creatures. His hair was long and red. His features were regular and his gaze was firm. He was handsome, cold and disturbing. His eyes were reptilian.

His name was Laedras and in his veins ran the blood of the Black Dragon.

The red carpet ran the entire length of the hall. Laedras strode to its end and, head bowed, and respectfully placed one knee on the floor before the tall steps of a large stone dais. To either side of these steps stood yet more sentinels in scarlet armour. All around the dais covered with crimson rugs were cold braziers. And upon it, there sat a black dragon.

An immense hydra, whose seven horned and scaly heads were almost exactly alike.

Orsak'yr.

The Dragon of Death and Night.

'Rise…' one head started to say.

'My son,' finished another.

Laedras stood up.

'Thank you, mother.'

He was one of the Black Hydra's offspring. A 'dragon-prince', as they were called. Some claimed there was one for each of the hydra's heads. Except for their eyes, they were human in appearance, but they did not grow old and bore within them part of their progenitor's power. That made them formidable adversaries, capable of unleashing a Dark force strong enough to cut down a rank of soldiers.

'The squadron is ready, mother.'

'Good…'

'You will…'

'Command it.'

'I will do so according to your orders, mother. But…'

'Yes?' asked one of the seven heads. They weaved incessantly but never took their eyes off Laedras.

The latter hesitated, and then asked:

'An entire battle squadron, mother? To escort one ambassador?'

The Black Dragon's eyes gleamed and, after a moment of silence, all of the heads said in unison:

'Diplomacy is war before the cannons sound.'

2

'In order to travel to the Free Cities, the queen decided to descend the course of the Eirdre and embarked on the splendid vessels of the Floating Palace, which, in the opinion of the wise, was one of Imelor's greatest and most magnificent wonders.'

Chronicles (The Book of the Knight with the Sword)

Lorn and his mount plunged into the wood at a gallop. Two riders were chasing him. Like his own, their mounts were excellent. Purebred, highly strung, and powerful. They too were running flat out.

Bent forward over the neck of his horse, Lorn raced along a narrow path. Branches brushed against him from the right and the left and passed just over his head. He risked a glance back and saw that the faster of the two riders was catching up with him.

He smiled, pleased and confident.

As long as he stayed on the path, none could pass him.

'You're cheating!' Alan shouted to him.

Lorn started laughing.

'Really? Who forced you to follow me into the wood?'

The prince scowled but consoled himself with the thought that Elenzio too had taken the same route without thinking. Curiously enough, knowing that he was not alone in falling into such a crude trap was somehow comforting.

Lorn saw that the path suddenly divided in front of him.

He picked the right-hand fork; Alan immediately took the left.

'Wrong choice!' Lorn yelled.

'We'll see about that!'

As for Enzio, he continued to pursue Lorn. And since the Sarmian heir kept his mind on his riding and the path, rather than shouting challenges, he was gaining ground. Lorn was a little late in realising this, too busy tracking Alan's progress among the trees and branches.

Lorn and Alan burst out of the wood at the same time, trailed closely by Enzio.

'It's Enzio who's cheating!' exclaimed Lorn. 'He's too serious!'

'As always!' Alan shouted gleefully.

The Sarmian gentleman simply smiled and spurred his mount.

The three riders were now galloping up a hill towards the tree that stood at the top. Lorn and Alan were riding almost boot to boot, but Enzio remained focused and his mount still had reserves which his friends had already used up. He drew level, wormed his way between them, and then edged ahead by a neck. His two friends urged their horses on, to no avail. The neck became a length, and stride by stride Enzio outdistanced them.

With a leap, his horse cleared a hedge in front of which Lorn and Alan finally gave up.

They halted their horses.

'How does he do that?' marvelled the prince.

Gasping for breath and wearing an admiring expression, he watched Enzio moving off in a cloud of dust.

'No idea,' confessed Lorn. 'Of course, a stranger might suspect that Enzio rode better than we did...'

They began to detour, at a walk, around the hedge.

'Nonsense,' said Alan. 'I would argue that he had the better horse.'

'And the better saddle.'

'And the better bridle...'

The prince smiled.

'Just look at that big pillock, he hasn't realised the race is over.'

Elenzio was indeed still galloping his horse towards the tree at the top of the hill.

'You'll see,' said Lorn, 'he'll even have the nerve to claim he's won.'

'Winning a race when there are no other riders? A handsome feat!'

'But he'll claim we were racing him...'

'The cheeky devil! But now that I think of it: if he had the better mount, perhaps it was because he chose better than us.'

'I see what you mean. I think we agree that we allowed him to have the better mount. Out of charity.'

'And the better saddle.'

'And the better bridle...'

They arrived at the tree feeling quite pleased with themselves, finding Enzio there, who had dismounted and was only half-annoyed with them.

'You're such poor losers,' he said, looking off into the distance.

Of the three of them, he was most often the victim of the two others' pranks and japes. He'd assumed this role good-naturedly for years now and even exaggerated his air of outraged dignity. As a child, he had always been the trio's voice of reason.

Lorn and Alan leapt down from their saddles and, standing to either side of Enzio, they looked out in the same direction as him. The three young men remained silent and still, admiring a unique spectacle beneath an immense, sunny sky.

Adorned with glorious multi-coloured banners, a city of canvas and wood was descending the course of the Eirdre River. It was composed of dozens of barges, tightly moored together in groups of four of five, forming what seemed like distinct neighbourhoods. The size of these barges – or ships – varied. Some bore splendid structures rising three storeys or more, with balconies, galleries and vast canopies covering terraces. Others, more modest, formed clusters at a remove from the grander vessels.

This city, which appeared to be drifting upon the slow waters of the river, was just as much a royal residence as the Citadel or the former palace of the Langrian kings in Oriale. It was carrying the High Kingdom's court, which was accompanying Queen Celyane and her minister Esteveris to Angborn. The royal barges were the longest and the tallest vessels, with the High King's Ship – which some now called the 'Queen's Ship' – dominating them all. They were surrounded by barges from the Imelorian kingdoms: Alguera, Vestfald, Loriand, Sarme, Iredia, Valmir and others – with the notable exception of Yrgaard. Even the Church of the Dragon-King had its own barge, which looked like a floating cathedral.

Superbly bedecked with bunting and flags, the High King's Ship was the heart of this mobile mosaic, whose disposition shifted according to practical requirements, but also according to intrigues, diplomacy and the whims of a proud and temperamental sovereign. Having one's vessel moored to that of the queen was an honour which could be granted and withdrawn, so that one could measure the degree of royal favour bestowed on a given personage by the position of their barges. To that was added the complex game of traditions, alliances and rivalries, the vessels gathering together according to political or religious affinities, and changing according to the evolution or – sometimes – sudden reversals of diplomacy. The layout of the Floating Palace was thus constantly changing for both frivolous and serious motives: a quarrel over etiquette at an official ceremony, the opening of trade talks, or the declaration of a war. The rapprochement of two vessels, the distancing of another, or the arrival of a fourth, was never innocent. Each mooring line tied or untied, each gangway set down or raised, was a signal, a salute, or a warning to one's allies and enemies alike. To the point that the arrangement and rearrangement of the Floating Palace's layout, on an almost daily basis, was a faithful portrait, in outline and in fine detail, of the diplomatic relations among the Imelorian kingdoms.

Lorn's attention was drawn to Valmir's vessel.

Made of light-coloured wood, hung with grey and gold drapes, it advanced ahead of the High King's Ship and never left that position. Small but tall, it was without a doubt the most important of all. For if the vessels could interlock with one another in an infinite number of combinations, if they could navigate without oar or sail as though moved by the river's sole will, it was the result of both magic and the genius of their design. The bonds between Valmir and the High Kingdom were solid and their treaties ancient. The Floating Palace was the product of one of those treaties and it was thanks to the art of the mages aboard the Valmirian vessel, steady as a lighthouse, that the ensemble was proceeding safe and sound, preserving its cohesion, balance and harmony.

It had been two weeks since the Floating Palace had left Oriale. For the most part, it had been two weeks of parties and games. The days stretched out as long as the course of the Eirdre, in indolence and idleness, while the evenings were filled with dinners, balls and spectacles aboard one vessel, then another, each kingdom and delegation trying to outshine its rivals in terms of luxury and excess to make an impression. Thus the royal court devoted itself to dancing, drinking, eating and making merry until dawn, and then spent the following day commenting and comparing notes on the previous receptions, and discussing those to come.

Lorn had never had much taste for these pleasures.

So one evening, he went to find Alan and Enzio and bluntly said to them:

'A ride. Tomorrow. The three of us.'

Which in fact sounded more like an announcement than a proposal.

Alan and Enzio had both raised their heads from their game of chess. They exchanged an amused glance and then the Sarmian gentleman seemed to hunt for something on the floor. The other two had then joined him in looking beneath the table and all around, but without comprehending the purpose.

'Did you lose something?' Alan had asked.

'I'm searching for Lorn's verbs. They must have gone astray somewhere, because he speaks like a Vestfaldian sergeant,' Enzio had said, before standing up with a wide grin.

Alan had chuckled and even Lorn had smiled.

'Very funny. But I'm going mad. I can't stand these courtiers and this diplomatic circus.'

'A ride? Now that's an idea,' Enzio had acknowledged. 'We could certainly use the exercise. But where would we find horses?'

'The Azure Guard has some.'

Lorn had turned to Alan, who pulled a face and said:

'It could be arranged. But it would not be just the three of us.'

Besides the fact that Alan was a prince of the High Kingdom, Enzio was a wealthy foreign gentleman who was representing his father at the head of the delegation from Sarme and Vallence. An escort would necessarily be assigned to them as a cautionary measure.

'Here they are,' said Lorn, turning round in his saddle.

Leaving off their examination of the Floating Palace, the two others did likewise.

Their escort, which they had momentarily shaken off, was emerging from the wood and ascending the hill to join them. It was composed of armoured riders wearing white and blue. Previously the palace guard at Oriale, the Azure Guard had become the queen's own. Esteveris had personally recruited each of its members.

The troop came to an orderly halt at a distance from the tree beneath which Lorn, Alan and Enzio stood. It was led by the Azure Guard's captain, who prodded his horse closer. Tall, heavy and imposing, Dol Sturich looked like the brute that he was. He had carried out various dirty deeds on behalf of the minister and was devoted to him.

'Well, Sturich?' Lorn called out to him. 'Finished dilly-dallying?'

The captain, out of breath and perspiring, was angry. He looked daggers at Lorn but did not answer him, addressing Alan instead:

'That was very… imprudent, my lord. That… That sudden cavalcade…'

Like Lorn, Alan did not care much for Sturich.

'You command our escort, Sturich,' he said in a severe tone. 'Confine yourself to escorting us.'

The captain was forced to bow his head.

'Yes, my lord,' he said.

He turned his horse and went to wait with his men.

'Say, what's that…?' said Enzio, squinting at something in the distance.

Lorn and Alan looked in the same direction as their friend and saw a cloud of dust. A troop was approaching on the road that ran alongside the Eirdre. It formed a long column of armoured horsemen and infantrymen. They marched to the beat of a drum and were preceded by banners that Alan was the first to recognise.

'It's Yrdel!' he exclaimed happily before spurring his mount. 'It's my brother! Let's go and greet him!'

The two others exchanged a glance.

'I thought Yrdel wasn't expected for several more days…' said Enzio.

'So did I,' replied Lorn.

They set off at a gallop in pursuit of Alan, heedless of their escort.

3

Prince Yrdel had journeyed to the Free Cities several weeks before the queen and it had been agreed he would come out to meet her, from Samarande, so that they might make as solemn and spectacular an entry as possible at Angborn.

As Elenzio had pointed out, Yrdel was not expected so soon. He had in fact left Samarande several days in advance and, taking the most minimal escort possible for the heir to the High Kingdom's throne, he'd travelled quickly. A vast round-up having permitted the arrest of the last opponents to Angborn's cession, all had finally been made ready to receive the queen, the numerous foreign ambassadors and delegations accompanying her to witness this historic event, and above all, the envoys sent by the Black Hydra. Every paragraph, every line, every word of the treaty had been weighed, studied and debated in three languages – Langrian, Yrgaardian and Old Imelorian – by armies of jurists and diplomats over the course of days and nights, each modification of one version or another giving rise to further discussions and revisions.

But the treaty had been drawn up at last.

All that remained was to affix the seals of the two kingdoms and the signatures of Queen Celyane and of Prince Laedras at the bottom of this impressive document, the one acting as proxy for the High King and the other as that of the Black Hydra. Angborn would become Yrgaardian, as some maintained it had always been. Yrgaard would pay a heavy tribute to the High Kingdom in compensation. And diplomatic relations would officially resume between these two powerful, hereditary enemies, whose rivalry had shaped the history of Imelor for centuries.

*

Yrdel's arrival was feted that evening aboard the Queen's Ship, with a magnificent banquet in which Lorn was obliged to partake. He was more than weary of parties and balls, but he was the First Knight of the Realm and it was his duty to take his seat at the high table: his presence was expected and his absence would have drawn notice. He was part of the royal procession by virtue of being the High King's delegate. It was why he'd insisted on coming along, despite the resistance of the queen, who wished to make Angborn's cession her personal political triumph and was furious to learn that her husband would be officially represented at the ceremony. But that was precisely the mission Erklant had assigned to Lorn: be present, be seen, and speak in the king's name.

During the banquet, with Yrdel presiding and Alan sitting between them, the queen treated Lorn just as she had since the beginning of the voyage and their forced proximity. Unable to drive him away, she ignored him. She did not speak to him, did not respond to him and did not see him. She even pretended not to hear or not to understand when someone made the mistake of mentioning Lorn in her presence. That hardly ever occurred, however. For scarcely any members of queen's entourage considered Lorn worthy of respect. Most ignored him with varying degrees of disdain, the most skilful managing to never have occasion to speak with him at all. Esteveris was a notable exception. He alone behaved normally, while feigning not to notice the cold treatment meted out to the First Knight of the Realm by a jealous queen and her fawning courtiers. Even the foreign ambassadors, without being too obvious about it, found it prudent to avoid contact with him for the moment.

Being treated as a pariah suited Lorn.

He hated what the High Kingdom's court had become: a nest of intrigue, and of envy, hypocrisy and cravenness, of ostentatious luxury where everyone owed their position to the queen, to her alone and not to one's own merits – nor even one's birth, which Lorn might have understood. This whole small, servile world made the most of its privileges and enriched itself, revelled and spent entire fortunes with no greater care than to please the queen and flatter her vanity, for she could bring about the disgrace of her favourites just as quickly as she had promoted them.

During the banquet, while the dishes were served and artists performed their entertainments, Lorn watched the courtiers with a cynical eye, as they only laughed and applauded when the queen did. But above all, he used the time to observe Prince Yrdel who was only sitting a few places away from him and hardly seemed to have changed over the past three years. His temples had greyed slightly. Otherwise he was the same gentleman whose Algueran pedigree was undisputable. Tall, slim and very dark, he was the son of the High King's first wife, a royal princess of Alguera who had died giving birth to him. The contrast with his half-brother Alan, ten years younger, was stark. Blond, joyful and full of energy, Alan was the complete opposite of his elder sibling. At this table where both princes were sitting, only the younger drew notice, for he was one of those solar beings who attracted light and made it seem to glow brighter and warmer.

Lorn noted that Yrdel was not drinking and ate very little. He smiled when others roared with laughter. He lent an attentive ear to his table companions, answering them politely but in the end saying little, and he hardly seemed to enjoy the show put on by the jugglers, dancers and entertainers. No doubt his journey had exacerbated the fatigue brought on by the delicate negotiations he had conducted with Yrgaard. But more than that, Yrdel was behaving in accordance with his nature. Quiet and reserved, he had no fondness for the pleasures of food and drink, nor for festivities and luxury. And he did not seek to please, unlike Alan who – unconsciously – felt a need to shine.

As the banquet came to a close, the gazes of Lorn and Yrdel met and lingered for a moment. Lorn read weariness and resignation in the prince's eyes and he understood that it was almost a confession that Yrdel was making to him. Why to Lorn and not another? They did not know one another well, truth be told. But the prince had perhaps guessed that they both would rather be eating stew with one of the guard units. That they both wanted to escape this drunken celebration and these smug smiles. That they felt the same disgust for this gaudy extravagance. Although Yrdel put on a better face than Lorn, they alone – with the exception of Esteveris – were not enjoying themselves, looking and listening rather than laughing and chattering.

But what made them even more alike was that both of them, in their own way, were strangers at this court. A silent observer, Yrdel had been the first to realise this, but Lorn, in turn, came to the same opinion soon enough. To be sure, Yrdel received all the signs of respect that were his due. He was lauded and flattered. But that was mere hypocrisy and pretence. He was the son of a queen whose memory was hateful to Queen Celyane, jealous of the love the High King had long borne for her predecessor. Despite the smiles and the attention she bestowed upon Yrdel in public, there was no doubt that Celyane preferred her own son Alan. The courtiers made no mistake on this score and knew that, in order to please the queen, it was wise to attach themselves to Prince Alderan. Besides, which of them did not actually prefer Alan, who made Yrdel seem so dull in comparison?

When Yrdel turned away to join his laughter to that which Alan had just provoked with some jest, Lorn recalled something Father Domnis had told him upon their arrival at Samarande. It concerned Alan: '*Some parties are starting to dream that he will inherit the throne upon the death of the High King.*' And the white priest had added that the people were hoping for a great king and feared that '*Yrdel is not that king*' .

Lorn's gaze slowly swept over those present at the banquet, wondering how many here would rejoice, or at least raise no objection, if Alan seated himself upon the Onyx Throne instead of his elder brother.

His eyes slid over Esteveris who was watching him.

And then they came to rest upon the queen.

After the banquet, a magnificent display of fireworks was launched from a barge situated behind the Floating Palace. When the torches and lanterns were extinguished, Lorn used the darkness to slip away. He snatched a bottle of wine and went off on his own to a terrace exposed to the warm breeze, but just when he had sprawled out in an armchair with his feet crossed upon a low table, Yssaris nimbly leapt upon his thighs.

Lorn smiled.

'So there you are. How are you?'

In guise of a reply, Yssaris pushed its small triangular head under Lorn's hand.

Lorn had hesitated over whether to bring it along on this journey, the ginger cat having quickly made itself at home in the Black Tower and its surroundings. But then Lorn realised he was more attached to the cat than he believed and, above all, that the fits brought on by the Dark had ceased since the Emissary had entrusted it to Lorn's care.

Was it a coincidence?

Lorn wasn't sure. He only knew that the young cat's presence relaxed him, and now once again, the heat and Yssaris's gentle purring did not take long to soothe him as Lorn sat there with the cat in his lap and drinking from his bottle of wine.

Behind him the night lit up, the rockets splashing the Great Nebula's pale constellations with bright colours.

4

The following day, Lorn made a point of joining his men for training. The Onyx Guards had obtained exclusive use of the fencing room on the Princes' Ship for two hours per day, early in the morning and late in the evening.

Vahrd was missing from roll call.

'Anyone know where the Old Man is?' asked Lorn.

No one knew, but Dwain, who shared a cabin with the blacksmith, said:

'Somebody knocked on the door this morning. It was Vahrd who opened. I was still sleeping and it woke me up.'

'Did you see who it was?'

'No. And since the Old Man seemed acquainted with them, I didn't worry about it. After all, he still knows a lot of people. They spoke in low voices, and then they went off together.'

'Did Vahrd say anything to you?'

'Only that he'd be back in time for training.'

Lorn raised an eyebrow.

'I don't like the sound of this.'

'I'm sorry,' said Dwain. 'Perhaps I should have—'

'No,' Lorn curt him short. 'Vahrd doesn't need a chaperone.'

'It's barely been an hour since he left,' noted Logan.

'That's true,' Lorn admitted.

But it worried him, and it could be read upon his face.

'We could try asking around,' proposed Liam.

Lorn hesitated but then saw all their eyes urging him to agree; they wanted to help.

'Very well,' he said. 'But discreetly and carefully. I don't need to remind you that we're not exactly popular around here: if Alan hadn't invited us, we'd be sleeping down in the hold. So don't make matters worse if the Old Man has got himself in a fix.'

'Don't bother,' said Vahrd. 'I'm here.'

Everyone turned towards the doorway, where the old black-smith had just appeared.

'All right?' asked Yeras.

Vahrd nodded, but he had sombre look and his face was drawn.

'What's going on?' asked Lorn.

'May I speak with you?'

'Of course.'

The others understood and withdrew, exchanging nods with Vahrd, who seemed grateful for their support.

'It'll be fine, lads. Thank you.'

'Logan!' Lorn called.

'Yes?'

'Guard the door, will you?'

'Yes, knight.'

The mercenary with the twin swords shut the doors behind him, leaving Lorn and Vahrd alone in the fencing room.

'It's Naé,' said the blacksmith in a low voice. 'She's been arrested.'

'Naé? But why?'

'She was part of the group of insurgents who wanted to prevent Angborn's cession.'

'Idealists.'

'Patriots!' Vahrd corrected Lorn in a harsher tone than he intended and which he immediately regretted. 'Sorry,' he said, pulling himself together. 'I knew it was a terrible idea.'

'Is it this group she went to join, when she left the Citadel?'

'Yes.'

'So you knew. And you let her do it.'

The old blacksmith did not appreciate the reproach.

'I told you I raised her to be independent. To make her decisions on her own. Good or bad.'

'This one was bad, obviously.'

Vahrd grew heated.

'I bloody well know that!' he exclaimed.

Logan had to have heard that outburst. Lorn and Vahrd turned towards the door, but it remained closed.

'All right,' said Lorn after a moment. 'What happened?'

'They were all rounded up a few weeks ago. Naé along with the rest.'

'And where is she right now?'

'Here. She arrived yesterday with Prince Yrdel's baggage. A little gift for Esteveris.'

'How do you know that?'

'I still have a few friends. Reliable friends.'

Lorn rubbed his face and thought.

'We can't leave Naé in Esteveris's hands,' said Vahrd in an almost pleading tone.

'I know,' said Lorn as he continued to mull over the matter. 'I know...'

'So what are we going to do?'

Lorn made up his mind.

'You'll do nothing at all,' he said. 'I'll speak with Alan.'

'I'm coming with you.'

'No.'

'Lorn, please. Naé's my daughter.'

Lorn hesitated, but gave in.

'All right. But keep your mouth shut, understood?'

'Understood. Thank you, Lorn.'

'You'll thank me when we've got Naé out of this mess.'

Lorn asked to see Alan. Since it was still early, the prince had just woken up. Nevertheless he received Lorn and Vahrd in his private apartment, as he was finishing his washing up.

He was in an excellent mood.

'What brings you here at such an early hour, Lorn? Good morning, Vahrd.' Alan paused and gave the old blacksmith a circumspect glance. 'I'm not certain I've ever seen you outside the Citadel...'

Vahrd bowed.

'We need your help,' Lorn announced gravely.

His expression worried the prince, whose smile faded.

'One moment,' he said.

He went to close the door leading to his bedroom, Lorn just having time to catch a glimpse of a young blonde woman still asleep behind the gauzy veils of a four-poster bed, in a tangle of white sheets and plump pillows. Alan then invited Lorn and Vahrd to sit with him around a small low table, on which was placed a platter of fruit. Still in his shirtsleeves and unshaven, he said:

'I'm listening. What's this all about?'

Lorn outlined the situation in a few words. Alan listened, attentive and concerned. Like Lorn, he had been close to Naé during the summers spent within the Citadel's austere walls, until life had drawn them apart. No doubt he felt less affection for the young woman than Lorn did. But special bonds – which neither Lorn nor Vahrd knew about – still linked him to her.

'She was with Dorsian?' Alan asked Vahrd.

The blacksmith nodded.

'You know about this?' Lorn exclaimed in surprise.

'I didn't know Naé had been arrested. But yes, I was aware of the operation that captured Dorsian and his accomplices, although I believed they were all being held in the gaol cells at Angborn or its fortress. Yrdel told me yesterday.'

Upon hearing the word 'accomplices' Vahrd grew tense, but held his tongue.

Lorn turned to him.

'Naé followed Dorsian?' And incredulous, he insisted: 'Cael Dorsian?'

'Yes. You know him?'

The old blacksmith did not understand the look of astonishment and annoyance that he read upon Lorn's face.

Lorn and Alan exchanged a glance.

'We know him, yes,' said the prince.

'It doesn't matter,' said Lorn, trying to dismiss the problem. But speaking to Vahrd again, he asked: 'But don't tell me he and Naé...'

He did not finish.

'What?' asked Vahrd.

He was slow to comprehend, before blurting out:

'Naé and... No! Of course not!' He hesitated. 'Well... Yes,

perhaps…' And then he finally protested: 'But I'm her father! How do you expect me to know that kind of thing?'

Alan rose to his feet, putting an end to the meeting.

'Well,' he said, 'I'll take care of this.'

Imitated by Vahrd, Lorn also stood, and asked:

'What do you intend to do?'

'First of all, get dressed. Then I'll speak to Esteveris.'

'You can't ask your brother to set her free?'

'The official version is that Dorsian's arrest was my brother's doing. The truth is that all credit should go to Dalk, Esteveris's henchman.'

'I don't know him,' said Lorn.

'Believe me, you will. The fact remains that it's Esteveris who is actually holding Naé, if I understand correctly. Not Yrdel. Nor even the justice of the High Kingdom.'

Vahrd had a question burning his lips but he dared not ask it. Lorn saw this and, with a nod, urged him to speak. So the old blacksmith cleared his throat and, embarrassed, said to the prince:

'There's one thing I don't understand, my lord.'

'What's that?'

'If all the others are being guarded in the dungeon cells at Angborn or Saarsgard, why did Esteveris have my daughter brought here? Why make an exception for her?'

Saarsgard was the massive fortress defending Angborn.

'Because Esteveris knows who Naé is,' explained Alan. 'So he knows what she's worth, which is both good news and bad…'

'What she's worth?' interjected Lorn.

'She's the daughter of the royal blacksmith. Perhaps Esteveris sees her as a means of implicating the Citadel and the High King, albeit indirectly, in a scandal. Or else he plans to use her to put pressure on you, Vahrd. Or on you, Lorn. Or perhaps even on me. Because you can be sure that fat snake knows what Naé means to us…'

Lorn and Vahrd returned to the quarters assigned to the Onyx Guards, where they found the others waiting. The old blacksmith having agreed, Lorn explained to his men what was going on. They listened gravely, occasionally exchanging astonished glances and casting rather admiring ones at Vahrd.

'She has courage, your girl,' commented Liam when Lorn had finished.

'You can say that again!' exclaimed Vahrd with a mixture of pride and anxiety.

'She's not afraid of anything and she's as stubborn as a mule,' added Lorn. 'You know who she gets that from.'

'So what are we going to do?' asked Dwain.

'Alan said to do nothing until we hear from him,' Lorn replied. 'And that's exactly what we're going to do.'

'Nonetheless,' said Yeras, 'we could find out exactly where she's being held, and tonight, one or two of us—'

'No. No raids, no clever tricks. We wait.'

So they waited and two hours passed before Alan sent someone to fetch Lorn. The two friends met again in a discreet spot on the Princes' Ship, away from prying ears.

'I don't have a lot of time,' said Alan. 'I'm lunching with my brother and mother.'

'Did you see Esteveris?'

'I'm a prince of the High Kingdom,' replied Alan in an amused tone which contained a hint of pride. 'I see whomever I want.'

Lorn did not dispute the point.

'That's true. So?'

'So I spoke to Esteveris, but I did not obtain Naé's freedom. Indeed, I did not ask for it.'

'What?' Lorn exclaimed angrily, while trying to keep his voice down. 'Why not? You said—'

'I said I would take care of this matter and that's what I'm doing.'

'Really? Because you seem to be going about it the wrong way.'

'And you don't seem to know what you're talking about. It's not a question of taking a bastion by assault. Or of intimidating some militia leader.'

Surprised, Lorn stared at Alan.

Was he referring to Andara? And if so, how much did he know?

The tension between them having dropped a notch, Alan looked Lorn straight in the eye and calmly explained:

'The first thing we must do is ensure this whole story is true and we're not charging headlong into a trap. Believe me when I tell you that one can never be too careful with Esteveris. What I did not say in front of Vahrd, earlier, is that if Esteveris had Naé brought to the Floating Palace, it's because we're here. You and I. He must know we'd learn of Naé's presence, and he's playing some game where only he knows the rules and the stakes...'

Lorn was forced to acknowledge that Alan was right.

'I see,' he said. 'Forgive me.'

'Do you trust me?'

'Yes.'

'Esteveris admits he's holding Naé: that's a start. The game has begun and we'll need to play skilfully. It will take days, perhaps weeks, but I have a good chance of winning. All right?'

'All right.'

'I want to see Naé freed as much as you do. But don't try anything. Let me handle it. Before anything else, I need to discover what Esteveris really wants.'

Lorn nodded reluctantly.

Knowing that Naé was close by and being unable to save her was unbearable. He felt helpless, caught in an incomprehensible scheme, and he hated that. He had been a patient man, but now, fed by his anger, he was filled with a constant sense of urgency. He needed to act, to be doing something to further his aims, and to let none stand in his way.

5

That evening, Alan gave precise orders and then with a worried air went to the dinner to which his brother had invited him, accompanied by a few gentlemen of his entourage. He did his best to keep up his end of the conversation during the meal, but suffered moments of silence and distraction that betrayed him. He was preoccupied, and it was all the more difficult to hide the fact in such a small gathering.

'What's wrong?' his brother asked him quietly as another guest started a song.

'Nothing.'

'You seem worried. Distracted.'

The two princes liked and respected one another but had never been close. They were separated by ten years and by their very different, almost opposing, personalities. Alan sometimes had the impression they were strangers or distant cousins who shared some memories and had the pleasure of meeting on occasion, but who didn't miss one another when they were apart. They had never confided in one another, so Alan hesitated before saying:

'Forgive me. It's... It's just that I have the feeling that one of my friends is about to commit an error.'

'This friend, is it Lorn?'

'Yes.'

'Perhaps you should be warier of him...'

'Lorn would never do anything to harm me.'

'Even without meaning to, some people bring misfortune to those around them. Lorn is like that.'

Alan's first reflex was to protest, to defend his friend. But he kept silent and thought over what Yrdel had just said. He knew that his brother was a shrewd judge of character. Like all those endowed with great intelligence and of a reserved nature leading them to keep silent, listen and observe, Yrdel possessed a lucidity that rarely missed its mark.

As the song came to an end, a toast interrupted Alan's train of thought. He lifted his glass and, with a forced smile, clinked it with the others before seeing Odric who was trying to catch his eye from across the room.

'I'll be back,' said Alan to his brother.

He stood up and hurried to join his faithful servant.

'Is it Lorn?' he asked.

'No, my lord.'

Preceding Odric who trotted to keep up, Alan walked along briskly without even glancing at the sentries who saluted him as he passed. The last two opened a pair of doors for him and he entered a room lit by a lantern.

The captain commanding the guards assigned to the Princes' Ship was waiting for him there.

'He tried to sneak aboard the Azure Guard's vessel,' he said. 'He gave them a hard time but they finally subdued him. And in accordance with your orders, they delivered him to us.'

The captain stepped to one side.

Between two guards, Vahrd was sitting upon a stool with his hands tied behind his back. His head tilted forward so that his face was invisible, he swayed slightly as if the vessel were gently rocking. He was dishevelled, and his short collar and a sleeve of his doublet were torn. A cut on his brow was still bleeding.

Alan drew closer and wrinkled his nose: Vahrd stank of cheap wine.

'I told you to do nothing.'

'I wan' my daugh'er,' slurred the blacksmith without lifting his head.

Alan felt anger rising with him.

'You old fool…'

And turning to the captain, he said:

'Sling him in a cell. And find Lorn.'

The captain nodded.

'Yes, my lord.'

But the guards had barely started to hoist Vahrd from his stool when there was an explosion outside.

Then another.

And a third.

Worried, Alan raced up on deck and, leaning upon the rail, saw rockets lighting up the sky.

'Alarm rockets!' he exclaimed.

The captain, who had followed him, pointed to the barge floating on the far side of the Queen's Ship.

'They were fired from the Azure Guard's vessel,' he said.

'Yes,' replied the prince sombrely. 'And they're illuminating us.'

A rocket fell close by them and almost set fire to a tent on deck.

Less than half an hour later, the captain of the Azure Guard requested an urgent audience with Prince Yrdel. By then, the entire Floating Palace was in an uproar. The alarm rockets had done their job so well they had almost started a panic. Some had believed they were under attack, before other rumours started to spread, including one about a bold escape under the very noses of the Queen's Guard.

Yrdel met Captain Sturich in the presence of Alan and the captain of his own guard. After the customary salutes, Sturich bowed and said:

'My lords, this evening a man sneaked onto the Azure Guard's vessel and helped a prisoner being held there to escape. The pair of them were surprised as they were fleeing and they had to jump overboard. Thanks to the rockets we fired, we saw them swimming away and we have reason to believe they sought refuge on your vessel, if they didn't drown.'

'Who is this prisoner?' asked Yrdel.

'Naéris Vahrd, my lord. An outlaw. An accomplice of the rebel Cael Dorsian.'

'And the man who freed her, do we know who he is?'

'He could not be recognised,' replied Sturich, before realising that Yrdel had turned to look at his brother, as if the question were addressed to him instead.

Alan withstood his brother's gaze without blinking.

It was not a gaze of reproach, but a calm, steady look, almost regretful, and which said: *It didn't take him long, did it?*

'I imagine you wish to search this vessel,' said Yrdel.

'Indeed, my lord. With your permission.'

Dumbfounded, Alan straightened up.

'You?' he said furiously. 'Search the Princes' Ship? Absolutely not!'

'My lord, I'm acting on the queen's orders.'

'Who do you think you are, Sturich?'

As a worthy prince of the High Kingdom, Alan was making this a question of principle and honour. Permitting the Azure Guard to search the Princes' Ship would be granting it higher authority, or else tolerating being suspected of harbouring fugitives. Each vessel was a fiefdom with its own laws, its own privileges, and its own justice. From Alan's point of view, Sturich's mere request — even coming from the captain of the Queen's Guard — bordered on lese-majesty.

'I have my orders,' insisted the captain.

Alan turned to his brother. Would Yrdel have the backbone to stand up to the queen and Esteveris?

'My brother is right,' said Yrdel. 'There can be no question of anyone, other than ourselves, searching the Princes' Ship.'

Surprised, Alan smiled.

'My lord—' Sturich ventured again.

But Yrdel bade him to be silent by raising a hand.

'However,' he added, 'I will not oppose hunting down two fugitive criminals.' He turned to the captain of his own guards. 'Captain, I order you to conduct a thorough search of this vessel.'

And addressing Sturich, he said:

'I invite the Azure Guard to join its efforts to our own so that the fugitives may be apprehended as quickly as possible.'

Sturich bowed.

'Thank you, my lord.'

'Don't thank me, captain. I will not tolerate criminals taking refuge under my authority to escape royal justice.'

'Yrdel!' protested Alan. 'You cannot allow—'

'I've made my decision, Alan. See that my orders are carried out. I will be on the Queen's Ship.'

With those words, Yrdel rose and left the room.

The search of the Princes' Ship was cut short by a headbutt to Captain Sturich's face, which caused him to topple backwards.

'No one passes,' said Dwain, blocking the door to the Onyx Guard's quarters.

He wasn't alone. His fellow guards stood at his back, ready for a fight if necessary. Only Lorn and Vahrd were missing.

Sturich struggled to rise, stunned and furious, bleeding from the nose.

'But... But... How dare you?' he spluttered as his men helped him to his feet.

'You weren't listening,' Dwain explained evenly.

'You'll pay for this! I'll... I'll have you before a court martial.'

'Or we can settle this between men, right now,' proposed the red-headed colossus. 'I still have a forehead. Do you still have a nose?'

He took a step forward.

Sturich retreated.

'You cannot stand against an order from the queen and Prince Yrdel!'

'Yes,' said Logan. 'We can.'

'You're mad.'

'Possibly,' admitted Liam.

'But we're also the Onyx Guard,' said Lorn, stepping up behind his men.

They stood aside to let him pass and immediately closed ranks at his back. Unarmed, he stood before them, facing a seething Sturich.

'Neither you nor any of your men shall set foot in our quarters.'

The captain of the Azure Guard was starting to have doubts

but he was in the presence of his own men and several of the Princes' guards. Pride won out. He drew his sword.

'That's not a good idea,' said Yeras, in a voice too calm to be unthreatening.

Sturich looked at the one-eyed man anxiously.

Then at the other Onyx Guards and, finally, Lorn, who lifted his fist strapped in leather and said:

'Do you see this signet ring? I received it from the High King's own hand. It says that I am First Knight of the Realm. You are a brute with an officer's tassels. So, take your orders from Esteveris, your orders from the prince, you even take the queen's orders, and stuff them up your arse. Understood?'

Standing firm, Lorn saw that Sturich, humiliated, was about to commit a foolhardy act.

'That's enough!'

It was Alan.

The intervention of a prince of the High Kingdom quickly calmed everyone down. Embarrassed, Sturich resheathed his sword and wiped away the blood clinging to his mouth. Both his men and the Onyx Guards backed away, as if caught doing mischief. Only Lorn remained impassive, displaying an indifference tinged with arrogance.

To prevent himself from exploding with anger, Alan avoided meeting anyone's gaze. He was furious and it could be read in his eyes and his livid face.

And it could be heard, as well.

'Get the hell out of here,' he said to Sturich in an adamant tone. 'Get the hell out of here, you and your men, and don't let me see you again.'

The captain of the Azure Guard left without arguing, while the Onyx Guards also retired upon a sign from Lorn.

Alan waited until he was alone with Lorn to look him up and down with an icy air, and said to him:

'You're bleeding.'

Lorn looked down to see a trickle of blood running from beneath his right sleeve towards his ring finger. When he raised his eyes, Alan had already turned his back and was walking away.

6

Naé sat on Lorn's bunk, her features strained from worry and fatigue. She was toying nervously with a dagger, uncertain how she would use it if anyone except Lorn came through the door and tried to take her away. Should she defend herself and fight to the bitter end? Threaten to open her veins? She would not go without resisting.

She stood up when Lorn entered and, immediately reassured, smiled at him. Without a word, he wiped away the blood that ran from the slight wound he'd received on his shoulder when, just before diving into the river with Naé, a crossbow bolt had grazed him. Then he poured himself a glass of wine, drank a gulp, and thought for a moment. Seeing that he was preoccupied, Naé grew worried again. She did not dare say anything, but gave Lorn a questioning gaze. He glimpsed it out of the corner of his eye and said to her rather curtly:

'You're in no danger. For the moment.'

She felt somewhat relieved, but Lorn's annoyed expression and tone made her bow her head, as if ashamed.

'I... sorry,' she finally said. 'I... I didn't mean to bring you trouble. Neither to you, nor to Papa...'

Her hair was still damp and she looked smaller and more fragile than she actually was, wearing the clothing Lorn had lent her. The shirt, far too big, bared one of her shoulders.

Softening, Lorn sighed and smiled.

'Why don't you tell me about it?' he suggested.

The young woman nodded in agreement.

'I belong... That is, I used to belong to Cael Dorsian's group. But there's nothing left of it, now. We... We were all arrested.'

'Cael Dorsian…' repeated Lorn in a tone that was both ironic and scornful.

Naé stiffened.

'Well, what of it?'

'Dorsian is a mercenary. A criminal. Do you know how he earns his keep?'

'Yes. Smuggling kesh.'

'If it were only that! He sold arms to the Dalatian barbarians. His steel and powder killed the High Kingdom's soldiers.'

'That's not true!'

'Oh, come now!' Lorn snapped. 'And between deals, in his idle hours, he maintains his fortune by leaping from one bed to another. The man's half gigolo, half pimp. You wouldn't be the first your Cael's seduced!'

Naé stood up abruptly.

'He's not *my* Cael!' she exclaimed. 'And my relationship with him is none of your concern!'

Lorn fell silent.

Naé was right, of course. He was reacting like this because her recklessness had almost cost her own life and had caused problems which would no doubt have heavy consequences for others: himself, Vahrd, the Onyx Guards. But he wasn't just driven by reason. A stab of jealousy was goading him, although he was not in love with Naé. She was intelligent, lively and pretty, despite her scar, and perhaps even more touching because of it. But his feelings for her were purely brotherly.

Or so he'd believed up until this day.

For he knew that Naé loved him. She'd loved him since their adolescence and the summers they had spent with Alan in the Citadel, and he was now realising that this continuing love had been a constant source of comfort to him, flattering his pride and buoying his spirits. What could be more soothing and more stimulating than knowing he was irremediably and patiently loved by someone waiting in the wings? Men quickly become used to this state of affairs and feel betrayed when it ceases, even though they have done nothing to make that love endure. What was in fact an immense privilege now seems their due, and the loss of that privilege is a theft, which leaves

414

them suffering but still selfish. And so here was Naé, who no doubt now loved another man. She had given herself to him and turned away from Lorn.

Suddenly aware of the ambiguity of his feelings, Lorn pulled himself together. And very calmly, he said:

'Put that down, would you?'

Naé saw that she was still holding her dagger. She had not threatened Lorn with it but the reflexes were there. She knew how to wield a weapon and fight. In standing to protest, she had firmly gripped the dagger by the hilt, her thumb on the blade, ready to strike.

She looked down at the knife and, exasperated with herself, flicked it into the air, caught it by the tip, and hurled it against the door.

Where it planted itself deep.

Lorn looked from the blade to Naé with the same wondering and amused glance. She knew she was impulsive, but preferred to joke about it rather than rein in this side of her character.

'Sorry about the door,' she said, not sounding at all contrite.

To seal their reconciliation, Lorn poured a second glass of wine which he proffered to Naé and she readily accepted. They clinked glasses, drank, and exchanged a knowing look before Lorn finally relaxed a little.

'Is Papa really in trouble?' asked Naé, circling the lip of her glass with her index finger.

'No. I'll get him freed tomorrow. After all, he's done nothing wrong.'

'And you? Your men?'

'Me? What could they do to me?' Lorn lifted his left fist to show her the onyx signet ring on his finger. 'It would be the same as going after the king,' he added in a tone that Naé found disturbing.

More than a warning, it was a barely veiled threat against anyone who could hear him, or not. His gaze was fixed for an instant and his jaw was clenched.

The young woman hesitated before speaking.

'You're... You're not thinking of... of abusing your...'

She did not complete her sentence and Lorn stared at her, shocked.

'What?' he exclaimed in surprise. 'Me? Abuse my... No! Of course not!' He gave her a reassuring smile. 'I assure you that the only people who have reason to fear me are the enemies of the High Kingdom.'

'And not those of the High King?'

'No,' said Lorn gravely. 'It's not the same thing.'

Those words, more than anything else, worried Naé.

She had been raised to respect, even revere, the High King. To be sure, she knew he was not infallible. But his person, his word and his will were sacred. And to her they were indistinguishable from the High Kingdom.

One king, one throne, one kingdom.

Sensing Naé's turmoil, Lorn changed the subject.

'Do you know what became of those who were arrested with you?'

'Some preferred to be killed rather than captured. The others... The others, I don't know. I was quickly separated from them. Dalk knew exactly who I was. He knew it even before I was captured. Indeed, I believe orders were given that I should not be harmed... Not all of us were so lucky.'

The young woman's gaze darkened.

'Dalk was well informed,' observed Lorn.

'He is Esteveris's best spy. His principal henchman.'

'Who else knew who you were? Apart from Dorsian...'

'Dougall,' replied Naé without hesitating. 'Cael's right-hand man.' A wave of hatred overwhelmed her for an instant. 'He's the one who betrayed us. But I'll find him again.'

'You are going to lay low,' said Lorn, as he went to tug out the dagger buried in the door. 'You've caused enough trouble already, and you're a fugitive. Not to mention that Dalk and Esteveris are well aware you're aboard this barge. They know you are here, in my quarters.'

Naé remained silent for a moment, and then said:

'He deserves to be avenged, don't you see? If they've hurt him, if they've executed him, Cael deserves to be avenged. Whatever he may have done, whatever you blame him for, he

416

sought to oppose Angborn's cession. And there weren't many like him...'

Lorn looked at her without replying. She continued:

'He risked his freedom and his life, Lorn. For a cause that is also yours.'

Lorn reflected, expressionless. Then he said:

'I doubt he'll be executed.'

'Truly?'

'He's not just anybody. Esteveris cannot simply have him hanged one morning like some vulgar thief. Besides, if he really wanted Dorsian dead, he would have given orders to that effect when the man was arrested. Dorsian was captured because Esteveris and the queen want him alive. Otherwise, he would have suffered an unfortunate dagger stab, or had a fatal fall while trying to escape: it was then or never. Now it's too late for that.'

Lorn was simply putting forward a theory, one he only partly believed. But it was what Naé wanted and needed to hear, so he did his best to comfort her.

And who knew?

Perhaps Esteveris did have plans involving Dorsian. He was a prize that an able strategist like the prime minister would not hesitate to exploit. Perhaps he planned to use him as a bargaining chip or a means to exert pressure. Perhaps he intended to convict Dorsian in a resounding trial that would serve as a warning to all those thinking of defying the queen's authority.

'Do you think they're torturing him?' Naé asked in a fierce tone, as if daring Lorn to lie to her.

He paused before replying.

It was the final scenario explaining why Cael Dorsian still lived: Esteveris wanted to make him talk. In that case, there was no doubt he would be subjected to torture. In all likelihood, his ordeal had already begun and Lorn would have preferred not to speak of it. But Naé was neither an idiot, nor naive. Of course it had occurred to her, if only because she had feared being tortured herself.

That had not happened, thankfully.

'I don't know,' said Lorn.

Which was not exactly a lie.

'Perhaps you could help him,' ventured Naé.

'Help Dorsian?'

'You're on the same side. Maybe you could have him freed. Or at least make sure he has a fair trial.'

Lorn felt the pain of his own judgement rekindle. For a brief instant, he wondered if, by alluding to an equitable trial, Naé was deliberately pressing a particularly sensitive nerve. But he dismissed the notion; Naé wasn't that manipulative.

'I'm not sure I have the power to do that,' he temporised.

'But if you had, would you do it?'

Naé's eyes were locked with his and he knew he could not lie. So he thought about it, and said:

'Yes.'

The young woman smiled.

And that smile did not simply express a relief born of renewed hope. It also expressed her joy at knowing the Lorn she remembered and loved had not died in Dalroth; he was still capable of justice and compassion.

She threw herself at him before he could react, hugging him with all her might.

'Thank you,' she murmured, her head buried in his neck. 'Thank you...'

Lorn didn't know what to do.

He awkwardly enfolded the young woman in his arms, his hands barely brushing her back. But he felt her warmth, her body against his. Disturbed by the desire he felt rising within him, he gently pushed Naé away.

'It will all turn out well in the end,' he said. 'All right?'

She nodded, her eyes damp.

'Lock up behind me,' he advised, showing her the bolt on the door. 'Don't leave here. And don't open the door for anyone except me, understood?'

'You're leaving me?'

'I'll go and sleep with the lads, in your father's hammock. You'll be fine here.'

'Thank you, Lorn. For everything.'

Almost laughing, he shrugged.

418

'Bah! We couldn't leave you in Esteveris's clutches, now could we?'

He placed a kiss upon Naé's brow and, just before leaving, he said:

'And don't forget the bolt. Until tomorrow.'

Naé pushed the bolt home and leaned back against the door.

Then she slowly slid down to sit on the deck, her knees folded, as she suffered alone with the memories of everything Dalk had subjected her to.

7

Meanwhile, Dol Sturich, still furious, had only stopped to wash his face before going to see Esteveris in his apartment. The minister was relaxing, sipping a glass of flavoured wine. A light silk robe covered his obese body, still damp from a steaming-hot bath which had turned his skin coppery. He was not wearing his rings and his plump fingers, ordinarily weighted with precious stones, seemed strangely naked.

'Well, then?' he asked in an almost mocking tone.

In a few brief but evocative words, the captain recounted how the Onyx Guards had prevented the search of their quarters, how Lorn had asserted the authority of the High King, and how Prince Alderan had ended the dispute. Esteveris listened with a thin smile upon his lips, his eyes shining as if he were thoroughly enjoying the tale. The minister's amusement intrigued Sturich but then started to annoy him and stoke his anger. It required an immense effort on his part to keep calm.

Finally, no longer able to contain himself, he said:

'You're... You're smiling?'

'Indeed. Good evening, captain. That will be all...'

Sturich retired, still bemused.

'May I ask what amuses you?' enquired Dalk, emerging from the shadows. 'Sturich was acting on your orders. Your authority has been flout—'

'I know, I know...' Esteveris interrupted.

The minister rose and signalled for Dalk to lend him his arm. They passed through gauzy veils stirred by a warm breeze and walked out onto the terrace, beneath a Great Nebula so bright it made the night seem grey.

The terrace was deserted, covered by sections of light cloth that formed a long canopy leading to a railing against which they leaned. It overlooked thin air, far from any eavesdroppers. Moreover, the dull roar rising from the river covered the sound of their voices, as long as they did not speak too loudly.

'How do you think the blacksmith learned we were holding his daughter?' asked Esteveris.

'That was your doing?' Dalk exclaimed. 'But why?'

'Because the girl was ultimately of little value to us. She cannot tell us anything. And as leverage... On whom? On her father? On Lorn? They are not the sort of men to give in. At best, it would establish a link between the Citadel and the insurgents. However, from there to implicating the High King...'

Dalk nodded with a sombre expression.

He was forced to admit that the minister was right, but he had been proud of capturing Naé on top of the success of his mission at Angborn, and he found it galling to be told that his prize was not one, in fact. Even worse, Esteveris had deliberately let him believe that she was. As a game? Out of cruelty? Out of suspicion, or calculation?

'Whereas if I arranged for the father to learn that his daughter was at my mercy, I knew that Vahrd, or Lorn, or more likely both of them, would try something. Something bold and illegal...'

'But why? I mean, what... what interest is there for you?'

'First, the possibility that the escape attempt would go wrong,' Esteveris said. 'If Lorn or one of his men were wounded and captured, the Onyx Guard would have been implicated in a scandal that would have led to his downfall and incriminated the High King himself. But that's not all. Suppose, just suppose Lorn had been killed during the operation...'

Esteveris let his sentence trail off with a dreamy air, before gathering his wits and resuming:

'Bah! The main thing is that it went just as I had imagined.'

'So you knew that...'

The minister shrugged.

'Of course I knew Lorn would fly to Naéris's rescue, I knew that the only place he could hide her was aboard the Princes'

Ship, I knew that the Onyx Guards would oppose any search of their quarters, and lastly, I knew that Prince Yrdel and Prince Alan would be forced to take sides.'

'It was Prince Alderan who intervened.'

'Did he seem to be Lorn's accomplice?'

'No.'

'Perfect.'

'Nonetheless, the prince came down in favour of Lorn.'

'Yes. So now he must account for his actions to Prince Yrdel. Which means he will ask Lorn to do the same. You'll see.'

Dalk understood.

'So,' he said, 'Naé became the heart of a quarrel…'

'This fire may catch light now. Perhaps it will catch light later. But I can assure you that, in the end, its coals will come to life…'

8

The following morning, Lorn met with Alan again as the prince was having his breakfast alone, on a balcony of the Princes' Ship, in the shade of a canopy which rippled in the wind. Alan barely broke off eating to greet Lorn. He did not invite the knight to sit down, much less to share his meal.

So Lorn remained standing and waited.

He noted the prince's face, his tight features, his black gaze. He also noted that Alan was drinking wine laced with kesh and that he'd already made inroads on the carafe next to his glass. But that did not explain his friend's agitated state. On the contrary, kesh usually had a soothing effect.

Despite that, Alan seemed furious.

Two servants, silent and still, stood a short distance away. When one of them advanced to fill the prince's glass, Lorn – who was starting to grow annoyed – decided he had waited long enough.

'I've come to ask you to release Vahrd,' he said.

Alan took the time to swallow a mouthful which he did not savour and, without raising his eyes from his plate, replied:

'And why would I do that?'

'Because he's not guilty of anything.'

'He tried to sneak aboard the Azure Guard's vessel. That is something.'

'He was drunk. And worried about his daughter. He drank one glass too many and did something stupid, that's all. He's had all night to reflect on the error of his ways and sober up. Don't you think that's enough?'

Angrily, Alan threw his knife down upon his plate and sat back in his chair, looking at Lorn with a disdainful eye.

'You really have some nerve…' he finally said.

Lorn remained impassive.

'After all that happened last night,' continued the prince, 'you still want me to believe that Vahrd wasn't acting in concert with you? That he wasn't creating a diversion while you freed Naéris? Do you take me for a fool, Lorn?'

Lorn remained silent; Alan rose and came round the table.

'Look me in the eye and swear you didn't help Naé escape. Tell me she's not on this barge right now, and that she didn't spend the night in your cabin…'

Lorn glanced at the two footmen, who, beneath the canopy, stood to either side of the prince's chair, acting as though they saw and heard nothing. Alan took the hint and dismissed them with a gesture. They immediately withdrew, with the prudent haste adopted by the best servants.

Lorn waited until Alan and he were alone, and then said:

'Naé is in my cabin. You knew that full well last night, when you forbade any search of the Onyx Guard's quarters.

'Don't ever pull another stunt like this on me again, Lorn! Last night was a fait accompli; you knew perfectly well that I would support you against Esteveris, but you left me no choice. You manipulated me.'

'No,' protested Lorn. 'I didn't mean—'

'You did!' exploded Alan. 'You knew exactly what would happen! You knew I would take your side if necessary!'

'But you don't find it shocking for a minister's thugs to be searching the Princes' Ship?' Lorn asked calmly. 'Your brother never should have agreed to it.'

'Don't change the subject! My brother conducts his affairs as he sees fit. No doubt he has a reason to avoid a quarrel with Esteveris and I don't believe you have any say in the matter.'

They were standing face to face, almost nose to nose, Alan quivering with anger while Lorn remained completely still.

'You're right, Alan. But—'

'No! No buts. That signet ring doesn't make you a king. Or a prince.'

Alan turned away and went to lean against the balcony's

424

railing. Exasperated and upset, he drew in a few deep breaths, taking the time to calm himself.

Lorn joined him and stood silently at his side.

'You... You took advantage of our friendship, Lorn...'

'That's true. Forgive me. But we both know that's not the only question, don't we?'

The prince frowned.

'What?'

'The real reason you're angry,' said Lorn, 'isn't because I put your back to the wall. It's because I didn't warn you we were preparing to rescue Naé...'

It was true; Alan was feeling excluded. Almost betrayed.

'But how could I tell you?' Lorn continued. 'You don't really think you could have been involved in it? You're a prince of the High Kingdom. By hiding our plans from you—'

'Don't you dare,' Alan interrupted, his voice rich with anger. 'Don't you dare say you were protecting me. You didn't trust me, that's all there is to it.'

'I swear that's not the case.'

Lorn was sincere but Alan wasn't listening, saying:

'You're wrong about me, Lorn. Entirely wrong. After all, I've always been a prince, haven't I? So what difference does it make? To me, none. But to you?'

The prince left his question hanging and moved on, saying:

'You don't make things easy for your friends, Lorn...'

The knight gave no reply.

Although both sorrowful and angry, Alan nevertheless felt a resurgence of hope when Lorn called out to him.

'Alan!'

The prince had almost left the balcony. He hesitated, then turned back towards Lorn who, standing at the railing, kept his gaze fixed on the horizon.

Alan waited.

'I am sorry,' said Lorn.

The prince departed without saying another word.

9

*'He had been a great king, and a valiant one, feared and respected
by all, allies and enemies alike. He'd waged many a battle and
won immense victories. But as his reign drew to a close, his glory
and his strength waned beneath the weight of his faults, while his
throne tottered. Yet pride, rather than remorse or the warnings of
Destiny, made him unwilling to die leaving his kingdom to ruin.'*

Chronicles (The Book of the Knight with the Sword)

From the throne room's balcony, seated beneath a canopy which
protected him from the chalk-laden drops, the High King
watched the white downpour falling upon the Citadel. More
melancholy than ever, he sat perfectly still.

'Why do these rains never cease?' he asked in a weak,
scratchy voice.

'I don't know,' said the white drac who was standing beside
him.

'Have I not obeyed the will of the Dragon of Destiny? Have
I not redeemed my faults?'

'I'm only an Emissary, sire.'

'But what do the Guardians say?'

'Emissaries do not attend the Council's meetings.'

The old king smiled faintly behind the black veil which hid
his cadaverous face.

'Come now, I know your ways,' he said. 'Do you imagine
you're the first Emissary I've met? I know full well that you're
better informed than you admit…'

Skeren hesitated.

In his role as Emissary, there was indeed a difference between
what he knew and what he was supposed to know. And what

he had the right to reveal was yet another thing. Jealous of its secrets, the Assembly of Ir'kans was always careful to say as little as possible. It sometimes obliged its emissaries to conceal truths, or even to lie in order to further its aims and encourage the fulfilment of Destiny.

The white drac could not admit that the Guardians had deceived him, and were still doing so, but he was reluctant to lie again.

So he kept silent.

'Norfold believes freeing Lorn from Dalroth was an error,' said King Erklant. 'And that entrusting him with the fate of the High Kingdom was sheer folly. He thinks I never should have summoned him back. Or made him my First Knight. Or authorised him to reform the Onyx Guard... In short, he thinks I never should have listened to you. Norfold hates Lorn, that's understood. But he doesn't like the Assembly of Ir'kans and its emissaries much more, mark my words.'

Skeren nodded, with a knowing smile.

'I'm aware of that.'

'All the same, is he really wrong to be wary of you?'

'How can I answer such a question, sire?'

'And was I wrong?'

'I beg your pardon, sire? Wrong? Wrong about what?'

'To have listened to you! Wrong to have trusted the Guardians and carried out their will.'

The Emissary considered his reply, and then said:

'It's a question of the Grey Dragon's will, sire...'

The High King's bony shoulders shook with a small laugh that sounded like a hiccough.

'You... You're slippery as a... as a...'

The drac guessed which word the old king did not dare to utter.

'As a snake, sire?'

The High King hesitated.

'It's the usual expression,' added Skeren in a friendly tone. 'I see no reason to take offence.'

'Yes,' said King Erklant, scowling a little. 'As a snake...'

He fell into one of his misleading silences.

The High King had absent spells and could remain silent like this for long moments: his mind escaped and deprived his mummified body of the small life that still animated it. But sometimes he simply fell asleep, closing his eyelids behind the concealing black veil. In both cases, he sat unmoving and indifferent, inaccessible, his wheezing breath slowly lifting his meagre chest.

Uncertain, Skeren waited while the rain redoubled in strength.

Whiter and heavier, its drops pattered and burst upon the grey stones. The roofs were covered with milky water which overspilled from the gutters and fell in cold white trickles. Puddles drowned the paving stones. Streams raced down the streets, drawn to the deserted Citadel's lower regions.

'Does any of it really matter?' the old king suddenly said. 'If Norfold is partly right? That Lorn never should have been set free? Does it really matter?'

The Emissary carefully refrained from responding.

Did the king truly expect a reply? Probably not. He was probably thinking aloud, carried away by the train of his thoughts, his doubts and his fears.

'Guilty or not, what does it matter? That's what Norfold doesn't want to understand. In his eyes, a traitor is a traitor and he's convinced that Lorn betrayed the Grey Guard and the High Kingdom. That he betrayed me,' added the High King, sounding disillusioned. 'And that's something a man like Norfold cannot forgive.'

He paused for a moment and reflected.

'For my part, I know that Lorn is innocent,' he said. 'But the truth is, that is no longer of any importance…'

Once again, the white drac made no reply. First he wanted to learn where the old king's thoughts were leading him.

'Because the common interest outweighs all else, doesn't it?' continued Erklant II. 'What do a man's faults and crimes matter, if his actions save a multitude?'

The Emissary raised an eyebrow.

He wondered whom the High King was trying to convince. Was his question rhetorical?

'There's no doubt that Lorn has a destiny, sire.'

'And this destiny is to save the High Kingdom, is it not?'

Skeren chose his words carefully.

'I believe so. But all I know is that the destiny of the High Kingdom cannot be freely fulfilled without Lorn. That is what the Guardians affirm. It's what they were told by the Grey Dragon.'

Suddenly irritated, the High King made a gesture with the back of his hand, as if shooing away a fly.

'That remains to be seen!'

'Sire?'

'The Guardians never tell us what they actually want, do they? They don't confide in you or in me. Or in anyone else. And that's how it's always been.'

'That's true.'

The drac knew that the king's wariness towards the Assembly of Ir'kans was shared by almost everyone. The Guardians, however, did not deserve all of the accusations voiced against them and certainly not to be the target of a fearful hostility which, occasionally, was deflected onto their emissaries. Still, Skeren thought the Guardians had their share of blame to bear. The secrecy they surrounded themselves with, their arrogance and their refusal to explain or justify their decisions, all contributed to arousing suspicion.

What were they hiding, exactly? And why? To what end?

These questions were the ones being pondered by the High King and the Emissary was forced to acknowledge their legitimacy. Skeren was the one the Assembly of Ir'kans had entrusted with informing the king that Lorn should be freed from Dalroth and given all the means necessary to fulfil his destiny, as it was bound up with the future of the High Kingdom. Erklant II had enough experience and wisdom not to take the Guardian's pronouncements lightly. Nevertheless, he remained a proud king whose decisions determined the fate of Imelor's most powerful nation, and he did not intend to let his actions be dictated by anyone.

The truths that were subsequently revealed to him mattered little.

The Prophecy of the Princes and, as troubling as it might be, the secret of Lorn's origins mattered little.

There was no question of the High King taking the assertions and promises of the Assembly of Ir'kans at face value. He wanted guarantees and had only obtained one, but it came from the best and the worst of his allies.

Serk'Arn, the Dragon of Destruction.

'She was beautiful,' said the old king, who had once again silently drifted off into the meanders of his thoughts again. 'Very beautiful. A queen. A Skandish queen. A warrior queen.'

The Emissary realised after a moment's delay that the High King was talking about Lorn's mother. In an almost dreamy tone, Erklant continued:

'I think I loved her. In my fashion, but I did love her. As I loved so many others,' he said with a hint of regret.

Then he declared more forcefully:

'But I did not know. I didn't know Lorn was my son. I never even imagined it until...'

Until I told you, thought Skeren. *And the idea grew within you, that the innocent man rotting in Dalroth was perhaps indeed your son. A bastard, to be sure. But one you might have spared, or rescued during those three long years.*

'But of that,' said the old king, returning abruptly to the wariness that the Assembly of the Ir'kans inspired in him, 'of that I am sure, now. On this point, the Guardians have not lied. They could not have done so. Lorn is my son. My blood runs in his veins. That of my lineage.'

The drac gave no reply and thought of the detachment with which the High King had exposed Lorn to the Dragon of Destruction. Since it had been subjugated by magic, it could not harm a descendant of its vanquisher, the first King Erklant. The High King had therefore envisaged bringing Lorn before Serk'Arn, to see if the dragon spared him. For the old king, it a way to obtain proof of Lorn's origins. The idea that he might be delivering an innocent victim to the Dragon of Destruction did not even cross his mind, or at least had not stopped him. Would he have even felt any remorse, if – based on a lie by the Guardians – Sark'Arn's fire had consumed Lorn?

430

The Emissary doubted it. And this was not cruelty. Or even cynicism. Just indifference: that of a dying king threatened by madness, who no longer cared about anything except saving his kingdom.

'Where is he?' asked the old king.

'Sire?'

'Lorn. Where is he?'

'With Prince Alderan on the Floating Palace, which is taking the queen and her suite to Angborn.'

'And why are you not in Angborn?'

'I'll go, perhaps, but there's nothing left to be done now. All is ready, and the storms ahead cannot be averted.'

10

'Having completed its voyage upon the Eirdre, the Floating Palace halted before Samarande where the entire royal court came ashore in all its glory and pomp. For the three whole days, the town paid homage to the queen and the princes of the High Kingdom. Then the anniversary of the battle of Tears approached, along with the first cool weather of autumn. Whereupon Queen Celyane and her suite embarked on ten superb vessels, bedecked with banners and bunting, to go and greet Prince Laedras at Angborn, the city promised to Yrgaard.'

Chronicles (The Books of the Cities)

The ships sailed north upon the calm waters of the small Sea of the Free Cities. They soon arrived at Angborn, which, from its island, guarded the strait opening onto the Sea of Mists. From the prow of the royal caravel, holding Yssaris in his arms, Lorn observed the town and its citadel, now visibly growing near. The afternoon was drawing to a close.

Angborn had always been the most Yrgaardian of the Free Cities. The Black Hydra had pampered and favoured it, even making it the capital of the annexed province. After the reconquest carried out by Erklant II, not all links had been broken with Yrgaard. On the contrary, Angborn had made use of the new freedoms granted by the High King to remain as close as possible to the most powerful realm of the north. Despite the passing years, Angborn's political and commercial elites had never stopped considering themselves Yrgaardians, and had gladly welcomed the planned cession. But for its part, the general population feared being subjected to Orsak'yr again, the Black Dragon of Death and Night.

As for the High King...

He had liberated the Cities conquered by Yrgaard's armies. It had been one of his first deeds of glory and now, at the end of his reign, he was seeing one of the Free Cities returned to the Black Dragon. For the queen, it represented a victory, the crowning of her policy, since this cession would mark the resumption of diplomatic relations between the High Kingdom and Yrgaard. But for the king, it was an especially bitter defeat.

'If Yrgaard were to retake Angborn in battle, at least,' he'd said to Lorn. 'But no... That which the High Kingdom paid in blood to conquer and then defend, the High Kingdom now cedes with the stroke of a quill... Do you know how many men died on Saarsgard's ramparts? Returning Angborn to Yrgaard is like pissing on their graves. It's an insult. It's... It's shameful. Shameful for us all...'

Lorn had then thought he guessed the High King's intentions, as unrealistic as they might seem.

'Do you want me to prevent Angborn's cession, sire?'

'No. No, of course not. It would be folly and, besides, it's too late for that... You see, the queen thinks only of her triumph, of succeeding where all others have failed, in signing a peace treaty with Yrgaard. Esteveris, on the other hand, sees further. He does not believe a lasting peace is possible with the Black Dragon, but he knows a rapprochement between the High Kingdom and Yrgaard gives him what he needs most.'

'And what's that?'

'The freedom to devote himself to the kingdom's internal troubles. And the money he is cruelly lacking right now.'

Indeed, the High Kingdom's coffers were quite empty.

Nevertheless, it had never been a question – officially – of the High Kingdom selling Angborn. It had simply been agreed that Yrgaard would settle an old debt. Following the reconquest of the province of the Free Cities, the High Kingdom had imposed the payment of a heavy tribute upon its defeated opponent. Yrgaard had only transferred the first half of the stipulated amount, and it was the second half that it was offering to pay now, upon signature of the Angborn treaty, as a gesture of good

433

will. It was a fortune that was particularly welcome to the High Kingdom. No one was fooled, but appearances were saved.

'Esteveris knows they he will soon need money, Lorn. A lot of money. To secure loyalties, but also to raise the armies needed for safeguarding the High Kingdom.'

His train of thought interrupted by the flapping of a sail, Lorn raised his eyes towards the fortress overlooking Angborn. Massive, sombre and menacing, Saarsgard resembled Dalroth. Indeed, it had been built in the same period and for the same reasons, during the Shadows. And although it had not been exposed to the Dark, the sight of it made a chill run down Lorn's spine.

'Sinister-looking, isn't it?' said Esteveris.

Unlike Yssaris who had lifted its head, Lorn had not heard the minister approach. With a quick glance, Lorn assured himself they were alone, or almost: the minister's counsellors and guards – including Sturich – were waiting a short distance away, far enough not to hear anything over the sounds of the rigging in the wind and the ship's hull cleaving the waves.

'Its architecture must bring back bad memories,' added Esteveris.

'Indeed,' said Lorn.

'But all that is behind you now...'

'You really think so?'

'I hope so, for your sake, at least.'

Lorn made no reply.

'I'm glad to know your slight disagreement with Prince Alderan has been settled,' said the minister after a brief silence.

Lorn remained expressionless.

'What slight disagreement?'

'You know, after that deplorable escape.'

Esteveris was alluding to the altercation between Lorn and Alan the day after Naé's escape. At the time, the two friends had parted without being completely reconciled, but time had done the rest and everyone could see, during the final days of the voyage on the Eirdre, that together with Enzio they were more inseparable than ever. In truth, things were not so well between Alan and Lorn, but they put on an act which convinced everyone of the contrary and had almost fooled themselves. Lorn wondered if they were simply refusing to admit that the years had gone by and they had changed. They were still firm friends, to be sure. However, that friendship's initial innocence had given way to nostalgia for that innocence. For they now realised that their bond was vulnerable to rancour as well as doubt.

'I don't know what you're referring to,' said Lorn.

The minister smiled.

'As you please… Permit me, however, to express my concern for your friend, Vahrd. No one seems to have seen him since he was arrested that famous night. Perhaps Prince Yrdel is unwilling to set him free? In that case, it would be my pleasure to…'

'That will not be necessary, thank you.'

Lorn contained a small smile and caressed Yssaris's head.

He was well aware that Esteveris knew that Alan had kept Vahrd locked up for a few days, before releasing him when the Floating City reached Samarande. On the other hand, the minister was surely unaware of what had become of the old blacksmith since then.

Or of his daughter.

Lorn had taken advantage of the commotion created by the court's landing at Samarande to smuggle Naé off the Princes' Ship. Disguised as a servant, and armed with a few pieces of silver and a letter of recommendation, she had immediately taken the road to Oriale, where, Lorn being convinced the Black Tower was under surveillance, she would ask Sibellus for his hospitality. Vahrd had disembarked the same day, just as discreetly.

'I would imagine,' said Esteveris, 'that a father would want to accompany his daughter on a long and perilous journey.'

Lorn kept silent but pondered the minister's words.

The journey to the capital was not so perilous as all that. Had Esteveris realised that Naé was going to Oriale, and insinuating that the roads were being watched? Or was he simply trying to worry Lorn in the hope of reading some sign of the truth upon his face?

435

'We're arriving,' the minister said. 'I don't know if we will have the opportunity to speak again, over the next few days. I will be very busy and I imagine you will be too. Whatever you are here to do,' he added, before walking away with a steady step.

Lorn did not bid him farewell and raised his eyes again towards the Saarsgard's ramparts and black towers, as the ship approached the port, greeted by ceremonial salvos.

'I want you to go to Angborn and represent me there,' the High King had said. 'I want you to be seen. It tears at my heart, but the cession of Angborn must take place. The High Kingdom needs this semblance of peace with Yrgaard. And it also needs the tribute Yrgaard is willing to pay... The treaty must be signed. You must convince Teogen of this, and then make sure that no one intervenes to prevent it in Angborn. The High Kingdom's future depends on it, Lorn. This treaty is dishonourable. But it's our only hope, do you understand?'

Lorn took a moment to think it over.

And then he nodded in agreement.

11

Queen Celyane proceeded at a walk, mounted upon a magnificent white mare and protected from the pale autumn sun and the warm drizzle by an azure canopy held aloft on golden poles by eight servants. Ahead of her, horsemen from the Azure Guard opened the parade with fifes, drums and heralds bearing banners. The official procession followed. First came the escort riders in blue and yellow, then the royal princes, the great lords and dignitaries of the High Kingdom, the members of the clergy, and the foreign ambassadors and delegations, all of them moving forward at the same solemn pace.

The procession had started off from the port, acclaimed by a vast crowd. It had then followed the route to Angborn's fortress, through streets decorated with bunting, where the onlookers became less numerous and less enthusiastic. It was obvious the bravos and the hurrahs that had greeted the queen were neither spontaneous nor sincere. Esteveris's agents had done what they could, but the illusion had not lasted long. Despite the garlands and the pennants, despite the applause of some, one could not help seeing the empty balconies, the closed shutters, the sparse ranks of onlookers at the foot of the buildings' façades. The procession even received a few boos from within the houses, while passers-by doffed their caps but were silent and grave-faced – which was as much as they could do without openly expressing their disrespect for the High Kingdom's sovereign. Unlike Angborn's civic leaders and bourgeoisie who welcomed a handover of power from which they hoped to reap great profit, the common people could not forgive the queen for returning the city to Yrgaard. They felt abandoned, sacrificed, and knew – having previously endured it – that they would suffer under the Black Dragon's yoke.

Sitting pale and upright on her mount, the queen simmered with rage, furious at not being cheered, and glad that she would soon be rid of this ungrateful city. She let none of it show, however. Looking straight ahead, only her eyes flashed with a murderous fire. As though it were not enough that she had to put up with the High King's representative...

Lorn was riding a short distance away, at Alan's side, behind Prince Yrdel and his barons. He wore the armour of the Onyx Guard, while his jet-black mount wore a splendid grey caparison embroidered in silver with the wolf's head, the crossed swords and the royal crown. Unknown to the crowd, he cut an intriguing figure, all the more so since he stood out among the silk clothes, the embroidered robes, the brocades and lace trimmings, the plumes and ornaments. Dressed in black, he seemed to be in mourning on behalf of the king, for the lost glory of the High Kingdom.

The procession crossed the city and, via a fortified road, reached Saarsgard. The fortress in fact stood apart from the rest of Angborn. Backed by forbidding rocky escarpments, it had its own port and served less to guard the town than the strait, its ramparts and cannons looking primarily out to sea. Like Dalroth, Saarsgard comprised several enclosures defended by towers, portcullises and drawbridges. It was a formidable citadel. Whoever possessed it controlled Angborn. And whoever controlled Angborn threatened the other Free Cities by dominating their sea.

Ceding Angborn and its fortress to the Black Dragon was clearly an act of folly, Lorn said to himself. A folly desired by all, including the High King himself – regretfully, to be sure. But despite its promises, despite the treaties, Yrgaard remained the High Kingdom's hereditary enemy. Ceding Angborn to it was like muzzling one's dogs and entrusting the sheepfold to the wolf because it pretended to accept a pat on the head.

Saarsgard's governor-general was waiting for the queen and her retinue in the main courtyard of the fortress. He was a courtier without military experience appointed by Esteveris to this post because he was docile and pro-Yrgaard. The queen and her minister had no desire for a commander who might create difficulties at the last minute. With the Baron of Gharn, there was no risk of that. His predecessor, on the other hand, had been an old general loyal to the High King, who'd been speedily removed once the plan for Angborn's cession began to take shape.

The queen paid scarcely any heed to the speech given by Saarsgard's governor before the garrison drawn up in ranks. Still angry, she'd even shortened it with an annoyed expression and then shut herself up in her quarters along with several close companions, who tiptoed about her. The brass band that was supposed to play was sent away, the garrison troops dismissed and the procession dispersed, disappointed by the queen's bad temper.

Lorn felt oppressed as he passed beneath the low black archway and entered the ancient fortress. He left Alan and rejoined his own men with relief. Liam informed him they had taken up their quarters and found a quiet stable for the horses. They had also had time to scout the site and take their bearings. In short, all was ready.

'The fortress is almost deserted,' said Dwain.

'The garrison has already started to withdraw,' explained Yeras. 'Only the Castel is still occupied. The rest is empty.'

'The High Kingdom is really in a hurry to rid itself of this place,' noted Logan bitterly. 'Yrgaard will be able to take possession a few hours after the treaty signing.'

They knew what that meant.

The next day, before nightfall, the colours of the Black Hydra would be waving over Saarsgard.

Lorn led his men to the Castel, through deserted streets which gave the impression that the sinister stronghold had been abandoned after falling victim to a sudden curse. He was lodging there, along with the queen, the princes, Esteveris and all of the most noteworthy guests, and he knew the way perfectly well.

This was not his first visit to Saarsgard.

For it was here that Yrgaard and the High Kingdom had

held the clandestine negotiations whose smooth conduct he had been charged with protecting, when he was still one of the High Kingdom's bright young hopes. Despite the passage of time, the old fortress held few secrets from him and he could honestly claim he knew each building, each hallway, each room of the Castel, after having guarded them night and day while the representatives of the two kingdoms laboured to draw up a peace treaty.

More than three years had passed since then.

An eternity…

They arrived.

The Castel was the heart and the most ancient part of Saarsgard, a fortress within the fortress, created centuries before the rest of it was built. It stood upon a rocky base, surrounded by a vertiginous crevasse whose walls plunged down into shadows haunted by the backwash of the Sea of Mists. Its bridge, its portcullises and its ramparts sheltered a maze of towers and courtyards joined by archways and flights of steps hollowed by wear. Its walls were thick, pierced by low doors and cruciform embrasures. Its keep, known as the 'Sanctuary', was massive and austere, as sinister as it was menacing, and seemed to have been carved from a single column of crenellated granite.

Still leading his men, Lorn traversed the bridge that crossed the gulf and disappeared into the Castel.

While the High Kingdom's court finished settling in, Lorn watched the sun set over Saarsgard from his windows. His apartment was on the same floor of the keep as those of the queen and the two princes, Esteveris having been forced to give up his place.

With Yssaris purring in his arms, Lorn reflected that having been sentenced to die in Dalroth, he had been rehabilitated by the High King in the Citadel – the very place where he had been judged and convicted. A first whim of Destiny. Now – by a second whim – he had returned to Saarsgard for the signing of a treaty much like the one prepared here three years earlier, in the greatest of secrecy and under his guard. Lastly – a third whim – he knew that, in this very same place, his life was about to take as dramatic a turn as the day when he was arrested for high treason. He'd survived Dalroth but he might very well die here, in another fortress inherited from the Shadows.

'The Grey Dragon definitely has a taste for irony, doesn't he?' he said in a low murmur.

The cat looked at him as if waiting for him to say something more.

12

The following day, as the final preparations for the ceremony kept the High Kingdom's court busy, Lorn was finishing lunch with Alan and Enzio in his apartment when Liam entered.

'My lords, please forgive me,' he said, bowing first to the prince.

'What is it?' asked Lorn.

'You need to see this for yourself, knight,' replied the veteran, crossing the room hurriedly.

He went to the window.

Intrigued, the three friends rose to join him there and saw what it was about. Below, a column of prisoners was filing into a small courtyard. Under close guard, the captives were marching slowly, hobbled by the weight of their chains and exhaustion. They disappeared one by one through a low door in the keep.

'They've just arrived,' explained Liam. 'They're the rebels who fought against the cession.'

'The ones Naé joined?' asked Alan.

'Yes, my lord. Until this morning, they were held in Angborn's prison.'

'So why transfer them here?' Lorn wondered out loud.

'That's Esteveris through and through,' said Alan.

'Esteveris cannot liberate them or have them murdered in their cells,' said Enzio. 'But I doubt he wants a trial that would allow others to take their side.'

'And,' added the prince, 'he cannot execute them without making them martyrs.'

'So he's handing them over to Yrgaard along with the

fortress,' concluded Lorn. 'Letting the Black Dragon decide their fate.'

'You have to admit it's a neat solution,' said Alan, turning away from the window.

He seemed both resigned and admiring. With a less steady gait than he would have wished, he went to the table, filled the first glass he saw with wine and drained it in a single gulp. His two friends exchanged a glance but said nothing.

Lorn turned back to look at the sparkling horizon and the Sea of Mists to the north. He caught a glimpse of a bright object reflecting the sun, revealing the location of the waiting Yrgaardian fleet.

'Ten ships,' said Enzio, who had seen the same glint. 'An entire battle squadron. So that's what Yrgaard sends to escort a diplomatic mission.'

'Officially,' said Alan from behind them, 'they're there to protect the dragon-prince from possible attacks by Skandish pirates.'

'As if Skandish sails had ever been sighted this far east in the Sea of Mists!' exclaimed Lorn.

'Perhaps they didn't take the most direct route...' Enzio joked.

There was a moment of silence, during which Alan emptied the last bottle of wine and said:

'It's time to go, Enzio. The general rehearsal is starting soon and we don't want to keep the queen waiting, do we?'

'Certainly not,' replied Enzio.

'And we can't let anything spoil the celebration, can we...' the prince added with a bitterness that intrigued Lorn.

Alan and Enzio left, leaving Lorn and Liam alone.

But the Sarmian gentleman soon returned to fetch his dagger, which he had removed to sit more comfortably at the beginning of their lunch.

It was merely a pretext, however.

As he tucked his weapon into his belt, he glanced at the open door and drew Lorn aside by the elbow. Liam understood and withdrew.

'I must be quick to rejoin Alan,' said Enzio. 'But you noticed, didn't you?'

'I think so.'

'How many glasses of wine did you drink?'

'Two.'

'Me too. And how many empty bottles do you see?'

Lorn glanced at the table which the servants had started to clear away.

'Three,' he answered gravely.

'He'd already been drinking when I met him this morning. And this isn't the first time it's happened. It's become a habit over the past few weeks.'

Lorn remained silent, full of concern.

In contrast to Enzio, he'd hardly seen Alan before embarking on the Floating Palace. But indeed, it seemed that almost every time they'd been together, the prince was drinking a little more than was reasonable. And that wasn't the worst of it. Lorn knew – and hadn't wanted to admit it to himself until now – what Enzio was about to tell him.

'I think Alan has started using kesh again.'

Lorn recoiled slightly and looked away from his friend.

'I know he drinks wine laced with kesh,' he acknowledged. 'It's not wise, but—'

'I'm not talking about that. I'm talking about kesh liquor. I think he started drinking it again aboard the Floating Palace. Since his… return, he's had plenty of time to see what the High Kingdom's court has become and I think he's finding it more and more unbearable.'

Lorn sighed, his jaw clenched in anger, but he said nothing.

'Alan isn't well, Lorn. Something is gnawing at him. He needs help, and you know he'll only confide in you.'

13

That evening, Lorn felt increasingly anxious as he advanced into the bowels of Saarsgard. They reminded him of the dungeons of Dalroth, making him feel he was back there. Everyone agreed that the Dark's influence had not been felt at Saarsgard for centuries, but was that in fact true? And what did the scholars really know about what lurked in these cellars and catacombs, these vaulted underground chambers condemned to eternal night? Had they revealed all their secrets?

Lorn gripped the hilt of his sword to resist the temptation to work the joints of his marked hand. It did not hurt. It did not even bother him. But despite that he felt an urge to rub it, as when the memory of an old pain comes to mind, even though the wound itself has long since healed.

He had not suffered any symptoms of the Dark for months now.

His last fit was the one he'd had during the return of the expedition against the Ghelts in the Argor Mountains, yet he did not believe he'd been cured and still feared a relapse. He knew the Dark was a patient monster still curled within him. If it had spared him recently, he owed it firstly to the Watchtowers, which had protected Oriale and its population from the Dark during the Shadows and continued to centuries later. But he was also convinced he owed something to Yssaris, who hardly ever left him now and was currently prowling the roofs of Saarsgard beneath the light of the Great Nebula.

Lorn regretted not having the cat with him now.

When they reached the bottom of a stairway, the gaoler pushed open a gate and, lantern in hand, entered a corridor.

Lorn followed him to a door whose massive lock the man turned thanks to one of the keys hanging from his belt.

The gaoler pushed the door open and stood back, holding out the lantern.

Lorn took it, and had to bend down to enter.

Lorn did not remove his hood until he was inside and the door shut behind him. He breathed in a foul air he recognised only too well, stinking of despair and the rank odours of filth, shit and fear.

In the light from the dark lantern, he discovered a cell that was longer than it was wide, with a low ceiling and a flagstone floor. Men were shackled to the walls, a single chain running through rings riveted to the stone. All of them were attached by the neck and could only sit, lie down, or stand, but never move more than three feet from the wall. Runnels intended to carry away the prisoners' urine and excrement converged on a hole only a few inches wide at the centre of the room.

Arm outstretched, Lorn directed the beam from his lantern towards the prisoners and inspected them one by one. Some of them – gaunt and haggard, with bushy beards and hair, their bodies covered with sores and vermin – looked back with the wild gazes of spooked beasts. More turned away or protected their eyes with their hands. Those were the prisoners that Lorn had seen arriving. They were dirty and weak, their faces hollowed by fatigue. Some were wounded and all had clearly been beaten. But they were in better shape than those who had been rotting here for years. In the light, Lorn caught one of those unfortunate wretches glaring at him, and for an instant thought he'd glimpsed the madman he'd become at Dalroth.

'Are you looking for me?' asked one prisoner before the lanternlight reached him.

He rose with a clanking of the chain as Lorn turned and illuminated his face. Dazzled, Cael Dorsian blinked and lifted his arm to shield his eyes, while trying to look sideways at the knight.

'Lower that, would you?'

Lorn complied.

'Good evening, Cael.'

The other man hesitated.

'Lorn? Is that you?'

'It's me.'

'Shit. If I'd been expecting you... You'll excuse me for not saluting you,' said Dorsian, jiggling the chain.

'Don't trouble yourself,' Lorn replied coldly.

Dorsian eyed him for a moment.

Tall, blond and broad-shouldered, Dorsian was the same age as Lorn. He had a certain bearing about him, despite present circumstances, his filthy clothing, his greasy, tangled hair, and the bruises from blows to his face. But his pretended nonchalance – which was in fact just vanity – spoiled the effect.

'I see you've not changed much,' he said, sitting back down against the wall.

Lorn gave no reply.

'Gentlemen,' said Dorsian to all present, 'allow me to introduce Lorn Askarian, the fine flower of the High Kingdom. Unjustly accused and convicted, now absolved of all charges and appointed First Knight of the Realm. We respectfully salute you.'

Still seated, he gave the caricature of a bow, tilting his head forward and twirling his right hand in the air.

'Are you finished?' asked Lorn.

'Why are you here? To gloat, now that you're high and mighty, and I'm reduced to this state? Just like the good old days. You always liked to lord it over me with your grand airs and lofty sentiments...'

Lorn and Dorsian had attended the royal military academy together, where the most worthy sons of the High Kingdom – by merit or by birth – were sent for training. Gifted but lazy, and resistant to authority, Dorsian had been expelled after being accused of raping a girl. He was convinced Lorn had falsely denounced him and had nursed a tenacious hatred for him ever since. A few years later, the two young men had crossed paths once again in the border region of Valmir, where Lorn was fighting under the banner of the High Kingdom and Dorsian commanded a company of mercenaries, selling themselves to the highest bidder and engaging in a variety of criminal activities.

'Bah!' he continued. 'It would be wrong for you not to enjoy this... If you knew the pleasure I felt when I learned that the noble, valiant, irreproachable Lorn Askarian had been convicted of high treason... But it was just a tragic mistake, wasn't it? And here you are.'

'Naé is well,' said Lorn. 'She's free and in good health.'

That piece of news took Dorsian aback.

'Na... Naé?' he stammered. 'Free?'

'Yes. And safe.'

Dorsian collected his wits.

'So you know,' he said.

'That you almost got her killed? Yes, I know.'

'I didn't want that. I even tried to convince her not to—' He interrupted himself. 'But don't you think she's strong and intelligent enough to make her own choices?'

Lorn made no reply and returned Dorsian's stare. The rebel leader finally smiled and said:

'It troubles you, our relationship, doesn't it?'

'You're raving.'

'I'm trying to work out why you're here. I'm already puzzled why I'm here. Until today, they seemed happy enough keeping us locked up in the city prison. Our gaolers had plenty of fun beating and starving us. And suddenly, this morning, they brought us here. Do you know why?'

'You and your companions are going to be handed over to Yrgaard.'

Silent at first, Dorsian absorbed this piece of news with real courage. Then he stood up and asked:

'So this is a farewell?'

Lorn turned to the door and called:

'Gaoler!'

The door opened to reveal the gaoler, who entered with two large baskets and started to distribute the food – bread, wine, meat, cheese – to the famished prisoners.

'I can't do more for you right now,' said Lorn. 'Regain what strength you can. You'll be needing it soon.'

14

Upon leaving Saarsgard's dungeon, Lorn felt an urgent desire for fresh air and went, on his own, for a walk upon the ramparts. The fortress seemed strangely silent. The night was clear and cool, the Great Nebula spreading across a cloudless sky.

From the ramparts, Lorn was able to make out, a long way off to the north, the lights of the Yrgaardian fleet accompanying the dragon-prince who would represent the Black Hydra at the treaty signing. Alan had said this battle squadron was meant to protect against attacks by Skandish pirates. But in truth, Lorn told himself, all of Yrgaard was aboard that fleet. It spoke of pride and wariness, the desire to be feared and to impress others with its power.

Ten ships.

And perhaps more, further out to sea.

How many men could they carry? Enough to take rapid possession of Saarsgard. The inhabitants of Angborn would soon feel Orsak'yr's yoke.

His gaze filled with bitterness, Lorn contemplated the dark horizon for a moment.

The rivalry between Yrgaard and the High Kingdom had endured for centuries. It had political, diplomatic, military and commercial motives. But above all, it was rooted in the hatred Orsak'yr bore for Eyral, the High Kingdom's tutelary dragon. As Lorn saw matters, Yrgaard and the High Kingdom could sign all the treaties they liked but true peace would be impossible until the day the Dragon of Death and Night ceased to hate the Dragon of Knowledge and Light…

Lorn sighed.

Making its presence known with a meow, Yssaris leapt into Lorn's arms. The knight smiled and, rubbing its head, asked:

'Had a good prowl?'

The young cat started to purr.

'You're right,' said Lorn. 'It's time to go inside.'

The cession of Angborn would be signed the following day.

Lorn returned to the Sanctuary.

At nightfall, all of the doors were closed except the main one, which was guarded by sentries from the Azure Guard. Lorn passed them without a glance, as they stood to attention for the representative of the High King.

Oil lamps burned in the corridors, where a deep silence reigned. Lorn wanted to take the stairway, but at the bottom of the steps, Yssaris nimbly escaped from him and walked away in a tranquil fashion, tail held high, with the air cats have when leading the way.

Lorn hesitated.

Then he followed the young feline.

Yssaris entered the keep's hall and disappeared into the shadows. The next day, the immense chamber would host the ceremony of Angborn's cession.

His eyes adapting easily to the dim light, Lorn strolled after him.

Everything was ready.

The scents of sawdust, wax and fresh paint still floated in the air. Lit by a few night-lights, hangings with the colours of the High Kingdom and of Yrgaard decorated the walls and tiers of seats. A gallery ran round the room at the height of the first floor, from which dozens of banners hung – from there, heralds with trumpets and drummers would accompany the ceremony. Cordons marked out squares for the audience. A long carpet ran from the door to the dais upon which the queen, the princes and Lorn – as First Knight – would take their places. A seat beside the queen was reserved for the dragon-prince, who would preside with her over the festive banquet after the ceremony.

Lorn heard a noise.

At first he thought it was Yssaris who had upset something but he sensed a presence in the darkness and immediately reached for his sword.

'No need to panic,' said Alan, revealing himself. 'It's only... only me.'

His voice was slurred and he walked unsteadily. Unkempt, his eyelids drooping, he held a half-full bottle in his hand.

'So, you came to have a look too?' he asked. 'Before tomorrow's great triumph?'

He made a clumsy gesture and staggered. Lorn moved to assist him, but the prince managed to catch himself on his own.

'It's all right,' he said. 'All right...' Grumbling, he let himself fall onto a bench and swigged from the neck of his bottle. 'A triumph... What rubbish! We're going to witness a tragic error tomorrow, Lorn. A tragic error... And the only... the only real question is: is it the last of my father's reign, or the first of my mother's?'

'You can't stay here, Alan. Not in this state.'

Suddenly despondent, the prince shrugged and murmured something. Unable to hear, Lorn approached and crouched before him.

'What did you say?'

'I... I hate what the High Kingdom has become, Lorn. I hate it... All these courtiers. The intrigue, the ambition, the lies. And the flattery, Lorn. All the flattery... If you knew how weary I am of it...'

Alan's eyes were full of distress and guilt.

'You aren't to blame for that,' Lorn told him. 'It's not your fault if—'

'I know Yrdel has done what- he could,' the prince continued without hearing a word. 'But he's alone... Alone against Esteveris. Alone against... against my mother... She hates him, you know.'

'Yes, I know.'

'Because he's not her son. While me... Me! You'll see... One day, she'll want me on the throne in his place...'

The sentence died in a bitter snicker.

Lorn felt guilty. No one knew Alan better than he. He knew

451

that behind the charm, the carefree manner and dashing grace lay hidden doubts, faults and pain that Alan sought to forget, or soothe, with kesh. He was fragile and subject to crises of self-doubt that laid him low, but he concealed them out of a sense of decency as much as pride. And because he had been raised with the idea that a prince of the High Kingdom must never be weak.

Lorn had believed that Alan had been cured of these crises when he had freed himself from the kesh. Or at least he'd wanted to believe that, out of his own selfishness. But evidently the prince was not free from the doubts eating away at him.

Or from kesh.

'Odric!' Lorn called.

He was convinced the old servant was waiting somewhere nearby and he was right: Odric was not long in appearing. He bore the mark of a recent blow to his face. Seeing that Lorn had immediately understood the situation, he looked away, ashamed for his master who had struck him in a fit of anger.

Lorn pretended not to notice.

'Help me.'

Together they lifted the prince. Then, when Lorn was sure he had a firm hold on him, with an arm around his shoulders, he said to Odric:

'Go on ahead and make sure we don't run into anyone.'

'Yes, my lord.'

The old servant left and Lorn waited.

'He did not ask to see me,' Alan muttered. 'Not once since my return. He could have written. Asked for my news... But no.'

Lorn did not immediately understand whom Alan was referring to.

'The king?' he finally asked.

'My father, yes. Does he even know I'm alive?'

'Of course!'

'Then he couldn't care less about me...'

Lorn had no reply. He wanted to find words to comfort the prince, but he searched in vain. Moreover, even if he felt sorry for his friend, he was also angry with him. Seeing Alan this way, knowing that he had succumbed once again to the lure of kesh, revolted him. He could not help holding it against his friend. There were people who had done everything, tried everything in their power, to help the prince. And he'd relapsed, betraying the trust placed in him.

'He despises me,' Alan continued. 'He's forgotten me. I might just as well never have returned from that monastery where they had me locked up...'

Screaming with pain, sometimes begging to be put out of his misery, maddened by fever and delirium while his muscles, his bones and his guts formed one massive ache, Alan had endured a martyrdom during the long months needed to purge his body of kesh.

And all that, for what?

Seized by a sudden loathing for himself, the prince threw away his bottle, which smashed in the darkness. The smell of kesh soon began to pervade the room.

'I... I suffered, you know? In that lost and lonely monastery.'

'I know,' Lorn said.

'But you...' murmured Alan, once again finding the thread of his chaotic thoughts. 'He called you back to his side. He... He summoned you and made you First Knight of the Realm... Why does he prefer you to his own son? A king should prefer his own blood, shouldn't he?'

Lorn, yet again, had no reply.

Luckily, Odric returned and, from the door, signalled that the way was clear.

'You need to sleep,' said Lorn, helping the prince walk.

Seated in the shadow of the throne destined for the queen, with its paws straight ahead and its head held high, Yssaris watched them move away.

15

The following morning, beneath Yssaris's tranquil gaze, Lorn did something he had not done for a long while. Unsure if he even believed in the divinity of the Great Dragons, and without addressing any one of them in particular, he prayed, kneeling in his armour before a window in the pale light of a fragile dawn. He did not pray for himself or to be forgiven, but for the souls of those who had faith and were going to die, unaware of the lies of Destiny.

In less than an hour, an Yrgaardian war fleet would enter the port of Saarsgard.

16

The ceremony lasted three hours and proceeded without incident.

It commenced with the entrance of Queen Celyane and the princes to the sound of brass trumpets, and their solemn speeches before an impatient but respectful audience. Then the ambassadors, together with their delegations, presented themselves one by one at the royal dais before regaining their assigned seats. All of them saluted the queen as though she had just been crowned and now reigned over the High Kingdom. This was not said openly, but Esteveris had carefully arranged for the ceremony to have all the trappings of a coronation, and no one was left in any doubt on that point. Celyane's reign was being celebrated and her authority recognised. Each homage paid to her by the representative of a foreign power confirmed her regency and conferred an additional layer of legitimacy upon her.

Other treaties were even signed.

The one the High Kingdom and Yrgaard were about to conclude effectively disrupted existing coalitions and required prior adjustments. For centuries, the High Kingdom's entire diplomacy had been founded on its antagonism towards Yrgaard. Every accord – diplomatic, commercial, or other – it had previously made contained clauses hostile to Yrgaardian interests. It was therefore necessary for the High Kingdom to sign new treaties – or amend older ones – with its historic allies, so that nothing should contradict the conditions for peace with the Black Dragon. No one knew what would happen now that the two most powerful realms of Imelor claimed to be enemies no longer. But each kingdom, each foreign province, each free city, would be forced to redefine the terms of its alliances with the High Kingdom.

So the ambassadors came forward again and the queen signed 'Celyane, Queen of the High Kingdom' on the various documents that had been hammered out in prior negotiations and were now presented to her, one after another, opened to the last page. Immediately after signature, the seal of the High Kingdom was solemnly affixed next to the queen's. Only the High King's seal, stamped in black wax, was missing.

But the queen seemed to have no concern about that.

Happy and radiant despite the natural haughty coldness which she never managed to completely shed, she had a kind thought, a compliment, a smile for each and every diplomat. To her left stood the king's empty throne. To her right was another seat, also empty, reserved for the dragon-prince who would soon be making his entrance. She was therefore the focus of all attention, sitting proudly in the middle, wearing her crown and a low-cut gown that clasped her waist and straightened her back while lifting her bosom.

She was beautiful, and savouring her triumph.

Having also taken his place on the dais, Prince Yrdel cut a pale figure in comparison. Reserved and austere, he seemed ill at ease. Prince Alderan looked positively unwell. Although he forced himself to keep up appearances and act as befitted his rank, his smiles were artificial and his gaze often distracted. To the point that some, among the ambassadors and foreign dignitaries, were already asking themselves if Alan opposed the treaty with Yrgaard. Or did he have another reason not to share his mother's joy? He had distanced himself from the court for more than two years, which he had spent travelling and educating himself. What role would he play in the High Kingdom, now that he had returned? And what exactly was his relationship with the First Knight of the Realm?

Lorn was standing behind the High King's vacant throne, as if forbidding anyone from sitting there. He had the right to take the seat himself, thanks to the signet ring on his finger. But he'd told Esteveris that he preferred to remain in the background. The minister had seen it as a gesture of appeasement, a willingness to assert his rank discreetly, without causing friction. The queen, for her part, had been pleased that she would thus occupy centre stage with the two princes. Some mean-spirited observers would interpret the vacant seat as a sign of the king's disapproval, but who would care about that for much longer?

She was not wrong on that score.

Having initially drawn gazes and provoked interest, Lorn's presence behind the throne, unmoving and impassive, was soon forgotten. The court only had eyes for the queen and for the magnificence and dignity of the ambassadors and other royal emissaries.

Moreover, the person who everyone was waiting to see had not yet appeared. Wrapped in a great black-and-red cloak whose hood completely hid his face, the dragon-prince had disembarked that morning from the Yrgaardian flagship and, surrounded by a large escort which prevented anyone from approaching, had gone directly to the Castel's keep, where – still closely guarded he had shut himself away in the quarters reserved for his use.

Only his name was known: Laedras. It was said he was 'Third Dragon-Prince', although no one was certain what the term actually meant. None had seen him and there was much anxious and far-fetched speculation about him, with no way to separate fact from rumour and legend.

So when the trumpets and the drums announcing his arrival fell silent, a great hush came over the immense hall as the Yrgaardian delegation made its entrance.

The great doors opened and a single gentleman appeared.

Laedras was tall and slender, athletic in build and broad of shoulder. He looked about thirty years old, perhaps less, when in fact he had already lived for a century. He wore black and red, the colours of Yrgaard, and boots and gloves of fine leather. A cape hung from the shoulders of his embossed breastplate. His hair was long and red. He was handsome and had a noble bearing. His step was firm, brave and regular.

He made a deep impression.

For many of those present, it was the first time they had

seen a dragon-prince. And for most, it would be the last, as dragon-princes rarely appeared outside Yrgaard, unless they were leading armies.

Laedras preceded four drac lancers whose armour was as black and as gleaming as their scales. Then came a dozen men who bore, with the help of shafts passed through rings, two enormous carved ebony chests encrusted with rubies. Priests followed them, in rows of threes, their hands in their sleeves, wearing black-and-scarlet robes, and with their heads covered by obsidian caps that hugged the shape of their bald skulls. Four human lancers closed the march, equipped like the first but mounted on giant caparisoned lizards whose forked tongues lashed the air.

A shiver ran through the audience as the Yrgaardian procession advanced behind Laedras. A shiver of dread and excitement, like that experienced when one stands – vulnerable and unarmed – before a superb, deadly beast. The queen straightened in her seat and, aware of the moment's importance, displayed more confidence than she felt. The princes also grew tense.

Lorn, standing behind them, showed no sign of emotion but unerringly identified what was dimly sensed by everyone else: the presence of the Dark. It awakened old echoes of feelings which were both familiar and frightening, while the stone seal on his left hand began to prickle. In the dragon-prince's veins ran the blood of the Black Hydra, his mother. Intelligent and cruel, he was a creature of the Dark, and one of the most formidable to be found.

The queen felt a confused turmoil steal over her when Laedras, having saluted her, straightened up and directed his hypnotic reptilian gaze upon her. A man left the group of priests and advanced, his robe's hem brushing against the thick carpet in a silence disturbed only by the hissing war lizards. He waited, and then began to translate the dragon-prince's speech from High Yrgaardian, a language no longer spoken anywhere except in the Black Hydra's palace, into the common Imelorian tongue. Melodious and rhythmic, the language was derived from Draconic and was primarily used for incantations.

Lorn did not listen to the dragon-prince, or to the queen's response. Their declarations might as well have gone untranslated. Anyone who had witnessed the reception of an extraordinary ambassador would have heard them before. Moreover, the texts of both speeches had been drafted and agreed well in advance. Not a single comma was improvised. Both parties played their parts perfectly.

Lorn watched Laedras carefully, though, more curious than fascinated. He too was seeing a dragon-prince for the first time and wondered to what degree his human appearance reflected the truth. Was it his ordinary form, the one most natural for him? Or did he prefer the draconic form; the one he bore when summoning the Black Hydra's power? That power emanated from him like an icy aura. What did it become, when he liberated it? According to the *Chronicles*, many courageous men had fallen before it, swept away by their fear.

The dragon-prince made a gesture, beckoning the porters to approach. They deposited the two chests before the queen and the princes, removing the shafts with which they had transported their burdens, and retreated without a word. Laedras gave another signal and four priests advanced. They opened the chests' heavy locks, but waited for the dragon-prince – through his translator – to express Yrgaard's satisfaction at finally paying 'an old debt of honour' as a token of good will and friendship, with no expectations regarding the future relations between the two kingdoms.

Which was a way of formally indicating that Yrgaard was not paying for Angborn. This was a war tribute, delivered after some delay but paid in accordance with the treaty signed following the reconquest of the Free Cities, whose clauses Yrgaard had never fulfilled completely. The hypocrisy was blatant but appearances were thereby saved for the High Kingdom: it was not selling its city. And Yrgaard was not buying it.

No one was fooled.

The priests opened the two chests at the same time, and the gold coins and jewels which filled them to the brim shone in the light with the same victorious gleam as could be seen in Queen Celyane's eyes. She was looking at a fortune. Enough to replenish her kingdom's coffers. Enough to finance a war. Enough to serve her ambitions and impose her authority, by fire and sword if necessary.

A murmur of surprise and wonderment ran through the gallery, the terraced seats and then the rest of the chamber. In the audience, those unable to see jostled their neighbours for a glimpse. There was the beginning of a crush, quickly calmed by the Azure Guard.

Lorn only saw the price of a city and its inhabitants.

The price of the High Kingdom's honour.

Smiling, the queen bowed her head and thanked Yrgaard in the precise terms agreed in advance, which the dragon-prince received with polite indifference. The priests withdrew, leaving the chests open before the royal dais. It had been agreed that they would remain there until the end of the ceremony.

Finally, the moment had come for the cession treaty.

More formal speeches were exchanged, and then one of the Yrgaardian priests brought forward a casket encrusted with precious stones which he held like a reliquary. Placing a knee upon the ground before the queen, he opened the casket, whose sides fell away while the base lifted to reveal a heavy parchment scroll, which the Black Hydra had already signed with her claw, next to her seal.

The desk appeared again, along with an inkpot and a large gold and blue quill which Esteveris dipped into the ink before handing it respectfully to the queen. Measuring each of her gestures to better savour the solemnity of the moment, convinced she would be celebrated in the *Chronicles* for concluding peace with Yrgaard and restoring the High Kingdom to its state of glory, Queen Celyane thanked her minister with a cold smile, took the quill and, as the kingdom's seals and wax were being conveyed to the desk, she prepared to sign, when…

'One moment, pray…'

The queen froze, speechless.

Then, incapable of accepting what she had just heard, she shook her head and placed the quill upon the parchment, as if she had fallen victim to some illusion, as if the astonished

460

hush which had fallen over the hall were another figment of her imagination.

But Lorn stepped forward and said:

'Ma'am, if you please?'

The queen turned to him.

'You! By what right do you dare to speak?'

'By right of being First Knight of the Realm, ma'am. And because the High King himself speaks through my mouth.'

Dumbfounded, the queen stammered a few words which died upon her lips. Then she turned to her minister:

'Esteveris?'

It was an appeal for help, to which the minister was at a loss to reply. Muttering, he shrugged his shoulders haplessly.

'Ma'am, I only know—'

The queen's furious gaze, however, forced him to summon all his wits. He swallowed and asked Lorn:

'Knight, what is the meaning of this?'

But his voice was covered by the noise from the hall, where incredulous murmurs were gathering in strength. A hubbub was rising beneath the vaulted ceiling and echoed there. It was already difficult to be heard and the uproar simply added to the confusion.

'Silence!'

The order rang out and was immediately obeyed, although the source took some time to identify.

It was the dragon-prince.

'Who are you?' he demanded, staring at Lorn.

He spoke perfect Imelorian.

'I am Lorn Askarian, First Knight of the High Kingdom.'

'So?'

Laedras's voice was glacial. Sharpened by scorn, his response cut like steel.

'This treaty will not be signed,' announced Lorn.

He descended from the dais, passed between the two great chests and planted himself before the dragon-prince.

'The High King is opposed to it,' he added.

'But that can't be!' exclaimed the queen, rising to her feet.

461

'You can't claim that… Knight! Do you hear me! I order you to—'

'BE QUIET!' shouted the dragon-prince.

Stunned, the queen fell silent and retreated as if she had been slapped.

She sat back down.

Scandalised, Alan tried to intervene but Yrdel restrained him.

'No. Wait,' he murmured.

The dragon-prince called out to Esteveris:

'You!'

The minister came forward:

'My lord?'

'Does this man truly speak for the High King?' asked Laedras, his reptilian gaze looking deep into Lorn's eyes.

And as Esteveris hesitated, he insisted:

'Can he oppose this treaty? Does he have the right and the power to do so?'

The minister bowed his head and, trapped, was forced to admit:

'Yes. He has the right and the power, if this is the High King's will.'

'Angborn is and shall remain part of the High Kingdom,' Lorn said to the dragon-prince.

'That is still to be seen.'

'It will certainly not be a treaty that decides otherwise.'

'There are other means,' the dragon-prince hissed menacingly.

'Really?'

Laedras then noticed the men in black armour who were revealing themselves. One of them was standing on the gallery, behind Lorn. With one elbow resting on the barrier, he had shouldered a crossbow and was conspicuously aiming it right at Laedras's head. And a dragon-prince was not immortal: a crossbow bolt to the forehead could kill him when he was in human form.

Laedras gave up, and declared to all those present:

'This insult, this affront shall not go unpunished! No one

mocks Yrgaard in this fashion without paying the price! The crown of the High Kingdom shall soon render accounts!'

And making ready to leave, he signalled to the porters to take back the chests.

But Lorn opposed this as well.

'That gold no longer belongs to you.'

The dragon-prince was taken aback.

'I... I beg your pardon?'

'That gold is not yours,' repeated Lorn.

'You have just prevented the signing of this treaty. You cannot possibly lay claim—'

'I can and do lay claim. This is payment for Yrgaard's debt of honour, now finally redeemed, is it not? It has nothing to with Angborn's cession; your declaration was very clear on that point. Are you now going back on your solemn word?'

'I will not leave you this treasure!'

'Then blood will be spilled. Yours mixed with mine, no doubt, but if you try to reclaim this tribute you shall not leave this fortress alive.'

The dragon-prince's eyes narrowed and became two vertical slits behind which burned a furious brazier. He had ten lancers with him, some of them mounted upon war lizards. He could start a massacre, but would he survive it? This knight seemed prepared to go through with his threat. His black-armoured men would quickly be at his side. And then there was the crossbowman.

But the idea of leaving now, cheated, tricked and empty-handed...

No.

It was more than Laedras's pride could bear.

Lorn felt it and tensed.

Also sensing the danger, the Onyx Guards put the hands to their swords, ready to leap into action. Yeras firmly lodged the crossbow's stock against his shoulder: he would only get one shot. The priests backed away while the black dracs lowered their spears for combat.

Lorn narrowed his eyes. He had not foreseen the dragon-prince resorting to arms right here and now, and yet...

'Guards! Stand ready!'

Against all expectation, it was Esteveris who had given the order.

From the beginning of the ceremony, the Azure Guard had merely performed the role of an honour guard. But Laedras suddenly perceived the danger represented by the sentries posted at the doors and those, dressed in armour and with pikes in their hand, who were aligned along the walls and at the foot of each column. His troops were clearly at a disadvantage, and the crossbowman still had him in his sights.

Lorn realised that Esteveris had decided to save what he could: the treasure. All the same, would the prospect of the Azure Guard's intervention be enough to dissuade the dragon-prince from attacking?

Several very long seconds passed in an atmosphere of acute anxiety.

Then Laedras spun about and marched away, followed by his priests who had to hurry to keep up, and his lancers who backed away to the door, as if covering their retreat.

'The colours of Yrgaard shall fly above this fortress,' the dragon-prince swore. 'Anyone still here shall be put to the sword. You have until nightfall to leave this place!'

And turning back at the threshold of the great double doors, he cried:

'After that, it shall be war!'

Once the doors of the hall shut, there was general relief, at least until the dragon-prince's final words sank in. A feeling of urgency then took hold of the audience and the Azure Guard had to mobilise itself to calm and contain the most restless, the most selfish and the most eager to leave.

As for the queen, she rose and descended from the dais as if totally oblivious of the growing panic.

'Mother...' Alan said, attempting to hold her back.

But in vain.

She did not hear him. She did not hear anything.

With a slow step, she walked towards Lorn. Livid, her gaze furious, she stared at him for a long moment.

Before slapping him in the face with all her might.

Lorn's head jerked sideways, then his eyes locked with the queen's. His split lip was bleeding. But he remained calm and, as if nothing had happened, said:

'You should leave, ma'am. For your own safety. This evening we will be at war, and the first battle will take place right here.'

17

'For the Dragon had spoken to him, in the secret heart of the mountain that sheltered the tomb of the first High King, who had imprisoned and enslaved it in order to steal its power.'
Chronicles (The Book of the Knight with the Sword)

In the heart of the mountain against which Erklant I's mausoleum had been built, Lorn had forgotten the old king from the moment the Dragon of Destruction had addressed him, and only him. All his thoughts, his entire being, had been captured by it, and he'd been unable to tear his eyes away from Serk'Arn.

'You know what they all want you to believe, don't you?'

'Yes,' said Lorn.

'And you know why.'

'I do. Is the king—'

'Fooled by all this? Yes, I believe he is. There is no faith stronger than that of a madman who wants to believe. And this madman desperately wants to believe he is your father.'

Serk'Arn's voice filled Lorn's skull with a low, almost painful roar. It was the expression of an ancient power, which had declined over the years, to be sure, but still surpassed understanding. Serk'Arn was no longer a god. However, he had been one once and the vestiges of his might were still greater than anything Lorn had encountered so far.

'And the Guardians?' he asked. 'What do they believe?'

'Them? I don't know. I wonder... I can only tell you they expect something from you too.'

'The fulfilment of my Destiny.'

'Yes. And perhaps something more. Everyone wants something from you.'

'Even you?'

'The magic which binds me only protects Erklant I's descendants. If I wanted you dead...'

A shiver of horror ran through Lorn.

He was crushed by the power of this fallen god imprisoned by a spell. It was like standing in the shadow of an avalanche held back by a breath of air, like raising one's eyes towards the foamy crest of a tidal wave frozen by an enchantment. Lorn sensed the incredible power which a few runes and arcanium chains could not suffice to subjugate.

'Then what do you want?' he asked.

'To conclude a pact with you,' replied the dragon. 'A secret pact that will benefit both of us.'

'What can you offer me? I'm at your mercy. You can destroy me with a breath, but that is all you can do. And once I pass those doors, you can do nothing against me, or for me.'

'Don't be so sure of that, Lorn. There is much I can do for you.'

It seemed impossible, unreal.

And yet this really was Serk'Arn, the Dragon of Destruction, Lorn was speaking to.

'The Dark is in you. I sense it. It is stronger than anyone yet guesses and, one day, it will overwhelm you. But you already know that. You don't want to admit it, perhaps, but you know it's true.'

Lorn nodded gravely.

At that instant, he did not know what he was hoping for, but he could not prevent himself from doing so. A glimmer of hope, flickering and distant, had kindled within him. That of a man with an illness who wanted to believe in a miraculous remedy. That of the condemned man waiting for a pardon.

'I cannot free you from the Dark, Lorn. Any more than I can free myself from these chains.'

With those words, hope died within Lorn and was replaced by icy shadows.

'But I can let you dominate it,' continued Serk'Arn. 'I still have that power. The Dark is in you. With my help, however, you could control it. And who knows? Perhaps even use it for your own benefit…'

Lorn thought about it, hesitant and more troubled that he wanted to let on. The dragon's words kept returning to him: *'There is no faith stronger than that of a madman who wants to believe.'* Wouldn't they apply just as much to himself as to the old king, if he let himself be tempted?

'The Dark will cease to be a disease eating away at you, and become a strength,' the Dragon of Destruction added. 'Do I need to describe the Dark's power to you? Can you imagine if that part of the Dark that lies within you were subject to your will?'

It was enough for Lorn to imagine the Dark no longer corroding his body and soul. But the dragon's claims nevertheless struck home when he recalled the resurgent energy he'd felt in Bejofa, after he'd received a beating at the end of an alleyway. He had been lying there vanquished and broken, bleeding, when something had awoken inside him and made him stand up. His strength had returned to him, along with a savage determination that had rendered him cold, lucid and merciless. That determination, that renewed physical and mental vigour which had saved his life, he owed to the Dark.

'You've already tasted its power, haven't you?' said Serk'Arn.

Lorn nodded, aware that he could hide nothing from the dragon. Nevertheless, he voiced an objection:

'Nothing can dominate the Dark. Not even you. Sooner or later, it will destroy me.'

'As the sea wears away the cliff that will inevitably crumble, yes.'

'So what good will it do me?'

'Think of the time that is now allotted to you. Think of the self they stole from you. Do you want to simply brood and await death? Do you want to spend your remaining years in a futile combat against the Dark? Do you want to remain the condemned prisoner that you were at Dalroth?'

'No. I… I want to live.'

'Then become my ally.'

'And the Dark? How will I—'

'That does not depend entirely on you. But if I'm not mistaken, a moment will come. You'll recognise it. You'll understand. It's even possible – you'll foresee it... And when the moment arrives, you will need to return to me.'

'And if that moment never comes?'

'Then the Dark will slowly complete its work and kill you.'

Lorn thought about it.

Then, his decision made, he had looked directly into Serk'Arn's incandescent gaze.

'So be it. What do you want from me?'

'They are going to give you power,' the Divine Dragon had replied in the immense shadows of the hollow mountain. 'Use it.'

18

'"Since the king is so intent on keeping Saarsgard, let him see to its defence!" Those were the last words Queen Celyane, in her anger, uttered before embarking on her ship, abandoning Saarsgard to Yrgaard's wrath. The court followed her, worried and anxious to depart, and soon there were only a handful of men left to defend the fortress and the honour of the High Kingdom. A prince, however, was one of them.'

Chronicles (The Book of the Knight with the Sword)

The afternoon was drawing to an end.

From Saarsgard's ramparts, Lorn watched the High Kingdom's ships disappearing in the distance, upon waters which were already growing dark. Then his gaze fixed on the black-and-red sails of the Yrgaardian fleet at its moorings in the now otherwise deserted port.

'How many of them, do you reckon?' he asked.

Alan screwed up his face.

'Ten ships. Forty men per ship.'

'Four hundred, then.'

'Of which about a third are sailors. But they also know how to fight.'

'Four hundred...' repeated Lorn to himself. Then, straightening up: 'The sun will soon be setting, Alan. It's time for you to leave.'

'Out of the question.'

'And that goes for you as well,' added Lorn, turning to Enzio.

The latter, leaning against an enormous bombard which

pointed out to sea, was scribbling with a pencil lead in a note-book.

'Bad news, my friends,' he said. 'According to my calculations, we're well within range of the Yrgaardian cannons.'

'Naval guns,' objected Alan. 'Effective against a wooden hull. Less so against stone walls.'

'True. But their gunners will have plenty of time to adjust their aim, in the calm waters of the harbour. And thanks to the reserves in the port's arsenal, they won't be running out of powder or cannonballs any time soon…'

'Are you listening to me?' asked Lorn, raising his voice.

'No,' replied Enzio, correcting a trajectory. 'Siege warfare is a science which requires one's full attention.'

'Alan,' insisted Lorn. 'You are a prince of the High Kingdom. Your life is worth more than this fortress.'

It was not the first time Lorn had tried to persuade his friend to leave. And before him, Esteveris had pleaded in vain until the moment of embarkation. As for the queen, she had not said a word upon learning the news of her son's decision to remain behind.

'Lorn is right,' said Enzio without lifting his eyes from his notebook.

'Look who's talking!' protested Alan.

'I am merely a Sarmian gentleman. The blood of the High Kings does not run in my veins.'

'And now he's being modest, too…'

The elder son of the Duke of Sarme and Vallence gave a smirk.

'Lorn,' said Alan, 'you know as well as I do that we're not just defending a fortress here. And even if we were, isn't it the king's will that we do? My father's will? What sort of son would I be if I went against my father's will?'

If only you knew… thought Lorn.

'Yrdel did not have such scruples,' he said.

'Don't bring my brother into this. First, he is the crown prince. Second, I'm certain he's doing his utmost to persuade my mother to rethink her decision to abandon Saarsgard.

Believe me, if a fleet comes to our rescue, we'll owe it to Yrdel. And he will be commanding it.'

Lorn wanted to object but the prince did not give him the chance.

'My place is here, Lorn. Here. Upon these walls. I am sure of it as I have not been sure of anything for a long while now. We're going to defend Saarsgard and we're going to send that dragon-prince packing.'

Alan's almost naive confidence moved Lorn.

'Besides,' added Enzio, 'Alan's presence might actually save our lives. Without him, I can see no reason that might convince the queen to return here in order to do anything other than gather up our bodies.'

'That's right,' said Alan.

'So be it,' said Lorn. 'And you, Enzio? What's your valid reason for remaining?'

Enzio flashed a wide grin.

'It would be inconceivable for a Sarmian prince to run away when a prince of the High Kingdom chooses to make a stand.'

'Ah! You've become a prince again! What happened to the modest gentleman you were just a minute ago?'

'Bah! All gentlemen from Sarme and Vallence are more or less princes.'

'I thought it was the other way around,' said Alan in jest.

'Very funny. Remind me to kill you in a duel, once the siege is over.'

Alan and Enzio then became aware of Lorn's silence as he had turned back to watching the port again.

Their smiles faded.

'Enzio, how long do you think we can hold that gate?'

A road paved with flagstones led from the port to the fortress between two fortified gates at either end. Lorn was pointing to the first: the gate near the port.

'Not long,' said Enzio, becoming serious again. 'The men defending it will come under heavy cannon fire.'

'Speaking of which...' said Lorn, looking at the enormous bombard close to where they were standing.

In its haste to hand over the stronghold to Yrgaard, the High

Kingdom had not waited for the treaty to be signed to begin its withdrawal. Thus, most of its garrison troops had already departed, taking with them the fortress's cannons, with the exception of a dozen old bombards too bulky and heavy to be moved.

On the other hand, they could be turned around.

'We will never be able to hold these ramparts,' said Lorn. 'We'll need to fall back fairly quickly into the Castel. And in that case, it would be best if the enemy could not use these fire maws against us.'

'Let's stuff them full of mortar,' proposed Enzo. 'It's still the quickest method.'

'Why not use them against the Yrgaardian fleet?' asked Alan.

'Too risky,' said Lorn. 'They're unreliable. They might very well blow up in our faces.'

'Besides,' continued the prince, thinking out loud, 'if we used them ourselves, we might not have time to render them harmless against us.'

'Exactly.'

Liam arrived at that very instant, with Cael Dorsian hand-cuffed between two of the garrison's soldiers. They had arrived from the gaol cells, where Liam had gone to fetch the prisoner on Lorn's orders. Dorsian proudly endured Alan and Enzio's hostile appraisal.

'Unchain him,' said Lorn.

The soldiers freed Dorsian from the irons which bound his wrists together.

'To what do I owe this honour?' he asked.

'Look.'

Dorsian approached the parapet's embrasures. He saw the Yrgaardian fleet in the port and the sails of the last of the High Kingdom's ships disappearing in the distance. Then he turned back towards the fortress, which he found strangely silent.

'What's going on?'

Lorn outlined the situation and Dorsian listened, astonished at first, then admiring and... puzzled.

'So you've started a war between the High Kingdom and Yrgaard...'

'Only if we win this battle. If we lose, the High Kingdom will present its apologies, Yrgaard will accept them, and the treaty will be signed. If we win, on the other hand…'

'And what are your chances?'

'None to speak of.'

'I know that most of the garrison has already left. How many men do you have to defend this fortress?'

'Thirty-odd soldiers from the garrison.'

'Thirty!'

'Alan has the twenty soldiers forming his escort. Enzio, ten.'

'And your Onyx Guard? How many men?'

'Four.'

Dorsian snickered.

'Including you three, if I've done my sums right, that makes less than seventy blades. And opposing you, how many are there? Five hundred?'

'Less.'

'And they have cannons.'

Lorn did not reply.

Turning to look out to sea, Dorsian pondered for a moment, rubbing his chafed wrists.

'What am I doing here?' he asked gravely.

'You wanted to fight in order to prevent Angborn being ceded to the Black Dragon, didn't you?'

Dorsian stifled a small chuckle and displayed a cynical smile.

'So these are the choices you're offering us, my men and myself. Die defending these ramparts or wait to be executed in prison… Now I understand why you wanted us to regain our strength yesterday. I'd almost believed you brought us food out of the goodness of your heart…'

'Lorn is offering you the chance to fight and die as a gentleman,' said Enzio. 'It's already more than you deserve.'

Stung to the quick, Dorsian almost snapped a retort, but restrained himself.

'Moreover,' added Lorn, 'I'm only offering you this deal: either you fight at our side, or you return to the dungeon.'

'I don't understand. And my men?'

'They're free to leave or to fight. I won't force them to defend Saarsgard against their will.'

'Just me. Thanks for the special treatment.'

'And we want you to give us your word of honour that you'll be loyal, Cael,' demanded Alan.

Enzio raised his eyes heavenwards in exasperation.

'You have my word,' said Dorsian, after a moment's reflection. 'But I can't speak for my men.'

'I'll talk to them,' said Lorn.

Gathered together in a courtyard, everyone looked up at Lorn when he appeared on a gallery overlooking them. He was accompanied by Prince Alderan of the High Kingdom and Elenzio de Laurens, along with his lieutenant from the Onyx Guard and Cael Dorsian, who stood behind them.

Evening was approaching.

The great fortress was silent and already invaded by deep shadows.

Lorn spent a moment observing the men who had come to listen to him. They included the remnant of Saarsgard's garrison, the dark and impassive silhouettes of the Onyx Guard, Alan's and Enzio's bodyguards, and the prisoners freed from the fortress's gaol cells. In all several dozen men, most of whose names Lorn had not had time to learn.

Drawing a breath, he said:

'Once the sun sets, a dragon-prince will advance towards us. He will demand that we open Saarsgard's gates and abandon Angborn. He will demand that we lay down our weapons. He will demand that we surrender and deliver this stronghold to him.'

Lorn paused. The stone seal on the back of his left hand had been prickling for some time now, a fact which he hadn't mentioned to anyone. He discreetly worked his knuckles, wishing the incipient pain would cease.

'To that, I shall say "no"!' he resumed, striking the gallery's railing with a fist gloved in black leather. 'Despite his superior numbers. Despite his dracs and his war lizards. Despite his ships and his cannons aimed at us, who are but a handful, I will answer that to pass through these gates, he will have to knock them down and vanquish those defending them. Will you be at my side?' he asked in a loud voice.

He gestured towards Alan with his left hand and could not help grimacing as he lifted his arm. The Dark's mark was now truly hurting. The pain had rapidly invaded his whole hand and was rising towards his shoulder. Unfortunately, the sensation was all too familiar. Oriale's Watchtowers had protected Lorn from the Dark for several weeks, but they were a long way away.

Alan realised something was wrong. But pulling himself together, Lorn continued his speech.

'Will you stand at the side of the High King's own son?' he asked. 'Will you fight alongside him when Yrgaard tries to seize these ramparts? Or will you let another blood than your own be shed and be mixed with that of a prince?'

Once again, Lorn fell silent.

It seemed like an oratorical pause, but Lorn felt hot and his vision was blurring. Alan and Enzio noticed the sweat drenching his temples and exchanged a worried glance.

'If I ask this of you,' Lorn resumed, 'it's because I do not expect you to fight against your will. All of you are free to leave without disgrace, released from your oaths. For the battle we are about to engage is not a combat for victory. It is for honour. Our honour. The honour of the High Kingdom. And that of the High King, whose colours fly above us.'

All those present turned and raised their eyes when Lorn pointed at the wolf's head banner. It flew high above the keep, just above the High Kingdom's flag. Some of them had not seen that emblem for a long time.

Lorn was suffering. Nauseous now, leaning upon the railing, it took immense will power on his part not to faint. Enzio wanted to support him, if only by taking his elbow. But Lorn shook his head at him curtly. There could be no question of his showing the slightest weakness now.

'Do you want to see the colours of the Black Dragon replace them?' he exclaimed. 'Here, men will make a stand! Here, men will fight, suffer and die for their king! And if they do not win in the end, each hour spent resisting and fighting will be victory enough! And each wound received! And each blow struck, each drop of blood shed, each enemy slain! Will you be among those men?'

He almost faltered but rallied his strength.

'The choice is yours,' he said in a softer voice. 'Search your hearts. Weigh your situation, but make up your minds soon. Destiny is here! It is watching and waiting, impatient. So decide. Decide today what kind of man you are and what kind of memory you will leave behind!'

With those words, Lorn retreated from view, his legs giving way beneath him as the hurrahs and warrior cries rose from the courtyard. Enzio hurried to support him. Meanwhile, Alan stepped forward to distract attention. Immediately acclaimed, he brandished his sword and shouted:

'Tomorrow, we shall be victorious or we shall die! Tomorrow, those of you who choose to fight can call themselves my brothers-in-arms! But know that the High King does not expect you to be soldiers! He expects you to be heroes!'

As Alan continued to elicit cheers, no one noticed Lorn being almost carried inside. With Liam guarding the door, the knight was laid out on a bench.

'Do you want something to drink?' asked Enzio.

Lorn nodded.

He was feeling pain in his flesh, but not only that. Against all logic and all reason, when he was in Oriale he had sometimes entertained the illusion that he was freed of the Dark. After all, the witch's ritual in the Argor Mountains might have been more effective than she claimed. And his long exposure to the beneficial influence of the Watchtowers might have completed his cure. Who could say? Of course, Lorn knew deep down that it was impossible. But how could he not believe? How could he not hope? But now there was no longer any room for doubt. The Dark was an evil and jealous mistress who had not abandoned him and seemed to take a malign pleasure in reminding him of her presence at the worst possible moment.

Enzio helped Lorn drink some cool water.

'Thank you,' said Lorn. 'I'm feeling better now.'

It was true.

The pain and the trembling were swiftly subsiding.

'But what's wrong with him?' asked Dorsian.

'Nothing,' snapped Enzio.

'What do you mean, nothing?'

'Lorn's exhausted, that's all.'

'I know a fit brought on by the Dark when I see one, Enzio.'

'Then why are you asking the question?' the Sarmian gentleman rounded on him irritably.

Alan came in.

'I think I have the right to know, don't I?' insisted Dorsian. 'As do all those who might decide to follow Lorn in this adventure.'

Alan immediately saw what was going on.

'If you say a single word about any of this to the troops,' he threatened, 'I will gut you. Understood?'

Dorsian gave no reply.

'Stop it!' ordered Lorn, who was now rapidly recovering.

He sat up.

'It's not a fit,' he added. 'Just a… warning…'

'All right, then?' enquired Enzio.

'Much better, thanks. Soon there will be no trace of it.'

And addressing Dorsian:

'You see, there's no cause for alarm.'

'Was it Dalroth…?'

Dorsian did not complete his question.

'Yes,' replied Lorn. 'But I'm fine, I assure you.'

He rose to his feet without wobbling too much.

Liam then opened the door slightly and, putting his head inside, announced:

'Night has fallen, knight.'

'We're coming, Liam.'

Lorn removed his spectacles. He no longer needed them.

With his cape covering the rump of his mount, Laedras presented himself on horseback before the fortified gate defending the road which ran from the port to the fortress. Wearing black steel armour decorated with blood-red patterns, he was escorted by four torch bearers and two dracs mounted on war lizards.

Taking care to remain a respectable distance from the embrasures behind which silhouettes could be made out, he halted, waiting long enough to make sure he'd been noticed, and then called out in a loud, calm voice:

'Have you come to your senses? Saarsgard will fall; you know it as well as I do. So save your lives. Don't sacrifice them for the folly of a reclusive, dying king who has already abandoned you!' The dragon-prince steadied his mount, which was champing at the bit. 'In the name of Yrgaard, I command you to open these doors and deliver the fortress. Leave now, and I guarantee your lives and your liberty!'

A moment went by in silence, after which the doors shuddered and opened slightly before Laedras. A man emerged with a bowed head, then another, a third and others after them, who had all decided to live.

'Twenty,' counted Enzio.

'I was expecting worse than that,' Lorn confessed.

'But we're only fifty now,' said Alan.

They stood at the top of one of the crenellated towers flanking the fortified gate. In the torchlight, they watched as the column of those who refused to stay, fight and probably die so that the High King's banner would continue to fly over Saarsgard moved off. For the most part, it consisted of soldiers belonging to the garrison, as well as some of Dorsian's partisans.

'It's difficult to blame them,' said Alan.

'And who can say: we might regret not joining them,' said Enzio.

'Close the gate!' ordered Lorn.

Slowly, the heavy oak panels sheathed in steel closed again, and the portcullis dropped.

'You have chosen!' cried the dragon-prince before turning his horse round and riding away. 'Nothing will save you now!'

The three friends remained silent for a moment.

'They won't attack before sunrise,' said Enzio. 'That leaves us the night to prepare and get some rest.'

Just as he uttered these words, a Yrgaardian vessel fired a cannon salvo. Most of the cannonballs passed over the gate with a humming sound but some struck home. One of them even destroyed a merlon at the top of the tower where Lorn, Alan and Enzio were standing. They were not wounded and the impact surprised them more than anything else.

'I don't think we'll get any rest,' said Lorn before taking cover as a second volley of cannonballs arrived.

The barrage lasted the entire night.

19

Laedras's troops attacked at dawn, after having bombarded Saarsgard without respite. In the darkness the cannonballs often fell at random but their purpose was less to inflict damage upon the defences than to harass the fortress's defenders. As the sun rose, the cannons ceased firing and a strange silence, as fragile and tense as a thread of spider silk between two branches in the wind, settled over the scene.

Exposed to direct fire, the fortified gate guarding the road towards Saarsgard had suffered greatly. Its merlons had all been blown away or were crumbling. The top of one of its towers had collapsed and the heavy oak panels that closed the archway had been smashed in. But the portcullis had resisted. Although holed and twisted, with three cannonballs lodged between its iron bars, it remained planted in the ground and prohibited passage.

'No more cannon fire?' asked Yeras in surprise, keeping his ears open.

'So it seems…' said Lorn.

With his Onyx Guards and fifteen soldiers, Lorn had spent the night in the fortified gatehouse, sheltered from the cannonballs but not from the incessant detonations and the dull impacts which had shaken the solid building each time a cannonball reached its target. They had stood watch and relieved one another on the wall walk, maintaining a vigilant guard despite the incoming shots, in case the Yrgaardians attempted a night attack. Under the command of Alan and Enzio, the thirty other defenders occupied the fortress, ready to intervene in order to cover Lorn's retreat.

For Lorn knew he could not hold this gate. It was a matter

of resisting for as long as they could, and inflicting as many enemy casualties as possible, then withdrawing. And then fighting some more before falling back again.

Until they finally found themselves at bay.

Or dead.

Lorn knew the last stand would take place within the Castel...

He and his Onyx Guards joined the sentries at the embrasures in the remaining tower. The silence that reigned worried them and, because they all had experience of combat, they understood that the assault was imminent.

'To ARMS!' ordered Lorn, drawing his Skandish blade. 'THEY'RE COMING!'

The Yrgaardian soldiers approached in good order, men and dracs mixed together, armed with axes, spears and swords, clad in leather and chain mail which clanked in time with their steady footsteps. Drums marked the beat of their advance.

'I don't see Laedras,' Liam remarked.

'I don't either,' said Lorn, squinting behind his dark glasses. 'Yeras?'

Although one-eyed, the former Vestfaldian scout still had the keenest sight among them. No details escaped him.

'No,' he said.

'He knows this assault is only the first,' Lorn surmised. 'No doubt he's holding himself in reserve for the final combat.'

For the killing blow, he thought to himself.

A horn sounded and the Yrgaardians came to a halt, just beyond crossbow range. They waited, immobile, their black-and-red banners fluttering in the wind. Silence fell once again.

Upon an order from Lorn, the crossbowmen placed themselves at the embrasures.

'Don't shoot until you hear my command,' he said.

A few long minutes went by.

Then a ship fired one of its guns, projecting a cannonball which, at the end of a flattened arc, whistled by just above the heads of the defenders.

Lorn was perplexed.

Was the dragon-prince going to bombard them as his troops were trying to take it by assault? Did he have so little regard for the lives of his own soldiers?

But Lorn did not have time to ponder the matter.

A horn sounded three long notes and the Yrgaardians charged, screaming.

'Crossbowmen, wait!' shouted Lorn above the growing clamour. 'The rest of you, stand ready!'

The crossbowmen shouldered their weapons. There were ten of them and if they shot at the right moment, they would have no trouble mowing down the front rank of the assailants. Out of the corner of his eye, Lorn watched Yeras who had also shouldered his crossbow. They had agreed that Lorn would give the order to shoot as soon as Yeras signalled to him...

But Lorn never gave that order.

For just when the assailants came into range and Yeras was about to alert Lorn, the ship which had previously fired started up again, this time with all its cannons.

Lorn realised that the first shot was only to determine the aim of those that followed.

He yelled:

'Take cover!'

But it was too late.

A volley of cannonballs struck the parapet with full force. Some of them came whizzing between the merlons and killed three men, projecting them into thin air, dismembered and bloody. The others smashed into stones and rubble. The impact was dreadful, deafening. A cloud of dust and loose mortar rose and then rained down upon the stunned and disorganised defenders. During this time, having reached the foot of the fortified gate, the Yrgaardians raised ladders and swarmed upwards to attack.

Grey with dust, a trickle of crusted blood running from a wound to his forehead caused by a stone shard, Lorn had just regained his wits when he saw a big black drac setting foot upon the parapet. A furious melee was under way. Yrgaardians and High Kingdomers fought hand to hand in total chaos. Brandishing his Skandish sword with both hands, Lorn rushed towards his adversaries. He struck to the right, to the left, to the right again, killing or maiming three men before reaching the drac. The latter turned to face him. He gripped in his scaly fist the hilt of a great scimitar which a man would have difficulty lifting. The blade was chipped, and already covered in blood. Lorn delivered two blows which the drac parried before riposting. It was a stroke powerful enough to break a blade or a wrist, but Lorn evaded it rather than try to block it. He stepped back and counterattacked, wounding the drac in the side. The drac screamed and slashed at shoulder level. Lorn ducked, stood up after the broad blade had passed over him, and drove his heavy Skandish weapon beneath the drac's arm, where the armour had a weak point. Lorn had trouble freeing his blade, which had sunk in as far as the guard. He finally managed to draw it clear, sticky with cold black blood, before toppling his opponent out into empty space with his foot. As he fell, the drac struck and carried off two men who were ascending a ladder. Picking up a halberd, Lorn tried to use the weapon to push the whole thing away. But more Yrgaardians were already climbing up and he strained against it in vain.

'To ME!' he called.

Almost immediately, Dwain, Logan and a soldier from Saarsgard's garrison came to lend him a hand. Together, they forced the ladder to a vertical position just as an Yrgaardian reached the top, and then tipped it backwards along with those clinging to its rungs.

A small victory, and one which Lorn was unable to savour.

He heard an awful grinding of twisting metal, added to the grating and cracking of splitting stones.

'What was that?' asked Logan.

The same sounds were repeated.

Leaning out from an embrasure, Lorn saw that the assailants had attached chains to the portcullis and four of Laedras's war lizards had been harnessed to those chains. They were slowly, inexorably, pulling together, joining their strength to rip away the fortified gate's last defence.

Lorn did not hesitate.

'Retreat!' he yelled, although it galled him. 'Retreat!'

484

They had repelled the Yrgaardians' assault and were once again masters of the parapet. And at least that would permit them to withdraw in good order and take their wounded with them.

As a second wave of attackers scrambled up the ladders, the Onyx Guards covered the flight of the remaining soldiers, fighting and retreating one step at a time towards the trapdoor which, opening onto a spiral staircase, constituted the only exit.

'Your turn, knight!' said Liam, just before he split open a skull with his big sword.

Lorn did not argue. Taking a lit torch from the wall as he passed, he dashed down the staircase which ended beneath the great archway. The defenders had erected a barricade there during the night. But this final obstacle seemed quite ludicrous against the giant lizards, which, before Lorn's eyes, were tearing away the portcullis in a deafening din which echoed in the covered space.

The soldiers had been given time to leave the gate and were now running along the road towards the fortress. Worried about his own men, Lorn turned back to the staircase. He saw Yeras, Logan, Dwain and Liam all come hurtling down. Liam, wounded in the shoulder, said:

'The trapdoor's shut, but they're already attacking it with axes.'

'To the fortress, quickly,' said Lorn. 'Go on ahead.'

'Knight…' Liam started to object.

'I said: go on ahead!'

The guards knew what Lorn intended to do.

But they reluctantly left him, with a torch in one hand and his Skandish sword in the other, facing the lizards, which, ridden by lancers, were opening the way for the soldiers massed behind them, crushing the barricade and passing through the thick dust cloud raised by the removal of the portcullis.

Lorn waited until the last moment.

And threw his flaming torch to the ground, on top of a bundle of braided fuses. The fuses were set alight and Lorn was already running for the exit when the small, lively, crackling flames took their separate paths, each of them climbing the cord which they devoured and travelling up the archway's walls.

The lancers were too late in spotting the barrels of powder attached to the vaulted ceiling. They voiced their alarm, giving the infantry troops following them a chance to run away, but their mounts, too ponderous and already enmeshed in the barricade, could not flee as quickly. One lizard tried to climb over another in order to turn round. The beasts snapped at one another and a scaly tail, as wide and as heavy as a tree trunk, struck when...

Lorn had only run about twenty yards before the whole scene exploded. The blast threw him to the ground as the deflagration destroyed the fortified gate, lifting enormous pieces of rubble into the air at the same time as three immense balls of flame blossomed, one upwards and the other two from the extremities of the blackened archway.

Time seemed to stand still. Strange seconds stretched out in a false silence. Then a rain of debris came down, a mixture of stones and burning coals, which crackled on the ground amidst a hail of pebbles.

Lorn staggered to his feet and saw that the door and its towers were now mere ruins. He contemplated them in almost drunken astonishment, as if unable to comprehend what his eyes beheld. Then he felt helping hands holding him upright. The Onyx Guards had come back for him. He recognised them, or at least he thought they looked vaguely familiar.

'Are you all right?' asked a red-headed colossus.

'Are you wounded?' enquired a short one-eyed man.

'Let's not hang about!' said a guard who had a veteran's face and air of confidence.

Lorn let them move him along at a trot towards the fortress.

20

The Onyx Guards were the last to pass through the fortress's gates. Dwain and Yeras helping Lorn, and Liam supporting a straggler wounded in the thigh. The double doors slammed shut. A portcullis dropped just in front of them. And two bars as thick and solid as master beams slid into their lodgings. The next troops to come through this gate would be led by a dragon-prince.

Lorn was taken into a guardroom where he could lie down on a cot. His ears stopped ringing and he managed to gather his wits while Liam firmly inspected him to verify that he wasn't injured. Yssaris, seated close by, seemed to be keeping an eye on the proceedings.

Lorn finally pushed Liam away and sat up.

'I'm fine. But I'm dying of thirst.'

Dwain was handing him a glass of wine when Alan and Enzio arrived. Logan, who was guarding the entrance, glanced in to make sure everything was all right and closed the door behind them. They had watched the battle from the ramparts, and then they had seen Lorn come running out of the fortified gate just before it exploded. They'd been aware of Lorn's plan. Realising that the gate would not hold for long, they had decided to destroy it rather than abandon it to Laedras and allow him to install cannons there. The risks entailed were nevertheless enormous and Alan and Enzio had anxiously witnessed their friend being engulfed by the thick cloud thrown up by the explosion.

'You gave us quite a scare!' exclaimed the prince of the High Kingdom. 'Are you all right?'

'I'm as fit as a fiddle.'

'Truly?'

'Well, a fiddle with a terrible headache.'

'But nothing broken?'

'Ask him,' said Lorn, jerking his thumb at Liam.

The veteran shook his head, which finally convinced Alan.

'Did you really need to wait so long?' asked Enzio in a tone of reproach.

'Well…' said Lorn, shrugging his shoulders. 'At the time, it seemed like a good idea. How many men did we lose?'

'Seven. Dead or seriously wounded.'

Lorn's face darkened and he nodded sadly. The terrible toll had started and it would continue to mount until the last among them fell, unless some providential rescue arrrived from the heavens.

Or by way of the sea.

'It wasn't in vain,' announced Lorn. 'The war lizards were under the archway when the whole place blew up.'

'All four of them?' asked Enzio.

'Yes.'

'Excellent news,' said Alan. 'Those filthy monsters can climb walls.'

'And it's a blow for Laedras,' added Enzio. 'He lost at least twenty men in this assault. If you include his lizards…'

'But we can't afford to lose seven men for only twenty of his.'

Lorn immediately understood what the prince was driving at. During the night, they'd had a long discussion about the wisdom of defending Saarsgard's ramparts, without reaching an agreement.

'Do we have a choice?' he asked, rising to his feet.

As far as he was concerned, the question was entirely rhetorical. But Alan was of a different mind.

'This fortress is immense, Lorn. And at present, we have barely more than forty men to defend it. It's impossible! Untenable!'

'It's simply a question of resisting. If we fall back to the Castel straight away, we lose the chance to slow Laedras down and inflict more losses on him.'

'But we end up retreating into the Castel all the same. Only there will be fewer of us to defend it.'

'Each hour gained is a victory, Alan.'

'I was there when you gave your speech, thank you.'

Lorn put on his belt, which his men had removed before they laid him out upon the cot.

'You're misguided if you're hoping for a triumph,' he said.

Annoyed, Alan turned to Enzio.

'What do you think?'

The Sarmian gentleman did not reply right away. His mind was made up, but the exchange between Alan and Lorn had been sharp and he wanted to smooth matters over.

'I say that a stronghold under siege can only have one general, and Lorn is ours.'

Alan sighed.

Calmly, he addressed Lorn:

'You really insist on defending every stone of this fortress?'

'Yes.'

'At whatever cost?'

When Lorn didn't reply, the prince resigned himself.

'So be it.'

'Our walls are too high for their ladders and solid enough to resist their cannons for a long while. Without his lizards, Laedras can no longer take them by assault. The battle will be concentrated at this great gate. And thirty men would be enough to defend it. We have forty. That's ten too many.'

Alan smiled at his cockiness and, only half convinced, called on Enzio as his witness:

'What can anyone possibly say in response to that?'

Lorn approached the prince, placed his hands upon his friend's shoulders and looked him straight in the eye.

'You father's banner flies above our heads, Alan. It can only be seen here, and over the Citadel. Each hour gained...'

'...is a victory, I know.'

The door opened to reveal Dorsian, who, from the threshold, asked:

'How's our heroic arsonist?'

'As you can see,' replied Lorn.

'Perfect. Then you should come with me.'

*

489

The soldiers who were not standing watch upon the ramparts had assembled in a vast guard hall whose thick columns supported cross-arched vaults. They were eating there, relaxing, or taking care of their equipment. Some were praying, and the wounded were resting.

It was there that Dorsian led Lorn, standing aside before the door to let the knight pass through first.

Lorn entered.

And despite the dead and the wounded, despite those who had fallen and those who would fall soon, he was cheered loudly by all present.

21

The bombardment resumed and lasted all day.

The cannonballs struck Saarsgard's ramparts or passed over them to fall upon the rooftops, into the courtyards, or against the buildings' façades – one of them, breaking a window, traversed an entire floor, which was fortunately deserted. They caused damage but did not threaten to create a breach in the defences. On the other hand, they did wear on the defenders' nerves. There was the noise of the cannons. There was that of the impacts. And there was the constant risk of a ball mowing down a man or taking off his head. The sentries had to remain under cover. Any movement required creeping from one shelter to another.

The Yrgaardians, however, did not try anything else and, when the cannons suddenly fell silent, calm settled over Saarsgard along with the dusk.

'Laedras is licking his wounds,' Logan said in a sinister tone as he patiently sharpened his twin blades.

Everyone knew the dragon-prince had not given up.

At nightfall, beneath a black sky haunted by the distant pallor of an almost absent Nebula, a long and massive silhouette, its long tail snaking behind it, approached Saarsgard's ramparts. Slow but sinuous, the war lizard threaded a silent path between the big boulders which, at this particular spot, cluttered the steep slope. It opened the way for a group of equally silent men. Most of them proceeding on foot, they wore supple leather and were armed with cutlasses and short swords. Sailors. And agile and formidable fighters.

The lizard reached the bottom of the wall and waited, its

forked tongue lashing the air. It was hurt. One eye had been punctured and there were gleaming wounds on its flanks. Its breathing was laboured and wheezing. Blood ran from its maw, a sign that it was dying from internal injuries and would not long outlive its fellows, buried beneath the rubble of the fortified gate.

It was no longer fit for battle, but Laedras had realised it could still serve and perhaps even bring victory. Not possessing the numbers to maintain an adequate watch, the besieged were obliged to rely on the ramparts' height to protect them.

An error.

The men accompanying the lizard attached a long rope to its harness. Then the giant reptile began to climb the rampart. Its powerful claws had no difficulty finding holds in the stone. Its belly brushing against the wall and its body slithering quickly, it took only an instant for the beast to climb up to the deserted rampart walk.

Unable to sleep, Lorn went out onto the ramparts. He took a spiral staircase that led to the embrasures on top of the main gate and, from there, observed the Yrgaardian ships in the port, aboard which several lights were burning.

Dwain was on duty here.

Having turned to see his captain arrive, he gave Lorn a nod and resumed his watch. Lorn placed himself on Dwain's right, one hand on the pommel of his sword and the other hooking a thumb to the buckle of his belt.

The two men kept silent for a moment.

'You never asked me why I was sentenced to the galleys,' Dwain said suddenly, without ceasing to look off into the distance.

Lorn gave him a sideways glance.

'No,' he said, after a brief pause. 'Is it important?'

'It was because of the fellow I killed.'

Lorn greeted this news without blinking.

'Did he deserve to die?'

'No,' said the red-headed colossus. But then he added: 'Not for what he did to me, at any rate.'

Lorn nodded and gave the matter a little further thought.

'If you were sentenced to the galleys for murder in Ansgarn, then you would have been condemned for life.'

'I wasn't sent to the galleys for murder. But I know, deep inside, that it was the reason why the Dragon of Destiny wanted me sentenced to the galleys.'

Lorn told himself this explanation was as good as another.

'Did the Dragon of Destiny also want the Onyx Guard to recruit you?

'No doubt about it.'

'Why?'

'I have no idea. But it's not necessary to understand it in order to accept one's destiny.'

Lorn had no reply, and Dwain broke the silence again after a moment.

'We fought well today.'

'Yes.'

'Thanks to you.'

Lorn directed his gaze towards the shimmering horizon.

'Until tomorrow, Dwain,' he said as he turned away.

'Until tomorrow, knight.'

Lorn did not see the crossbow bolt.

He only saw, out of the corner of his eye, a gleaming line pass through Dwain's throat, and then the guard shuddered as two other bolts struck him in the back. The blood gushing from the wound spattered Lorn, who stood dumbfounded for an instant. Choking, Dwain fell to his knees and was dead before he toppled forward.

Then everything sped up and Lorn's reflexes took over.

Glimpsing a crossbowman taking aim at him, he drew his Skandish sword and, in the same movement, sliced through the bolt speeding towards his chest. He would have liked to bend over Dwain's body for a moment, but Yrgaardians in leather armour were already charging at him. He deflected a cutlass, severed a wrist, removed a head, tripped a third opponent and, turning his sword, pinned him to the ground with a quick jab.

'To ARMS!' he yelled, before rushing to the spiral stairs. 'To ARMS!'

The enemy was within the stronghold, but how? Since when? And in what strength? The questions jostled around in his head, but, caught up in the action, Lorn had trouble thinking. And besides, what did it matter now? He needed to react, take stock of the situation, and save whatever still could be.

'To ARMS! TO THE MAIN GATE! TO ARMS!'

On the stairs, Lorn came nose to nose with an Yrgaardian who was climbing to meet him. He propelled the man backwards with a kick to the chest and finished him off in passing with a backhanded sword stroke, before the man could recover.

'To ARMS!' the knight yelled again, once he reached a landing.

The sentry who had been posted here to keep watch through an arrow slit over the approaches to Saarsgard, was lying in a pool of blood at the end of the corridor. Lorn did not pause to see if he was still breathing: he had just heard a frightening sound, that of the chains and cogs controlling the portcullis.

The entrance to the fortress was defended by two sets of double doors closing off either end of a wide and long archway which passed through the main wall. The outer set of double doors was reinforced by a heavy portcullis...

...which was now being raised.

'To THE PORTCULLIS! TO THE PORTCULLIS!'

Lorn could only imagine the assailants massed at the foot of the ramparts, just waiting to enter the stronghold. For there was no doubt that the men who – one way or another – had managed to infiltrate Saarsgard only had one goal: opening the gate to the main body of their troops. This could still be prevented, Lorn hoped. But if the portcullis were raised, the enemies outside would need no further assistance. A few explosive mines would be enough to blow open the double doors that would be the last remaining obstacle blocking their path.

The tocsin finally sounded.

When he arrived beneath the archway, Lorn had to throw himself to one side in order to avoid two crossbow bolts. Then, brandishing his sword, he attacked.

Some Yrgaardians were toiling at the portcullis's winch and had already succeeded in raising the barrier halfway. Others had already partially opened the inner set of double doors. And lastly, still more were standing ready to face Lorn. They were twenty in all, but he felt no fear. He had to prevent the portcullis from being raised at any cost. In any event, he had to prevent it long enough to allow his men time to arrive.

Even if he found himself alone.

One against twenty.

Lorn attacked, parried, riposted, sliced open a face, the torchlight casting twisted shadows which flickered across the archway's rounded ceiling. A stroke from a short sword grazed him. A second scored a solid hit, but his leather and chain mail armour saved him. Varying cuts and thrusts, he slashed through a shoulder and pierced a chest. His heavy blade ravaged his enemies. In the heart of the melee, he wielded it with both hands and found the legendary fury of Skandish warriors boiling within his blood. Three more soldiers fell before his heels came up against a dead body. He staggered and almost fell, coming away with a long gash to the arm. Feinting, he killed one Yrgaardian and wounded another.

But there were too many of them.

The portcullis was still rising and Lorn realised he would not stop it. Raging, surrounded by enemies on all sides, he heard a clamour echoing beneath the archway.

Help was arriving.

With Alan and the Onyx Guards at their head, the besieged had forced their way through the inner doors and charged. The Yrgaardians retreated, offering Lorn an unexpected respite. Thinking he could catch his breath, he did not see a crossbowman aiming at him from the top of a flight of steps. The bolt whistled and struck Lorn in the shoulder.

The blow was dreadful.

'Lorn!' cried Alan, throwing himself into the melee.

But Yeras was already dragging Lorn away from the fighting, with Liam and Logan covering them.

'Is it serious?' asked Yeras, seating Lorn upon a bollard.

Lorn shook his head. His spaulder had resisted the blow,

absorbing most of the impact, and the bolt's point had penetrated less than an inch into the flesh. Painful, but not dangerous. Lorn gritted his teeth and pulled the projectile from the wound himself.

At that moment, the portcullis came to a halt at the top of the archway.

'THE PORTCULLIS!' ordered Lorn. 'QUICKLY! LOWER IT BEFORE THEY OPEN THE DOORS!'

And without waiting, he picked up his sword and leapt into action.

'WITH ME!'

The Onyx Guards followed him. Together, they joined Alan, Enzio, Dorsian and the other defenders in the battle. They numbered about thirty in all, but against them the Yrgaardians, half that number, presented a savage resistance. Backed up against the outer set of doors, they would not give in, killing and wounding as many of their enemies as they could. Lorn and Alan fought side by side. The prince was exemplary. He received a wound but killed three men, even saving the life of a soldier whom he helped drag out of harm's way. Dorsian and Enzio did their fair share of fighting and, little by little, the ranks of Saarsgard's defenders advanced. Trapped, the Yrgaardians realised they were doomed but did not lay down their arms. They had to be killed one by one. The smell of blood filled the archway as sticky puddles spread across the flagstone pavement.

Without a qualm, Yeras finished off the last Yrgaardian with his dagger, while Logan pulled the lever that was supposed to release the portcullis.

To no avail.

Liam examined the mechanism.

'It's blocked,' he said.

'Nothing we can do,' confirmed Logan, giving up. 'Those bastards jammed up the works!'

Alan swore.

'We can't break the chains,' said Enzio. 'They're as thick as my arm.'

An odour caught Yeras's attention.

Lorn also caught scent of it, and cried:

'OUT! EVERYBODY OUT!'

He had just seen the grey smoke seeping from beneath the double doors. The odour he and Yeras had detected was that of gunpowder.

'IT'S GOING TO BLOW UP!'

Everyone raced towards the exit. A twenty-yard dash beneath the archway, which echoed with their shouts. Some of the soldiers, further away from the outer doors, remained unaware of the danger and were slow to react. Lorn and his companions yelled at the top of their lungs as they ran.

'Get out!'

'Quickly!'

'Everybody out!'

Instinctively, Lorn realised that not all of them would escape the archway in time.

'Down!' he ordered, pulling Alan into the recess of a door. 'Take cover!'

Those who did not obey quickly enough were flattened by the blast of a deafening deflagration which shook the whole rampart and made the half-opened inner doors fly wide apart. The other set of doors had exploded behind them, converting the archway into a corridor full of incandescent debris which whirred, hissed and crackled against the walls.

Lorn and Alan stumbled away from their shelter.

Their ears buzzing, they groped about for the others in the dust and the chaos, making themselves understood by gestures, helping the wounded stand, and renouncing the idea of taking away their dead. Lorn caught a glimpse of Yeras and Logan carrying Liam who looked badly hurt, but he did not have time to worry about it.

The Yrgaardians were entering Saarsgard. He could already see silhouettes cautiously advancing through the thick cloud thrown up by the detonation.

The defenders withdrew from the archway.

Lorn was the last to leave. Hoping they were not leaving anyone behind, he helped close the set of inner doors and spared a thought for Dwain lying in his own blood on the rampart walk. Only this death affected Lorn personally. It seemed cruel and unfair, and it was with the terrible feeling of abandoning a brother-in-arms on the field of battle that he watched the bars slide home across the twin door panels.

Those, however, would only keep the dragon-prince's troops pent up long enough to allow the besieged to fall back and prepare to defend the Castel. Driving Dwain's dead body from his thoughts, Lorn quickly gave the necessary orders. He ordered Dorsian to lead the retreat and his Onyx Guards to close up the rear. But he detained both Alan and Enzio, saying to the prince:

'No, Alan. Not you.'

'What?'

'We have no choice. We must fall back into the Castel. And once we do that, we'll be trapped. We will resist, but there's no hope.'

'You don't know that.'

'Yes, I do. And so do you.'

'Lorn's right,' said Enzio, keeping an eye on the gate.

The last set of doors would not hold for long. Moreover, the Yrgaardians would soon overrun the ramparts via the stairs running up from the gate's archway.

'You must leave while there's still time,' Lorn urged. 'Laedras is not yet master of this fortress. Take advantage of that. Escape.'

'No. There's no question—'

Lorn seized Alan brusquely by the neck and shoved him against a wall.

'Come to your senses, Alan!'

'Let go of me, Lorn!'

'Start by listening! I was mistaken, all right? I thought we could hold the ramparts for a few days, but I was wrong. Now the game's up. Those who lock themselves away in the Castel will either be killed or taken prisoner.'

'Let go of me...' Alan said in a menacing tone.

But Lorn wasn't paying any heed.

'You are a prince of the High Kingdom, Alan. If tomorrow we die alone, people will remember us, remember our battle here, and our deaths will not be in vain. But if you stay, if you are captured or killed, our defeat will be complete. It… It will be a catastrophe. The High King's own son, a prisoner of the Black Dragon? Can you even imagine it?'

Alan brutally freed himself.

At that same moment, the sound of muffled pounding against the doors reached their ears.

'Listen to Lorn,' Enzio intervened. 'You're wounded. You fought for as long as you could. Now, you must think of the High Kingdom.'

The prince hesitated.

'It's your duty, Alan,' said Lorn. 'Besides, perhaps you'll have time to raise troops and return with reinforcements. You can still save us. You alone.'

Defeated, resigned, Alan nodded.

'All… All right. But I will return. With troops.'

Lorn smiled.

'I'm counting on it.'

They exchanged an embrace.

Out of the corner of his eye, Lorn glimpsed silhouettes outlined on top of the ramparts.

'Get out of here, now.'

'Stand fast. I promise you I'll—'

'I know.'

Lorn turned to Enzio.

'Go with him. Make sure nothing happens to him?'

The Sarmian gentleman nodded. They too exchanged an embrace, and Enzio murmured in Lorn's ear:

'You know we won't return in time, don't you?'

Lorn did not reply, but his gaze said that he knew.

'Knight!' called Logan. Despite Lorn's orders, he had waited. 'We must go!'

Lorn nodded.

After a last salute, the three friends separated and moved off quickly in different directions.

Alan and Enzio escaped across the ramparts.

Chance led them to the spot where the Yrgaardians had climbed the wall. They found the body of the giant lizard which had collapsed there, dead from exhaustion. They made use of the ropes left by the assailants and quickly covered a good distance in the darkness, keeping well away from the road along which the dragon-prince's troops were marching in an orderly fashion.

They arrived at the city's port and knew they were out of danger when Alan turned back towards Saarsgard with a sorrowful expression. Enzio guessed what he was thinking and told him in a compassionate tone:

'We can do nothing more for them, Alan. Come on.'

22

Lorn and Logan caught up with some stragglers whom they accompanied as far as the old tower guarding the sole bridge linking the Castel to the rest of the fortress. It was a massive structure, its thick walls pierced with arrow slits. Crossing it was the only means of reaching Saarsgard's heart, by way of a long and narrow stone arch straddling a deep abyss. The besieged, as a last resort, could take refuge within the Castel. But a battle could still be waged from this guard tower, which a handful of men sufficed to hold.

Lorn found Dorsian there, organising its defence.

'How many men do we have left?' the knight asked him.

'Thirty or so.'

'Select the fifteen most valiant among them. They will stay behind to defend the tower with me. I want you to fall back with the others into the Castel's keep and place the most seriously wounded, the ones who can't fight, in a safe spot. Perhaps they will be spared. I'm going up to see how the Yrgaardians are progressing.'

Dorsian seized Lorn's arm.

'Wait.'

'What?'

Dorsian led Lorn slightly apart within the great hall, where men – sombre and attentive – were preparing to fight, bandaging their wounds, and awaiting orders.

'Does it make sense to resist any longer?' asked Dorsian in a low voice.

'You want to surrender?'

'How much longer can we hold out? A few hours? If we only had the means to fall back and blow up the bridge...'

'We're out of powder,' said Lorn. 'And besides, if we did that we'd trap ourselves. And it would allow Laedras to take the rest of Saarsgard without a fight. He would not even need to raze the Sanctuary with his cannons. He would simply let us die of hunger.'

'I know,' said Dorsian. 'We needed to put up a fight. But only as long as it had a meaning.'

'It still does.'

'Really? Where's Alan?'

Lorn realised that Dorsian already knew the answer.

'I told him to flee,' he acknowledged nonetheless.

'You were right to do so. But that means the game is lost, doesn't it?'

Lorn gave no reply.

'I'm not speaking for me,' added Dorsian. 'I'm speaking for them. These men have displayed great courage. They followed you when they knew this battle could not be won. They deserve not to die in vain. To not be sacrificed. And what difference does it make if Saarsgard falls now or in an hour's time? Everyone will know what you accomplished in the High King's name, Lorn. Isn't that enough?'

'Because you believe I'm doing this for glory?'

'Then for what? For whom? For them?'

Lorn turned towards the men in the hall.

'Soldiers!' he called out. 'Soldiers!'

The men fell silent. Some stood. All of them waited.

'What we have done here will be recorded in the *Chronicles*,' said Lorn to all those present. 'It will be written that we have fought and that we have suffered and that we have resisted for an ideal: that of the High Kingdom. And for a cause: that of the High King whose banner flies above this fortress. Now we face a choice.' He paused. 'We can surrender now, and all will remember that we fought well. Or we can go on fighting, and people will remember that we were victorious.' He paused again. 'You are free to beg clemency from a dragon-prince.' Then Lorn suddenly raised his voice. 'But I shall not surrender! I shall not give up! I shall never lay down my sword!' He drew forth his Skandish blade. 'So, I ask you this: are you with me?

Will you be at my side when Yrgaard charges? Will you be at my side when my blood is spilled? And will you fight so that once more, just once more, the sun shall rise at Saarsgard above the colours of the High King?' He brandished his blood-stained sword. 'For the High King!' he cried.

'For the High Kingdom!' the soldiers roared back.

Lorn turned to Dorsian.

'You've just condemned these men to death,' the latter said.

Lorn did not blink.

'Your fifteen bravest,' he reminded the rebel leader before making his way to the stairs, with Logan at his heels.

Liam and Yeras were at the top of the tower.

'Well?' asked Lorn.

Instead of replying, Yeras motioned with his chin towards the torches of the column which was entering Saarsgard and advancing towards them accompanied by the slow, steady beat of war drums. A rider wearing a scarlet cape rode at their head. It could only be the dragon-prince.

'Do you think they're going to attack tonight?' asked Liam.

'I think Laedras will want to deliver the final blow, yes.'

Lorn then noticed his lieutenant's pallor, and recalled seeing Logan and Yeras helping him leave the archway, in the smoke and dust, after the explosion of the outer doors. Liam had his left arm in a sling and his hand wrapped up to the elbow in a bloody rag.

'Show me,' said Lorn.

The veteran shook his head.

'I'm fine,' he said.

Yet he was visibly suffering. His eyes shone and sweat beaded upon his brow.

'Is it serious?' asked Lorn. 'Don't lie to me!'

Liam hesitated, and then nodded regretfully.

'I want you to go down and get that properly bandaged,' said Lorn firmly. 'Then go and assist Dorsian in the keep.'

'But—'

'That's an order, Liam. We'll hold on as long as we can here, but we'll end up falling back towards the keep and we'll need help then. I want to be able to count on you when the time comes. Understood?'

Liam resigned himself to the assignment.

'Yes, knight.'

He withdrew just as fifteen men arrived.

'Did Dorsian send you?'

They nodded.

'Are you all volunteers?'

'Yes, knight,' one of them answered.

'Good. You five, remain with me here. The rest of you, at the arrow slits. Yeras, position them as you see best and make sure they all have enough munitions. Grab all the arrows and bolts you can.'

'Yes, knight.'

Yeras left with the men under his command.

'Logan,' said Lorn, turning towards the mercenary with the twin swords. 'You will fight at my side.'

The guard tower could be reached by means of a ramp which rose between two walls. It was otherwise inaccessible, backing onto thin air, the bridge spanning the abyss resting upon the upper portion of its structure.

The drums still beat.

Leaning on the parapet, Lorn watched the Yrgaardian troops who were now merely waiting for an order to attack. Patient and disciplined, unmoving, they were perfectly silent in the torchlight. Their numbers would favour them insofar as Laedras could launch wave upon wave of assaults, but the ramp would force them to present themselves only ten or twelve abreast at the bottom of the tower and Lorn planned to make the most of this advantage.

His gaze moved further out, to the ramparts, and he wondered if Alan and Enzio had managed to escape. He hoped so...

The drums beat on. Slow and steady as the pulse of a sleeping giant.

What time was it?

Lorn raised his eyes towards the Great Nebula, which seemed

very pale and very distant to him. It would be daylight in a few hours, but Lorn did not know whether he would see the sun rise and – strangely enough – that did not seem to matter much.

All was ready within the tower.

The men were at their posts and waiting in a silence punctuated by the drums. An uneasy silence soaked in the sour odour of sweat exuded by fear. The silence that comes before steel, screams and bloodshed.

Lorn reviewed the events that had led him here, to this hour. He had endured some of them and provoked others, sometimes urged on by a destructive impulse, sometimes by a desire for justice, and sometimes by a thirst for vengeance. And at times, that impulse, that desire and that thirst had all been one and the same sentiment that moved him. Lorn wondered if he really sought peace, as all those who had suffered were supposed to be seeking. He had believed that at first, but now he doubted whether it was true. Was it because he had changed so much? Only a few months had gone by since he had been liberated from Dalroth. That had been in the spring, and now it was autumn. Yet an eternity seemed to have passed between the two seasons. An eternity that was the beginning of a new life.

For his liberation had been a rebirth.

In pulling him out of its Dark-infested depths, Dalroth had given birth to him.

Lorn lifted his hand wrapped in leather and looked at it carefully, as if discovering it for the first time. Slowly he unwound the strap which concealed the mark of the Dark.

He would not wear it any longer.

The drums suddenly fell silent, leaving behind an emptiness which filled the night.

In the tower, each of the defenders held their breath.

Lorn exchanged a grim glance with Logan who was positioned on his left. Then he turned to the young soldier who stood to his right and who gripped his crossbow in his damp hands.

'What's your name, soldier?'

'Glenn, knight. Esko Glenn.'

'Why are you here? Why didn't you leave with the others when it was still possible?'

The young man thought about it before replying. He could hear his heart beating, and his answer almost astonished him.

'My father. He... He would have been proud, I think. He would have stayed, if it were him.'

'Thank you,' said Lorn. 'I wish you luck, Esko Glenn.'

Horns sounded.

The drums abruptly resumed at a mad tempo and, in one mighty warrior clamour that gripped the guts, the Yrgaardians charged.

23

They repelled the first assault.

Without having even placed a single ladder against the wall,
the Yrgaardians retreated, leaving behind a dozen bodies and
carrying away an equal number of wounded. The defenders
gave victorious hurrahs and Lorn let them, although he knew
this assault had only been intended as a test of their resistance.
At least they hadn't suffered any casualties, as he confirmed by
yelling down the stairs:

'REPORT!'

Yeras, who was in charge of the crossbowmen at the arrow
slits on the lower floors, answered:

'NO DEAD, NO WOUNDED.'

Lorn returned to the parapet.

'Here they come again,' Logan said.

Indeed, the Yrgaardians were already returning in greater
numbers, along with two large ladders, a battering ram and
broad shields to protect those who were carrying it.

'Aim at the men with the battering ram,' said Lorn, shoul-
dering his crossbow. 'On my command...'

The assailants ran up the ramp screaming, backed by the
frantic beat of the drums.

'Now!'

Lorn, Logan and the five soldiers defending the parapet
loosed their bolts together, almost immediately imitated by
the crossbowmen below, Yeras having waited until the same
moment before giving the order to fire. Fifteen bolts sped
towards the soldiers carrying the forward end of the ram.
Some buried themselves with a thump in the shields. A few
scored hits. Two leading men collapsed and caused the others

to stumble. The ram fell heavily to the ground and rolled on the paving while the charge continued.

'Reload!' ordered Lorn.

The crossbows were tautened by their levers and shouldered. The attackers had almost reached the foot of the tower.

'The ladder bearers!' yelled Lorn. 'Shoot them d—'

Lorn did not finish, surprised by the sound of cannons being fired from the fortress's ramparts.

'Take cover!'

But cannonballs were already striking the tower and its parapet, passing over their heads or whizzing between the merlons. Laedras had deployed cannons on Saarsgard's outer ramparts, aimed inwards at the Castel's defenders. That was why he had waited to attack, allowing the defenders time to organise themselves.

He had been preparing too.

Lorn stood up, feeling slightly dazed, but quickly recovered his wits. The dragon-prince's troops had placed their ladders against the towers and were climbing up them.

'With me!'

Drawing forth his heavy Skandish blade, he killed the first man to appear at the embrasures, smashed the shield of the next, and, still striking with both hands, split his skull. Three soldiers moved to support him while Logan and two others drove back the assailants who were climbing the second ladder.

Dull blows struck the gate below: the battering ram was at work despite the bolts shot by the crossbowmen from their slits. When one man fell, another immediately replaced him.

'Hold them back!' Lorn cried. 'Don't let them set foot on the parapet!'

The cannons fired a new salvo as Logan pushed a ladder out into thin air and took a wound to the side. The cannonballs' impacts shook the tower. One of them lodged itself in an arrow slit, sending stone shards flying which killed a crossbowman. Another whizzed past Lorn and decapitated a soldier fighting on the parapet. A third smashed a merlon into a cloud of dust.

The ram was still battering at the gate.

With his men, Lorn pushed off the second ladder. Then he looked below, took stock of the situation, and turned to Logan.

'THE GATE IS GOING TO GIVE WAY SOON. HELP ME,' he said, before straining against a merlon that had been struck by a cannonball.

Logan pushed with him and the loosened blocks shifted, slowly tilted, leaning out above the gate, and finally toppled in an avalanche of stone and dust which crashed fifty feet below onto the men wielding the ram. It killed and maimed, crushing bone, flesh and metal. Horrible cries rose and the hammering against the great gate, at last, halted.

The respite, however, was of short duration.

Already, the cannons were thundering again.

Already, more ladders were being raised.

The fighting resumed at the embrasures. Abandoning the arrow slits, Yeras and his crossbowmen came up to assist Lorn and the others, who risked being overwhelmed. At the top of the tower, they loosed a last volley of arrows at the Yrgaardians straddling the parapet, then they drew their swords and threw themselves into the melee.

Their arrival made all the difference.

The assault was repelled, the ladders destroyed and the attackers who still remained on the tower were quickly eliminated, launched into space without there being any question of taking prisoners. But the Yrgaardians had dragged the battering ram clear, pushed the bodies out of the way and, once again, under the orders of a big black drac, the gate was subjected to the device's mighty blows.

Lorn realised they would have to abandon their positions if they did not want to be trapped here once the doors below gave way. Moreover, of the fifteen men who had been defending the tower with him, seven were dead and three were no longer capable of fighting.

His gaze fell on the body of young Glenn.

'We're falling back,' he said, just as the tower suffered another salvo of flaming cannonballs.

'Knight!' Yeras called, while Logan led the men down the stairs, supporting the wounded. 'Come and see.'

Lorn cautiously approached the ruined parapet.

He noticed that the horizon was growing lighter, and then saw what Yeras was pointing out.

Laedras was heading towards the tower, leading fresh troops marching to the beat of drums, all perfectly aligned, their red-and-black banners floating above them.

'Quickly,' said Lorn.

They hastened to the stairs.

On the bridge side, the tower could be closed by a portcullis. The latter was half-lowered, propped up by a solid wooden beam that Lorn and his men had placed there, just before destroying the mechanism keeping the barrier raised.

Lorn made sure they had not left anyone behind in the tower. Then, with the help of Logan and Yeras, he removed the beam and the portcullis slammed down into place, Yssaris passing beneath it with a bound before streaking, belly to the ground, towards the Sanctuary.

At the same instant the gate opened, smashed apart by the battering ram.

They were running across the bridge when Lorn heard a loud squealing of tortured metal that chilled his blood. Letting the others outdistance him, he turned and saw the portcullis twisting, opening up as if claws had dug into the middle of it and were spreading it apart.

The soldiers continued to flee towards the Sanctuary whose gate stood wide open for them, but Yeras and Logan had also halted and were coming back, cautious and worried.

'What is it?' asked Yeras.

'Laedras is fed up with the damage we've inflicted upon him,' Lorn replied.

'Somehow, that idea comforts me,' remarked Logan.

'He's using his Dark powers.'

'The ones that come to him from the Black Hydra,' Yeras thought aloud.

'From his mother, yes...'

'Then we'd better hurry,' said Logan. 'We'll be a lot safer behind the Sanctuary's walls.'

The soldiers and the wounded were entering the keep while, at the embrasures on top, Liam and Dorsian observed the scene without comprehending.

'Those walls won't hold him back,' said Lorn. 'Not while he has possession of his Dark powers. Fortunately they'll be used up quickly.'

He was perfectly calm.

'Knight?' Yeras asked anxiously.

Lorn watched the dragon-prince who was now crossing the ripped-open portcullis. Laedras was in armour but bare-headed, his red hair falling upon his cape and his spaulders. He walked alone, his sword unsheathed, surrounded by a mist which shifted about as if animated by a life of its own and took on the appearance of a dragon made of shadow and night.

So that's the form the Dark puts on for you, thought Lorn, not moving an inch.

'Knight!' snapped Yeras.

The blasts of a horn could be heard coming from the Sanctuary. They seemed to be desperately calling Lorn to fall back.

In vain.

Lorn looked down at his marked hand.

A feeling of warmth had invaded his fist and then his arm, radiating from the stone seal engraved in his flesh. It was a burning, familiar heat, but this time it was beneficent.

The Dark was calling the Dark.

'Leave,' said Lorn. 'Join the others in the Sanctuary.'

'You can't defeat a dragon-prince, knight,' said Logan.

'I can slow him down. If he reaches the Sanctuary while in this form, it will be a massacre. And believe me, it's better to be killed by Yrgaardian steel than by the Dark...'

Yeras tried to protest but, without taking his eyes off the dragon-prince, Lorn overrode him:

'Leave, now. That's an order. No turning back. Tell Dorsian that I'm giving him command. It's been an honour to have fought at your sides.'

Yeras hesitated but Logan took his arm, signalling to him not to insist, and led him away.

They jogged off, leaving Lorn alone in the middle of the

stone arch, standing at its highest point above the crevasse. A lugubrious groaning rose from its apparently bottomless depths.

The sun was rising.

Lorn took out his dark spectacles. One of the lenses was cracked, but he put them on anyway. His wounded shoulder no longer hurt. He was calm and almost confident.

In fact, he was perfectly indifferent to his own fate. Didn't he have a destiny?

He drew his sword and waited.

'You don't actually imagine you can stop me, do you?' Laedras asked in amusement.

'I can always try.'

'Surrender. I promise you a quick and honourable death.'

Lorn smiled.

The dragon-prince stared at him and Lorn was unable say which of the two, Laedras or the Dark dragon surrounding the Yrgaardian, was examining him more closely. He could make out two bright eyes in the statue of living mist.

'Then I should like you to answer a question for me… Did you really do all this…' Laedras made a gesture that encompassed the fortress all about them '…for that?' He pointed a finger at the High King's banner which floated in the light from the rising sun. 'For the High King and the High Kingdom?'

'They're not the same thing,' said Lorn.

But the dragon-prince wasn't listening.

'Or did you do it, as I believe, to set all the Imelorian kingdoms on fire?'

'Why does it matter?'

Laedras pulled a face.

A few yards still separated the two adversaries. Only the two of them seemed to exist in the whole world, on a great stone arch spanning nothingness.

'Farewell,' said the dragon-prince.

Lorn adopted a defensive stance, his sword gripped in both hands. Laedras raised his towards the sky, before pointing it at the knight. The Dark dragon accompanied this movement. It reared up…

And spat out a black, opaque fire which engulfed Lorn.

The malevolent blast went on and on, obscuring its victim – in flesh and in soul – entirely. A terrible metallic scream bore into the temples and stirred the guts of those witnessing the scene. The air vibrated and the bridge itself seemed to tremble, dust escaping from beneath its stones.

Finally, Laedras lowered his sword and his dragon ceased to belch.

There should have been nothing left but a broken, deformed being, a cringing and wretched madman pleading to be killed with whatever sanity he still retained.

But instead Lorn pounced, delivering a slashing stroke to the middle of the dragon-prince's chest with enough strength to split a tree stump.

Laedras reeled under the impact.

The dragon arched its back and screamed in pain.

The dragon-prince's armour had saved him, but he was wounded. Astonished that Lorn had somehow withstood the full force of his Dark blast, he barely managed to counter a flurry of attacks.

What had just occurred was impossible.

Unless they were protected by the Dark, no one could...

The dragon-prince was unable to solve this conundrum, being too busy saving his own life. Transported, exalted, Lorn gave him no respite. The moment that Serk'Arn had spoken of had arrived. The Dark within him was triumphing. Pressing his advantage, carried away by his fury, he struck and struck again without letting up.

Upon the Sanctuary's walls, horror and then incredulity had given way to delight. Hurrahs and cries of encouragement rang out from the defenders. In the guard tower, on the other hand, there was fearful consternation...

Laedras attempted to riposte, but again, Lorn surprised him. The knight dodged, grabbed the dragon-prince by the wrist and delivered a violent headbutt to his face. Laedras staggered backwards. The Dark dragon vanished, as if carried away by a whirlwind which tore it into shreds. Lorn continued his onslaught, delivering a hook to the jaw with the fist holding his sword. The basket guard of the Skandish weapon stunned the dragon-prince, who dropped a knee to the ground. Then Lorn spun him round to face the tower and, seizing him by the hair with his left hand to force the Yrgaardian to lift his chin high, he slid his sword under the other's throat and waited.

The dracs belonging to the dragon-prince's personal guard were already coming out onto the bridge. But they halted on seeing their master at Lorn's mercy. With a single gesture, the knight could slaughter their commander.

Would he dare?

Lorn heard the Sanctuary's doors opening behind him. He glanced back and saw his own men emerging but hesitating to advance too far, in case they provoked a catastrophe.

'And now?' asked the dragon-prince, his teeth pink with blood.

From the top of the guard tower, fifteen crossbowmen had taken aim at them.

'I won't let you capture me,' continued Laedras. 'If you try, I will order them to shoot.'

'They won't obey you.'

'Oh yes they will. No one takes a dragon-prince prisoner.'

'But if your men advance, I'll slit your throat.'

'You'll condemn yourself to death.'

'Do you think I'll even hesitate?'

'No.' The dragon-prince stifled a chuckle. 'A strange victory, isn't it?'

Indeed, Lorn thought to himself, the situation was scarcely ideal.

His life depended on a stalemate which could not be maintained indefinitely. Moreover, the slightest incident – a cry, a misheard order, an arrow loosed by one side or another – was all it would take for hostilities to resume.

Lorn pondered his options.

And hesitated.

With nothing to lose, he considered leaping into the abyss with Laedras. The authors of the *Chronicles* would love that. A First Knight of the Realm carrying a dragon-prince to their deaths was the stuff of legend, much less history...

A shadow passed over the bridge.

Then another.

And a third, and then a fourth…

All eyes were lifted towards the sky to see the wyverns arriving out of the rising sun. Enthralled by the duel between Laedras and Lorn, no one had seen them approaching and now here they were, in great numbers, circling over Saarsgard.

They were war wyverns. A hundred of them, harnessed, armoured and ridden by the best wyverners in the world.

On their flanks they bore the colours of Argor.

Count Teogen of Argor was the first to land on the bridge. Then Vahrd, Orwain and others, while the remainder continued to turn in the sky, the shadow of their leathery-winged mounts casting menacing shadows over Saarsgard.

Wearing armour, with his famous mace at his side, Teogen advanced towards Lorn, who released Laedras and allowed him to stand up. And in a calm, firm voice, the count said:

'I don't believe, prince, that you'll be taking this fortress today. Surrender your sword to the knight, please.'

With the dragon-prince at their head, the Yrgaardians retreated and before evening came had re-embarked for the kingdom of the Black Dragon. Saarsgard was saved and, when night fell, the High King's banner still flew over the fortress.

Just above that of the Onyx Guard.

Epilogue

End of Autumn 1547

'Who will tell of the loneliness of dying kings? Who will tell of their regrets and their wounds? Who will tell of their fear?'

Chronicles (The Book of Defiant Heroes)

In the Citadel's throne room, beneath its immense vaults, large candelabra burned in the darkness. Carrying his helmet under his arm, Captain Norfold had placed one knee on the floor to draw as close to his king as possible. He spoke to him softly, as one speaks to dying men, in a voice strained by worry.

'Sire. You must answer me, sire. Was it upon your orders that Lorn prevented the signing of the Angborn treaty?'

The High King, unmoving, with his back straight and his hands gripping the armrests of his Onyx Throne, gave no reply. Behind the black veil concealing his corpselike face, he was staring at a distant point that only he could see.

'What difference does it make?' he asked at last.

'Sire! If Lorn disobeyed you, if he overstepped his...'

'What difference does it make?' repeated the king in a stronger voice.

The captain fell silent and bowed his head, torn between dejection and anger.

'He... He triumphed, didn't he?' the old king said. 'He stood alone against Yrgaard and he won.'

Norfold nodded reluctantly.

'Yes,' he said. 'But...'

'He'll be glorified,' the High King interrupted him. '*I* will be glorified,' he added, stressing the personal pronoun in a quavering voice. 'Lorn... Lorn has restored honour and pride to the High Kingdom. And to me. To us all. To you too, Norfold.'

The captain sighed.

He would have liked to speak at length with his king and bring him back to his senses, but clearly it was impossible.

'But at what price? The Black Dragon will not let this insult go unanswered. There will be war, sire. With Yrgaard. And it will happen when the High Kingdom is more divided than ever.'

The king mulled this over.

Then he turned his head slowly towards Norfold, and said:

'At what price?' His eyes sparkled beneath the veil held in place by a crown adorned with dark jewels. 'And just what is the price of the High Kingdom's honour, do you think?'

'I beg you, sire,' the captain tried one last time in desperation. 'Tell me. Did you order Lorn to oppose the treaty's signing in your name, or…?'

Or is your First Knight of the Realm a man devoured by anger and the Dark, capable of provoking the High Kingdom's ruin? he thought, unable to say the words aloud.

The High King was once again staring off into space with a rocklike stillness.

And then he lied:

'Yes. I gave the order.'

2

There was a triumphal parade in Oriale.

Given in honour of the heroes of Saarsgard, it passed along Erklant I Street, from the Langre Gate to the palace. The building façades were magnificently bedecked in the High Kingdom's colours to mark the occasion. Beneath a blazing sun, the gold and azure shone out in garlands, pennants, banners and silk ribbons thrown out as the procession passed by. The people thronged below the houses, at the windows, on balconies, on rooftops and even in the trees.

Everyone wanted to see the heroes of Saarsgard.

But above all, everyone wanted to see and acclaim the man who had led them to victory.

That is to say: Prince Alderan of the High Kingdom.

Alan led the parade upon a grey horse, head bare and smiling, clad in shining ceremonial armour. He was cheered. People shouted his name and gave hurrahs. He waved greetings to one side and the other, trying to appear modest and dignified, as befitted a prince. The sun gleamed on his blond hair. He was young, handsome and victorious. Men and women had eyes only for him, and young girls fell in love at the sight of him.

Esteveris had done his work well.

As soon as news of the victory had reached Samarande, where the royal court had taken refuge, heralds had taken the roads to report how Yrgaardian treachery had been discovered at the last moment, causing the High Kingdom to refuse to sign the treaty. To which Yrgaard, adding brutality to duplicity, had responded by trying to take Angborn by force. Fortunately, Prince Alderan had led a handful of courageous men

521

in defending the realm. And he had won after putting up a heroic resistance, thanks to Argor's providential help.

This version of events had been circulated, repeated and embroidered upon throughout the High Kingdom for weeks. Of course, the ambassadors of all the nations had witnessed Lorn's dramatic intervention so no one in the various capitals of Imelor's kingdoms was ignorant of the truth. But Esteveris knew that people were always hungry for good news and glorious feats, and that was all that mattered. What difference did it make if the truth were slightly twisted? Besides, there was no truth except what was written in the *Chronicles*, and the Palace's historians were already busy establishing that.

'Don't count on your merits being recognised today, knight,' said Teogen.

Lorn, Enzo and he were riding side by side, at the front of the parade but ten yards behind Alan. They were the brave souls who had fought with the prince for the honour and integrity of the High Kingdom. Tribute was paid to their courage and their loyalty, but they were merely subordinates.

'That's fine,' replied Lorn. 'Alan is being celebrated. Loved. He embodies a new hope for the High Kingdom.'

'Besides,' interjected Enzo, 'all those who matter know what really happened. You will soon be much sought after, Lorn.'

'It's already started. The ambassadors of Alguera and Vestfald have already asked to meet me.'

'And what was your reply?'

Lorn shrugged.

'Nothing, yet.'

'You should be more wary of politics than of steel,' advised Teogen.

'More wary?' asked Lorn in surprise.

'There's no armour against politics,' said Enzo.

The queen and her court were waiting for the procession at the Palace gates, seated on tribunes clothed in blue and yellow. Alan went first, to pay his respects to his mother, then it was the turn of the Count of Argor, Enzo and Lorn to place a knee to the ground before her.

The queen embraced her son and held out her hand to be

522

kissed by the others, before inviting them in an amiable tone to stand. She had a kind word for each of them, even for Lorn to whom she said with a smile:

'I know your true merits, knight. And I thank you for them.'

Lorn was astonished.

It would have sufficed to save appearances if the queen – who detested him – had simply smiled at him. No one could hear them over the loud cheers from the crowd.

Lorn probed the gaze of Celyane of the High Kingdom for an explanation, to no avail.

During the banquet, with Lorn sitting at the high table between Alan and Esteveris, the queen continued to be friendly.

She smiled, laughed and seemed relaxed and joyful. And why shouldn't she be? She suddenly had the people's support, thanks to her son whose popularity was unrivalled, and the kingdom's treasury was full, thanks to the tremendous tribute just received from Yrgaard. She would be able to conduct policy as she saw fit, both within and beyond her country's borders. And her enemies now knew they could fear war.

'When one thinks about it,' commented Esteveris, offering Lorn a platter of meat, 'the Grey Dragon has envisaged a strange destiny for you. The Angborn treaty you prevented was not so very different from the one we prepared with Yrgaard, three, no, four years ago…'

Lorn turned to him.

'That *we* prepared?' he repeated.

'Well, yes! I was one of the secretaries serving the High Kingdom's representatives. You were unaware of that?'

'There were so many of you…'

'That's true.'

'And how far you've come, since then.'

It did not sound like a compliment, but Esteveris did not appear to have heard him.

'So, the same treaty,' he continued. 'More or less… Four years ago you were falsely accused of compromising it, and you were tried and convicted for doing so. Yet today, here we are celebrating the fact that you have achieved exactly the same result…'

'It's Alan who is being celebrated.'

'No doubt, no doubt… What can I say? He is the prince.'

Another prince was seated at their table, Yrdel sat on the queen's right and yet seemed to go unnoticed. Grave, withdrawn and subdued, he spoke little. His dull personality did him no service and his inglorious role during the Angborn crisis had completed his isolation. Alan had already, naturally, tended to draw all the light to himself. But this evening, Yrdel seemed even more self-effacing than usual.

Lorn wondered what he was thinking.

By following the queen to Samarande, leaving behind a fortress which could not be defended and choosing not to recklessly engage the High Kingdom in an open conflict with Yrgaard, Yrdel had done nothing less than what his duty as crown prince required. For a prince of the High Kingdom could not risk his life in such a fashion as his half-brother had done. He could not expose himself to being captured, wounded or killed by the enemy. He could not throw himself into an adventure whose political and diplomatic consequences might prove catastrophic for the High Kingdom. Yet Alan had done all of that. Without forethought. And now he was being feted for it.

'I must congratulate you, Lorn,' said Esteveris. 'Obviously, you prepared your scheme very carefully and you played me admirably by letting me believe that Sir Vahrd had run off with his daughter, when instead you sent him to seek the aid of Count Teogen. Bravo! I mean that.'

'Thank you.'

'However… However, I must urge you not to consider me your enemy.'

Lorn smiled.

'You're amused…' said Esteveris. 'I understand why. Do you want proof that we are allies?'

'I'm listening.'

'I know Naéris is hiding with your friend the master archivist. I could have had both of them arrested, but I chose not to do so. Better, this morning I signed a decree clearing Naéris of all charges against her. She is no longer a fugitive.'

Lorn looked at Esteveris.

'You'll receive a copy of that document,' the minister promised.

'Thank you, for Naé's sake. But you won't win my trust with a scrap of paper.'

'That goes without saying. But consider my offer, knight. You will need powerful allies, ones equal to your enemies…'

Lorn thought he caught a flicker in Esteveris's gaze towards the queen, who, looking radiant, was laughing at some jest.

At the end of the meal, almost all of the lights were extinguished in preparation of a show. Drums and cymbals began to beat a lively rhythm, before dancers and fire-eaters came on stage, leaping, twirling and grimacing like elemental creatures. Acrobatics and feats of dexterity followed, performed according to a dizzying choreography, punctuated by admiring murmurs and spontaneous applause.

The spectacle, however, soon began to bore Lorn. Indeed, he was thinking about retiring for the night when a servant – leaning over him to fill his glass – discreetly slipped him a note.

Lorn gave no sign that anything unusual had taken place.

He unfolded the small piece of paper beneath the table, then pressed his shoulders slightly against the back of his chair and looked down. To no avail. It was too dark for him to read anything at all.

'I'll be back,' he said to Alan. 'I need some fresh air.'

'Don't you feel well?'

'I have a headache and those cymbals are hurting my ears. I think I've had too much wine.'

'I'll call Odric to accompany you.'

'No need. I'll go for a little walk and I'll be fine.'

Lorn stood up.

'You're abandoning us already, knight?' asked Esteveris, without taking his eyes from the show.

Lorn did not reply.

He left the banquet hall and was finally able to read the

mysterious note in the light from a candelabrum. He pondered it. Someone had taken the pain of contacting him in this clandestine fashion. So time was of the essence, for one reason or another.

Lorn recognised the secret code.

It was one employed by Irelice, which brought some very bad memories to mind. This code had been used to encrypt some compromising letters that had been found among his possessions after his arrest, and had led to his conviction for treason.

At the time, he'd sworn that he knew nothing of those documents or the code protecting them.

In vain.

Four years later, Lorn was surprised by the ease with which he deciphered the note.

3

Duke Duncan of Feln was waiting on a bench in a quiet garden within the Palace. Lit by a torch planted in the ground, he appeared to be alone and stood when he heard Lorn approach.

'Good evening, knight. Forgive me for arranging a meeting with you in this fashion, but I must leave Oriale and it would be best, for your sake, if we weren't seen together.'

With a gesture, he invited Lorn to take a seat. But the knight remained standing and, using the torch to set alight the note that had brought him here, he said:

'Employing that Irelice code was hardly prudent.'

'I wanted to be sure I caught your attention,' explained Feln. 'As I told you, my time is short. I hoped to see you at the banquet, but Esteveris made it clear at the last moment that my presence was no longer desirable. A minor humiliation for my daughter and myself. Pointless, but very much in the manner of Her Majesty Queen Celyane of the High Kingdom…'

Lorn waited until the paper was almost entirely consumed before letting it go and watching it disintegrate, its glowing particles carried off by a breath of air.

'You are returning to your lands?' he asked.

'Yes. Thanks to you, the moment has come to make myself scarce.'

'I'm sorry to hear that.'

'The queen is enjoying her newfound popularity and the kingdom's coffers are full. Knowing her, none of that will last, but for now she's in control. Her allies are increasing in number, while even my staunchest supporters are wavering…'

Feln heaved a fatalistic sigh and smiled.

'What can I say, knight?' he resumed. 'The wheel turns and turns again. Would you care to take a stroll?'

It was already night.

Lorn considered the dark and silent garden around them, and asked in an ironic tone:

'Should I expect to be abducted? After Samarande, and the fortified inn on the road to Brenvost, that would be a little much...'

'So you guessed.'

'That Irelice was behind it? I didn't need to guess. Your henchmen were careless and talkative. Besides, who else would want me to disappear? Who else would be worried that I had been rescued from the dungeon where I was rotting?'

The duke shook his head contritely.

'I did not order you to be abducted. And I certainly didn't want to make you disappear. I know what services you rendered us and I know what they cost you. I have many faults, but I'm not ungrateful. I am loyal.'

'Is that all you wanted to say to me this evening?'

'In a manner of speaking. I wanted you know to you have nothing to fear from Irelice. On the contrary, I ask you to regard us as your ally.'

The proposition amused Lorn.

After Esteveris, Feln was the second person to hold out a hand to him this evening. They were disputing his favours. Even the queen was casting smiles his way, although he was not fooled by them, any more than he believed the minister's or the duke's sincerity. Both men were guided by their interests, by their political calculations. These offers only proved one thing: Lorn now occupied a key place on the High Kingdom's chessboard.

'I also want you to know,' added Feln, 'that your secret is safe with me. No one will ever know the charge of treason was well founded. No one will ever know the truth.'

Lorn smiled, but the look in his mismatched eyes was ice-cold. Too calmly not to be menacing, he approached Feln, who became frightened, held his breath, and froze. Lorn pressed up against him, chest to chest, gripped his neck firmly, and murmured in his ear:

'And who would believe you? A loyal and devoted knight, unjustly accused of treason, returns from hell and saves the kingdom at the request of its ruler. That's the tale. It's beautiful, too beautiful for people to have any desire to hear another. And it matters little what you know. It matters little what I did. And besides, I've more than paid for it.'

Lorn let go of Feln and stepped back, allowing the duke to breathe.

'Safe journey,' he said as he walked away. 'My regards to your daughter.'

Feln swallowed, and then called out:

'No one can explain it and some don't want to believe it, but it seems the Dark protects you, knight. Take care that it doesn't guide you!'

Lorn walked off with a tranquil step into the shadows.

Lorn left the Palace thinking about the duke's parting words. The Dark had indeed protected him from the dragon-prince's fire. Steel against steel. Fire against fire. The Dark against the Dark.

He did not know how or why, but the fact remained.

He was alive and had never felt such well-being before. As the Dragon of Destruction had predicted, his body had let itself be taken over by the Dark rather than resisting it, and he had emerged stronger, tougher and capable of unequalled feats.

Like surviving a Dark blast.

And his soul?

In truth, he didn't care about that, convinced that if he possessed a soul, it had died in Dalroth. Perhaps that was the price to be paid.

An exorbitant price, whatever his crimes had been.

Yes, Lorn had betrayed the High Kingdom.

Four years earlier, he'd revealed the content of the secret treaty the High Kingdom was preparing with Yrgaard, which had prevented it from being signed. That did not warrant his incarceration in Dalroth, or enduring what he'd endured, alone against madness, death and oblivion.

Alone against the Dark.

Moreover, he had been denounced. Betrayed. But by whom and why? He didn't know, but now that he had the power he was going to find out. He was influential enough at present to manage it and had every intention of using his advantage, starting with obtaining the minutes of his secret trial from Sibellus.

After that, whoever had brought about his ruin would pay for it with their life.

4

Midnight.

Lorn considered finding his men in the tavern where they had agreed to celebrate the victory at Angborn, and to pay tribute to Dwain, whose remains now rested in the cemetery at Saarsgard. Only Vahrd, Yeras and Logan had returned to Oriale with Lorn. Liam had remained at Samarande, confined to bed by a fever which the doctors assured them was not serious. Anyway, it was better that he rest while his wounded arm healed. He would rejoin the others later.

Lorn's steps took him almost of their own accord to the Black Tower, through a Redstone district filled with rejoicing crowds. He walked with his head down, but was recognised several times and invited to have a drink, which he refused politely by saying he would take up the offer later. He was, in fact, anxious to go home and shut himself away in the quiet of his new quarters. Following Andara's death, restoration work in the tower had resumed unhindered and Lorn had been pleasantly surprised upon his return to find it was almost completed. Scaffolding still surrounded the keep, but it was now perfectly functional and inhabitable. Proudly flying a banner with the wolf's head and crossed swords at its summit, a Black Tower once again stood in all its glory in Oriale.

Lorn found the place plunged into darkness and silence. But it was not deserted, which surprised him.

'Daril?'

The boy was there, dozing in a chair on the keep's ground floor, with a candle stub burning in a saucer at his feet.

'What are you doing here?' asked Lorn.

Daril stood up, rubbing his eyes.

'I... I was waiting for you, my lord.'

'Why?'

'To see if you needed me. Do you need me?'

'No. Run along and amuse yourself. You're at liberty like the others.'

'But—'

'Go! Have a drink. Dance. Play. Get your hands on a girl or a boy...'

'A boy?'

'Do whatever you like, but scarper. Do you know where Cadfeld is?'

Although mostly recovered, the old bookseller still enjoyed the Onyx Guards' hospitality.

'He went out with the others, my lord.'

'Perfect. Then go and join them,' said Lorn, starting up the spiral staircase.

'Until tomorrow, my lord!'

'That's right.'

The unkempt boy went off, with his eyes sparkling and a huge grin on his face

Lorn lived on the keep's last floor.

He entered his quarters unwarily and just had time to see Yssaris's small body lying in a pool of blood before he received one, two, three dagger stabs in his side.

He collapsed.

Men emerged from the shadows. Dressed in black and shod in supple boots, they wore finely crafted leather masks whose harmonious and complex patterns shifted about.

'Take him,' said one of the men.

Lorn wanted to move but found himself incapable of doing so.

He realised that some kind of poison had paralysed him. The wounds he'd received would be fatal, but not until all of his blood had drained into his own entrails.

The assassins carried him down the stairs and deposited him in the large fencing room which occupied almost the entire first floor of the keep.

'Set him up,' said the one who seemed to be the leader.

Two assassins sat Lorn on the floor, with his back against a wooden bench, and spread his arms wide so that his hands rested flat upon the piece of furniture.

The one in command crouched before Lorn. He was tall, very slender and graceful. And his eyes were a grey so pale they seemed white.

Lorn knew he would never forget those eyes.

'I've been asked to make you suffer,' the man said, as the other assassins emptied goatskin pouches of lamp oil over the walls and the floor.

Lorn could not yell but an atrocious pain shot through him when they nailed his left hand to the bench.

Then his right hand endured the same fate.

'Suffer a lot,' added the assassin's leader in a gentle, compassionate voice.

His eyes filling with tears of anger, suffering and impotence, Lorn saw one of the killers bringing Daril into the room.

'My lord!' the frightened boy implored. 'Help me!'

They forced him to kneel and slowly slit his throat before the knight's eyes.

Lorn was barely able to moan, barely able to lift his shoulders when all he wanted was to scream, rise up, tear himself from the bench and throw himself on the assassins to kill them with his tortured hands.

Daril fell, choking, his throat opened and his hands bound behind his back, his eyes frozen in an expression of incredulous terror. He thrashed in his own blood, until the last bit of life he desperately clung to finally left him.

'That's fine,' said the assassin's leader.

Alone with Lorn, he leaned over him, lifted the bottom of the leather mask and placed a kiss upon the knight's still lips. After which he set fire to the floorboards which burst into sudden flames, and walked away.

'Farewell,' he said.

Lorn vowed to return from hell to seek his revenge.

ED LEISURE+CULTURE